NEUROTICA

Jewish Writers On Sex

edited by

Melvin Jules Bukiet

Broadway Books • New York •

A hardcover version of this book was originally published in 1999 by W. W. Norton & Company. It is here reprinted by agreement with W. W. Norton & Company.

Broadway Books titles may be purchased for business or promotional use or for special sales. For information, please write to: Special Markets Department, Random House, Inc., 1540 Broadway, New York, NY 10036.

BROADWAY BOOKS and its logo, a letter B bisected on the diagonal, are trademarks of Broadway Books, a division of Random House, Inc.

Visit our website at www.broadwaybooks.com

Library of Congress Cataloging-in-Publication Data Applied For

First Broadway Books trade paperback edition published 2000.

ISBN 0-7679-0650-0

00 01 02 03 04 10 9 8 7 6 5 4 3 2 1

To Jill,

the mother of
Madelaine, Louisa, and Miles

(I hope they're mine)

Contents

ex is a universal phenomenon
irds do it; bees do it; even Co
orteron his knees do it. Bu
ney all do itdifferently. Not on
o differen **NEUROTICA** in di
rent eras perceive the desirab
images of their own constru
on, but so do differ **Jewish** ion
Vhereas the Christian **Writers**
owedly unrealized by a **On** t th
rongest vessels, is cel **Sex**y, Ju
aism has rarely disclaimed th
ody. Not only is sex unshunne
y the Jewish tradition; it's ofte
onsidered a positive mitzvah t
ave sex on Sabbath. Besides,
ork is prohibited and you can'
o to the movies, how else ca
ou spend your holy time? Whe
er this serves a Darwinian func
on: to wit, the increase of th
ibe; or is a real-politik cor
ession that rabbis make to the

Introduction

Sex is a universal phenomenon. Birds do it; bees do it; even Cole Porter on his knees do it.

But they all do it differently. Not only do different nationalities in different eras perceive the desirable in images of their own construction, but so do different religions. Whereas the Christian ideal, avowedly unrealized by all but the strongest vessels, is celibacy, Judaism has rarely disdained the body. Not only is sex unshunned by the Jewish tradition; it's often considered a positive mitzvah to have sex on Sabbath. Besides, if work is prohibited and you can't go to the movies, how else can you spend your holy time? Whether this serves a Darwinian function: to wit, the increase of the tribe; or is a real-politik concession that rabbis make to their wayward flocks, I leave to anthropologists, but from the ancient Aramaic ketubah (marriage contract) that guarantees conjugal interaction to an early societal acceptance of divorce when things just didn't work out, it's been understood: Jews do it, too.

Although biblical narrative is full of sex (Abraham and Sarah, Jacob and his two wives, Lot in Sodom, Joseph and Potiphar's wife, Tamar, Dina, Onan, etc., etc.) most post-exilic Jewish writing was liturgical or legal. During the long millennia until the advent of the Haskalah (Jewish enlightenment) in the middle of the nineteenth century, every hint of eroticism had to be justified as an analogy for presumably more ecstatic intercourse with deity. But then the novelists and poets and short-story writers of Eastern Europe discovered another use for language. Instead of parsing the ineffable nature of God, men like Sholom Aleichem and Mendele Mocher Seforim wrote about the all-too-effable nature of Jews who lived in a world of privation and violent oppression and, occasionally, small, secret moments of comfort. For them, as for their non-Jewish peers throughout Europe, life itself became the subject of literary contemplation. And in the beginning was sex.

Think of Tevye's three daughters, seduced away from their father's expectations of a normative future by three young men, each inappropriate in his own way, each as predestined as the turn of the calendar. Think of the subversive passions of S. Ansky's *Dybbuk* and the young woman whose body he inhabits. Look further beyond the shtetl to the terse irony of Isaac Babel who trades words for sex in "My First Fee" or the shabby garrison affairs of Joseph Roth's *The Radetzky March* and the weird, sublimated frenzy of Franz Kafka and Bruno Schultz. In every case, the writer walks a high wire between learning and instinct. Inhabiting a world about to be consumed, they focus on the internal flames of their characters. Sex thus represents the defiant embodiment of the impulse to life even as the external, thanatotic powers of czars, commissars, and Germans try their best to deny life.

And then came America.

Arrived at Ellis Island during the great migrations, immigrant Jews bred children whose new native language was English. From the start of American Jewish literature in Anzia Yezierska's febrile longings and Henry Roth's harsh awakening, the simple perception of what it feels like to be alive provided the connective tissue for larger social issues. Michael Gold, excoriating the evils of capitalism in *Jews Without Money*, cannot help but gaze lustfully at the whores on the Grand Concourse, while the more psychologically curious yellow star, Delmore Schwartz, sees his parents necking on the screen of his mind. Fiction begs for flesh.

To the extent that craving is the human condition and commentary the Jewish position, *Neurotica* aims to reflect the abundant varieties of one people's sexual experience in all its glorious and fertile catholicity. It includes straight sex, gay sex, married and unmarried sex, satisfied and frustrated sex, guilty and innocent sex, carnal, platonic, and pathetic sex. Some of the stories you are about to read are graphic, some ethereal, some hilarious, some tragic. In style, they range from the social realism of the slums to the magic realism of the skies. In substance, some explore conflicts between the sexes while others forge deep, enduring connections among the sexes.

Religion and sex are not contradictory modes of human endeavor; in fact, they function analogously; they just situate redemption in different loci. Sex, like religion, is a placating power that dissolves social inequities. In both its sensual and procreative operations, human intercourse (in both its two grandest incarnations; that is, fucking and writing fiction) provides this world's compensation for loss, lack, and, especially, mortality. Sex and storytelling are the gifts that make of a tailor a king, a seamstress a queen. The sheet, like the writer's page, is a clean, white throne available to all, and also, because every gift has its price, as dangerous for all. And as Jewish writers have wrestled intensely with divinity through the ages, from the story of the angel and Jacob (whose name God would change to Israel to give birth to the tribe), *Neurotica* seeks out those works that reveal this one culture's rapturous communion between biology and theology.

Witness the people of the book, in bed.

It's a strange process, anthologizing, and for the editor of this project who is so befuddled by biology's blunt imperatives that he still believes that a stork delivered his three children, it probably seems stranger than for most. Reading through this . . . stuff for the last few months, I've felt like Adam in the Garden, but unlike Adam, the *only* fruit I'm picking are the apples. No pomologist I, all I can tell you is the flavors I've tasted. Some are tart, some sweet, all juicy. And what abundance!

Probably the first thing worth noticing is that a lot of these stories are funny. I won't try to analyze humor or I'll break its leg, but why is sex the subject of more humor than any other topic? Maybe the propositions that stroke our bodies also strike the funny bone because we are seldom more ridiculous than en flagrante or engaged by the torments of the soul that often precede and sometimes preclude that condition.

Let the reader beware, though; not all are funny. In fact, not even the funny ones are untainted by the bitter awareness of life's uncertainty.

Maybe it's the ability—or the necessity—to see the tragic and the comic as a single rather than a two-sided coin that makes particular stories intrinsically Jewish more so than the author's last name or native soil. Starting with Woody Allen's "The Whore of Mensa," wit and yearning commingle here with an abandon that bespeaks the ongoing—Alarm! Alarm! Fancy word at o' three hundred. Duck and cover!—dialectic between the anxiety of powerlessness and the assertion of potency. Thus, many stories tamper with opposing stereotypes of Jewish asexuality or Jewish hypersexuality. It was that hard-to-describe but easy-to-recognize Jewish texture that I looked for in making my choices.

Even then, however, there were far too many excellent works to include. Lines had to be drawn and the first line was historical; I could have commenced with "Song of Songs" and inched through from the medieval *Alphabet of Ben Sidra* to arrive at the turn of the millennium, but I wasn't putting together a survey. Likewise, I decided that I would not use foreign authors, because I could not possibly cover that particular waterfront and a handful of entries would seem tokenistic. Then, limited by the confines of the continental United States (it may lose me a grant from the National Endowment for Identity Politics, but I also decided to ban all Alaskans of the Hebrew persuasion), generational questions arose. Several writers like Stanley Elkin who came of literary age in the same era as the Jewish Literary Trinity were not included because it seemed vital to cede space to youth.

At this point, I was compelled to deal with genre issues. Preferring stories (and one single one-act play by Saul Bellow) to excerpts, I was torn between Cynthia Ozick's "The Pagan Rabbi" and a portion of her first novel, *Trust*, which includes the following astonishing scene. "The union of the lovers takes place on the floor . . . I crouch on the ledge of the world and am their witness . . . I think of . . . seeing how his stream falls from a tender fat creature with a short neck scalloped out of the head, and in the head a pouring cyclops-eye—the Jews are different . . . she cleaves herself wide for him, his stud charges and misses, retreats, assesses, charges, misses . . . he . . . reaches a single vast hand curved and spread to contain her and takes the swell of her crotch and fast and brutally, before she can sprawl, he flips her over. And penetrates." Although this was especially, well, penetrating in the light of Ms. Ozick's later, less wanton career. I nonetheless chose her story for the sake of its completeness. In other cases certain writers I admired (Henry Roth) never wrote stories while still others provided sections of novels that were essentially interpolated tales, and I had to make my peace with their pieces.

Most importantly, there was the question of subject matter. Because I wished to hit 100 on both the Jew-o-meter and the sex-o-meter, I regretfully passed over writers like Norman Mailer, whose fiction was more nominally than theologically Jewish, as well as those like Grace Paley who do write out of a deep Jewish ethical sensibility, yet are not so much of the body.

Ultimately, what links the works that are in *Neurotica*—like any anthology—must be the editor's taste. In other words, some decisions were based on merit, some were based on friendship, and the rest were arbitrary. Sue me.

But first notice the way in which the place of the various writers—and many of their characters—within the tribe echoes the place of the tribe within the world. The Jewish writer is the outsider's outsider, whose role has often been, as the former senator from New York might have said, a putzhead. Inherently untrustworthy, heedlessly heeding only the voice from within, these secular prophets court danger by daring to speak the truth as they see it. In fact, they cannot help but notice that although much of Jewish law has to do with the separation of the clean and the unclean, the sacred and the profane, the rabbis who have sought to safeguard the former from the intrusions of the latter must fail when it comes to human behavior precisely because sex is inherently messy, unconfined, unconfinable, and, yes, unclean. Life is what it is. Thus, the antinomian principle for inclusion in *Neurotica* became something like this: if the author would really get under the skin of the authorities, then he or she was welcome. Finally, you've got a bunch of dirty Jews at play in the swamps of the land.

I think it's a law that the introduction to every anthology of Jewish writing must refute the late Irving Howe's assertion that Jewish literature had already chronicled its encounter with America, and was therefore on the verge of exhaustion by the 1960s. With due respect, history has proven Mr. Howe wrong. Not only is there more overtly Jewish literature being written now, but I'd suggest that it's even more Jewish than before. Acculturation has allowed writers to dwell on the sinister side of the Jew-ish/American hyphenate.

Why now? Why not? So what if modernity may prove a more im-placable enemy to faith than fascism. Why therefore can't proverbial Jewish stiff-neckedness, which displayed itself pridefully against Roman centurions, Spanish Inquisitors, and in the Warsaw ghetto, act the same in the face of assimilation as it once did at the risk of immolation? If you prick them, do they not bleed? If you arouse them, do they not know?

So look at them . . . behold these vulgarians. Consider a young man writing about naked rabbis or an elderly Nobelist craning for one last look at an elderly lady's private parts while a bebanged, middle-aged woman dressed in a schoolgirl's jumper and saddle shoes skulks around a placid Bronx park, peeking at a scholarly rabbi's sad affair with a tree. Have they no shame?

Thank God, the answer is "No."

In choosing these stories, I was delighted to span the gamut from the cool analysis of Rebecca Goldstein, for whom seduction is a branch of philosophy, to Harold Brodkey's amazing thirty-page description of a single sex act that can hardly be mentioned; suffice to say that thinking about it makes the jaw drop.

It's also a great pleasure to present fiction by younger writers like Ger-ald Shapiro and S. L. Wisenberg beside groundbreaking works like Erica Jong's *Fear of Flying*. Twenty-five years after Ms. Jong's incendiary land-ing during the so-called sexual revolution, her sex may seem tame, but the vision of a planeful of shrinks is still one of the most terrifying things I can imagine.

Geographically, *Neurotica* hops from the hip downtown scene of Cheryl Pearl Sucher where, despite black pants and nose rings, one can never escape from ancestral ways, to Helen Schulman's uptown Ivy cam-pus to Janice Eidus's Bronx and Leonard Michaels's Brooklyn. But it also includes stories written in the heart of America that take place else-where: Steve Stern's Eastern Europe, Enid Shomer's Israel, Michael Lowenthal's Germany, Bernard Malamud's Italy, Francine Prose's France, and Jerzy Kosinski's no-man's land.

Inevitably, picking up where Kosinski leaves off, the ghosts of the Holocaust hover in the work of Thane Rosenbaum and Binnie Kirshenbaum. After the Shoah, life goes on, with memory, with suffering—and with filth.

Others stories venture more gently through time, from Max Apple's personal journey back to the crucial second week of his protagonist's life to Benjamin Taylor's early century Galveston, which is just as exotic as I. B. Singer's pre-War shtetl of the same period.

And what congregation is complete without a Shabbos goy? Because so many of the stories here are about transgression (prostitutes and perversions galore, step right up) it seemed only right to transgress *Neurotica*'s own rules and include Gilbert Sorrentino's "The Moon in Its Flight," an utterly sweet story that says practically everything about Jews and non-Jews, Brooklyn and the Bronx, money and no money.

I haven't mentioned them all, but they're here, in raucous, orgiastic unity, wailing like . . . oh, there's one more, I nearly forgot; there's Roth. One can't do sex without Roth; one can't do Jews without Roth; one can't understand how the Swedish Academy can wake up in the morning and look itself in the face without Newark's martyr and patron saint of the corpus Judaicus. But what to choose? Pick a page, any page. In the piece here, Roth presents Henry Zuckerman, a suburban dentist and his new assistant. After a hard day of fillings and extractions, Zuckerman suggests that they pretend to be dentist and assistant. "But," the untutored Wendy giggles, "I *am* the assistant." Patiently, the doctor evokes just the tiniest bit of the power of the imagination. And so they pretend, and the walls between man and woman, labor and management, imagination and actuality come tumbling down. Roth's exhortation might as well serve as a call to see what's really inside us, as a people and as persons. After all, all that writers are really doing is pretending that life makes a difference and trying to have a good time. So what the Gehenna, let's pretend.

Woody Allen

"The Whore of Mensa"

One thing about being a private investigator, you've got to learn to go with your hunches. That's why when a quivering pat of butter named Word Babcock walked into my office and laid his cards on the table, I should have trusted the cold chill that shot up my spine.

"Kaiser?" he said. "Kaiser Lupowitz?"

"That's what it says on my license," I owned up.

"You've got to help me. I'm being blackmailed. Please!"

He was shaking like the lead singer in a rumba band. I pushed a glass across the desk top and a bottle of rye I keep handy for nonmedicinal purposes. "Suppose you relax and tell me all about it."

"You . . . you won't tell my wife?"

"Level with me, Word. I can't make any promises."

He tried pouring a drink, but you could hear the clicking sound across the street, and most of the stuff wound up in his shoes.

"I'm a working guy," he said. "Mechanical maintenance. I build and service joy buzzers. You know—those little fun gimmicks that give people a shock when they shake hands?"

"So?"

"A lot of your executives like 'em. Particularly down on Wall Street."

"Get to the point."

"I'm on the road a lot. You know how it is—lonely. Oh, not what you're thinking. See, Kaiser, I'm basically an intellectual. Sure, a guy can meet all the bimbos he wants. But the really brainy women—they're not so easy to find on short notice."

"Keep talking."

"Well, I heard of this young girl. Eighteen years old. A Vassar student. For a price, she'll come over and discuss any subject—Proust, Yeats, anthropology. Exchange of ideas. You see what I'm driving at?"

"Not exactly."

"I mean, my wife is great, don't get me wrong. But she won't discuss Pound with me. Or Eliot. I didn't know that when I married her. See, I need a woman who's mentally stimulating, Kaiser. And I'm willing to pay for it. I don't want an involvement—I want a quick intellectual experience, then I want the girl to leave. Christ, Kaiser, I'm a happily married man."

"How long has this been going on?"

"Six months. Whenever I have that craving, I call Flossie. She's a madam, with a master's in comparative lit. She sends me over an intellectual, see?"

So he was one of those guys whose weakness was really bright women. I felt sorry for the poor sap. I figured there must be a lot of jokers in his position, who were starved for a little intellectual communication with the opposite sex and would pay through the nose for it.

"Now she's threatening to tell my wife," he said.

"Who is?"

"Flossie. They bugged the motel room. They got tapes of me discussing *The Waste Land* and *Styles of Radical Will*, and, well, really getting into some issues. They want ten grand or they go to Carla. Kaiser, you've got to help me! Carla would die if she knew she didn't turn me on up here."

The old call-girl racket. I had heard rumors that the boys at headquarters were on to something involving a group of educated women, but so far they were stymied.

"Get Flossie on the phone for me."

"What?"

"I'll take your case, Word. But I get fifty dollars a day, plus expenses. You'll have to repair a lot of joy buzzers."

"It won't be ten Gs' worth, I'm sure of that," he said with a grin, and picked up the phone and dialed a number. I took it from him and winked. I was beginning to like him.

Seconds later, a silky voice answered, and I told her what was on my mind. "I understand you can help me set up an hour of good chat," I said.

"Sure, honey. What do you have in mind?"

"I'd like to discuss Melville."

"*Moby Dick* or the shorter novels?"

"What's the difference?"

"The price. That's all. Symbolism's extra."

"What'll it run me?"

"Fifty, maybe a hundred for *Moby Dick*. You want a comparative discussion—Melville and Hawthorne? That could be arranged for a hundred."

"The dough's fine," I told her and gave her the number of a room at the Plaza.

"You want a blonde or a brunette?"

"Surprise me," I said, and hung up.

I shaved and grabbed some black coffee while I checked over the Monarch College Outline series. Hardly an hour had passed before there was a knock on my door. I opened it, and standing there was a young redhead who was packed into her slacks like two big scoops of vanilla ice cream.

"Hi, I'm Sherry."

They really knew how to appeal to your fantasies. Long straight hair, leather bag, silver earrings, no makeup.

"I'm surprised you weren't stopped, walking into the hotel dressed like that," I said. "The house dick can usually spot an intellectual."

"A five-spot cools him."

"Shall we begin?" I said, motioning her to the couch.

She lit a cigarette and got right to it. "I think we could start by approaching *Billy Budd* as Melville's justification of the ways of God to man, *n'est-ce pas?*"

"Interestingly, though, not in a Miltonian sense." I was bluffing. I wanted to see if she'd go for it.

"No. *Paradise Lost* lacked the substructure of pessimism." She did.

"Right, right. God, you're right," I murmured.

"I think Melville reaffirmed the virtues of innocence in a naïve yet so-phisticated sense—don't you agree?"

I let her go on. She was barely nineteen years old, but already she had developed the hardened facility of the pseudo-intellectual. She rattled off her ideas glibly, but it was all mechanical. Whenever I offered an insight, she faked a response: "Oh, yes, Kaiser. Yes, baby, that's deep. A platonic comprehension of Christianity—why didn't I see it before?"

We talked for about an hour and then she said she had to go. She stood up and I laid a C-note on her.

"Thanks, honey."

"There's plenty more where that came from."

"What are you trying to say?"

I had piqued her curiosity. She sat down again.

"Suppose I wanted to—have a party?" I said.

"Like, what kind of party?"

"Suppose I wanted Noam Chomsky explained to me by two girls?"

"Oh, wow."

"If you'd rather forget it . . ."

"You'd have to speak with Flossie," she said. "It'd cost you."

Now was the time to tighten the screws. I flashed my private-investigator's badge and informed her it was a bust.

"What!"

"I'm fuzz, sugar, and discussing Melville for money is an 802. You can do time."

"You louse!"

"Better come clean, baby. Unless you want to tell your story down at Alfred Kazin's office, and I don't think he'd be too happy to hear it."

She began to cry. "Don't turn me in, Kaiser," she said. "I needed the money to complete my master's. I've been turned down for a grant. *Twice*. Oh, Christ."

It all poured out—the whole story. Central Park West upbringing, So-cialist summer camps, Brandeis. She was every dame you saw waiting in line at the Elgin or the Thalia, or penciling the words "Yes, very true" into the margin of some book on Kant. Only somewhere along the line she had made a wrong turn.

"I needed cash. A girl friend said she knew a married guy whose wife

4

wasn't very profound. He was into Blake. She couldn't hack it. I said sure, for a price I'd talk Blake with him. I was nervous at first. I faked a lot of it. He didn't care. My friend said there were others. Oh, I've been busted before. I got caught reading *Commentary* in a parked car, and I was once stopped and frisked at Tanglewood. Once more and I'm a three-time loser."

"Then take me to Flossie."

She bit her lip and said, "The Hunter College Book Store is a front."

"Yes?"

"Like those bookie joints that have barbershops outside for show. You'll see."

I made a quick call to headquarters and then said to her, "Okay, sugar. You're off the hook. But don't leave town."

She tilted her face up toward mine gratefully. "I can get you photographs of Dwight Macdonald reading," she said.

"Some other time."

I walked into the Hunter College Book Store. The salesman, a young man with sensitive eyes, came up to me. "Can I help you?" he said.

"I'm looking for a special edition of *Advertisements for Myself*. I understand the author had several thousand gold-leaf copies printed up for friends."

"I'll have to check," he said. "We have a WATS line to Mailer's house."

I fixed him with a look. "Sherry sent me," I said.

"Oh, in that case, go on back," he said. He pressed a button. A wall of books opened, and I walked like a lamb into that bustling pleasure palace known as Flossie's.

Red flocked wallpaper and a Victorian décor set the tone. Pale, nervous girls with black-rimmed glasses and blunt-cut hair lolled around on sofas, riffling Penguin Classics provocatively. A blonde with a big smile winked at me, nodded toward a room upstairs, and said, "Wallace Stevens, eh?" But it wasn't just intellectual experiences—they were peddling emotional ones, too. For fifty bucks, I learned, you could "relate without getting close." For a hundred, a girl would lend you her Bartók records, have dinner, and then let you watch while she had an anxiety attack. For one-fifty, you could listen to FM radio with twins. For three bills, you got the works: A thin Jewish brunette would pretend to pick you up at the Museum of Modern Art, let you read her master's, get you involved in a screaming quarrel at Elaine's over Freud's conception of women, and then fake a suicide of your choosing—the perfect evening, for some guys. Nice racket. Great town, New York.

"Like what you see?" a voice said behind me. I turned and suddenly found myself standing face to face with the business end of a .38. I'm a guy with a strong stomach, but this time it did a back flip. It was Flossie, all right. The voice was the same, but Flossie was a man. His face was hidden by a mask.

"You'll never believe this," he said, "but I don't even have a college degree. I was thrown out for low grades."

"Is that why you wear that mask?"

"I devised a complicated scheme to take over *The New York Review of Books*, but it meant I had to pass for Lionel Trilling. I went to Mexico for an operation. There's a doctor in Juarez who gives people Trilling's features—for a price. Something went wrong. I came out looking like Auden, with Mary McCarthy's voice. That's when I started working the other side of the law."

Quickly, before he could tighten his finger on the trigger, I went into action. Heaving forward, I snapped my elbow across his jaw and grabbed the gun as he fell back. He hit the ground like a ton of bricks. He was still whimpering when the police showed up.

"Nice work, Kaiser," Sergeant Holmes said. "When we're through with this guy, the F.B.I. wants to have a talk with him. A little matter involving some gamblers and an annotated copy of Dante's *Inferno*. Take him away, boys."

Later that night, I looked up an old account of mine named Gloria. She was blond. She had graduated *cum laude*. The difference was she majored in physical education. It felt good.

Max Apple

"The Eighth Day"

I was always interested in myself, but I never thought I went back so far. Joan and I talked about birth almost as soon as we met. I told her I believed in the importance of early experience.

"What do you mean by early?" she asked. "Before puberty, before loss of innocence?"

"Before age five," I said.

She sized me up. I could tell it was the right answer.

She had light-blond hair that fell over one eye. I liked the way she moved her hair away to look at me with two eyes when she got serious.

"How soon before age five?" She took a deep breath before she asked me that. I decided to go the limit.

"The instant of birth," I said, though I didn't mean it and had no idea where it would lead me.

She gave me the kind of look then that men would dream about if being men didn't rush us so.

With that look Joan and I became lovers. We were in a crowded restaurant watching four large goldfish flick their tails at each other in a display across from the cash register. There was also another couple, who had introduced us.

Joan's hand snuck behind the napkin holder to rub my right index finger. With us chronology went backwards. Birth led us to love.

2

Joan was twenty-six and had devoted her adult life to knowing herself.

"Getting to know another person, especially one from the opposite gender, is fairly easy." She said this after our first night together. "Apart from reproduction it's the main function of sex. The biblical word 'to know' someone is exactly right. But nature didn't give us any such easy and direct ways to know ourselves. In fact, it's almost perverse how difficult it is to find out anything about the self."

She propped herself up on an elbow to look at me, still doing all the talking.

"You probably know more about my essential nature from this simple biological act than I learned from two years of psychoanalysis."

Joan had been through Jung, Freud, LSD, philosophy, and primitive religion. A few months before we met, she had re-experienced her own birth in primal therapy. She encouraged me to do the same. I tried and was amazed at how much early experience I seemed able to remember, with Joan and the therapist to help me. But there was a great stumbling block, one that Joan did not have. On the eighth day after my birth, according to the ancient Hebrew tradition, I had been circumcised. The circumcision and its pain seemed to have replaced in my consciousness the birth trauma. No matter how much I tried, I couldn't get back any earlier than the eighth day.

"Don't be afraid," Joan said. "Go back to birth. Think of all experience as an arch."

I thought of the golden arches of McDonald's. I focused. I howled. The therapist immersed me in warm water. Joan, already many weeks past her mother's postpartum depression, watched and coaxed. She meant well. She wanted me to share pain like an orgasm, like lovers in poems who slit their wrists together. She wanted us to be as content as trees in the rain forest. She wanted our mingling to begin in utero.

"Try," she said.

The therapist rubbed Vaseline on my temples and gripped me gently with Teflon-coated kitchen tongs. Joan shut off all the lights and played in stereo the heartbeat of a laboring mother.

For thirty seconds I held my face under water. Two rooms away a tiny flashlight glowed. The therapist squeezed my ribs until I bruised. The kitchen tongs hung from my head like antennae. But I could go back no farther than the hairs beneath the chin of the man with the blade who pulled at and then slit my tiny penis, the man who prayed and drank wine over my foreskin. I howled and I gagged.

"The birth canal," Joan and the therapist said.

"The knife," I screamed, "the blood, the tube, the pain between my legs."

Finally we gave up.

"You Hebrews," Joan said. "Your ancient totems cut you off from the centers of your being. It must explain the high density of neurosis among Jewish males."

The therapist said that the subject ought to be studied, but she didn't think anyone would give her a grant.

I was a newcomer to things like primal therapy, but Joan had been born for the speculative. She was the Einstein of pseudoscience. She knew tarot, phrenology, and metaposcopy the way other people knew about baseball or cooking. All her time was spare time except when she didn't believe in time.

When Joan could not break down those eight days between my birth and my birthright, she became, for a while, seriously anti-Semitic. She used surgical tape to hunch my penis over into a facsimile of precircumcision. She told me that smegma was probably a healthy secretion. For a week she cooked nothing but pork. I didn't mind, but I worried a little about trichinosis because she liked everything rare.

Joan had an incredible grip. Her older brother gave her a set of Charles Atlas Squeezers when she was eight. While she read, she still did twenty minutes a day with each hand. If she wanted to show off, she could close the grip exerciser with just her thumb and middle finger. The power went right up into her shoulders. She could squeeze your hand until her nipples stood upright. She won spending money arm wrestling with men in bars. She had broken bones in the hands of two people, though she tried to be careful and gentle with everyone.

I met Joan just when people were starting to bore her, all people, and she had no patience for pets either. She put up with me, at least at the beginning, because of the primal therapy. Getting me back to my birth gave her a project. When the project failed and she also tired of lacing me with pork, she told me one night to go make love to dark Jewesses named Esther or Rebecca and leave her alone.

I hit her.

"Uncharacteristic for a neurotic Jewish male," she said.

It was my first fight since grade school. Her hands were much stronger than mine. In wrestling she could have killed me, but I stayed on the balls of my feet and kept my left in her face. My reach was longer so she couldn't get me in her grip.

"I'll pull your cock off!" she screamed and rushed at me. When my jab didn't slow her, I hit her a right cross to the nose. Blood spurted down her chin. She got one hand on my shirt and ripped it so hard she sprained my neck. I hit her in the midsection and then a hard but openhanded punch to the head.

"Christ killer, cocksucker," she called me, "wife beater." She was crying. The blood and tears mingled on her madras shirt. It matched the pattern of the fabric. I dropped my arms. She rushed me and got her hands around my neck.

"I must love you," I said, "to risk my life this way."

She loosened her grip but kept her thumbs on my jugular. Her face came down on mine, making us both a bloody mess. We kissed amid the carnage. She let go, but my neck kept her fingerprints for a week.

"I'd never kill anyone I didn't love," she said. We washed each other's faces. Later she said she was glad she hadn't pulled my cock off.

After the fight we decided, mutually, to respect one another more. We agreed that the circumcision was a genuine issue. Neither of us wanted it to come between us.

"Getting to the bottom of anything is one of the great pleasures of life," Joan said. She also believed a fresh start ought to be just that, not one eight days old.

So we started fresh and I began to research my circumcision. Since my father had been dead for ten years, my mother was my only source of information. She was very reluctant to talk about it. She refused to remember the time of day or even whether it happened in the house or the hospital or the synagogue.

"All I know," she said, "is that Reb Berkowitz did it. He was the only one in town. Leave me alone with this craziness. Go swallow dope with all your friends. It's her, isn't it? To marry her in a church you need to know about your circumcision? Do what you want; at least the circumcision is one thing she can't change."

Listening in on the other line, Joan said, "They can even change sex now. To change the circumcision would be minor surgery, but that's not the point."

"Go to hell," my mother said and hung up. My mother and I had not been on good terms since I quit college. She is closer to my two brothers, who are CPAs and have an office together in New Jersey. But, to be fair to my mother, she probably wouldn't want to talk about their circumcisions either.

From the United Synagogue Yearbook which I found in the library of Temple Beth-El only a few blocks from my apartment I located three Berkowitzes. Two were clearly too young to have done me, so mine was Hyman J., listed at Congregation Adath Israel, South Bend, Indiana. "They all have such funny names," Joan said. "If he's the one, we'll have to go to him. It may be the breakthrough you need."

"Why?" my mother begged, when I told her we were going to South Bend to investigate. "For God's sake, why?"

"Love," I said. "I love her, and we both believe it's important to know this. Love happens to you through bodies."

"I wish," my mother said, "that after eight days they could cut the love off too and then maybe you'd act normal."

South Bend was a three-hundred-mile drive. I made an appointment with the synagogue secretary to meet Hyman Berkowitz late in the afternoon. Joan and I left before dawn. She packed peanut butter sandwiches and apples. She also took along the portable tape recorder so we could get everything down exactly as Berkowitz remembered it.

"I'm not all that into primal therapy anymore," she said as we started down the interstate. "You know that this is for your sake, that even if you don't get back to the birth canal this circumcision thing is no small matter. I mean, it's almost accidental that it popped up in primal; it probably would have affected you in psychoanalysis as well. I wonder if they started circumcising before or after astrology was a very well-developed Egyptian science. Imagine taking infants and mutilating them with crude instruments."

"The instruments weren't so crude," I reminded her. "The ancient Egyptians used to do brain surgery. They invented eye shadow and embalming. How hard was it to get a knife sharp, even in the Bronze Age?"

"Don't be such a defensive Jewish boy," she said. "After all, it's your pecker they sliced, and at eight days too, some definition of the age of reason."

For people who are not especially sexual, Joan and I talk about it a lot. She has friends who are orgiasts. She has watched though never participated in group sex.

"Still," she says, "nothing shocks me like the thought of cutting the foreskin of a newborn."

3

"It's no big deal," Berkowitz tells us late that afternoon. His office is a converted lavatory. The frosted glass windows block what little daylight there still is. His desk is slightly recessed in the cavity where once a four-legged tub stood. His synagogue is a converted Victorian house. Paint is peeling from all the walls. Just off the interstate we passed an ultramodern temple.

"Ritual isn't in style these days," he tells Joan when she asks about his surroundings. "The clothing store owners and scrap dealers have put their money into the Reformed. They want to be more like the goyim."

"I'm a goy," Joan says. She raises her head proudly to display a short straight nose. Her blond hair is shoulder length.

"So what else is new?" Berkowitz laughs. "Somehow, by accident, I learned how to talk to goyim too." She asks to see his tools.

From his desk drawer he withdraws two flannel-wrapped packets. They look like place settings of sterling silver. It takes him a minute or two to undo the knots. Before us lies a long thin pearl-handled jackknife.

"It looks like a switchblade," Joan says. "Can I touch it?" He nods.

She holds the knife and examines the pearl handle for inscriptions.

"No writing?"

"Nothing," says Berkowitz. "We don't read knives."

He takes it from her and opens it. The blade is as long as a Bic pen. Even in his dark office the sharpness glows.

"All that power," she says, "just to snip at a tiny penis."

"Wrong," says Berkowitz. "For the shmekel I got another knife. This one kills chickens."

Joan looks puzzled and nauseated.

"You think a person can make a living in South Bend, Indiana, on newborn Jewish boys? You saw the temple. I've got to compete with a half dozen Jewish pediatricians who for the extra fifty bucks will say a prayer too. When I kill a chicken, there's not two cousins who are surgeons watching every move. Chickens are my livelihood. Circumcising is a hobby."

"You're cute," Joan tells him.

H. Berkowitz blushes. "Shiksas always like me. My wife worries that someday I'll run off with a convert. You came all this way to see my knife?" He is a little embarrassed by his question.

I try to explain my primal therapy, my failure to scream before the eighth day.

"In my bones, in my body, all I can remember is you, the knife, the blood."

"It's funny," Berkowitz says, "I don't remember you at all. Did your parents make a big party, or did they pay me a little extra or something? I don't keep records, and believe me, foreskins are nothing to remember."

"I know you did mine."

"I'm not denying. I'm just telling you it's not so special to me to remember it."

"Reverend," Joan says, "you may think this is all silly, but here is a man who wants to clear his mind by reliving his birth. Circumcision is standing in the way. Won't you help him?"

"I can't put it back."

"Don't joke with us, Reverend. We came a long way. Will you do it again?"

"Also impossible," he says. "I never leave a long enough piece of foreskin. Maybe some of the doctors do that, but I always do a nice clean job. Look."

He motions for me to pull out my penis. Joan also instructs me to do so. It seems oddly appropriate in this converted bathroom.

"There," he says, admiringly. "I recognize my work. Clean, tight, no flab."

"We don't really want you to cut it," Joan says. "He just wants to re-live the experience so that he can travel back beyond it to the suffering of his birth. Right now your circumcision is a block in his memory."

Berkowitz shakes his head. I zip my fly.

"You're sure you want to go back so far?"

"Not completely," I admit, but Joan gives me a look.

"Well," Berkowitz says, "in this business you get used to people mak-ing jokes, but if you want it, I'll try. It's not like you're asking me to com-mit a crime. There's not even a rabbinic law against pretending to circumcise someone a second time."

4

The recircumcision takes place that night at Hyman Berkowitz's house. His wife and two children are already asleep. He asks me to try to be quiet. I am lying on his dining room table under a bright chandelier.

"I'd just as soon my wife not see this," Berkowitz says. "She's not as up to date as I am."

I am naked beneath a sheet on the hard table.

Berkowitz takes a small double-edged knife out of a torn and stained case. I can make out the remnants of his initials on the case. The in-strument is nondescript stainless steel. If not for his initials, it might be mistaken for an industrial tool. I close my eyes.

"The babies," he says, "always keep their eyes open. You'd be surprised how alert they are. At eight days they already know when something's happening."

Joan puts a throw pillow from the sofa under my head.

"I'm proud of you," she whispers. "Most other men would never dare to do this. My instincts were right about you." She kisses my cheek.

Berkowitz lays down his razor.

"With babies," he says, "there's always a crowd around, at least the family. The little fellow wrapped in a blanket looks around or screams. You take off the diaper and one-two it's over." He hesitates. "With you it's like I'm a doctor. It's making me nervous, all this talking about it. I've been a mohel thirty-four years and I started slaughtering chickens four years before that. I'm almost ready for Social Security. Just baby boys, chickens, turkeys, occasionally a duck. Once someone brought me a captured deer. He was so beautiful. I looked in his eyes. I couldn't do it. The man understood. He put the deer back in his truck, drove him to the woods, and let him go. He came back later to thank me."

"You're not really going to have to do much," Joan says, "just relive the thing. Draw a drop of blood, that will be enough: one symbolic drop."

"Down there there's no drops," Berkowitz says. "It's close to arteries; the heart wants blood there. It's the way the Almighty wanted it to be."

As Berkowitz hesitates, I begin to be afraid. Not primal fear but very contemporary panic. Fear about what's happening right now, right before my eyes.

Berkowitz drinks a little of the Manischewitz wine he has poured for the blessing. He loosens his necktie. He sits down.

"I didn't have the voice to be a cantor," he says, "and for sure I wasn't smart enough to become a rabbi. Still, I wanted the religious life. I wanted some type of religious work. I'm not an immigrant, you know. I graduated from high school and junior college. I could have done lots of things. My brother is a dentist. He's almost assimilated in White Plains. He doesn't like to tell people what his older brother does.

"In English I sound like the Mafia, 'a ritual slaughterer.' " Berkowitz laughs nervously. "Every time on the forms when it says Job Description, I write 'ritual slaughterer.' I hate how it sounds."

"You've probably had second thoughts about your career right from the start," Joan says.

"Yes, I have. God's work, I tell myself, but why does God want me to slit the throats of chickens and slice the foreskins of babies? When Abraham did it, it mattered; now, why not let the pediatricians mumble the blessing, why not electrocute the chickens?"

"Do you think God wanted you to be a dentist," Joan asks, "or an insurance agent? Don't be ashamed of your work. What you do is holiness. A pediatrician is not a man of God. An electrocuted chicken is not an animal whose life has been taken seriously."

Hyman Berkowitz looks in amazement at my Joan, a twenty-six-year-old gentile woman who has already relived her own birth.

"Not everyone understands this," Berkowitz says. "Most people when they eat chicken think of the crust, the flavor, maybe Colonel Sanders. They don't consider the life of the bird that flows through my fingers."

"You are indeed a holy man," Joan says.

Berkowitz holds my penis in his left hand. The breeze from the air conditioner makes the chandelier above me sway.

"Do it," I say.

His knife, my first memory, I suddenly think, may be the last thing I'll ever see. I feel a lot like a chicken. I already imagine that he'll hang me upside down and run off with Joan.

She'll break your hands, I struggle to tell him. You'll be out of a job. Your wife was right about you.

The words clot in my throat. I keep my eyes shut tightly.

"I can't do it," Berkowitz says. "I can't do this, even symbolically, to a full-grown male. It may not be against the law; still I consider it an abomination."

I am so relieved I want to kiss his fingertips.

Joan looks disappointed but she, too, understands.

"A man," Hyman Berkowitz says, "is not a chicken."

I pull on my trousers and give him gladly the fifty-dollar check that was to have been his professional fee. Joan kisses his pale cheek.

The holy man, clutching his cheek, waves to us from his front porch. My past remains as secret, as mysterious, as my father's baldness. My mother in the throes of labor is a stranger I never knew. It will always be so. She is as lost to me as my foreskin. My penis feels like a blindfolded man standing before the executioner who has been saved at the last second.

"Well," Joan says, "we tried."

On the long drive home Joan falls asleep before we're out of South Bend. I cruise the turnpike, not sure of whether I'm a failure at knowing myself. At a roadside rest stop to the east of Indiana beneath a full moon, I wake Joan. Fitfully, imperfectly, we know each other.

"A man," I whisper, "is not a chicken." On the eighth day I did learn something.

Saul Bellow

"A Wen"

A dark stage. Upper left we see a regularly beating light. It descends and is revealed as the cage of an elevator. Inside is SOLOMON ITHIMAR, PH.D., a celebrated scientist, middle-aged. As the elevator door opens the stage lights up. We are in the lobby of a third-class Miami Beach resort hotel. A LADY is seated alone at a coffee table. She is of an age with ITHIMAR and has an ample, swelling figure, curving lips and a heavy head of kinky golden hair. Her name is MARCELLA VANKUCHEN, née MENELIK. The hour is sunset. Hurricane Clara has recently passed through. We now hear the first gusts of Hurricane Delia.

ITHIMAR: (eagerly advances, then stops): You are . . . !

MARCELLA: (turning, she presses the many strands of beads to her bosom): Yes . . . ?

ITHIMAR: Mrs. Vankuchen? Marcella?

MARCELLA: You are the gentleman who rang my room and said he was a friend of my brother Julius?

ITHIMAR: I am Solomon Ithimar. (He waits, keenly excited, for the name to take effect. He is disappointed.)

ITHIMAR: From Detroit originally, now Washington, D.C.

MARCELLA: I was born in Detroit.

ITHIMAR: Of course. You and your brother Jemby, both.

MARCELLA: Jemby! His family name. No one has used it in more than thirty years.

ITHIMAR: You lived on Singleton Street, before it was paved. There were still horses.

MARCELLA: What was that name again?

ITHIMAR: Solomon Ithimar. That means nothing? (*Sighs, but is determined to continue.*) And you are Marcella Menelik!

MARCELLA: Was.

ITHIMAR: To me always will be. Your father was Marcus Menelik, the butcher. A red shop front with a golden bull's head.

MARCELLA: Brass.

ITHIMAR: Golden. Your mother's name was Faigl. She owned a player piano.

MARCELLA: Poor Mama—gone. Papa too.

ITHIMAR: Your dog's name was Gustave. He must have had a hernia. He groaned when he ran.

MARCELLA: It's all very far away, isn't it.

ITHIMAR: Your grandfather had a long beard. He had a newsstand. Your uncle Selig was a cigarmaker. Then there was your grandmother. She was called Basha. I have never forgotten any fact about your family. She wore a wig. I think she must have been a great beauty once. She had a dark, lovely, tender, even magical spot on her cheekbone.—It has meant a lot to me. Right here it was. (*Taps under his eye.*)

MARCELLA (*to herself*): Ithimar? Ithimar? Must have been neighbors. (*Shrugs.*)

ITHIMAR: You had two maiden aunts, Dunya and Manya. Both nice. Dunya taught Russian. She was very *kulturny*. Manya was more *sympathisch*, however. (*He lowers his voice to accommodate a most significant feeling.*) She had the same little spot on her face as your granny, a speck of mulberry color. Hers was on the upper lip, close to the nose. Or maybe she was a small bit cross-eyed. But terribly vivacious and charming. What a sharp little laugh! And the way she would rest her hand on her belt and draw a breath—such a bosomy breath! To watch her breathe made me feel like an astronaut. I believe we used to say an aeronaut, in those days. Anybody who went up in a plane or a balloon. Ah! (*Rubs his hands in sheer excitement. Moves his feet, sways somewhat.*)

MARCELLA: You do just like a chained elephant with your feet. First the right, and then the left, and then you knock them together. So you were a playmate of Jemby?

ITHIMAR: I was your playmate even more, Marcella.

MARCELLA: I didn't play with boys often.

ITHIMAR: Yes. Not often. But you played—you played.

MARCELLA (*a little impressed by the forcefulness of the assertion*): Ithimar. . . . Was your father in the ice business?

ITHIMAR: No, he was the watchmaker on Windsor Street.

MARCELLA: Of all things! I remember him. He had one of those clocks under the glass bell. And you've kept in touch with Julius all this time?

ITHIMAR: Not really close touch. No.

MARCELLA: He did a smart thing.

ITHIMAR: What was that?

MARCELLA: Giving up the shoe store, becoming a photographer.

ITHIMAR: Art for business?

MARCELLA: Art? Crap! Excuse me. But no Detroit wedding is a wedding unless it has an album by Menelik. We thought his diabetes would slow him up. Uh-uh! And have you noticed how photographers push people around? And that they all take it? Even the greatest in the land. And what do you do, Mr. Ithimar? Are you married? Children? In business? I think they used to say the watchmaker's son was a prodigy.

ITHIMAR: An exaggeration.

MARCELLA: But you look well. That's no twenty-two-fifty jacket you're wearing. What's the label? Tailor-made. Three hundred dollars. Let me see that stitching. So, then, why are you staying in this dump? Let me see if I can figure you out. You've made a hobby of old times in Detroit. But you're not common. You must have done all right for yourself. (*Sips her drink.*) You don't boast. I'm from the small world, where everybody talks big. You must be from the big world, where you can afford to be modest. Just look how modest and conservative he is. My only criticism is that a man with such large feet shouldn't wear tapering trousers. I can't place you, except that your father fixed clocks. Oh, wait! You must be the scientist. Ye gods! You! A famous man. The clockmaker's son. You won the Nobel Prize!

ITHIMAR: Not I. My team.

MARCELLA (*shrieks*): You're eminent! You made the atom bomb in Chicago.

ITHIMAR: I was in the Manhattan Project. (*He is unwilling to speak of this.*)

MARCELLA: Oh! (*Presses her painted nails to her brow.*) I could kick myself in the head! It's Iggy. Little Iggy. Iggy the Genius. Einstein's protégé. Truman's scientific brain. The kid who put our neighborhood on the map. How would I know what! I'm just a vulgar painted *yachna*, bad at canasta, so I could never understand high mathematics. (*Looks about.*) What are you doing in a joint like this? Though I'm glad to see you, and it's even kind of an honor, I have to ask myself, do angels smell of garlic? I mean, does a great scientist stay in a fourth-rate Miami dump, with bad sewage? And does he pick the hurricane season when nobody in his right mind comes?

ITHIMAR: I am on my way to an international conference. I thought I'd fly by way of Florida and take a very short holiday in the sunshine.

MARCELLA: What is this conference?

ITHIMAR: I can't say.

MARCELLA: Is it classified information?

ITHIMAR: Top secret.

MARCELLA (*guessing*): You came to this loathsome place to avoid publicity—the press. (*She thinks.*) But then again. . . .

ITHIMAR: I knew you were here. (*The phone rings very loudly. He starts and exclaims:*) I won't take any calls!

MARCELLA: But you don't have to. Anyway, the clerk is out. This is the hour when the guy comes from the Syndicate and they do their bookie accounts in the men's room. You wouldn't know about such things. You take the big view. Overall. International. Cosmic. Nature.

ITHIMAR: Nature? I don't know Nature. I only know certain mathematical structures. Nature I don't understand. (*Silence.*)

MARCELLA: You're here alone. Of course. . . .

ITHIMAR: But I'm married. Children. That's what you want to know.

MARCELLA: I too. I have a son. Six foot four, two hundred ten pounds. Size sixteen shoes. Size twenty collar. How strange your breathing sounds. Is it something allergic? Or is the evening air too sweet for your nose? It's tropical evening, plus low tide, plus the septic tank. They're expecting Hurricane Delia.

ITHIMAR: You *are* marvelous! I was not wrong. I couldn't have been wrong. I should have had more confidence in my instincts.

MARCELLA: And should you ask what am I doing here, the doctor sent me.

ITHIMAR: You aren't sick, are you, Marcella?

MARCELLA: The doctor is my husband. He's a mere chiropodist, but he gets very angry if you call him mister.

ITHIMAR: What is he like?

MARCELLA: Oh, he doesn't have a very piercing personality. He likes being typically American. He wears only white silk socks, which he buys by the gross. He smokes bad cigars. Is pompous about his chiropody. He's lazy—won't go down the hall; he pees in the sink. I don't hold it against him. It's all the usual good and bad. He acts cheerful but feels gloomy. Drives a Cadillac. And you have to call him Doc, or he blows up. It's an ordinary life. Boring. It'll kill us by and by. Maybe that's what we deserve. I don't know what it's all about.

ITHIMAR: Don't be sad. You're not dead, and life can always start again.

MARCELLA: Never the same, Iggy. You can't fool a woman with that sort of talk. Only men can deceive themselves that way. This is a swampy hotel. I stay here because my husband does all the feet for the management. But you. . . .

ITHIMAR: The literature made it sound attractive.

MARCELLA: No, Iggy, you have another reason. Are you in trouble? Running away from the Pentagon? Mixed up in a spy plot?

ITHIMAR: Of course not.

MARCELLA: I can't believe it! You came here because of me. (*She stands.*) Me! (*She bursts out laughing.*) Me, me, me! (*She screams like a night bird.*) Dull old me!

ITHIMAR: That's right, Marcella. You.

MARCELLA: Me, with this face, with this figure! Are you out of your mind?

ITHIMAR: It's true I shouldn't be here, Marcella. It's wrong. Infantile. Illegal. Grotesque. Everybody will be sore. The thing is dangerous. It gives me a sick ache to think of it. But here I am. Everything is green, indigo, swampy. Palms. Mangroves. The moon. I should have landed in Geneva, Switzerland, this morning. I was expected. This will be serious. . . .

MARCELLA: Is it a government matter?

ITHIMAR: Multigovernmental. International. Disarmament. Top secret. Take my word for it. I can't say a word more.

MARCELLA: Instead, you flew to Detroit, looking for me, after thirty-five years. You saw Jemby. He told you where I was. . . . Because you were in love with me three dozen years ago?

ITHIMAR: I want you to listen to me. (*Strides to desk and looks behind it. Shuts a door. Tries to draw curtains, which blow out of his grasp.*) Something I haven't been able to get out of my mind.

MARCELLA: Iggy, I am a faithful wife. It's a fantastic and yet basically uninteresting fact nobody cares about. Still, the mind of a genius might discover what *is* interesting about me. According to certain ideas in the world there's nothing to me. Even I share those same ideas. They make me tiresome, more tiresome. But the intelligence of a man of distinction might see that after all . . . but I don't know after all what.

ITHIMAR: There *is* something extraordinary.

MARCELLA: Don't tell me here. I couldn't bear for other people to come in. I want it to be in private. (*Takes him by the hand.*) What's in your attaché case?

ITHIMAR: Documents, a slide rule. Things like that. My Rollax Razor. I never carry valises. (*They go toward elevator.*)

MARCELLA: Did you really know Einstein?

ITHIMAR: Yes. (*They enter elevator.*)

MARCELLA (*laughing as stage darkens and the elevator begins to rise*): Oh, what a thing! What an occasion! All this way to see a childhood darling. And finding *me!* A square old creature. Only *you* remember. (*The light throbs in the cage. A blast of wind is heard and simultaneously the current is cut off.*)

ITHIMAR (*after a long silence in the darkness*): What is it?

MARCELLA: A power failure. (*Ithimar turns on a flashlight.*) Where did you get that?

ITHIMAR: The reading light is poor on the jets. I designed this, with a lens attached to magnify. (*He demonstrates on his own face. We see, about eight feet from the ground, a distorted mask of* ITHIMAR. *He turns the light on her and we see a similarly distorted mask of* MARCELLA.)

MARCELLA: Don't do that, Iggy. Please.

Scene Two

The light goes on. ITHIMAR *and* MARCELLA *enter* MARCELLA's *room.*

ITHIMAR: May I pour myself a drink? (*He gulps from the bottle.*) Now, Marcella. (*She seats herself on large sofa, center.*) For old times' sake, listen without prejudice. Just consider the peculiarities of another human being, the strange twists of his life. No reflection on you. I had to come here.

MARCELLA (*enjoying the word*): *Was it a compulsion.*

ITHIMAR: Why else would I risk my security clearance, forget my official duties, to say nothing of the cause of international peace and who knows what else!

MARCELLA: Iggy, my husband banished me here, ostensibly to take off weight. But life surprises everyone. All I expected in Florida was ashes and gloom. So this is a gift from heaven. What unknown relationship have I enjoyed with you? Or do you want to drop it all, now that you see me in the flesh.

ITHIMAR: No, Marcella! Your color has changed—a *little*—since those days. But then, both organisms have undergone such transformations as all human tissue must.

MARCELLA: Yes, your eyes seem to lean against your nose. They used to be more independent.

ITHIMAR: But as you will see, I have not ignored the years. But I'd better plunge straight in. What good is lecturing. Marcella, on your grandfather's back stairs in Detroit we played a game called "Show," I believe.

MARCELLA: Called Show? Just you and me?

ITHIMAR: We showed each other things.

MARCELLA: What things! (ITHIMAR *sighs deeply, shakes his head.*) This is quite a thing to remember, four decades later in Florida before a storm. A reason to be absent from Geneva. Oh, Iggy! You, a Stockholm Laureate—me, a poor ordinary member of Hadassah. And *this* is our common ground . . . that you showed me your . . . that I showed you . . . that's what *you* say, anyway.

ITHIMAR: You did.

MARCELLA: I was not like that.

ITHIMAR: It's stamped into my memory—the green clumsy staircase. Noise from the house. Then the secret moment of intimacy which silenced the whole world. When you disclosed that personal object, you and I were sealed in stillness. Then my soul took form, a distinct form. I experienced all the richness and glory of existence for the first time consciously. I recognized beauty. And I loved it. With love came worship. I showed you what I had. It throbbed. It filled. It brought all being to a point, and that point could only aim toward you. . . .

MARCELLA: And that never happened again?

ITHIMAR: Repeatedly, but only approximately, and never so purely, with such perfection or clarity of vision. There have been moments, in certain discussions of Quantum Theory. With Niels Bohr, at times, I felt similar things. But that was sublimation. Not the thing itself.

MARCELLA: Quantum?

ITHIMAR: Listen to the rest, and listen with sympathy, please. I never forgot. It has been of tremendous influence in shaping my mind. And here is a strange aspect of that vision—that you have a little birthmark—a wen.

MARCELLA: Do I?

ITHIMAR: You're not aware of it?

MARCELLA: Absolutely not!

ITHIMAR: What your grandmother had on her cheek, and your Aunt Manya on her lip, that charming, colorful spot. My spirit has attached itself to it and gravitates about it. To the scientist only a drop of pigment, perhaps, a small concentration of melanin, a purplish or rosy or mulberry discoloration; but to me a fixed star, an electromagnetic potency, a phenomenon which makes me ache, adore, throb, long to merge, and in fact seems to contain the secret of life.

MARCELLA: Oh! And where is it?

ITHIMAR: It *was* to the left as I faced . . . (*stammers*) that little . . . apricot-colored; soft . . . I didn't touch. I refrained. But a sense of softness entered my fingertips of itself.

MARCELLA: It even gives me an odd sensation now.

ITHIMAR: Don't you have a corresponding memory?

MARCELLA: You know how one-sided life is. We're all in business by ourselves.

ITHIMAR: May I have another drink?

MARCELLA: Help yourself. (ITHIMAR *swigs again from the bottle*.)

ITHIMAR: There have been times, as I was roller-skating to my laboratory, or talking to the President, when that little mark would suddenly appear to me. Sometimes like a closed bud or tinier. Sometimes the size of an egg. Or as if you held that egg to a powerful light, all transparency. Finally, the same diameter as the sun. The sun itself, where the fusion process goes on, pouring out subatomic particles. Lastly, explosions within me like whole novae, scattering my matter through sidereal space to cool again. Finally, I had to see you. I had to fly. I was driven. I had to know.

MARCELLA: To know what?

ITHIMAR: Whether I could still feel as I felt on that day.

MARCELLA: At your age?

ITHIMAR: I am not offended. That's also what I have said to myself. And yet, a vision is a vision. They say bliss is no miracle, only instinctual. I, however, do not believe in schematic approaches. My way is to test things out, not to decide beforehand on the basis of general experience. Who knows?

MARCELLA: I can't believe you would really ask me. . . . (*She titters, then says sternly:*) Impossible! (*She gathers herself up.*) There are limits, Dr. Ithimar. Because my husband is a mere chiropodist, don't think you can hold me cheap.

ITHIMAR: Don't talk yourself into a false attitude, Marcella. I think I understand how such a request must strike you. But how can you deny me! Think what I may recover. And if me, why not you?

MARCELLA: You're trying to work me up with illusions.

ITHIMAR: There are powerful forces at work, forces of all magnitudes. I mean my desire is *pure*. I am prepared to die without recovering that dimension of experience if it is irrevocable. But would you ask me to go to the grave resigned never to attempt the recovery?

MARCELLA: Why not resigned? What are you so special, Iggy? Are you too good for the common lot?

ITHIMAR: The matter isn't entirely personal.

MARCELLA: It might be different if you said, "Marcella, I once loved you. And after all these years I love you still. Madly!" But it isn't me. It's just a wen or something. I don't remember it. I don't even know if I have it.

ITHIMAR: Why shouldn't you have it?

MARCELLA: Maybe it's all in your mind.

ITHIMAR: There's only one way to find out.

MARCELLA: It's not I personally who inspires you with this passion.

ITHIMAR: Who knows what will result.

MARCELLA: This is one of those menopause ideas that drive people to destruction. I'm not ready for that yet. And thank God I have a little dignity left yet. There isn't much I do have left. I'm reduced to bragging about my son's weight. Iggy, it's true, I'm very unhappy. I don't like to admit that unhappiness has broken me down to the point of absurdity.

ITHIMAR: But, Marcella, after all we mustn't expect to understand these deeper motives. The Prince was mad for Cinderella's foot. And think of King David and the virgin. How that poor kid must have felt when the old man applied her to himself. We have to tolerate these seemingly absurd things. Marcella, let me see.

MARCELLA: No. I'm sure it's changed. Everything has become different. There's a difference of forty years, nearly.

ITHIMAR: I beg you, Marcella. (*Carefully kneeling.*) I throw myself at your feet. (*Fastidiously, even pedantically, he extends himself before her.*) We are both unhappy. (*She tries to move away and he takes her foot.*) Marcella, don't refuse me.

MARCELLA: To tell the honest truth, Iggy. It's too grotesque for me.

ITHIMAR (*sits up, still holding her foot*): Now you've said it.

MARCELLA: What have I said.

ITHIMAR: I've been trying to purge life of its grotesque elements. Ordinary life has a grotesque dimension, and this has become a theme of the times. The human mind is the slave of its own metaphors. When I sit at the White House in conference, I think of this. Individual fantasy collaborates with the grotesque inventions and achievements of the public realm. I see how people rejoice in their grotesqueness, and I see that reason must sever its dependency on the grotesque. We thrust the same distortion upon conscious events as we experience in dreams. The purpose of this distortion is to show that we must passively submit, as in dreams. So we remove all occasions of action and decision by making them grotesque. The grotesque is therefore our form of Quietism. It is the American form of Hindu Quietism.

MARCELLA: I don't follow that at all.

ITHIMAR: I was at Göttingen in 1931, studying Physics. One day I fell in the street and a fellow student tried to help me up. I yelled at him, "Let me alone!"

MARCELLA: Why was that?

ITHIMAR: I had been thinking out a problem, and as I was falling a new mathematical expression entered my head. I didn't want to be disturbed. You see the occasion seemed grotesque, but it was redeemed by an ecstasy, by devotion to pure truth, by the ennoblement of reason.

MARCELLA: I still can't see where *I* come in.

ITHIMAR: Oh Marcella, let me see—let me see! *(He kisses the hem of her skirt.)*

MARCELLA *(to herself, bitterly)*: Well, nobody else cares about it at all. Just the gynecologist, once a year or so. *(To* ITHIMAR:*)* Suppose we do look—big deal! And what then. I don't want to exaggerate, but I do lose something. Respectfully means something to me. Not much. But it's better than absolutely nothing. I have to live, too. So I'll be making a sacrifice. And what will you sacrifice for me?

ITHIMAR: I'm in trouble already.

MARCELLA: You can claim amnesia. You may be able to get out of it easily. No, you must give up something of value, too.

ITHIMAR: Humble me.

MARCELLA: Don't carry on. I don't think you're very proud anyway. No, we'll put this thing on a real basis. You want me to give up my dignity? You must tell me. . . . Yes, you must tell me a classified secret. A top secret.

ITHIMAR: You want me to betray my country? Our country?

MARCELLA: Betray? Am I a Communist? Do I belong to any organization besides Hadassah and my Temple Sisterhood? No. I will swear to you never to tell, but you must give up one major secret. We don't know what goes on, the people of this country. What do they really do in Washington? The Invisible Government. The C.I.A. The Joint Chiefs. What about Flying Saucers. Are there really Flying Saucers?

ITHIMAR: Not that I know of.

MARCELLA: You aren't leveling with me. That wasn't truthful. What is this thing worth to you?

ITHIMAR: Ask me for any *personal* sacrifice. Ask me to inject something into my veins. To bail out with a parachute. To take a sailboat out in this hurricane. I'll do that.

MARCELLA: What do you tell President Johnson when you confer?

ITHIMAR: We talk about Atoms for Peace. We talk about detection devices, limited test bans, things like that.

MARCELLA: This I can read in the papers. You must tell me something I don't know.

ITHIMAR: All right. But. . . .

MARCELLA: I'll make good. Right behind this sofa . . . to conceal you from any possible intrusion. Now tell me.

ITHIMAR: There is a device. Electronic. So minute it's invisible. Can be introduced anywhere. Works on the germanium diode principle. No bigger than a grain of pollen. It floats after the person one wants to watch. There are these invisible units which tell us, for instance, what Khrushchev is doing, any time of the day or night. Or Castro. Or Mao Tse-tung. The information is received in a special chamber of the Pentagon. On a screen.

MARCELLA: Great God! Is this true?

ITHIMAR: What would you like me to swear by?

MARCELLA: Who knows what those devils carry on. While they feed us nonsense. How many of these devices are there?

ITHIMAR: I don't know. I can go to prison for revealing this.

MARCELLA: No one will ever find it out from me.

ITHIMAR: Well? Now?

MARCELLA: Please don't be rough, Iggy. (*The hurricane is howling.*)

ITHIMAR: Why behind the sofa.

MARCELLA: You must make some concession to my feeling for propriety. Don't expect me to be brazen. With an extraordinary request like this. . . . Oh, the gullibility of women. The things we go along with! (*She leans against the sofa.* ITHIMAR *is now out of sight.*) You'd better remove my stockings. What are you doing with those buckles.

ITHIMAR: Perhaps you'd better remove your own girdle.

MARCELLA: Don't ask that. I can't. No, don't pull from the bottom. Here. From the top. You can't say I didn't humiliate myself. I hope you'll have the decency to keep all comments to yourself. (*She reaches under her dress to help.*) I never expected *ever* to find myself in such a situation.

ITHIMAR (*from below*): Ah!

MARCELLA: Well? (*A pause.*) Not the way you remember, I'll bet.

ITHIMAR: I didn't expect it to be.

MARCELLA: You'll be happy to go back to your Quantum Theory.

ITHIMAR: There'll have to be a search.

MARCELLA: You don't intend to use that flashlight.

ITHIMAR: I'm terribly sorry.

MARCELLA: Your hands are shaking.

ITHIMAR: Well, it's pretty dense here, in places.

MARCELLA: I know you're going to be horribly disappointed and let down. If I had an illusion like yours, I wouldn't have taken such a risk.

ITHIMAR: May I ask you to bend just a little backward.

MARCELLA: Kindly be careful. I have a slipped disc. (*She bends further over back of sofa.*) You can be positive of one thing: I'll never give away any secret of yours, with what you're getting on me. Dr. Ithimar, for heaven's sake, stop. What are you getting into. I won't permit any more. You must stop!

ITHIMAR (*gives a cry*): It's here! (*His arms with flashlight flung up from behind sofa.*) I have it! Bless you, Marcella, you have it. You have it. You still have it!

MARCELLA: Where did you find it.

ITHIMAR: Here—here! Just where I remembered.

MARCELLA: I'll add it to my blessings on the next count. (*Hurricane noises. Clashing of fixtures.*)

ITHIMAR: With this point for a compass, I could make a new sweep of the universe.

MARCELLA: Is it having a result?

ITHIMAR: Marcella, it's happening again to me. Just as it did on those ancient stairs. I am beating—like a metronome. Beating.

MARCELLA: I will not look. That was not part of the bargain. (*Hurricane. The lights go out.*) I wonder if this old building will stand. Hurricane Clara slashed off the roof. Hurricane Delia may push the whole rotten place over. (*By flashlight, the two stare at each other.*)

ITHIMAR: This is a moment of awe. The dead years have shifted aside. Again I feel like that immature boy. You must look, too, Marcella. The results must be verified.

MARCELLA: I will not! (*But she does.*) Iggy, what are we going to do with it?

ITHIMAR: I don't know.

MARCELLA: Iggy, those invisible gadgets you told me about, no bigger than a grain of pollen, is one of them trained on you? Are you important enough?

ITHIMAR: At Los Alamos, I had two bodyguards. So perhaps I am.

MARCELLA (*in a shout*): In a secret room at the Pentagon, is someone watching you and me on a screen.

ITHIMAR: Maybe. I've been in government service for so long, though. They must remember all I've done.

MARCELLA: But you're being seen. You're in danger.

ITHIMAR (*cries out*): I don't care. I don't care. It's worth the price.

We have recovered life. We were lost and now are found again. Found in a spout of blood as powerful as this hurricane!

MARCELLA (*piercingly*): Iggy! What are you *doing!* This is grotesque. (*Great hurricane noise.*)

ITHIMAR: Let me alone. I have found the expression. I have it! (*Flashlight extinguished. There is a great roar as the curtain falls down, and afterward the sound of cracking beams.*)

MARCELLA (*screaming*): It's ending. We're falling. It's crashing. (*After silence, throatily:*) Oh, Iggy—This is the end!

CURTAIN

Harold Brodkey

"Innocence"

1   ORRA AT HARVARD

Orra Perkins was a senior. Her looks were like a force that struck you. Truly, people on first meeting her often involuntarily lifted their arms as if about to fend off the brightness of the apparition. She was a somewhat scrawny, tulip-like girl of middling height. To see her in sunlight was to see Marxism die. I'm not the only one who said that. It was because seeing someone in actuality who had such a high immediate worth meant you had to decide whether such personal distinction had a right to exist or if she belonged to the state and ought to be shadowed in, reduced in scale, made lesser, laughed at.

Also, it was the case that you had to be rich and famous to set your hands on her; she could not fail to be a trophy and the question was whether the trophy had to be awarded on economic and political grounds or whether chance could enter in.

I was a senior too, and ironic. I had no money. I was without lineage. It seemed to me Orra was proof that life was a terrifying phenomenon of surface immediacy. She made any idea I had of psychological normalcy or of justice absurd since normalcy was not as admirable or as desirable as Orra; or rather she was normalcy and everything else was a falling off,

a falling below; and justice was inconceivable if she, or someone equivalent to her if there was an equivalent once you had seen her, would not
sleep with you. I used to create general hilarity in my room by shouting
her name at my friends and then breaking up into laughter, gasping out,
"God, we're so small time." It was grim that she existed and I had not had
her. One could still prefer a more ordinary girl but not for simple reasons.

A great many people avoided her, ran away from her. She was, in part,
more knowing than the rest of us because the experiences offered her had
been so extreme, and she had been so extreme in response—scenes in
Harvard Square with an English marquess, slapping a son of a billionaire
so hard he fell over backwards at a party in Lowell House, her saying then
and subsequently, "I never sleep with anyone who has a fat ass." Extreme in the humiliations endured and meted out, in the crassness of the
publicity, of her life defined as those adventures, extreme in the dangers
survived or not entirely survived, the cheapness undergone so that she
was on a kind of frightening eminence, an eminence of her experiences
and of her being different from everyone else. She'd dealt in intrigues,
major and minor, in the dramas of political families, in passions, decep-
tions, folly on a large, expensive scale, promises, violence, the genuine
pain of defeat when defeat is to some extent the result of your qualities
and not of your defects, and she knew the rottenness of victories that
hadn't been final. She was crass and impaired by beauty. She was like a
giant bird, she was as odd as an ostrich walking around the Yard, in her
absurd gorgeousness, she was so different from us in kind, so capable of
a different sort of progress through the yielding medium of the air,
through the strange rooms of our minutes on this earth, through the
gloomy circumstances of our lives in those years.

People said it was worth it to do this or that just in order to see her—
seeing her offered some kind of encouragement, was some kind of testimony that life was interesting. But not many people cared as much about
knowing her. Most people preferred to keep their distance. I don't know
what her having made herself into what she was had done for her. She
could have been ordinary if she'd wished.

She had unnoticeable hair, a far from arresting forehead, and extraordinary eyes, deep-set, longing, hopeful, angrily bored behind smooth,
heavy lids that fluttered when she was interested and when she was not
interested at all. She had a great desire not to trouble or be troubled by

supernumeraries and strangers. She has a proud, too large nose that gives her a noble, stubborn dog's look. Her mouth has a disconcertingly lovely set to it—it is more immediately expressive than her eyes and it shows her implacability: it is the implacability of her knowledge of life in her. People always stared at her. Some giggled nervously. *Do you like me, Orra? Do you like me at all?* They stared at the great hands of the Aztec priest opening them to feelings and to awe, exposing their hearts, the dread cautiousness of their lives. They stared at the incredible symmetries of her sometimes anguishedly passionate face, the erratic pain for her in being beautiful that showed on it, the occasional plunging gaiety she felt because she was beautiful. I like beautiful people. The symmetries of her face were often thwarted by her attempts at expressiveness—beauty was a stone she struggle free of. A ludicrous beauty. A cruel clown of a girl. Sometimes her face was absolutely impassive as if masked in dullness and she was trying to move among us incognito. I was aware that each of her downfalls made her more possible for me. I never doubted that she was privately a pedestrian shitting-peeing person. Whenever I had a chance to observe her for any length of time, in a classroom for instance, I would think, *I understand her.* Whenever I approached her, she responded up to a point and then even as I stood talking to her I would fade as a personage, as a sexual presence, as someone present and important to her into greater and greater invisibility. That was when she was a freshman, a sophomore, and a junior. When we were seniors, by then I'd learned how to avoid being invisible even to Orra. Orra was, I realized, hardly more than a terrific college girl, much vaunted, no more than that yet. But my god, my god, in one's eyes, in one's thoughts, she strode like a *Nike*, she entered like a blast of light, the thought of her was as vast as a desert. Sometimes in an early winter twilight in the Yard, I would see her in her coat, unbuttoned even in cold weather as if she burned slightly always, see her move clumsily along a walk looking like a scrawny field hockey player, a great athlete of a girl half-stumbling, uncoordinated off the playing field, yet with reserves of strength, do you know? and her face, as she walked along, might twitch like a dog's when the dog is asleep, twitching with whatever dialogue or adventure or daydream she was having in her head. Or she might in the early darkness stride along, cold-faced, haughty, angry, all the worst refusals one would ever receive bound up in one ridiculously beautiful girl. One always said,

I wonder what will become of her. Her ignoring me marked me as a sexual nonentity. She was proof of a level of sexual adventure I had not yet with my best efforts reached: that level existed because Orra existed.

What is it worth to be in love in this way?

2   ORRA WITH ME

I distrust summaries, any kind of gliding through time, any too great a claim that one is in control of what one recounts; I think someone who claims to understand but who is obviously calm, someone who claims to write with emotion recollected in tranquillity, is a fool and a liar. To understand is to tremble. To recollect is to reenter and be riven. An acrobat after spinning through the air in a mockery of flight stands erect on his perch and mockingly takes his bow as if what he is being applauded for was easy for him and cost him nothing, although meanwhile he is covered with sweat and his smile is edged with a relief chilling to think about; he is indulging in a show business style; he is pretending to be superhuman. I am bored with that and with where it has brought us. I admire the authority of being on one's knees in front of the event.

In the last spring of our being undergraduates, I finally got her. We had agreed to meet for dinner in my room, to get a little drunk cheaply before going out to dinner. I left the door unlatched; and I lay naked on my bed under a sheet. When she knocked on the door, I said, "Come in," and she did. She began to chatter right away, to complain that I was still in bed; she seemed to think I'd been taking a nap and had forgotten to wake up in time to get ready for her arrival. I said, "I'm naked, Orra, under this sheet. I've been waiting for you. I haven't been asleep."

Her face went empty. She said, "Damn you—why couldn't you wait?" But even while she was saying that, she was taking off her blouse.

I was amazed that she was so docile; and then I saw that it was maybe partly that she didn't want to risk saying no to me—she didn't want me to be hurt and difficult, she didn't want me to explode; she had a kind of hope of making me happy so that I'd then appreciate her and be happy with her and let her know me: I'm putting it badly. But her not being able to say no protected me from having so great a fear of sexual failure that I would not have been able to be worried about her pleasure, or to be concerned about her in bed. She was very amateurish and uninformed in bed, which touched me. It was really sort of poor sex; she didn't come or even feel much that I could see. Afterwards, lying beside her, I thought of her eight or ten or fifteen lovers being afraid of her, afraid to tell her anything about sex in case they might be wrong. I had an image of them protecting their own egos, holding their arms around their egos and not letting her near them. It seemed a kindness embedded in the event that she was, in quite an obvious way, with a little critical interpretation, a virgin. And impaired, or crippled by having been beautiful, just as I'd thought. I said to myself that it was a matter of course that I might be deluding myself. But what I did for the rest of that night—we stayed up all night; we talked, we quarreled for a while, we confessed various things, we argued about sex, we fucked again (the second one was a little better)—I treated her with the justice with which I'd treat a boy my age, a young man, and with a rather exact or measured patience and tolerance, as if she was a paraplegic and had spent her life in a wheelchair and was tired of sentiment. I showed her no sentiment at all. I figured she'd been asphyxiated by the sentiments and sentimentality of people impressed by her looks. She was beautiful and frightened and empty and shy and alone and wounded and invulnerable (like a cripple: what more can you do to a cripple?). She was Caesar and ruler of the known world and not Caesar and no one as well.

It was a fairly complicated, partly witty thing to do. It meant I could not respond to her beauty but had to ignore it. She was a curious sort of girl; she had a great deal of isolation in her, isolation as a woman. It meant that when she said something on the order of "You're very defensive," I had to be a debater, her equal, take her seriously, and say, "How do you mean that?" and then talk about it, and alternately deliver a blow ("You can't judge defensiveness, you have the silly irresponsibility of women, the silly disconnectedness: I *have* to be defensive.") and defer to her: "You have a point: you think very clearly. All right, I'll adopt that as a premise." Of course, much of what we said was incoherent and nonsensical on examination but we worked out in conversation what we meant or thought we meant. I didn't react to her in an emotional way. She wasn't really a girl, not really quite human: how could she be? She was a position, a specific glory, a trophy, our local upper-middle-class pseudo Cleopatra. Or not pseudo. I couldn't revel in my luck or be unself-consciously vain. I could not strut horizontally or loll as if on clouds, a demi-god with a goddess, although it was clear we were deeply fortunate, in spite of everything, the poor sex, the differences in attitude which were all we seemed to share, the tensions and the blundering. If I enjoyed her more than she enjoyed me, if I lost consciousness of her even for a moment, she would be closed into her isolation again. I couldn't love her and have her too. I could love her and have her if I didn't show love or the symptoms of having had her. It was like lying in a very lordly way, opening her to the possibility of feeling by making her comfortable inside the calm lies of my behavior, my inscribing the minutes with false messages. It was like meeting a requirement in Greek myth, like not looking back at Eurydice. The night crept on, swept on, late minutes, powdered with darkness, in the middle of a sleeping city, spring crawling like a plague of green snakes, bits of warmth in the air, at four A.M. smells of leaves when the stink of automobiles died down. Dawn came, so pink, so pastel, so silly: we were talking about the possibility of innate grammatical structures; I said it was an unlikely notion, that Jews really were God-haunted (the idea had been broached by a Jew), and the great difficulty was to invent a just God, that if God appeared at a moment of time or relied on prophets, there had to be degrees in the possibility of knowing him so that he was by definition unjust; the only just God would be one who consisted of what had always been known by everyone; and that you could always identify a basically Messianic, a hugely religious, fraudulent thinker by how much he tried to anchor his doctrine to having always been true, to being innate even in savage man, whereas an honest thinker, a nonliar, was caught in the grip of the truth of process and change and the profound absence of justice except as an invention, an attempt by the will to live with someone, or with many others without consuming them. At that moment Orra said, "I think we're falling in love."

I figured I had kept her from being too depressed after fucking—it's hard for a girl with any force in her and any brains to accept the whole thing of fucking, of being fucked without trying to turn it on its end, so that she does some fucking, or some fucking up; I mean the mere power of arousing the man so he wants to fuck isn't enough: she wants him to be willing to die in order to fuck. There's a kind of strain or intensity women are bred for, as beasts, for childbearing when childbearing might kill them, and childrearing when the child might die at any moment: it's in women to live under that danger, with that risk, that close to tragedy, with that constant taut or casual courage. They need death and nobility near. To be fucked when there's no drama inherent in it, when you're not going to rise to a level of nobility and courage forever denied the male, is to be cut off from what is inherently female, bestially speaking. I wanted to be halfway decent company for her. I don't know that it was natural to me. I am psychologically, profoundly, a transient. A form of trash. I am incapable of any continuing loyalty and silence; I am an informer. But I did all right with her. It was dawn, as I said. We stood naked by the window silently watching the light change. Finally she said, "Are you hungry? Do you want breakfast?"

"Sure. Let's get dressed and go—"

She cut me off; she said with a funny kind of firmness, "No! Let me go and get us something to eat."

"Orra, don't wait on me. Why are you doing this? Don't be like this."

But she was in a terrible hurry to be in love. After those few hours, after that short a time.

She said, "I'm not as smart as you, Wiley. Let me wait on you. Then things will be even."

"Things are even, Orra."

"No. I'm boring and stale. You just think I'm not because you're in love with me. Let me go."

I blinked. After a while, I said, "All right."

She dressed and went out and came back. While we ate, she was silent; I said things but she had no comment to make; she ate very little; she folded her hands and smiled mildly like some nineteenth-century portrait of a handsome young mother. Everytime I looked at her, when she saw I was looking at her, she changed the expression on her face to one of absolute and undeviating welcome to me and to anything I might say.

So, it had begun.

3   ORRA

She hadn't come. She said she had never come with anyone at any time. She said it didn't matter.

After our first time, she complained, "You went twitch, twitch, twitch—just like a grasshopper." So she had wanted to have more pleasure than she'd had. But after the second fuck and after the dawn, she never complained again—unless I tried to make her come, and then she complained of that. She showed during sex no dislike for any of my sexual mannerisms or for the rhythms and postures I fell into when I fucked. But I was not pleased or satisfied; it bothered me that she didn't come. I was not pleased or satisfied on my own account either. I thought the reason for that was she attracted me more than she could satisfy me, maybe more than fucking could ever satisfy me, that the more you cared, the more undertow there was, so that the sexual thing drowned—I mean the sharpest sensations, and yet the dullest, are when you masturbate—but when you're vilely attached to somebody, there are noises, distractions that drown out the sensations of fucking. For a long time, her wanting to fuck, her getting undressed, and the soft horizontal bobble of her breasts as she lay there, and the soft wavering, the kind of sinewlessness of her legs and lower body with which she more or less showed me she was ready, that was more moving, was more immensely important to me than any mere ejaculation later, any putt-putt-putt in her darkness, any hurling of future generations into the clenched universe, the strict mitten inside her: I clung to her and grunted and anchored myself to the most temporary imaginable relief of the desire I felt for her; I would be hungry again and anxious to fuck again in another twenty minutes; it was pitiable, this sexual disarray. It seemed to me that in the vast spaces of the excitement of being welcomed by each other, we could only sightlessly and at best half-organize our bodies. But so what? We would probably die in these underground caverns; a part of our lives would die; a certain innocence and hope would never survive this: we were too open, too clumsy, and we were the wrong people: so what did a fuck matter? I didn't mind if the sex was always a little rasping, something of a failure, if it was just preparation for more sex in half an hour, if coming was just more foreplay. If this was all that was in store for us, fine. But I thought she was getting gypped in that she felt so much about me, she was dependent, and she was generous, and she didn't come when we fucked.

She said she had never come, not once in her life, and that she didn't need to. And that I mustn't think about whether she came or not. "I'm a sexual tigress," she explained, "and I like to screw but I'm too sexual to come: I haven't that kind of daintiness. I'm not selfish *that* way."

I could see that she had prowled around in a sense and searched out men and asked them to be lovers as she had me rather than wait for them or plot to capture their attention in some subtle way; and in bed she was sexually eager and a bit more forward and less afraid than most girls; but only in an upper-middle-class frame of reference was she *a sexual tigress*.

It seemed to me—my whole self was focused on this—that her not coming said something about what we had, that her not coming was an undeniable fact, a measure of the limits of what we had. I did not think we should think we were great lovers when we weren't.

Orra said we were, that I had no idea how lousy the sex was other people had. I told her that hadn't been my experience. We were, it seemed to me, two twenty-one-year-olds, overeducated, irrevocably shy beneath our glaze of sexual determination and of sexual appetite, and psychologically somewhat slashed up and only capable of being partly useful to each other. We weren't the king and queen of Cockandcuntdom yet.

Orra said coming was a minor part of sex for a woman and was a demeaning measure of sexuality. She said it was imposed as a measure by people who knew nothing about sex and judged women childishly.

It seemed to me she was turning a factual thing, coming, into a public relations thing. But girls were under fearful public pressures in these matters.

When she spoke about them, these matters, she had a little, superior in puckered look, a don't-make-me-make-mincemeat-of-you-in-argument look—I thought of it as her Orra-as-Orra look, Orra alone, Orra-without-Wiley, without me, Orra isolated and depressed, a terrific girl, an Orra who hated cowing men.

She referred to novels, to novels by women writers, to specific scenes and remarks about sex and coming for women, but I'd read some of those books, out of curiosity, and none of them were literature, and the heroines in them invariably were innocent in every relation; but very strong and very knowing and with terrifically good judgment; and the men they loved were described in such a way they appeared to be examples of the woman's sexual reach, or of her intellectual value, rather than sexual companions or sexual objects; the women had sex generously with men who apparently bored them physically; I had thought the books and their writers and characters sexually naïve.

Very few women, it seemed to me, had much grasp of physical reality. Still, very strange things were often true, and a man's notion of orgasm was necessarily specialized.

When I did anything in bed to excite her with an eye to making her come, she asked me not to, and that irritated the hell out of me. But no matter what she said, it must be bad for her after six years of fucking around not to get to a climax. It had to be that it was a run on her neural patience. How strong could she be?

I thought about how women coming were at such a pitch of uncontrol they might prefer a dumb, careless lover, someone very unlike me: I had often played at being a strong, silent dunce. Some girls became fawning and doglike after they came, even toward dunces. Others jumped up and became immediately tough, proud of themselves as if the coming was *all* to their credit, and I ought to be flattered. God, it was a peculiar world. Brainy girls tended to control their comes, doling out one to a fuck, just like a man; and often they would try to keep that one under control, they would limit it to a single nozzle-contracted squirt of excitement. Even that sometimes racked and emptied them and made them curiously weak and brittle and embarrassed and delicate and lazy. Or they would act bold and say, "God, I needed that."

I wondered how Orra would look, in what way she would do it, a girl like that going off, how she'd hold herself, her eyes, how she'd act toward me when it was over.

To get her to talk about sex at all, I argued that analyzing something destroyed it, of course, but leaves rotted on the ground and prepared the way for what would grow next. So she talked.

She said I was wrong in what I told her I saw and that there was no difference in her between mental and physical excitement, that it wasn't true her mind was excited quickly, and her body slowly, if at all. I couldn't be certain I was right, but when I referred to a moment when there had seemed to be deep physical feeling in her, she sometimes agreed that had been a good moment in her terms; but sometimes she said, no, it had only been a little irritating then, like a peculiarly unpleasant tickle. In spite of her liking my mind, she gave me no authority for what I knew— I mean when it turned out I was right. She kept the authority for her reactions in her own hands. Her self-abnegation was her own doing. I liked that: some people just give you themselves, and it is too much to keep in your hands: your abilities aren't good enough. I decided to stick with what I observed and to think her somewhat mistaken and not to talk to her about sex any more.

I watched her in bed; her body was doubting, grudging, tardy, intolerant—and intolerably hungry—I thought. In her pride and self-consciousness and ignorance she hated all that in herself. She preferred to think of herself as quick, to have pleasure as she willed rather than as she actually had it, to have it on her own volition, to her own prescription, and almost out of politeness, so it seemed to me, to give herself to me, to give me pleasure, to ignore herself, to be a nice girl because she was in love. She insisted on that but that was too sentimental and she also insisted on, she persuaded herself, she passed herself off as dashing.

In a way, sexually, she was a compulsive liar.

I set myself to remove every iota of misconception I had about Orra in bed, any romanticism, any pleasurable hope. It seemed to me what had happened to her with other boys was that she was distrustful to start with and they had overrated her, and they'd been overwrought and off-balance and uneasy about her judgment of them, and they'd taken their pleasure and run.

And then she had in her determination to have sex become more and more of a sexual fool. (I was all kinds of fool: I didn't mind her being a sexual fool.) The first time I'd gone to bed with her, she'd screamed and thrown herself around, a good two or three feet to one side or another, as she thought a sexual tigress would, I supposed. I'd argued with her afterwards that no one was that excited especially without coming; she said she had come, sort of. She said she was too sexual for most men. She said her reactions weren't fake but represented a real sexuality, a real truth. That proud, stubborn, stupid girl.

But I told her that if she and a man were in sexual congress, and she heaved herself around and threw herself a large number of inches to either the left or the right or even straight up, the man was going to be startled; and if there was no regular pattern or predictability, it was easy to lose an erection; that if she threw herself to the side, there was a good chance she would interrupt the congress entirely unless the man was very quick and scrambled after her, and scrambling after her was not likely to be sexual for him: it would be more like playing tag. The man would have to fuck while in a state of siege; not knowing what she'd do next, he'd fuck and hurry to get it over and to get out.

Orra had said on that first occasion, "That sounds reasonable. No one ever explained that to me before, no one ever made it clear. I'll try it your way for a while."

After that, she had been mostly shy and honest, and honestly lecherous in bed but helpless to excite herself or to do more to me than she did just by being there and welcoming me. As if her hands were webbed and her mind was glued, as if I didn't deserve more, or as if she was such a novice and so shy she could not begin to do anything *sexual*. I did not understand: I'd always found that anyone who *wanted* to give pleasure, could: it didn't take skill, just the desire to please and a kind of, I-don't-know, a sightless ability to feel one's way to some extent in the lightless maze of pleasure. But upper-middle-class girls might be more fearful of tying men to them by bands of excessive pleasure; such girls were careful and shy.

I set myself for her being rude and difficult although she hadn't been rude and difficult to me for a long time but those traits were in her like a shadow giving her the dimensionality that made her valuable to me, that gave point to her kindness toward me. She had the sloppiest and most uncertain and silliest and yet bravest and most generous ego of anyone I'd ever known; and her manners were the most stupid imaginable alternation between the distinguished, the sensitive, the intelligent, with a rueful, firm, almost snotty delicacy and kindness and protectiveness toward you, and the really selfish and bruising. The important thing was to prevent her from responding falsely, as if in a movie, or in some imitation of the movies she'd seen and the books she'd read— she had a curious faith in movies and in books; she admired anything that made her feel and that did not require responsibility from her because then she produced happiness like silk for herself and others. She liked really obscure philosophers, like Hegel, where she could admire the thought but where the thought didn't demand anything from her. Still, she was a realist, and she would probably learn what I knew and would surpass me. She had great possibilities. But she was also merely a good-looking, pseudo-rich girl, a paranoid, a Perkins. On the other hand she was a fairly marvelous girl a lot of the time, brave, eye-shattering, who could split my heart open with one slightly shaky approving-of-me brainy romantic heroine's smile. The romantic splendor of her face. So far in her life she had disappointed everyone. I had to keep all this in mind, I figured. She was fantastically alive and eerily dead at the same time. I wanted from my various reasons to raise her from the dead.

4   ORRA: THE SAME WORLD, A DIFFERENT TIME SCALE

One afternoon, things went well for us. We went for a walk, the air was plangent, there was the amazed and polite pleasure we had sometimes merely at being together. Orra adjusted her pace now and then to mine; and I kept mine adjusted to her most of the time. When we looked at each other, there would be small, soft puffs of feeling as of toy explosions or sparrows bathing in the dust. Her willed softness, her inner seriousness or earnestness, her strength, her beauty muted and careful now in her anxiety not to lose me yet, made the pleasure of being with her noble, contrapuntal, and difficult in that one had to live up to it and understand it and protect it, against my clumsiness and Orra's falsity, kind as that falsity was; or the day would become simply an exploitation of a strong girl who would see through that sooner or later and avenge it. But things went well; and inside that careless and careful goodness, we went home; we screwed; I came—to get my excitement out of the way; she didn't know I was doing that; she was stupendously polite; taut; and very admiring. "How pretty you are," she said. Her eyes were blurred with half-tears. I'd screwed without any fripperies, cooly, in order to leave in us a large residue of sexual restlessness but with the burr of immediate physical restlessness in me removed: I still wanted her; I always wanted Orra; and the coming had been dull; but my body was not very assertive, was more like a glove for my mind, for my will, for my love for her, for my wanting to make her feel more.

She was slightly tearful, as I said, and gentle, and she held me in her arms after I came, and I said something like, "Don't relax. I want to come again," and she partly laughed, partly sighed, and was flattered, and said, "Again? That's nice." We had a terrific closeness, almost like a man and a secretary—I was free and powerful, and she was devoted: there was little chance Orra would ever be a secretary: she'd been offered executive jobs already for when she finished college, but to play at being a secretary who had no life of her own was a romantic thing for Orra. I felt some apprehension, as before a game of tennis that I wanted to win, or as before stealing something off a counter in a store: there was a dragging enervation, a fear and silence, and there was a lifting, a preparation, a willed and then unwilled, self-contained fixity of purpose; it was a settled thing; it would happen.

After about ten minutes or so, perhaps it was twenty, I moved in her: I should say that while I'd rested, I'd stayed in her (and she'd held on to me). As I'd expected—and with satisfaction and pride that everything was working, my endowments were cooperating—I felt my prick come up; it came up at once with comic promptness but it was sore—Jesus, was it sore. It, its head, ached like hell, with a dry, burning, reddish pain.

The pain made me chary and prevented me from being excited except in an abstract way; my mind was clear; I was idly smiling as I began, moving very slowly, just barely moving, sore of pressing on her inside her, moving around, lollygagging around, feeling out the reaches in there, arranging the space inside her, as if to put the inner soft-oiled shadows in her in order; or like stretching out your hand in the dark and pressing a curve of a blanket into familiarity or to locate yourself when you're half-asleep, when your eyes are closed. In fact, I did close my eyes and listened carefully to her breathing, concentrating on her but trying not to let her see I was doing that because it would make her self-conscious.

Her reaction was so minimal that I lost faith in fucking for getting her started, and I thought I'd better go down on her; I pulled out of her, which wasn't too smart, but I wasn't thinking all that consequentially; she'd told me on other occasions she didn't like "all that foreign la-di-dah," that it didn't excite her, but I'd always thought it was only that she was ashamed of not coming and that made being gone down on hard for her. I started in on it; she protested; and I pooh-poohed her objections and did it anyway; I was raw with nerves, with stifled amusement because of the lying and the tension, so much of it. I remarked to her that I was going down on her for my own pleasure; I was jolted by touching her with my tongue there when I was so raw-nerved but I hid that. It seemed to me physical unhappiness and readiness were apparent in her skin— my lips and tongue carried the currents of a jagged unhappiness and readiness in her into me; echoes of her stiffness and dissatisfaction sounded in my mouth, my head, my feet; my entire tired body was a stethoscope. I was entirely a stethoscope; I listened to her with my *bones;* the glimmers of excitement in her traveled to my *spine;* I felt her grinding sexual haltedness, like a car's broken starter motor grinding away in her, in my *stomach,* in my *knees.* Every part of me listened to her; every goddamned twinge of muscular contraction she had that I noticed or that she should have had because I was licking her clitoris and she didn't have, every testimony of excitement or of no-excitement in her, I listened for so hard it was amazing it didn't drive her out of bed with self-consciousness; but she probably couldn't tell what I was doing, since I was out of her line of sight, was down in the shadows, in the basement of her field of vision, in the basement with her sexual feelings where they lay, strewn about.

When she said, "No . . . No, Wiley . . . Please don't. No . . ." and wiggled, although it wasn't the usual pointless protest that some girls might make—it was real, she wanted me to stop—I didn't listen because I could feel she responded to my tongue more than she had to the fucking a moment before. I could feel beads sliding and whispering and being strung together rustlingly in her; the disorder, the scattered or strewn sexual bits, to a very small extent, were being put in order. She shuddered. With discomfort. She produced, was subjected to, her erratic responses. And she made odd, small cries, protests mostly, uttered little exclamations that mysteriously were protests although they were not protests too, cries that somehow suggested the ground of protest kept changing for her.

I tried to string a number of those cries together, to cause them to occur in a mounting sequence. It was a peculiar attempt: it seemed we moved, I moved with her, on dark water, between two lines of buoys, dark on one side, there was nothingness there, and on the other, lights, red and green, the lights of the body advancing on sexual heat, the signs of it anyway, nipples like scored pebbles, legs lightly thrashing, little *ohs;* nothing important, a body thing; you go on: you proceed.

When we strayed too far, there was nothingness, or only a distant flicker, only the faintest guidance. Sometimes we were surrounded by the lights of her responses, widely spaced, bobbing unevenly, on some darkness, some ignorance we both had, Orra and I, of what were the responses of her body. To the physical things I did and to the atmosphere of the way I did them, to the authority, the argument I made that this was sexual for her, that the way I touched her and concentrated on her, on that partly dream-laden dark water or underwater thing, she responded; she rested on that, rolled heavily on that. Everything I did was speech, was hieroglyphics, pictures on her nerves; it was what masculine authority was for, was what bravery and a firm manner and musculature were supposed to indicate that a man could bring to bed. Or skill at dancing; or musicianliness; or a sad knowingness. Licking her, holding her belly, stroking her belly pretty much with unthought-out movements—sometimes just moving my fingers closer together and spreading them again to show my pleasure, to show how rewarded I felt, not touching her breasts or doing anything so intensely that it would make her suspect me of being out to make her come—I did those things but it seemed like I left her alone and was private with my own pleasures. She felt unobserved with her sensations, she had them without responsibility, she clutched at them as something round and slippery in the water, and she would fall off them, occasionally gasping at the loss of her balance, the loss of her self-possession too.

I'd flick, idly almost, at her little spaghetti-ending with my tongue, then twice more idly, then three or four or five times in sequence, then settle down to rub it or bounce it between lip and tongue in a steadily more earnest way until my head, my consciousness, my lips and tongue were buried in the dark of an ascending and concentrated rhythm, in the way a stoned dancer lets a movement catch him and wrap him around and become all of him, become his voyage and not a collection of repetitions at all.

Then some boring stringy thing, a sinew at the base of my tongue, would begin to ache, and I'd break off that movement, and sleepily lick her, or if the tongue was too uncomfortable, I'd worry her clit, I'd nuzzle it with my pursed lips until the muscles that held my lips pursed grew tired in their turn; and I'd go back and flick at her tiny clitoris with my tongue, and go on as before, until the darkness came; she sensed the darkness, the privacy for her, and she seemed like someone in a hallway, unobserved, moving her arms, letting her mind stroke itself, taking a step in that dark.

But whatever she felt was brief and halting; and when she seemed to halt or to be dead or jagged, I authoritatively, gesturally accepted that as part of what was pleasurable to me and did not let it stand as hint or foretaste of failure; I produced sighs of pleasure, even gasps, not all of them false, warm nuzzlings, and caresses that indicated I was rewarded—I produced rewarded strokings; I made elements of sexual pleasure out of moments that were unsexual and that could be taken as the collapse of sexuality.

And she couldn't contradict me because she thought I was working on my own coming, and she loved me and meant to be cooperative.

What I did took nerve because it gave her a tremendous ultimate power to laugh at me, although what the courtship up until now had been for was to show that she was not an enemy, that she could control the hysteria of fear or jealousy in her or the cold judgments in her of me that would lead her to say or do things that would make me hate or fear her; what was at stake included the risk that I would look foolish in my own eyes—and might then attack her for failing to come—and then she would be unable to resist the inward conviction I was a fool. Any attempted act confers vulnerability on you but an act devoted to her pleasure represented doubled vulnerability since only she could judge it; and I was safe only if I was immune or insensitive to her; but if I was immune or insensitive I could not hope to help her come; by making myself vulnerable to her, I was in a way being a sissy or a creep because Orra wasn't organized or trained or prepared to accept responsibility for how I felt about myself: she was a woman who wanted to be left alone; she was paranoid about the inroads on her life men in their egos tried to make: there was dangerous masochism, dangerous hubris, dangerous hopefulness, and a form of love in my doing what I did: I nuzzled nakedly at the crotch of the sexual tigress; any weakness in her ego or her judgment and she would lash out at *me*; and the line was very frail between what I was doing as love and as intrusion, exploitation, and stupid boastfulness. There was no way for me even to begin to imagine the mental pain—or the physical pain—for her if I should fail, and, then to add to that, if I should withdraw from her emotionally too, because of my failure and hers and our pain. Or merely because the failure might make me so uncomfortable I couldn't go on unless she nursed my ego, and she couldn't nurse my ego, she didn't know how to do it, and probably was inhibited about doing it.

Sometimes my hands, my fingers, not just the tips, but all of their inside surface and the palms, held her thighs, or cupped her little belly, or my fingers moved around the lips, the labia or whatever, or even poked a little into her, or with the nails or tips lightly nudged her clitoris, always within a fictional frame of my absolute sexual pleasure, of my admiration for this sex, of there being no danger in it for us. No tongues or brains handy to speak unkindly, I meant. My God, I felt exposed and noble. This was a great effort to make for her.

Perhaps that only indicates the extent of my selfishness. I didn't mind being feminized except for the feeling that Orra would not ever understand what I was doing but would ascribe it to the power of my or our sexuality. I minded being this self-conscious and so conscious of her; I was separated from my own sexuality, from any real sexuality; a poor sexual experience, even one based on love, would diminish the ease of my virility with her at least for a while; and she wouldn't understand. Maybe she would become much subtler and shrewder sexually and know how to handle me but that wasn't likely. And if I apologized or complained or explained in that problematic future why I was sexually a little slow or reluctant with her, she would then blame my having tried to give her orgasm, she would insist I must not be bored again, so I would in that problematic future, if I wanted her to come, have to lie and say I was having more excitement than I felt, and that too might diminish my pleasure. I would be deprived even of the chance for honesty: I would be further feminized in that regard. I thought all this while I went down on her. I didn't put it in words but thought in great misty blocks of something known or sensed. I felt an inner weariness I kept working in spite of. This ignoring myself gave me an odd, starved feeling, a mixture of agony and helplessness. I didn't want to feel like that. I suddenly wondered why in the Theory of Relativity the speed of light is given as a constant: was that more Jewish absolutism? Surely in a universe as changeable and as odd as this one, the speed of light, considering the variety of experiences, must vary; there must be a place where one could see a beam of light struggle to move. I felt silly and selfish; it couldn't be avoided that I felt like that—I mean it couldn't be avoided by *me*.

Whatever she did when I licked her, if she moved at all, if a muscle twitched in her thigh, a muscle twitched in mine, my body imitated hers as if to measure what she felt or perhaps for no reason but only because the sympathy was so intense. The same things happened to each of us but in amazingly different contexts as if we stood at opposite ends of the room and reached out to touch each other and to receive identi-

cal messages which then diverged as they entered two such widely separated sensibilities and two such divergent and incomplete ecstasies.
The movie we watched was of her discovering how her sexual responses
worked: we were seated far apart. My tongue pushed at her erasure, her
wronged and heretofore hardly existent sexual powers. I stirred her with
varieties of kisses far from her face. A strange river moved slowly, bearing us along, reeds hid the banks, willows braided and unbraided themselves, moaned and whispered, raveled and faintly clicked. Orra groaned,
sighed, shuddered, shuddered harshly or liquidly; sometimes she jumped
when I changed the pressure or posture of my hands on her or when I
rested for a second and then resumed. Her body jumped and contracted
interestingly but not at any length or in any pattern that I could understand. My mind grew tired. There is a limit to invention, to mine anyway: I saw myself (stupidly) as a Roman trireme, my tongue as the prow,
bronze, pushing at her; she was the Mediterranean. Tiers of slaves, my
god, the helplessness of them, pulled oars, long stalks that metaphorically
and rhythmically bloomed with flowing clusters of short-lived lilies at
the water's surface. The pompous and out-of-proportion boat, all of me
hunched over Orra's small sea—not actually hunched: what I was, was
lying flat, the foot of the bed was at my waist or near there, my legs were
out, my feet were propped distantly on the floor, all of me was concentrated on the soft, shivery, furry delicacies of Orra's twat, the pompous
boat advanced lickingly, leaving a trickling, gurgling wake of half-
response, the ebbing of my will and activity into that fluster subsiding
into the dark water of this girl's passivity, taut storminess, and self-
ignorance.

The whitish bubbling, the splash of her discontinuous physical response: those waves, ah, that wake rose, curled outward, bubbled, and
fell. Rose, curled outward, bubbled, and fell. The white fell of a naiad. In
the vast spreading darkness and silence of the sea. There was nothing but
that wake. The darkness of my senses when the rhythm absorbed me (so
that I vanished from my awareness, so that I was blotted up and was a
stain, a squid hidden, stroking Orra) made it twilight or night for me; and
my listening for her pleasure, for our track on that markless ocean, gave
me the sense that where we were was in a lit-up, great, ill-defined oval
of night air and sea and opalescent fog, rainbowed where the lights from
the portholes of an immense ship were altered prismatically by droplets

of mist—as in some 1930's movie, as in some dream. Often I was out of breath; I saw spots, colors, ocean depths. And her protests, her doubts! My God, her doubts! Her *No don't, Wiley's* and her *I don't want to do this's* and her *Wiley, don't's* and *Wiley, I can't come—don't do this—I don't like this's*. Mostly I ignored her. Sometimes I silenced her by leaning my cheek on her belly and watching my hand stroke her belly and saying to her in a sex-thickened voice, "Orra, I like this—this is for me."

Then I went down on her again with unexpectedly vivid, real pleasure, as if merely thinking about my own pleasure excited and refreshed me, and there was yet more pleasure, when she—reassured or strengthened by my putative selfishness, by the conviction that this was all for me, that nothing was expected of her—cried out. Then a second later she *grunted*. Her whole body rippled. Jesus, I loved it when she reacted to me. It was like causing an entire continent to convulse, Asia, South America. I felt huge and tireless.

In her excitement, she threw herself into the air; but my hands happened to be on her belly; and I fastened her down, I held that part of her comparatively still with her twat fastened to my mouth, and I licked her while she was in mid-heave; and she yelled; I kept my mouth there as if I were drinking from her; I stayed like that until her upper body fell back on the bed and bounced, she made the whole bed bounce; then my head bounced away from her; but I still held her down with my hands; and I fastened myself, my mouth, on her twat again; and she yelled in a deep voice, "*Wiley, what are you doing!*"

Her voice was deep, as if her impulses at that moment were masculine, not out of neurosis but in generosity, in an attempt to improve on the sickliness she accused women of; she wanted to meet me halfway, to share; to share my masculinity: she thought men were beautiful: she cried out, "*I don't want you to do things to me! I want you to have a good fuck!*"

Her voice was deep and despairing, maybe with the despair that goes with surges of sexuality, but then maybe she thought I would make her pay for this. I said, "Orra, I like this stuff, this stuff is what gets me excited." She resisted, just barely, for some infinitesimal fragment of a second, and then her body began to vibrate; it twittered as if in it were the strings of a musical instrument set jangling; she said foolishly—but sweetly—"Wiley, I'm embarrassed, Wiley, this embarrasses *me* . . . Please stop . . . No . . . No . . . No . . . Oh . . . Oh . . . Oh . . . I'm very sexual, I'm too sexual to have orgasms, Wiley, stop, please . . . Oh . . . Oh . . . Oh . . ." And then a deeper shudder ran through her; she gasped; then there was a silence; then she gasped again; she cried out in an extraordinary voice, *"I FEEL SOMETHING!"* The hair stood up on the back of my neck; I couldn't stop; I hurried on; I heard a dim moaning come from her. What had she felt before? I licked hurriedly. How unpleasant for her, how unreal and twitchy had the feelings been that I'd given her? In what way was this different? I wondered if there was in her a sudden swarming along her nerves, a warm conviction of the reality of sexual pleasure. She heaved like a whale—no: not so much as that. But it was as if half an ocean rolled off her young flanks; some element of darkness vanished from the room; some slight color of physical happiness tinctured her body and its thin coating of sweat; I felt it all through me; she rolled on the surface of a pale blue, a pink and blue sea; she was dark and gleaming, and immense and wet. And warm.

She cried, *"Wiley, I feel a lot!"*

God, she was happy.

I said, "Why not?" I wanted to lower the drama quotient; I thought the excess of drama was a mistake, would overburden her. But also I wanted her to defer to me, I wanted authority over her body now, I wanted to make her come.

But she didn't get any more excited than that: she was rigid, almost boardlike after a few seconds. I licked at her thing as best I could but the sea was dry; the board collapsed. I faked it that I was very excited; actually I was so caught up in being sure of myself, I didn't know what I really felt. I thought, as if I was much younger than I was, Boy, if this doesn't work, is my name mud. Then to build up the risk, out of sheer hellish braggadocio, instead of just acting out that I was confident—and in sex, everything unsaid that is portrayed in gestures instead, is twice as powerful—when she said, because the feeling was less for her now, the feeling she liked having gone away, "Wiley, I can't—this is silly—" I said, "Shut up, Orra, I know what I'm doing . . ." But I didn't know.

And I didn't like that tone for sexual interplay either, except as a joke, or as role-playing, because pure authority involves pure submission, and people don't survive pure submission except by being slavishly, possessively, vindictively in love; when they are in love like that, they can *give* you nothing but rebellion and submission, bitchiness and submission; it's a general rottenness: you get no part of them out of bed that has any value; and in bed, you get a grudging submission, because what the slave requires is your total attention, or she starts paying you back; I suppose the model is childhood, that slavery. Anyway I don't like it. But I played at it, then, with Orra, as a gamble.

Everything was a gamble. I didn't know what I was doing; I figured it out as I went along; and how much time did I have for figuring things out just then? I felt strained as at poker or roulette, sweaty and a little stupid, placing bets—with my tongue—and waiting to see what the wheel did, risking my money when no one forced me to, hoping things would go my way, and I wouldn't turn out to have been stupid when this was over.

Also, there were sudden fugitive convulsions of lust now, in sympathy with her larger but scattered responses, a sort of immediate and automatic sexuality—I was at the disposal, inwardly, of the sexuality in her and could not help myself, could not hold it back and avoid the disappointments, and physical impatience, the impatience in my skin and prick, of the huge desire that unmistakably accompanies love, of a primitive longing for what seemed her happiness, for closeness to her as to something I had studied and was studying and had found more and more of value in—what was of value was the way she valued me, a deep, and no doubt limited (but in the sexual moment it seemed illimitable) permissiveness toward me, a risk she took, an allowance she made as if she'd let me damage her and use her badly.

Partly what kept me going was stubbornness because I'd made up my mind before we started that I wouldn't give up; and partly what it was was the feeling she aroused in me, a feeling that was, to be honest, made up of tenderness and concern and a kind of mere affection, a brotherliness, as if she was my brother, not different from me at all.

Actually this was brought on by an increasing failure, as the sex went on, of one kind of sophistication—of worldly sophistication—and by the increase in me of another kind, of a childish sophistication, a growth of innocence: Orra said, or exclaimed, in a half-harried, half-amazed voice, in a hugely admiring, gratuitous way, as she clutched at me in approval, "Wiley, I never had feelings like these before!"

And to be the first to have caused them, you know? It's like being a collector, finding something of great value, where it had been unsuspected and disguised, or like earning any honor; this partial success, this encouragement gave rise to this pride, this inward innocence.

Of course that lessened the risk for this occasion; I could fail now and still say, *It was worth it,* and she would agree; but it lengthened the slightly longer-term risk; because I might feel trebly a fool someday. Also it meant we might spend months making love in this fashion—I'd get impotent, maybe not in terms of erection, but I wouldn't look forward to sex—still, that was beautiful to me in a way too and exciting. I really didn't know what I was thinking: whatever I thought was part of the sex.

I went on, I wanted to hit the jackpot now. Then Orra shouted, "It's *there!* It's *THERE!*" I halted, thinking she meant it was in some specific locale, in some specific motion I'd just made with my tired tongue and jaw; I lifted my head—but couldn't speak: in a way, the sexuality pressed on me too hard for me to speak; anyway I didn't have to; she had lifted her head with a kind of overt twinship and she was looking at me down the length of her body; her face was askew and boyish—every feature was wrinkled; she looked angry and yet naïve and swindleable; she said angrily, naïvely, *"Wiley, it's there!"*

But even before she spoke that time, I knew she'd meant it was in her; the fox had been startled from its covert again; she had seen it, had felt it run in her again. She had been persuaded that it was in her for good.

I started manipulating her delicately with my hand; and in my own excitement, and thinking she was ready, I sort of scrambled up and covering her with myself, and playing with her with one hand, guided my other self, my lower consciousness, into her. My God, she was warm and restless inside; it was heated in there and smooth, insanely smooth, and oiled, and full of movements. But I knew at once I'd made a mistake: I should have gone on licking her; there were no regular contractions; she was anxious for the prick, she rose around it, closed around it, but in a rigid, dumb, far-away way; and her twitchings played on it, ran through it, through the walls of it and into me; and they were uncontrolled and not exciting, but empty: she didn't know what to do, how to be fucked and come. I couldn't pull out of her, I didn't want to, I couldn't pull out; but if there were no contractions for me to respond to, how in hell would I find the rhythm for her? I started slowly with what seemed infinite suggestiveness to me, with great dirtiness, a really grownup sort of fucking—just in case she was far along—and she let out a huge, shuddering hour-long sigh and cried out my name and then in a sobbing, exhausted voice, said, "I lost it . . . Oh Wiley, I lost it . . . Let's stop . . ." My face was above hers; her face was wet with tears; why was she crying like that? She had changed her mind; now she wanted to come; she turned her head back and forth; she said, "I'm no good . . . I'm no good . . . Don't worry about me . . . You come . . ."

No matter what I mumbled, "Hush," and "Don't be silly," and in a whisper, "Orra, I love you," she kept on saying those things until I slapped her lightly and said, "*Shut up, Orra.*"

Then she was silent again.

The thing was, apparently, that she was arhythmic: at least that's what I thought; and that meant there weren't going to be regular contractions; any rhythm for me to follow; and, any rhythm I set up as I fucked, she broke with her movements: so that it was that when she moved, she made her excitement go away: it would be best if she moved very smally: but I was afraid to tell her that, or even to try to hold her hips firmly, and guide them, to instruct her in that way for fear she'd get self-conscious and lose what momentum she'd won. And also I was ashamed that I'd stopped going down on her. I experimented—doggedly, sweatily, to make up for what I'd done—with fucking in different ways, and I fantasized about us being in Mexico, some place warm and lushly colored where we made love easily and filthily and graphically. The fantasy kept me going. That is, it kept me hard. I kept acting out an atmosphere of sexual pleasure—I mean of my sexual pleasure—for her to rest on, so she could count on that. I discovered that a not very slow sort of one-one-one stroke, or fuck-fuck-fuck-Orra-now-now-now really got to her; her feelings would grow heated; and she could shift up from that with me into a one-two, one-two, one-two, her excitement rising; but if she or I then tried to shift up farther to one-two-three, one-two-three, she'd lose it all. That was too complicated for her: my own true love, my white American. But her feelings when they were present were very strong, they came in gusts, huge squalls of heat as if from a furnace with a carelessly banging door, and they excited and allured both of us. That excitement and the dit-dit-ditting got to her; she began to be generally, continuingly sexual. It's almost standard to compare sexual excitement to holiness; well, after a while, holiness seized her; she spoke with tongues, she testified. She was shaking all over; she was saved temporarily and sporadically; that is, she kept lapsing out of that excitement too. But it would recur. Her hands would flutter; her face would be pale and then red, then very, very red; her eyes would stare at nothing; she'd call my name. I'd plug on one-one-one, then one-two, one-two, then I'd go back to one-one-one: I could see as before—in the deep pleasure I felt even in the midst of the labor—why a woman was proud of what she felt, why a man might kill her in order to stimulate in her (although he might not know this was why he did it) these signs of pleasure. The familiar Orra had vanished; she said, "GodohGodoh-God"; it was sin and redemption and holiness and visions time. Her throbs were very direct, easily comprehensible, but without any pattern; they weren't in any regular sequence; still, they were exciting to me, maybe all the more exciting because of the piteousness of her not being able to regulate them, of their being like blows delivered inside her by an enemy whom she couldn't even half-domesticate or make friendly to herself or speak to. She was the most out-of-control girl I ever screwed. She would at times start to thrust like a woman who had her sexuality readied and well-understood at last and I'd start to distend with anticipation and a pride and relief as large as a house; but after two thrusts—or four, or six— she'd have gotten too excited, she'd be shaking, she'd thrust crookedly and out of tempo, the movement would collapse; or she'd suddenly jerk in mid-movement without warning and crash around with so great and so meaningless a violence that she'd lose her thing; and she'd start to cry. She'd whisper wetly, "I lost it"; so I'd say, "No, you didn't," and I'd go on or start over, one-one-one; and of course, the excitement would come back; sometimes it came back at once; but she was increasingly afraid of herself, afraid to move her lower body; she would try to hold still and just *receive* the excitement; she would let it pool up in her; but then too she'd begin to shake more and more; she'd leak over into spasmodic and oddly sad, too large movements; and she'd whimper, knowing, I suppose, that those movements were breaking the tempo in herself; again and again, tears streamed down her cheeks; she said in a not quite hoarse, in a sweet, almost hoarse whisper, "I don't want to come, Wiley, you go ahead and come."

My mind had pretty much shut off; it had become exhausted; and I didn't see how we were going to make this work; she said, "Wiley, it's all right—please, it's all right—I don't want to come."

I wondered if I should say something and try to trigger some fantasy in her; but I didn't want to risk saying something she'd find unpleasant or think was a reproach or a hint for her to be sexier. I thought if I just kept on dit-dit-ditting, sooner or later, she'd find it in herself, the trick of riding on her feelings, and getting them to rear up, crest, and topple. I held her tightly, in sympathy and pity, and maybe fear, and admiration: she was so unhysterical; she hadn't yelled at me or broken anything; she hadn't ordered me around: she was simply alone and shaking in the middle of a neural storm in her that she seemed to have no gift for handling. I said, "Orra, it's OK: I really prefer long fucks," and I went on, dit-dit-dit-dit, then I'd shift up to dit-dot, dit-dot, dit-dot, dit-dot . . . My back hurt, my legs were going; if sweat was sperm, we would have looked like liquefied snow fields.

Orra made noises, more and more quickly, and louder and louder; then the noises she made slackened off. Then, step by step, with shorter and shorter strokes, then out of control and clumsy, simply reestablishing myself inside the new approach, I settled down, fucked slowly. The prick was embedded far in her; I barely stirred; the drama of sexual movement died away, the curtains were stilled; there was only sensation on the stage.

I bumped against the stone blocks and hidden hooks that nipped and bruised me into the soft rottenness, the strange, glowing, breakable hardness of coming, of the sensations at the approaches to coming.

I panted and half-rolled and pushed and edged it in, and slid it back, sweatily—I was semi-expert, aimed, intent: sex can be like a wilderness that imprisons you: the daimons of the locality claim you: I was achingly nagged by sensations; my prick had been somewhat softened before and now it swelled with a sore-headed, but fine distention; Orra shuddered and held me cooperatively; I began to forget her.

I thought she was making herself come on the slow fucking, on the prick which, when it was seated in her like this, when I hardly moved it, seemed to belong to her as much as to me; the prick seemed to *enter* me too; we both seemed to be sliding on it, the sensation was like that; but there was the moment when I became suddenly aware of her again, of the flesh and blood and bone in my arms, beneath me. I had a feeling of grating on her, and of her grating on me. I didn't recognize the unpleasantness at first. I don't know how long it went on before I felt it as a withdrawal in her, a withdrawal that she had made, a patient and restrained horror in her, and impatience in me: our arrival at sexual shambles.

My heart filled suddenly—filled; and then all feeling ran out of it—it emptied itself.

I continued to move in her slowly, numbly, in a shabby hubbub of faceless shudderings and shufflings of the mid-section and half-thrusts, half-twitches; we went on holding each other, in silence, without slackening the intensity with which we held each other; our movements, that flopping in place, that grinding against each other, went on; neither of us protested in any way. Bad sex can be sometimes stronger and more moving than good sex. She made sobbing noises—and held on to me. After a while sex seemed very ordinary and familiar and unromantic. I started going dit-dit-dit again.

Her hips jerked up half a dozen times before it occurred to me again that she liked to thrust like a boy, that she wanted to thrust; and then it occurred to me she wanted me to thrust.

I maneuvered my ass slightly and tentatively delivered a shove, or rather, delivered an authoritative shove, but not one of great length, one that was exploratory; Orra sighed, with relief it seemed to me; and jerked, encouragingly, too late, as I was pulling back. When I delivered a second thrust, a somewhat more obvious one, more amused, almost boyish, I was like a boy whipping a fairly fast ball in a game, at a first baseman—she jerked almost wolfishly, gobbling up the extravagant power of the gesture, of the thrust; with an odd shudder of pleasure, of irresponsibility, of boyishness, I suddenly realized how physically strong Orra was, how well-knit, how well put together her body was, how great the power in it, the power of endurance in it; and a phrase—absurd and demeaning but exciting just then—came into my head: *to throw a fuck*; and I settled myself atop her, braced my toes and knees and elbows and hands on the bed and half-scramblingly worked *it*—*it* was clearly mine; but I was Orra's—worked *it* into a passionate shove, a curving stroke about a third as long as a full stroke; but amateur and gentle, that is, tentative still; and Orra screamed then; how she screamed; she made known her readiness: then the next time, she grunted: "Uhnnnnahhhhhh . . . " a sound thick at the beginning but that trailed into refinement, into sweetness, a lingering sweetness.

It seemed to me I really wanted to fuck like this, that *I* had been waiting for this all my life. But it wasn't really my taste, that kind of fuck: I liked to throw a fuck with less force and more gradations and implications of force rather than with the actual thing; and with more immediate contact between the two sets of pleasures and with more admissions of defeat and triumph; my pleasure was a thing of me reflecting her; her spirit entering me; or perhaps it was merely a mistake, my thinking that; but it seemed shameful and automatic, naïve and animal: to throw the prick into her like that.

She took the thrust: she convulsed a little; she fluttered all over; her skin fluttered; things twitched in her, in the disorder surrounding the phallic blow in her. After two thrusts, she collapsed, went flaccid, then toughened and readied herself again, rose a bit from the bed, aimed the flattened, mysteriously funnel-like container of her lower end at me, too high, so that I had to pull her down with my hands on her butt or on her hips; and her face, when I glanced at her beneath my lids, was fantastically pleasing, set, concentrated, busy, harassed; her body was strong, was stone, smooth stone and wet-satin paper bags and snaky webs, thin and alive, made of woven snakes that lived, thrown over the stone; she held the great, writhing-skinned stone construction toward me, the bony marvel, the half-dish of bone with its secretive, gluey-smooth entrance, *the place where I was*—it was undefined, except for that: *the place where I was*: she took and met each thrust—and shuddered and collapsed and rose again: she seemed to rise to the act of taking it; I thought she was partly mistaken, childish, to think that the center of sex was to meet and take the prick thrown into her as hard as it could be thrown, now that she was excited; but there was a weird wildness, a wild freedom, like children cavorting, uncontrolled, set free, but not hysterical, merely without restraint; the odd, thickened, knobbed pole springing back and forth as if mounted on a web of wide rubber bands; it was a naïve and a complete release. I whomped it in and she went, "UHNNN!" and a half-iota of a second later, I was seated all the way in her, I jerked a minim of an inch deeper in her, and went, "UHNNN!" too. Her whole body shook. She would go, "UHN!" And I would go, "UHN!"

Then when it seemed from her strengthening noises and her more rapid and jerkier movements that she was near the edge of coming, I'd start to place the whomps, in neater and firmer arrangements, more obviously in a rhythm, more businesslike, more teasing with pauses at each end of a thrust; and that would excite her up to a point; but then her excitement would level off, and not go over the brink. So I would speed up: I'd thrust harder, then harder yet, then harder and faster; she made her noises and half-thrust back. She bit her lower lip; she set her teeth in her lower lip; blood appeared. I fucked still faster, but on a shorter stroke, almost thrumming on her, and angling my abdomen hopefully to drum on her clitoris; sometimes her body would go limp; but her cries would speed up, bird after bird flew out of her mouth while she lay limp as if I were a boxer and had destroyed her ability to move; then when the cries did not go past a certain point, when she didn't come, I'd slow and start again. I wished I'd been a great athlete, a master of movement, a woman, a lesbian, a man with a gigantic prick that would explode her into coming. I moved my hands to the corners of the mattress; and spread my legs; I braced myself with my hands and feet; and braced like that, free-handed in a way, drove into her; and the new posture, the feeling she must have had of being covered; and perhaps the difference in the thrust got to her; but Orra's body began to set up a babble, a babble of response then—I think the posture played on her mind.

But she did not come.

I moved my hands and held the dish of her hips so that she couldn't wiggle or deflect the thrust or pull away: she began to "Uhn" again but interspersed with small screams: we were like kids playing catch (her poor brutalized clitoris), playing hard hand: this was what she thought sex was; it was sexual, as throwing a ball hard is sexual; in a way, too, we were like acrobats hurling ourselves at each other, to meet in mid-air, and fall entangled to the net. It was like that.

Her mouth came open, her eyes had rolled to one side and stayed there—it felt like twilight to me—I knew where she was sexually, or thought I did. She pushed, she egged us on. She wasn't breakable this way. Orra. I wondered if she knew, it made me like her how naïve this was, this American fuck, this kids-playing-at-twilight-on-the-neighborhood-street fuck. After I seated it and wriggled a bit in her and moozed on her clitoris with my abdomen, I would draw it out not in a straight line but at some curve so that it would press against the walls of her cunt and she could keep track of where it was; and I would pause fractionally just before starting to thrust, so she could brace herself and expect it; I whomped it in and understood her with an absurd and probably unfounded sense of my sexual virtuosity; and she became silent suddenly, then she began to breathe loudly, then something in her toppled; or broke, then all once she shuddered in a different way. It really was as if she lay on a bed of wings, as if she had a half-dozen wings folded under her, six huge wings, large, veined, throbbing, alive wings, real ones, with fleshy edges from which glittering feathers sprang backward; and they all stirred under her.

She half-rose; and I'd hold her so she didn't fling herself around and lose her footing, or her airborneness, on the uneasy glass mountain she'd begun to ascend, the frail transparency beneath her, that was forming and growing beneath her, that seemed to me to foam with light and darkness, as if we were rising above a landscape of hedges and moonlight and shadows: a mountain, a sea that formed and grew; it grew and grew; and she said "OH!" and "OHHHH!" almost with vertigo, as if she was airborne but unsteady on the vans of her wings, and as if I was there without wings but by some magic dispensation and by some grace of familiarity; I thunked on and on, and she looked down and was frightened; the tension in her body grew vast; and suddenly a great, a really massive violence ran through her but now it was as if, in fear at her height, or out of some automatism, the first of her three pairs of wings began to beat, great fans winnowingly, great wings of flesh out of which feathers grew, catching at the air, stabilizing and yet lifting her: she whistled and rustled so; she was at once so still and so violent; the great wings engendered, their movement engendered in her, patterns of flexed and crossed muscles: her arms and legs and breasts echoed or carried out the strain, or strained to move the weight of those winnowing, moving wings. Her breaths were wild but not loud and slanted every which way, irregular and new to this particular dream, and very much as if she looked down on great spaces of air; she grabbed at me, at my shoulders, but she had forgotten how to work her hands; her hands just made the gestures of grabbing, the gestures of a well-meaning, dark but beginning to be luminous, mad, amnesiac angel. She called out, "Wiley, Wiley!" but she called it out in a *whisper*, the whisper of someone floating across a night sky, of someone crazily ascending, someone who was going crazy, who was taking on the mad purity and temper of angels, someone who was tormented unendurably by this, who was unendurably frightened, whose pleasure was enormous, half-human, mad. Then she screamed in rebuke, "Wiley!" She screamed my name: *"Wiley!"*—she did it hoarsely and insanely, asking for help, but blaming me, and merely as exclamation; it was a gutter sound in part, and ugly; the ugliness, when it destroyed nothing, or maybe it had an impetus of its own, but it whisked away another covering, a membrane of ordinariness—I don't know—and her second pair of wings began to beat; her whole body was aflutter on the bed. I was as wet as—as some fish, thonking away, sweatily. Grinding away. I said, "It's OK, Orra. It's OK." And poked on. In mid-air. She shouted, *"What is this!"* She shouted it in the way a tremendously large person who can defend herself might shout at someone who was unwisely beating her up. She shouted—angrily, as an announcement of anger, it seemed—*"Oh my God!"* Like: *Who broke this cup?* I plugged on. She raised her torso, her head, she looked me clearly in the eye, her eyes were enormous, were bulging, and she said, *"Wiley, it's happening!"* Then she lay down again and screamed for a couple of seconds. I said a little dully, grinding on, "It's OK, Orra. It's OK." I didn't want to say *Let go* or to say anything lucid because I didn't know a damn thing about female orgasm after all, and I didn't want to give her any advice and wreck things; and also I didn't want to commit myself in case this turned out to be a false alarm; and we had to go on. I pushed in, lingered, pulled back, went in, only half on beat, one-thonk-one-thonk, then one-one-one, saying, "This is sexy, this is good for me, Orra, this is very good for me," and then, "Good Orra," and she trembled in a new way at that, *"Good* Orra," I said, *"Good . . . Orra,"* and then all at once, it happened. Something pulled her over; and something gave in; and all three pairs of wings began to beat: she was the center and the source and the victim of a storm of wing beats; we were at the top of the world; the huge bird of God's body in us hovered; the great miracle pounded on her back, pounded around us; she was straining and agonized and distraught, estranged within this corporeal-incorporeal thing, this angelic other avatar, this other substance of herself: the wings were outspread; they thundered and gaspily galloped with her; they half broke her; and she screamed, *"Wiley!"* and *"Mygodmygod"* and *"IT'S NOT STOPPING, WILEY, IT'S NOT STOPPING!"* She was pale *and* red; her hair was everywhere; her body was wet, and thrashing. It was as if something unbelievably strange and fierce—like the holy temper—lifted her to where she could not breathe or walk: she choked in the ether, a scrambling seraph, tumbling, and aflame and alien, powerful beyond belief, hideous and frightening and beautiful beyond the reach of the human. A screaming child, an angel howling in the Godly sphere: she churned without delicacy, as wild as an angel bearing threats; her body lifted from the sheets, fell back, lifted again; her hands beat on the bed; she made very loud hoarse tearing noises—I was frightened for her: this was her first time after six years of playing around with her body. It hurt her; her face looked like something made of stone, a monstrous carving; only her body was alive; her arms and legs were outspread and tensed and they beat or they were weak and fluttering. She was an angel as brilliant as a beautiful insect infinitely enlarged and irrevocably foreign: she was unlike me: she was a girl making rattling, astonished, uncontrolled, unhappy noises, a girl looking shocked and intent and harassed by the variety and viciousness of the sensations, including relief, that attacked her. I sat up on my knees and moved a little in her and stroked her breasts, with smooth sideways, winglike strokes. And she screamed, *"Wiley, I'm coming!"* and with a certain idiocy entered on her second orgasm or perhaps her third since she'd started to come a few minutes before; and we would have gone on for hours but she said, "It hurts, Wiley, I hurt, make it stop . . ." So I didn't move; I just held her thighs with my hands; and her things began to trail off, to trickle down, into little shiverings; the stoniness left her face; she calmed into moderated shudders, and then she said, she started to speak with wonder but then it became an exclamation and ended on a kind of a hollow note, the prelude to a small scream: she said "I *came* . . ." Or "I ca-a-a-ammmmmmmmme . . ." What happened was that she had another orgasm at the thought that she'd had her first.

That one was more like three little ones, diminishing in strength. When she was quieter, she was gasping, she said, "Oh you *love* me . . ."

That too excited her. When that died down, she said—angrily—"I always knew they were doing it wrong, I always knew there was nothing wrong with me . . ." And that triggered a little set of ripples. Some time earlier, without knowing it, I'd begun to cry. My tears fell on her thighs, her belly, her breasts, as I moved up, along her body, above her, to lie atop her. I wanted to hold her, my face next to hers; I wanted to hold her. I slid my arms in and under her, and she said, "Oh, Wiley," and she tried to lift her arms, but she started to shake again; then trembling anyway, she lifted her arms and hugged me with a shuddering sternness that was unmistakable; then she began to cry too.

Janice Eidus

"Elvis, Axl, and Me"

I met Elvis for the first time in the deli across the street from the elevated line on White Plains Road and Pelham Parkway in the Bronx. Elvis was the only customer besides me. He was sitting at the next table. I could tell it was him right away, even though he was dressed up as a Hasidic Jew. He was wearing a yarmulke on top of his head, and a lopsided, shiny black wig with long peyes on the sides that drooped past his chin, a fake-looking beard to his collarbone, and a shapeless black coat, which didn't hide his paunch, even sitting down. His skin was as white as flour, and his eyes looked glazed, as though he spent far too much time indoors.

"I'll have that soup there, with the round balls floatin' in it," he said to the elderly waiter. He pointed at a large vat of matzoh ball soup. Elvis's Yiddish accent was so bad he might as well have held up a sign saying, "Hey, it's me, Elvis Presley, the Hillbilly Hassid, and I ain't dead at all!" But the waiter, who was wearing a huge hearing aid, just nodded, not appearing to notice anything unusual about his customer.

Sipping my coffee, I stared surreptitiously at Elvis, amazed that he was alive and pretending to be a Hasidic Jew on Pelham Parkway. Unlike all those Elvis-obsessed women who made annual pilgrimages to Graceland and who'd voted on the Elvis postage stamp, I'd never particularly had a thing for Elvis. Elvis just wasn't my type. He was too goody-goody for me. Even back when I was a little girl and I'd watched him swiveling his hips on *The Ed Sullivan Show,* I could tell that, underneath, he was just an All-American Kid.

My type is Axl Rose, the tattooed bad boy lead singer of the heavy metal band Guns n' Roses, whom I'd recently had a *very* minor nervous breakdown over. Although I've never met Axl Rose in the flesh, and although he's *very* immature and *very* politically incorrect, I know that, somehow, somewhere, I *will* meet him one day, because I know that he's destined to be the great love of my life.

Still, even though Elvis is a lot older, tamer, and fatter than Axl, he *is* the King of Rock 'n' Roll, and that's nothing to scoff at. Even Axl himself would have to be impressed by Elvis.

I waited until Elvis's soup had arrived before going over to him. Boldly, I sat right down at his table. "Hey, Elvis," I said, "it's nice to see you."

He looked at me with surprise, nervously twirling one of his fake peyes. And then he blushed, a long, slow blush, and I could tell two things: one, he liked my looks, and two, he wasn't at all sorry that I'd recognized him.

"Why, hon," he said, in his charming, sleepy-sounding voice, "you're the prettiest darn thing I've seen here on Pelham Parkway in a hound dog's age. You're also the first person who's ever really spotted me. All those other Elvis sightings, at Disneyland and shopping malls in New Jersey, you know, they're all bogus as three-dollar bills. I've been right here on Pelham Parkway the whole darned time."

"Tell me *all* about it, Elvis." I leaned forward on my elbows, feeling very flirtatious, the way I used to when I was still living downtown in the East Village. That was before I'd moved back here to Pelham Parkway, where I grew up. The reason I moved back was because, the year before, I inherited my parents' two-bedroom apartment on Holland Avenue, after their tragic death when the chartered bus taking them to Atlantic City had crashed into a Mack truck. During my East Village days, though, I'd had lots of flirtations, as well as lots and lots of dramatic and tortured affairs with angry-looking, spike-haired poets and painters. But all that was before I discovered Axl Rose, of course, and before I had my *very* minor nervous breakdown over him. I mean, my breakdown was so minor I didn't do anything crazy at all. I didn't stand in the middle of the street directing traffic, or jump off the Brooklyn Bridge, or anything like that. Mostly I just had a wonderful time fantasizing about what it would be like to make love to him, what it would be like to bite his sexy pierced nipple, to run my fingers through his long, sleek, red hair and all over his many tattoos, and to stick my hand inside his skintight, nearly see-through, white Lycra biking shorts. In the meantime, though, since I had happily bid good-riddance to the spike-haired poets and painters, and since Axl Rose wasn't anywhere around, I figured I might as well do some heavy flirting with Elvis.

"Okay," Elvis smiled, almost shyly, "I'll tell you the truth." His teeth were glistening white and perfectly capped, definitely not the teeth of a Hasidic Jew. "And the truth, little girl, is that I'd gotten mighty burned out."

I liked hearing him call me that—"little girl." Mindy, the social worker assigned to my case at the hospital after my breakdown, used to say, "Nancy, you're not a little girl any longer, and rock stars like their women really young. Do you truly believe—I'll be brutal and honest here, it's for your own good—that if, somehow, you actually were to run into Axl Rose on the street, he would even look your way?" Mindy was a big believer in a branch of therapy called "Reality Therapy," which I'd overheard some of the other social workers calling "Pseudo-Reality Therapy" behind her back. Mindy was only twenty-three, and she'd actually had the nerve to laugh in my face when I tried to explain to her that ultimately it would be my womanly, sophisticated, and knowing mind that would make Axl go wild with uncontrollable lust, the kind of lust no vacuous twenty-three-year-old bimbo could ever evoke in a man. Axl and I were destined for each other precisely because we were so different, and together we would create a kind of magic sensuality unequaled in the history of the world and, in addition, I would educate him, change him, and help him to grow into a sensitive, mature, and socially concerned male. But Mindy had stopped listening to me. So after that, I changed my strategy. I kept agreeing with her, instead. "You're right, Mindy," I would declare emphatically, "Axl Rose is a spoiled rock 'n' roll superstar and a sexist pig who probably likes jailbait, and there's no way our paths are ever going to cross. I'm not obsessed with him any more. You can sign my release papers now."

"Little girl," Elvis repeated that first day in the deli, maybe sensing how much I liked hearing him say those words, "I ain't gonna go into all the grisly details about myself. You've read the newspapers and seen those soppy TV movies, right?"

I nodded.

"I figured you had," he sighed, stirring his soup. "Everyone has. There ain't been no stone left unturned—even the way I had to wear diapers after a while," he blushed again, "and the way I used my gun to shoot out the TV set, and all that other stuff I did, and how the pressures of being The King, the greatest rock 'n' roll singer in the world, led me to booze, drugs, compulsive overeatin', and impotence. . . ."

I nodded again, charmed by the way he pronounced it im*po*tence with the accent in the middle. My heart went out to him, because he looked so sad and yet so proud of himself at the same time. And I really, really liked that he'd called me *little girl* twice.

"Want some of this here soup?" he offered. "I ain't never had none better."

I shook my head. "Go on, Elvis," I said. "Tell me more." I was really enjoying myself. True, he wasn't Axl, but he *was* The King.

"Well," he said, taking a big bite out of the larger of the two matzoh balls left in his bowl, "what I decided to do, see, was to fake my own death and then spend the rest of my life hiding out, somewhere where nobody would ever think to look, somewhere where I could lead a clean, sober, and pious life." He flirtatiously wiggled his fake peyes at me. "And little girl, that's when I remembered an article I'd read, about how the Bronx is called 'The Forgotten Borough,' because nobody, but *nobody*, with any power or money, ever comes up here."

"I can vouch for that," I agreed, sadly. "I grew up here."

"And, hon, I did it. I cleaned myself up. I ain't a drug and booze addict no more. As for the overeatin', well, even the Good Lord must have one or two vices, is the way I see it." He smiled.

I smiled back, reminding myself that, after all, not everyone can be as wiry and trim as a tattooed rock 'n' roll singer at the height of his career.

"And I ain't im*po*tent no more," Elvis added, leering suggestively at me.

Of course, he had completely won me over. I invited him home with me after he'd finished his soup and the two slices of honey cake he'd ordered for dessert. When we got back to my parents' apartment, he grew hungry again. I went into the kitchen and cooked some kreplach for him. My obese Bubba Sadie had taught me how to make kreplach when I was ten years old, although, before meeting Elvis, I hadn't ever made it on my own.

"Little girl, I just love Jewish food," Elvis told me sincerely, spearing a kreplach with his fork. "I'm so honored that you whipped this up on my humble account."

Elvis ate three servings of my kreplach. He smacked his lips. "Better than my own momma's fried chicken," he said, which I knew was a heap-ful of praise coming from him, since, according to the newspapers and TV movies, Elvis had an unresolved thing for his mother. It was my turn to blush. And then he stood up and, looking deeply and romantically into my eyes, sang "Love Me Tender." And although his voice showed the signs of age, and the wear and tear of booze and drugs, it was still a beautiful voice, and tears came to my eyes.

After that, we cleared the table, and we went to bed. He wasn't a bad lover, despite his girth. "One thing I do know," he said, again sounding simultaneously humble and proud, "is how to pleasure a woman."

I didn't tell him that night about my obsessive love for Axl Rose, and I'm very glad that I didn't. Because since then I've learned that Elvis has no respect at all for contemporary rock 'n' roll singers. "Pretty boy wussies with hair," he describes them. He always grabs the TV remote away from me and changes the channel when I'm going around the stations and happen to land on MTV. Once, before he was able to change the chan-nel, we caught a quick glimpse together of Axl, strutting in front of the mike in his sexy black leather kilt and singing his pretty heart out about some cruel woman who'd hurt him and who he intended to hurt back. I held my breath, hoping that Elvis, sitting next to me on my mother's pink brocade sofa, wouldn't hear how rapidly my heart was beating, wouldn't see that my skin was turning almost as pink as the sofa.

"What a momma's boy and wussey *that* skinny li'l wannabe rock 'n' roller is," Elvis merely sneered, exaggerating his own drawl and grabbing the remote out of my hand. He switched to HBO, which was showing an old Burt Reynolds movie. "Hot dawg," Elvis said, settling back on the sofa, "a Burt flick!"

Still, sometimes when we're in bed, I make a mistake and call him Axl. And he blinks and looks at me and says, "Huh? What'd you say, little girl?" "Oh, Elvis, darling," I always answer without missing a beat, "I just said 'Ask.' Ask me to do anything for you, anything at all, and I'll do it. Just ask." And really, I've grown so fond of him, and we have such fun together, that I mean it. I *would* do anything for Elvis. It isn't his fault that Axl Rose, who captured my heart first, is my destiny.

Elvis and I lead a simple, sweet life together. He comes over three or four times every week in his disguise—the yarmulke, the fake beard and peyes, the shapeless black coat—and we take little strolls together through Bronx Park. Then, when he grows tired, we head back to my parents' apartment, and I cook dinner for him. In addition to my kreplach, he's crazy about my blintzes and noodle kugel.

After dinner, we go to bed, where he pleasures me, and I fantasize about Axl. Later, we put our clothes back on, and we sit side by side on my mother's sofa and watch Burt Reynolds movies. Sometimes we watch Elvis's old movies, too. His favorites are *Jailhouse Rock* and *Viva Las Vegas*. But they always make him weepy and sad, which breaks my heart, so I prefer to watch Burt Reynolds.

And Elvis is content just to keep on dating. He never pressures me to move in with him, or to get married, which—as much as I care for him— is fine with me. "Little girl," Elvis always says, "I love you with all my country boy's heart and soul, more than I ever loved Priscilla, I swear I do, and there ain't a selfish bone in my body, but my rent-controlled apartment on a tree-lined block, well, it's a once-in-a-life-time deal, so I just can't give it up and move into your parents' apartment with you."

"Hey, Elvis, no sweat," I reply, sweetly. And I tell him that, much as I love him, I can't move in with him, either, because *his* apartment—a studio with kitchenette—is just too small for both of us. "I understand, little girl," he says, hugging me. "I really do. You've got some of that feisty women's libber inside of you, and you need your own space."

But the truth is, it's not my space I care about so much. The truth is that I've got long-range plans, which don't include Elvis. Here's how I figure it: down the road, when Axl, like Elvis before him, burns out—and it's inevitable that he will, given the way that boy is going—when he's finally driven, like Elvis, to fake his own death in order to escape the pressures of rock 'n' roll superstardom, and when he goes into hiding under an assumed identity, well, then, I think the odds are pretty good he'll end up living right here on Pelham Parkway. After all, Axl and I are *bound* to meet up some day—destiny is destiny, and there's no way around it.

I'm not saying it *will* happen just that way, mind you. All I'm saying is that, if Elvis Presley is alive and well and masquerading as a Hasidic Jew in the Bronx, well, then, anything is possible, and I do mean *anything*. And anything includes me and Axl, right here on Pelham Parkway, pleasuring each other night and day. It's not that I want to hurt Elvis, believe me. But I figure he probably won't last long enough to see it happen, anyway, considering how out of shape he is, and all.

The way I picture it is this: Axl holding me in his tattooed, wiry arms and telling me that all his life he's been waiting to find me, even though he hardly dared dream that I existed in the flesh, the perfect woman, an experienced woman who can make kreplach and blintzes and noodle kugel, a woman who was the last—and best—lover of Elvis Presley, the King of Rock 'n' Roll himself. It *could* happen. That's all I'm saying.

Nathan Englander

"Peep Show"

T ouch," she says.

She is looking right at him, she can see him. This is not how Alan
Fein remembers past visits, not with the women looking back. He turns
to the other women seated on the carpeted platform, turns to them as if
for confirmation, and each, eyeing him, begins with the same thing.
"Touch," they say, "touch." Well, two out of the other three say it. The
last—sitting in her cheap plastic lawn chair, too wide for it; her thighs,
cut in half, drooping like her breasts in languid arcs toward the floor—
is reading a book. She's got glasses on and is holding a page, ready to turn
it, and he knows the motion will be slow and lazy, as weary as her posture.

They are all four on the stage naked, or almost so. The second woman
wears a bra, the third panties, and the fourth has the book and glasses.
It is the first one, the first that spoke, who is, to Alan, beautiful.

He has not been in a peep show since boyhood. Thirteen the last
time. Alan recalls things from then. The tiny window and the tiny room.
The way he used to stand and shiver, shiver so badly that his teeth chattered, his hands pressed between his legs for warmth. He had been afraid
he might freeze to death, actually expire from excitement and he'd often
indulged this nightmare, squandered precious viewing time on the darker

fantasy of dropping dead right there in the booth. Alan would picture the old man who used to run the old place banging and banging and banging on the door. Unlocking it and finding Alan's body, the old man would empty pockets, hold up a single house key, a stray bobby pin, while the other kids jockeyed for position—torn away from the more erotic fare by the captivating spectacle of sudden death.

It's not the same anymore. Change inevitable. The glass is gone from the windows, glass mirrored on one side. The windows had left you, the voyeur, invisible in your booth, dark and safe, as the women moved for the tiny mirrored echoes of themselves. And they had danced like they cared, moved to excite, to titillate the observer. The only time you saw anybody else was when you ran out to buy tokens from the old man. It was Alan's only contact with the outside world, his only interactions with strange boys, Gentile boys, boys who smoked cigarettes, whose fathers were mechanics, whose mothers had rocked them to sleep singing in Swahili or Chinese. The others were always dreamy. Drunk on fantasy, high on the chemicals that washed their brains and left them ether-slow when they opened the doors. There was also the tacit agreement that none of them were there: they were not cutting school, or spending money they had stolen out of their mothers' purses, or hard up, or the kind of people who would enter such a place. They were not themselves. They were nothing but eyes. Alan didn't remember any grownups. He didn't remember anyone else shaking either, when they bought their tokens from the man.

It is bright enough so that Alan can see into the other windows that circle the stage. The faces are both young and old, and still, like always, from every walk of life. The men are earnest, even the ones who stare at backs of chairs. The framed faces look like portraits. Alan is in a living portrait gallery, watching as the windows close, winking slowly, opening again, on a new face, a new honoree to be for a moment displayed on this bull ring of a wall.

There is the occasional twitch of facial muscle. There are shoulders that move and all they imply. One middle-aged, broad-headed man has a wide, open-mouthed smile going and is clearly masturbating with vigor. An asylum is brought to mind. He catches the eye of another man, Latino, hair-slicked, wearing the very same tie as his own. Alan puts his hand to his chest, feels the silk of his tie pulsing with his heart, like a feather held before a mouth, telling him he is alive. The man, the slicked man, such a good looking man, turns away first. Alan half expected that he would greet him in the language of the realm; "Touch," he had thought the man would say. He looks back at the three women he does not desire, so old and heavy and bored, so long naked that they don't even know. The second woman, the one next to the beauty, turns to the Latino man. "Touch," she says. Alan sees no visible response, but she goes over and the Latino man's hands come out, exiting the picture that frames him, penetrating the fantasy world. He has never seen it broached before, the world of dreams cracked open. He has never seen a woman leave and does not even know how one might, can not find anywhere, the handle to a door.

The first girl is perfection and when she looks at Alan he feels unworthy to watch. He can hardly bear having her acknowledge him, so skewed and corrupt does the whole situation seem. He wants to ask her what she is looking at. "Can I help you?" he would have said if they were anywhere else. He reddens when he looks away from her eyes, not because he can't maintain her stare, but because he is looking at her long bare legs, a deep black that accentuates the contours so much in contrast are they with the whiteness of the chair. He looks at her shoulders, smooth and round and strong, picking up the highlights even under the depressing green of the fluorescent bulbs. She is so young, so perfect and beautiful, and Alan wants her, desperately. He stares at her and feels sick. Her look beckons. Trained and insincere, he is sure, but wanting him nonetheless. "Touch," she says, and Alan thinks, yes, he wants to touch her, to see if she is real. But he hasn't yet responded, hasn't said a thing, and she is coming toward him, so long and graceful, the woman of his dreams.

Alan is shaking again, like when he was a boy. And why shouldn't he be? A loyal husband, who, reaching out, touching, had always honored his vows. He does not move his hands or his fingers, just presses them against her wonderful skin, so warm, almost hot, and is embarrassed as his hands tremble. She takes them in her own, presses them to her chest, and massages. It calms him. She does this like an expert, a masseuse, a doctor, someone trained in an art. He hasn't been so aroused in years. He wants to say something, to tell her, to climb through and be with her. But the window starts to come down, it is closing, and in the split second he has to make the choice, Alan takes back his hands.

Leaning up against the wall in a terror, a complete panic, he tells himself it was an aberration, just like his entering the place, his giving in to the feeling and coming up those stairs—each with a word painted on the front, a greater claim made with every step, so that before seeing the landing at the top Alan knew it promised ECSTASY.

Alan Fein had regained what he thought he would never feel again: the immaculate yearning that no woman of this world, with a name and a history, no woman who was anything but pure sex, pure lust, could ever rouse. It was wonderful and he feels horrible about it and about the young girl he has just violated. She had asked, hadn't she? Offered herself? But he shouldn't have touched her. Claire was in the car, at the bus stop, waiting. At some point he will touch Claire, press the same hands against his wife. Deception. He lets these thoughts overwhelm him. It is time to be sorry. Remorse is the antidote to joy.

He straightens his tie and picks up his briefcase, the four remaining tokens he holds in his other hand. He had only wanted one, had gone up the stairs with a stray quarter, already nearing rapture, already feeling guilty for what he was about to do. He had been on his way to Port Authority, was almost there, just like every day, no different than any other except that he had stubbed his toe, scuffed a shoe, looked up and took notice.

Alan Fein had put a nick in $250 of a $500 investment. It had maddened him and then shocked him, for he wondered how little Ari Feinberg had become Alan Fein, Esq., in fancy ox-blood wing tips that mattered if they were scuffed, a man, grown, on his way home to his loving wife, his beautiful blonde Gentile wife who laughed when he didn't know how to work the Christmas lights, who thought it was adorable when he was awed to learn that one bulb decides whether they flash or not, a woman who bought a candle with a picture of Jesus on it when it came time for the memorial of his father. "They were out of the little white ones," she had said. "Can't you just turn Jesus toward the wall?" And he wondered why he couldn't *just*. Looking down again, he wondered, once more, how he had come to be wearing half-a-thousand dollar shoes.

The scuffing, the nick, had bumped him from the flow to which he was accustomed. And he had looked around 42nd Street, at the regentrified theaters and all the new shops, well lit and friendly, the kind a family could enter in broad daylight. What had happened to all the hucksters who used to stand outside promising nirvana and shaken booty, forbidden acts and creamy thighs? So busy had Alan been with his own transformation that he hadn't noticed the one going on around him. Standing there, leaning against a wall, spit shining his toecap with a handkerchief, he wondered something. As polished, as straight, as middle class and on the up and up as 42nd Street now looked, Alan Fein wondered if it was still the same inside.

And then the man had said it.

"Buddy," he said. "Mac," he said. "Upstairs. Girls. Live girls inside."

"What?" Alan had said, as if the proposition was confusing. But it was more the "what" one says to a familiar voice, the hazy "what" of recognition.

There was the sign in the window. The neon token, round, with the 25 cents flashing in its center. "That's right, buddy," the man said. "Twenty-five cents. Two stages. Lots of girls. Follow the stairs, you can't get lost, all the arrows lead to one place—Paradise."

Alan's mind reeled with the thought of what waited upstairs. His desire charmed to raging by the idea of the naked body, of the lovely ache he would experience while watching the dancers move.

And he went up, glancing only for a second, to see if fate had mustered an office mate or neighbor to descry his ascent. He headed into the stairwell, painted black; the only light coming off the flashing neon arrows and illuminating the words on the stairs.

He found a quarter in his pocket. One shot, one quarter. He would tell Claire about it, like a joke, as if he had been there on a dare. Yes, if he felt guilty enough, he would tell Claire that he had been inside.

When he got to the top and entered the place, he had expected the old man from his childhood, had expected the other boys to be pooling pennies for a shared booth, to be hustling the old man for a token.

But here in front of him was a towering figure behind a podium. Alan could see where the hallway opened, where a single, massive, many-doored pillar reached from floor to ceiling. He looked back at the man, mammoth, truly too big to fit through one of the doors, his legs reach-

ing out past the width of the podium. A baseball bat, needle thin compared to the leg, leaned against the podium's side.

Alan had put his quarter on top of the podium, elevated enough that
he had to reach. The man had laughed.

"A dollar," he said.

"It says a quarter." Alan spoke octaves higher than the man, higher
than Alan himself usually did.

"A dollar," the man said. Alan, fumbling with his wallet, found some
twenties, and a fifty, and a five. He pulled out the five-dollar bill and took
five tokens, too bashful to ask for change.

A crime, he thought. False advertising. He saw himself taking the
case pro bono, a good Samaritan, Alan Fein and the Perverts of New
York State vs. The Place With The Flashing Arrows. He entertained
himself with the scenario, calmed himself on his way to the wheel of
doors.

Which to choose? A decision of mythic proportions.

Alan had gone to the right.

And now, minutes later, a different man: a violator of girls and wives and
matrimonial bonds. Alan clutches his briefcase more tightly, tokens more
tightly, and considers leaving, though his legs have gone cool and empty
so that they feel unreliable and hollow at their cores. And there is his
erection, diabolically hard, bringing to mind all the basest and most virile descriptions from pornographic magazines. Alan is so very close he is
afraid to move, careful not even to brush against his briefcase which he
holds before him like a shield. He wants to get away without climax, before he has to face the enormity of his pleasure. How much more absolute
would his sin be then? The briefcase back at his side, he remains still. His
other hand is clutched tightly. Should he open it, the tokens would not
drop, so deeply are they impressed into his palm. Empty thoughts. Peace-
ful thoughts. Sane, level, realistic thoughts. There is Claire, waiting.
But the girl is on the other side. So wonderful. Her legs and skin. The
way—the skill—with which she touched. The idea of her is so enticing
it pushes him past control. Alan lets go and, with every wave, lets the
shame rush in and fill the emptiness so that even the hollow legs feel
solid and full.

Immediately there is plotting. Already the deceit grows. A joke, he would say, A dare. Horrible. And to ride the bus home this way, to face Claire, soiled. She could drop him at the gym. The gym before dinner; that is the plan. He is waiting, locked in his pressboard sarcophagus, preparing to make an exit. But the erection, it endures. He is neither so old that it should disappear in an instant, nor so young, so new to it all, that it should remain—and in such a pronounced and steadfast state.

And why should it fade when she is so near and there are four more tokens and he has already crossed the threshold and made his way inside? The erection builds strength and, Alan worries, might never go away. He can not, will not, leave in this state. And he admits to himself, knows, that if he did not ever have to leave, if it meant spending all he had, giving up everything, and losing irretrievably the outside world, he would abandon it all if only that siren would stand up from her chair, take his hands, and guide them over her body one more time. But he won't allow himself such an indulgence. He will put in the token but he will not touch. He will look at his shoes, at the scuff mark that damned him. He will shake and picture his own heart attack, the fat man stepping on his briefcase and tearing at his suit pants to get at his wallet, the fat man calling Claire on the car phone to break, callously, the news. This is how he will occupy himself—without a whit more enjoyment. He will use up what he paid for but the penance, the penance will begin right now.

Checking his watch, making sure there is time, Alan drops in the second token and, closing his eyes, hearing the window give, falls against the wall.

There is silence. He waits, counting in his head. A dollar doesn't buy much, very soon the window will close.

"Hey!"

He hears it, the voice deep, raspy, and, he thinks, rather accusatory. "Hey, you. Feinberg. You want to touch?" Fein knows right away who it is. But it takes some time, an understandable pause. "Touch, Feinberg? You want to cop a feel?"

He raises his eyes and the old chatter returns. He goes cold. It is, in the first chair, the man who he imagined. It is, looking the same, though fifteen years older, Rabbi Mann. He is naked and fat, his chest hairy. Mann has become so overweight that his masculine breasts are bigger than were the girl's.

Down the row are three other rabbis from his old school. Rabbi Rifkin sits in the second chair wearing boxers, a bleached-out blue. Then there's Rabbi Wolf, so tall, his shoulders almost at the other man's head, only donning tzitzit, the fringes once white looking yellow against the chair. In the last seat is Rabbi Zeitler, a tractate spread across his lap, his glasses black and thick-lensed, distorting greatly, so that looking at his face it seems his eyes are tiny and his head deeply notched. He adjusts his glasses, pushing them higher on his nose.

Amazed at himself for not passing out, or losing, immediately, his mind, Alan wishes that his shrink, Dr. Springmire, was there to tell him if it was so. Anyone to help him along.

"Should I come over so you can lay a hand on me?" It is Mann. "You want me to come over by you?" Rabbi Mann puts his hands on the sides of the chair and begins to push himself up.

Alan is grabbing the window frame, scratching at the groove in the top, trying to get hold of the partition, to drag it down. "Please, Rabbi. Sit. Do sit."

"Of me you don't want a pinch?" He puts on a falsetto, puts up his arms and bends his hands and fingers delicately, as if to cast the shadow of a swan. He is trying to look dainty. "I'm not so good enough as the pretty girl with the long legs? Too hairy? Too Jewish to be touched by the big-shot lawyer? By Mr. Ari-Alan-Feinberg-Fein."

"That's not it," Alan says. "Not at all. I wasn't going to touch again. I was already done."

"Not true, Feinberg. I know better. Ari Feinberg isn't satisfied. He never is." Rabbi Mann addresses the moving windows, a rotating jury. "But does he ever stay to finish? No, he always turns to run."

A good idea, Alan thinks. He turns, forgetting his briefcase, is about to rush for the door.

"Hold it, Feinberg. Turn around. Look at me. Listen to me for a second."

Alan drops his hands, turns, looks, listens.

"Always so emotional," Rabbi Mann says, leaning forward so that his testicles hang off the end of the chair. "You've always been too emotional, Feinberg. Acting without thinking, doing what feels best, chasing around after your own heart." Rabbi Rifkin nods in agreement.

Rifkin has always agreed. "Listen, Fein—I'll even call you by your new name. Turn on your lawyer's head, Fein, and try and follow some logic. Do you think if I'm here, if I've brought the other rabbis and we're sitting up here like at the shvitz bath, that you can so easily turn around and tiptoe out the door?" Mann raises his knees so that his feet appear light and does a little ballet from his seat. He leans in further, practically yells. "Do you have any sense at all that you can maybe use to take even a guess at the situation? Use a bit of sechel," Rabbi Mann taps at his head, "and deal!"

Always more. The rabbis always want more from Fein than Fein gives. Is this not dealing? Is he not dealing spectacularly well? Is he screaming, "this can't be happening!" and pulling at his hair or letting his jaw go slack and his tongue loll as might one who gives in to insanity? No. He is listening with a fair amount of respect. After all, it's an invasion, and a personal embarrassment to Alan, who is only happy that they cannot see more than the window reveals. Whatever the rabbis think, the tokens, the neon signs, the man in the street, all promise live girls—which the rabbis are not. They are, in effect, stealing from him with every second they sit on stage. Looking at Mann, preparing to speak, Alan is confused, so much is there to process.

"Why," he says, "doesn't the window go down?"

Mann is as aggravated as he was trying to teach the boy Talmud fifteen years before. "That's the kind of idiocy I'm talking about. Do you think, Fein—do you really think that the window is supposed to go down?"

Fein's face goes long. He is forlorn. "No," he says, "I don't think the window is ever supposed to go down."

"So frustrating!" Mann goes back to the falsetto, flutters his fingers, and adds fake crying. "Oooh! It'll never go down." He slaps a hand against his leg and the sound bounces around the weird acoustics of the stage. "You know it won't stay open forever as well as you know it won't go down too soon. You've got a good head, Fein. You always have. So tell me why you're always acting like a dummy."

"You wonder why I don't talk to you? Listen to yourself, Rabbi. Always on the attack."

"What, I should hold you up as an example? Say that Fein made the right decision when he decided it was easier to live without God? Congratulate you on changing your name so that the boyish restaurant man doesn't make you repeat your reservations? Fein who goes to live in a town where there are no troubles and no Jews, so his son will be able to play soccer carefree on Shabbos morning."

"It's a boy?" Fein interrupts. "She's having a boy?"

"I don't know! Always the details, the little details. Boy? or Girl? What about the fact that it's not going to be a Jew."

"I'm all right with that," he says. "I've made my choices."

This is when another window comes up. The Latino man's window on the other side. Alan does not expect it to be him and is not surprised to see Dr. Springmire, his psychologist, standing there, scratching at his short, secular beard.

"Is he all right with his decisions, Mr. Doctor?" Mann throws the words over his shoulder without looking back. A witness, Mann has called a witness.

"First a token," the doctor says to Fein.

"A token?" Alan asks.

"I think it would be best for you if you paid for my peep. We have thus far in your therapy constructed a relationship based partly—and it is an important aspect that you may not have consciously acknowledged—on financial remuneration. We dare not put that trust in jeopardy, especially in a situation as peculiar as this." He offers an apologetic smile.

Alan is thinking, bless the doctor, and, after inserting a token on Springmire's behalf, he tries to force in the remaining pair. The last two do not fit. He is disappointed and, looking to Mann, can tell the Rabbi knows what mischief he attempts.

Mann rolls his eyes.

"Mr. Doctor, I ask you, is Fein all right with his choices?"

"He will be," says Dr. Springmire. "He has come a long way and will, I am convinced, one day adjust to the life he has made—it is a very nice life. He is a very nice man."

"Did I say he wasn't?" Rabbi Mann strains, twists in his chair, twists his fat neck, and even turns his eyes trying, but failing, to face the doctor behind him. "I wouldn't be here today if I didn't think Fein was a nice boy. I'm here for that very reason, because I want to know what makes a nice boy forget God; what makes it so a boy with a nice job and a nice life—as you say—doesn't question how he came to such comfort, doesn't even look at the streets he walks on every day? What makes such a darling boy, with such a nice little wife waiting for him at home with a baby on the way, what makes him climb the stairs into a place like this to fondle a young girl who has to sell her body to live? What is the math in that equation, Dr. of Psychology?"

It is Alan who answers.

"It's you."

Fein points a finger, reaches through the window, so that Rabbi Zeitler looks up from his book and says, absentmindedly, "Touch?"

"It's you who made me this way," Fein says. "I came here because of you."

"Really?" Mann says, a big smile on his face. "And all the time I thought it was the other way around."

"What choice was I left with, Rabbi? When I used to play at Benji Wernik's house, the grandson of the Galitzia Rebbe, he used to pull from the space between his father's bookcase and the wall, filthy magazines. This is where his father hid them. What am I to do if I learned the facts of life from Simcha Wernik's magazines—the pillar of our community who, in private, looks at women who do their business into glass toilet bowls?"

Dr. Springmire is raising a finger, already speaking, "If I may interject, it is normal to masturbate. Healthy even. Such pictures are of no importance if in the possession of an adult man."

"But the son of the Galitzia Rebbe? A wise man? A teacher of high-school mathematics?" He spoke to his shrink and then to the Rabbi. "What is a boy raised in a world of absolutes to do when he is faced with contradictions?"

"You question. That's what you do." The Rabbi is fed up. He waves a fist, the loose flesh of his upper arm shaking obscenely. "This is what intelligent people do. They question. They don't throw their religion away. They don't turn into the sick people who first shook their faith."

"I'm not sick!" Fein yells. "And I didn't throw anything away! You want truth and justice and for everything to fit in its place. Some things are in between, Rabbi. They are not right or wrong. Only natural."

"Who's saying different? There are many ugly vices in the world."

Mann chews at his top lip, rubs his palms along his thighs. "Did I need to come here for you to admit this to yourself? To learn that you abandoned God because the world is not the way you wanted it to be?"

"That's not what I said." Fein's voice breaks. He looks around for support, waits for one of the windows to open revealing someone on his side.

Rabbi Mann exhales.

"Then what did you say?"

"That I left religion because of people like you."

"Me," he says, voice booming. "Me?" Then, controlling himself, "If that's what you want to tell yourself, then that's what I wanted to know."

The window, easily, as if oiled, moves down. Fein, two tokens left, sick, grabs at the lock and slides the bolt back when he understands one thing Mann was saying. He knows the window will have to come up two more times. Mann is right and it kills him. And as much as he feels bitter and lied to and kept in the dark for all those years, he half wishes that he could live in their utopia. You are religious or you are not, a good husband or bad. He wants what they promised. Scales of justice that always dip to one side. Then he would know what to do with Mr. Wernik, the son of the Galitzia Rebbe, a clean man with a dirty magazine.

Running his thumb along the face of a token, Alan slides the bolt back the other way. He has figured it out. It's a test from the Rabbi. The Everlasting Gobstopper, the sword Excalibur, such things must be returned to their rightful places and rightful owners. Their bearers must prove their mettle. Fein will face the rabbis—will not run or hide only to find himself haunted. He does not want to suffer the rabbis every time he raises the garage door or discover them in the basement when a fuse blows. He is a free man and they have no right to sit in judgment. Alan checks his watch. There is time still, time enough to spend his tokens and reach the bus. And maybe it will be the girls again. Maybe Mann is gone. He said he found what he wanted to know.

Steeling himself, Alan drops in a token and it fits. He assumes this means he has won. As the window goes up and he sees the round leg of a woman, an older woman, he is overjoyed—as simple as that. It is over. When Alan sees that it is his mother, he again knows that he is wrong. He looks over to see Claire next to her, in a pair of panties, only the sides visible because of her massive pregnant belly and her bellybutton, her adorable bellybutton, giant, distended, on display. The other two women he does not recognize. Many of the windows are open, and he can see the men's arms moving, their expressions wide-eyed as if hypnotized. One is wearing a yarmulke. It is Benji Wernik, the glass toilet bowl boy.

Alan's mother is wearing stockings and garters. In the place where other such women keep tips, she has a wad of Kleenex, which she removes and with which she motions toward him.

"Do you need some tissue, Ari? Did you remember to bring?" She gets up to hand him some.

"Sit," he says. "Mother, sit down!"

"What, and let you spoil a fancy hanky? Let alone an expensive suit."

"Mother, please, what are you saying?"

"I'm saying that I washed your underwear every day and know from such things." She leans toward Claire, who has not said a word, puts a hand on Claire's hand. Alan can tell that his wife is not talking to him and that his mother who hates the very idea of his Gentile wife is now in cahoots. "He wants to know of what I speak. Underwear stiffer than starched, I scrubbed. Underwear that would shatter if you dropped them to the floor. I tell you, if the Russians had dropped a nuclear bomb when I was in that basement, I would have been safe surrounded by his dirty gatkes."

"You knew?"

"Of course, I'm a mother. What, you are the first in the world to do such a thing?"

"It's normal. The doctor says so. The Rabbi didn't even dispute—and he knows it's a grave sin." Fein is backpedaling, explaining it all away.

"Who said it wasn't normal?" His mother speaks to his wife.

Claire shrugs and spreads her legs, giving Benji Wernik a better view.

"All I'm saying," his mother says, tucking the tissues back into place, "is to have some sense about it. Why ruin a good suit? Why ruin a good marriage—"

She pauses.

Alan claws at the window frame to see if he can pull down the board hidden inside. Claire turns—waits. Alan waits even as he claws. They all wait for his mother to finish the sentence, to say it in its entirety: "Why ruin a good marriage, even if it's to her?" But she doesn't. She leaves it as it was. Claire smiles and moves her hand, placing it on top of her mother-in-law's. She gives it a little pat and says, "So true."

Alan stands open-mouthed, equally confounded by the presence of wife and mother as by the goodwill they share.

"Is this what the Rabbi means?" he asks them. "Is this how people learn to deal?"

But there is no time for an answer. The fourth dollar is spent and the window comes down.

Alan holds the last token lightly. How good it will feel to let it drop. He is actually eager to find the Rabbi and Dr. Springmire waiting for him, eager to show them both how resigned he is to finishing something, something difficult and taxing from which he would gladly have run. He wants to pull out his pockets, hold up for them his empty hands. With the greatest intent, Alan presses the last token into the slot.

But the window opens onto an empty chair. The other three are filled, not with rabbis but with the women first there when Alan arrived. Only his beauty is gone. The second lady talks to him, her accent strong, a native of the Bronx.

"You're up," she says and pats the chair.

Alan is already taking off his jacket and undoing his shoes. He uses one shoe to kick off the other, maybe for the first time since he was a boy in black Shabbos loafers, his father yelling at him not to break the backs.

When he is naked except for his watch, Alan reaches down and finds on the wall in front, a knob. He takes it, as if he had always known it was there, and opens his section of wall; the hinges, he assumes, hidden on the other side.

Alan Fein steps up onto the stage, sits in the empty chair.

He is embarrassed, most especially because his erection persists. When Alan hears the window open behind him, he does not need to look, knowing which of the two men it is. He turns anyway, gracefully, and looks at the Latino man, wearing the familiar tie, his hair perfectly slicked.

"Touch?" Alan says.

The man does not outwardly answer. Alan is surprised to find that the man's wishes are perceptible anyway. He is surprised by his own sensitivity in knowing, an art of sorts.

Standing up, he turns and moves toward the man, stepping carefully as if the carpet were rough and uncertain. He moves slowly and with an air of detachment. Just the right amount, he feels, befitting an object of desire.

Rebecca Goldstein

"The Courtship"

From *The Mind-Body Problem*

It was march when I saw Himmel again. I had just boarded the dinky, the two-car train that shuttles between Princeton and Princeton Junction to meet the trains going north to New York and south to Philadelphia, when I saw a figure loping down the hill toward us. That's what "galumphing" means, I thought, as I watched it approach: hair, tie, jacket, papers all flowing. I was surprised that something could move at once so awkwardly and so quickly. As the localized commotion got nearer, I saw it was Noam Himmel running to catch the train. Wouldn't it be exciting if he were to sit with me, I thought, and then dreaded that he might. How would I ever keep up a conversation with him?

He galumphed onto the train a second before it started. A girl and a boy holding hands glanced up at him, and then the boy whispered something to the girl and they both laughed. I was infuriated on Himmel's behalf. It was outrageous that these nitwits (in comparison, surely) should share a superior laugh at the expense of a genius. Like the prisoners in Plato's cave, I thought, laughing because the sundazzled philosopher can't see in their darkness. He spotted me immediately and came toward me. God help me, I thought, feeling stupid and inadequate, dreading the exposure to the bright light of his understanding. Many of the stories about Himmel were devoted to his intolerance of stupidity.

"Renee Feuer, isn't it? Graduate student, philosophy?"

Remarkable memory. But then what else should I have expected? He was looking very pleased as he sat down next to me. And then I remembered, with that small surprise I always feel when I consider myself from the outside, that what *he* was seeing was a delicate-featured young woman with long legs and waist-length honey hair. From that point of view I was acceptable. At least for the moment, I thought, until I start speaking.

"New York?" he asked.

"Yes, of course. You?"

"I'm giving a talk at NYU. You?"

"Oh, I'm just going in for my weekly fix of the city."

He simply smiled at that. I assumed it was a smile of comprehension.

"You're a New Yorker, aren't you?" I asked.

"Well, I grew up in Manhattan, but I've lived there only very occasionally during the past twenty-two years. New York's proximity to Princeton was one of the deciding factors in my coming here."

Common ground. *Terra sancta.* I feel an immediate closeness to anyone who loves New York or hates Los Angeles. Either condition is sufficient, but I've found that satisfaction of the one usually entails satisfaction of the other.

"I would never have lasted out this year in Princeton if I couldn't get into New York and breathe," I said.

"Oh, don't you like Princeton?"

"I find it difficult to breathe in an atmosphere in which one's intelligence is always being assessed. But of course you wouldn't know about that."

"What do you mean?" The blue eyes, which were so unexpected in that face, had a very powerful stare. Noam is a man who insists on eye contact. I was already finding this somewhat disconcerting and kept gazing slightly ahead of him. He, in response, kept moving his head forward to meet my gaze squarely. At this rate he'll be off his seat before the Junction, I thought.

"I don't suppose you ever feel stupid."

"On the contrary, I very often feel stupid. I often have the experience of not being able to understand what everyone else seems to. Somebody will say something and I'll think, Now what the hell does that mean?

That doesn't make any sense. And then someone else will answer and his response is as incomprehensible as the first one's statement. And back and forth they go, intelligible to one another, unintelligible to me. Obviously there must be some meaning there if they're understanding one another. And usually the things being discussed aren't even supposed to be deep." He laughed. His laugh was higher pitched than his speaking voice. "It's curious, but the things I find obvious other people find difficult. They're amazed that I can see them so easily, and it sometimes takes me a tremendously long time to get others to see what I saw instantaneously. But then fairly average people will have intuitions on a whole range of topics that I can't get a hold on at all."

"Maybe you're simply not interested in those topics."

"I'm not. However, it's impossible to tell which is a function of which. Am I uninterested because I'm dense or dense because I'm uninterested?" He laughed in a way that showed this question too didn't overwhelmingly concern him.

"Is it lonely to have one's mind work differently from most people's?"

The blue eyes widened: "Lonely? It's damned lucky. A lucky thing for me that it's been decided the things I can see are the important ones, so I turn out smart instead of stupid. Oh, I think maybe when I was very young I was lonely for a while. There weren't too many other kids interested in playing around with numbers all the time. But I discovered early on that I liked ideas much better than people, and that was the end of my loneliness. For one thing, ideas are consistent. And you can control them better than people." He smiled. "Hell, to be honest I've just always found them more interesting. Logical relations are transparent and lovely. Human relations, from what I can tell, always seem pretty muddy."

"I suppose you're right that human relations are rarely very pretty," I said hesitantly. "But there are reasons besides the aesthetic for valuing them, aren't there?"

He leaned toward me as I spoke. He seemed to want to suck all the contents from my comments, as if they mattered that deeply to him. There could be no greater reassurance for me, short of the declaration: "You are brilliant. Speak."

"I'm not talking about valuing them," he answered. "That's a psychological or perhaps an ethical question. I'm talking about thinking about them. One can think they're good things to have even if one doesn't think they're interesting to contemplate. I've just never found anything much to engage the mind there. Of course that might just be my particular brand of stupidity again." He grinned.

"What *about* the ethical questions? Do you think they're interesting?"

"Well, when you talk about ethics you change the subject. It's no longer human relations that are your objects, but rights and obligations. And those are, I would say, important topics. But for myself, I don't derive much pleasure from thinking about them. The properties of rights and obligations are not what I would call theoretically pleasing. They don't form lovely patterns." He smiled. "Of course, perhaps I ought to think about them anyway. That's yet another ethical question, whether we have an ethical obligation to consider ethical questions, including this very one. However, since I haven't considered the question, I don't know that we do have such an obligation and thus feel no obligation to consider this question. If you follow." He grinned.

Self-referring propositions, as I was to learn, are a favorite source of humor for Noam, and he loves constructing them.

I ought to mention that in the course of our conversation we had arrived at the Junction, had crossed the tracks and boarded the New York-bound train. Himmel had never stopped speaking, had paid no attention to the details of descending, crossing, and ascending, of finding new seats. I wondered how he managed when alone.

"I seem to remember a poem by someone, Edna St. Vincent Millay, I think, beginning, 'Euclid alone has looked on Beauty bare.' I can't remember the rest."

"Yes?" He smiled. "Well, surely others beside Euclid have had the privilege. Euclidean geometry isn't even the prettiest of the geometries. But Beauty bare. That's good. I like that. So many people have no sensibility whatsoever for mathematical beauty, are even arrogantly skeptical of its existence. But of course beauty is what math is all about, the most pure and perfect beauty."

"You're really an aesthetician," I said. Or a strange breed of hedonist, I thought.

"Yes? Perhaps. Perhaps all mathematicians are. I've never thought about it before. You see," he grinned. "At least I'm consistent. I don't find people in general very interesting to think about, so I don't find myself in particular an arresting object of thought. A lot of people seem to assent to the universal proposition but decline instantiation when it comes to themselves."

By now I was feeling quite comfortable holding his high-intensity gaze, and we both laughed into each other's eyes. It was a happy moment.

"Oh dear." I smiled. "We seem, you and I, only to talk about boring things."

"That's true." He smiled back. "I wonder why I'm enjoying it so much. I wonder why I'm wondering when I can discuss these mind-deadening issues with you again."

We made a date to meet for dinner the following evening.

The next evening, as I walked up Witherspoon Street toward Lahiere's, the restaurant I had suggested since Himmel was apparently unaware of the existence of any such establishments, I saw him coming up Nassau Street from the direction of Fine Hall, the mathematics building. He was walking very quickly, everything still flowing, including the pile of papers he was carrying under his arm—a figure which, even in a town like Princeton, attracted stares. He of course was oblivious to the attention, lost in his own head. As I watched him cross Nassau Street against the light, I thought surely God must love mathematical geniuses.

His brow was, I saw as he got nearer, deeply furrowed and his lips were moving slightly. He didn't notice me until he was right alongside and I put my hand gently on his shoulder to halt his full pace.

"Oh." He looked at me, blank for a moment, then focused that full beam of his in on me: "How are you? how are you? how are you?" Leaning toward me he searched my face for I knew not what.

"Just fine, just fine, just fine." I laughed.

"You know, it occurred to me that I never asked you what kind of philosophy you do."

"Oh, I guess right now I'm doing philosophy of body."

"Philosophy of body? I've heard of philosophy of mind, but not of body. Tell me about it."

He hadn't understood my comment as the joke I had meant it to be. I was embarrassed at having put forth a joke that didn't even succeed in making its presence felt, and tried to recoup.

"Well, if there's a philosophy of mind, why shouldn't there be a philosophy of body? After all, the main question in philosophy of mind is the mind-body problem. Why assume only the mind makes the relationship between them problematic? Why assume only mind needs analysis? Why prejudge the issue by approaching it only from the point of view of a philosophy of mind?" And I worried that I couldn't think on my feet.

"I see what you're saying. There really isn't any such established area in philosophy. What you're saying is, you're working on the mind-body problem and you believe it's body rather than, or perhaps as well as, mind that is problematic."

"Very problematic. Fraught with difficulties," I drawled in my most pedantic manner.

This conversation took place out on the sidewalk in front of Lahiere's. Himmel had made no move to go in, had become completely absorbed in our conversation out there, leaning toward me, concentrating on my comments. I realized that if we were going to eat at all I'd better take some initiative, so I moved toward the door.

I asked him, as we were being seated inside, whether he was interested in philosophy.

"Oh yes, very, though I've never had the time to read as much as I'd like. I've mostly read in those areas that are contiguous with math, you know, foundations of math, philosophy of logic. I've read a little Quine. I find his views baffling."

Noam then launched into a critical discussion of the views of Quine and Putnam, two Harvard philosophers, that logic is empirical and that it perhaps ought to be revised to overcome the paradoxes posed by quantum mechanics. Noam thought these ideas the height, or depth, of absurdity: "not worth considering, except that they have had, incredibly, some influence, especially among the physicists.

"Some of the most idiotic statements I've been forced to listen to have come from physicists talking about math and logic. It's hard to find one—especially among the younger set, whose minds have all been warped by quantum mechanics—who has sensible views. I have a feeling that they don't even know what they're saying, that they're just mouthing words. That's the most charitable interpretation I can give to their babble. Otherwise I'd just have to conclude that they're imbeciles. Is it anything but imbecile to believe that a truth like the law of noncontradiction is empirical? That the only grounds for its truth lie in the nature of experience? Of course, a lot of these characters don't even know how to make the elementary distinction between the psychological grounds for our *belief* that some fact is true and the actual grounds for its truth. All knowledge turns out to be trivially empirical then, although I wonder if they even realize this. Anyway, it seems this confusion is partly responsible for their imbecile views. Their arrogance seems to be another factor. Everything's empirical, it's all up to them." He was shaking his head and smiling, rather meanly. "They're going to get out their little measuring sticks and meters, and tell us which of the many logics is the empirically true one. As if it really were in the realm of possibility to adopt a new logic, a quantum logic. What's the realm of possibility supposed to *mean* if that's possible? You know, it's rather funny. Previous ages believed that only God is mysterious and powerful enough to transcend logic. God is the only being for whom it's all right to predicate contradiction. Now it's electrons. Irrationality hasn't been wiped out by the physical sciences, it's just been rechanneled."

Noam went on to a less polemical, more detailed analysis of this view he despised, showing how its proponents contradicted themselves, using the very logic they would abandon in the argument for its abandonment.

"Of course"—he laughed—"the charge of self-contradiction may not bother them. They can respond by just giving up the law of noncontradiction."

Noam's "little knowledge" of these philosophers sounded more coherent than anything I'd heard in the countless discussions of them in 1879 Hall, Princeton's philosophy building. And the topic came alive as Noam discussed it. The beauty of his conversation has always been the simplicity with which he discusses the most complex of subjects. Often, as I listened in the early days, there would come into my mind the image of a soggy piece of cloth, crumpled and beginning to mildew, being shaken out with one powerful *thwack*—Noam's intellect—and hung up flat in the sunshine.

His obliviousness to external details was contagious, and when the waiter came to take our orders neither one of us had yet opened the menu.

"I'll have the soft-shelled crabs," I told the waiter, having sampled them on previous occasions. "They're good here," I said to Noam, who was looking pitifully at bay. This transition from extreme intellectual confidence to just as extreme practical helplessness was the sharpest I had ever witnessed. One minute ago this pathetic specimen had been magisterially denouncing the views of the most influential American philosopher as contemptible. It's quite clear where the borders of his turf are drawn, I thought, feelings of protectiveness oozing up in me.

"Good. I'll have them, too." Noam looked as if he had solved a major problem.

"I bet I'll enjoy them more than you," I told him as the waiter left, emboldened to the point of flirtatiousness by the display of Himmel's awkwardness.

"Oh, why is that?"

"Because I was brought up an Orthodox Jew. For me they're seasoned with sin."

"I'm afraid I don't understand."

"They're *trayf*, unkosher."

"Crabs? I thought only pig products were unkosher."

Noam, it turned out, was amazingly ignorant of things Jewish for someone who had grown up in New York (a more relevant fact than his being Jewish). He, in turn, was amazed by my account of my upbringing, particularly the girls' yeshiva I had very hastily been enrolled in when non-Jewish boys from my public school began telephoning for dates. I had gone to public school only because my parents couldn't afford to send both my brother and me to the expensive day school, Hillel Academy, serving Westchester's conservative and (less populous) Orthodox communities. My brother, being male, got priority. And sending me to a yeshiva in the dangerous city had been out of the question. But not quite as out of the question as those boys calling nightly on the phone. So I was soon commuting to the Lower East Side, to one of the more right-wing of the all-girl schools. The teachers here checked our hemlines for modesty every morning, and the principal came into our biology class at the start of our lesson on evolution, informing us that although they were required to teach this for the New York State regents' exam, it was all unproved *apikorsus*, or heresy, and we shouldn't believe any of it. But, as my mother often wails, "It was too late. You were already an *apikoros*."

And so I was. The word is derived from the same source as the noun and adjective "epicurean"—from the Greek philosopher Epicurus, who taught that pleasure is the good and "the root of all good is the pleasure of the stomach; even wisdom and culture must be referred to this." Hence our "epicurean," although in practice the philosopher found that the pain of stomachaches outweighed the pleasures of indulgence and so kept to a diet of bread and water, with a little preserved cheese on feast days. "I am filled with pleasure of the body when I live on bread and water, and I spit on luxurious pleasures, not for their own sake but because of the inconveniences that follow them." Epicurus was really no epicurean. But he was an *apikoros*, even about his own Hellenistic religion. "We, and not the gods, are masters of our fate." Definitely an *apikoros*, this Epicurus. Dante found his followers in hell. *Apikoros* was a much used word in my high school, and it wasn't too difficult to be labeled one.

"We weren't supposed to go to college."

"Why not?" Noam asked. "What were you supposed to do?"

"Get married, of course. And be fruitful and multiply, God's very words to Abraham."

Noam was dumbfounded. "It's a world I never knew existed. I pretty much took it for granted that Jews are generally enlightened. It sounds like a description of the Middle Ages."

"Oh, much older than that. How about the Babylonian captivity?"

"And you didn't swallow any of it. What about your siblings? Do you have any?"

"My brother swallowed what they fed him and hollered for more. My parents had wanted him to go to college, but he wouldn't. He sits and learns."

"He what?"

"Sits and learns. That's the expression for studying Talmud. You have heard of the Talmud?" He nodded. "That's what he does, at a yeshiva in Lakewood, New Jersey. His wife supports him. It's a very accepted, even respected *modus vivendi*."

"And here you are studying philosophy at Princeton, having been suckled on all this irrationality. It's amazing. You're an amazing woman."

His words kindled my ever ready vanity, but I also felt that pinch of uneasiness I always get when people put rationality on one side and religion on the other. Not that I haven't been known to think in exactly those terms, especially when I'm in the company of my religious relatives. But people remote from religion, whether they were born there or struggled there, tend to simplify the other side. (It goes without saying that the religious do likewise.) I'm amused when people talk of the "religious mentality" or the "religious personality," and always think of my father, my mother, my brother and my sister-in-law, all of whose religious personalities had little in common apart from their being Jewish.

"Oh, I wouldn't say that I don't take any of it seriously, at least on a very primitive level. Sometimes, especially on insomniac nights, I start worrying that there may be a God, and worse, that he may be Jewish."

"So?"

"So, if there is and He is, I'm in a lot of trouble. You too, by the way." I bit down hard on a forkful of crab to give my statement emphasis.

Noam shook his head. "I just can't connect to any of this. It's a world I can't make any sense of."

"Unfortunately, I can. I can make sense out of both worlds: Lakewood, New Jersey, and Princeton, New Jersey. So I can't feel really comfortable in either."

Noam just shook his head and shrugged.

"Is it really so alien to you?" I asked him. "Aren't your parents at all traditional, or your grandparents?"

"My parents are both dead. They both hated religion—opiate of the people and all that. I never knew my grandparents."

"And you hate religion?"

"It doesn't arouse the passion in me it did in my parents, but then I've never had to deal with it. It just seems juvenile, a child's conception of reality. I'm always a little surprised when I find reasonably intelligent people who haven't outgrown it." Again he shrugged.

"Have you ever read *Moses and Monotheism?*" I asked.

"No, what's that?"

"Freud," I answered, again surprised. Noam and I would always amaze one another by what we didn't know. Of course, my shock was always the greater, since I expected so much more; nothing less, in those days especially, than omniscience.

"Oh, him." Noam's smile was nasty. "What's he say? Religion is an incestuous desire for the father?"

"You're not too far off target. It's a neurotic fixation on the repressed tribal memory of the murder of the primeval father."

"Don't bother to explain."

Noam finally gave his food some attention as our first silence fell upon us. I was regretting having brought Freud up. It occurred to me that perhaps this entire subject of religion was utterly boring to Noam and that I hadn't noticed the signs because of my own neurotic religious fixation, tribal or otherwise. But *he* continued the discussion:

"You know, come to think of it, my parents did name me after my paternal grandfather, who was killed in a pogrom in Russia. That's a piece of Jewish tradition, isn't it?"

"Getting killed in pogroms?"

"Cute." Noam laughed. "But what about it?"

"Yes, you're right. In fact, if Jews name after a person at all, it's someone who's dead."

"Why is that?"

"I'm not quite sure. To honor the dead, I guess, to keep their memory alive. It's taken very seriously. I've known people who actually had a child because there was a name they wanted to pass on." (This has always seemed to me an extraordinarily insufficient reason for creating a person. A *person*, for Godssakes. But then the awesomeness of this act of responsibility so impresses me that I don't know if I'll ever come up with a reason I can judge sufficient.) "Wait a minute. I remember once hearing of a superstition that in passing on the names you passed on the souls. That would explain why you shouldn't name after the living, too."

"What?" Noam said very loudly, leaning across the table, his beard grazing my broccoli.

"Well, you know, there was a lot of superstition in the old country."

"But tell me about this, about passing on the souls. I'd never heard that Jews believed anything like that."

"I'm afraid I don't know very much about it. It's not the sort of thing one studies in yeshiva. Jewish thinkers for the most part devote themselves to the interpretation of the law, not to metaphysical questions. It's very different in that regard from Catholicism."

"Is there a belief in transmigration of souls?" he asked impatiently. He was obviously excited, rocking back and forth in his chair. Funny, I thought, he looks like he's *shuckling*, making the rhythmic motions of Orthodox Jews in prayer. Could this too be genetic, another tribal inheritance? Let his *payess* (sideburns) grow, stick a yarmulke on his head, he'd be the perfect picture of a yeshiva *bocher*.

"I don't think so," I answered. "Not officially. Just like heaven and hell aren't official. But there might have been some such belief among the people. And for all I know, that might be the source of the naming tradition."

"Interesting." The self-absorbed *shuckling* was attracting glances and, again, those infuriatingly superior shared smiles. He asked me some more questions, none of which I could answer. It was his turn to be surprised by my ignorance. How could someone of my background have failed to apprise herself of the facts on the subject?

"It's just not the kind of thing, one studies in yeshiva," I repeated defensively.

Suddenly Noam (I was now thinking of him as Noam rather than Himmel) looked at his watch, which was fastened at one chink of its band with a paper clip. (Much of Noam's life is held together by paper clips.)

"Oh my God! I'm terribly late! This is really awful. I've got to run." And he pushed back his chair, almost toppling it, and galumphed out. Everybody in the vicinity but me was very pleased by the performance. I hadn't even given him the copy of the Millay poem I had xeroxed in Firestone Library. I paid the check and left.

He called me the next day, having gotten my phone number from the philosophy department. I was touched by these efforts, which I (rightly) suspected were preternatural.

"I'm sorry for rushing off like that yesterday. I had promised to speak at Fitzer's graduate seminar and I was terribly late. I realized after that I had left you with the check." He invited me to a party for the following evening, given by Professor Fitzer.

The party was pretty dreadful. (How much more dread would it have inspired had I realized how many similar parties awaited me.) Fitzer's small brick house was near Lake Carnegie, not far from the Harrison Avenue bridge. It was a modest, strictly Euclidean affair, rectangular from the outside and divided up inside into a few rectangles and squares. The majority of the house seemed to be on the subterranean level, in a paneled den that seemed to enjoy a larger area than the frame of the house would allow, extending out perhaps beneath the small square front garden. The party took place in the den, which was furnished entirely in Lucite, perhaps to minimize the furniture's interfering with the geometry.

After the initial fluttering around Noam, the men, all mathematicians, settled down to talk shop while the women spoke among themselves of children, grandchildren, travel and gardening. It was a party of the senior faculty—in fact, it seemed, the senior of the seniors, the departments' gray eminences. The women were all soft-spoken and sweet, cherishing, quite clearly, the appearance of unflappable exteriors. I tried to modulate my voice accordingly. There was nothing to be done about my obvious raw youth. I was gratified, though, by the women's discreet inquisitiveness about my relationship with Noam. They asked subtle, indirect questions, to which I gave subtle, indirect answers.

There was one amusing little outburst from (of course) the men. Noam and this fellow, Raoul, the only other non-gray mathematician there, had a disagreement over the terms "obvious" and "trivial." Raoul had said that something was obvious.

"No, it's not," said Noam. "It may be trivial, but it's not obvious."

"Obvious, trivial, what's the difference?"

"A great difference. A theorem is obvious if it's easy to see, to grasp. A theorem is trivial if the logical relations leading to it are relatively direct. Generally, theorems that are trivial are obvious. If the logical relations leading to it are straight, it's easy to get to. And conversely. Thus the sloppy conflation of the terms." He glanced darkly at Raoul. "But the meanings are different, as are the extensions. Sometimes the logical relations are direct but not so accessible. You know the old joke about the professor who says that something is trivial and is questioned on this by a student and goes out and works for an hour and comes back and says, 'I was right. It is trivial'?" He paused for the laughter to stop. "Well," he concluded, "you couldn't substitute 'obvious' for 'trivial' in that joke."

"But of course there's another sense of 'trivial,' " someone said. "Insignificant, undeep."

"Yes, of course," Noam said. "That's a secondary sense." This secondary sense is a great favorite of Noam's. Events, ideas, people—oh, definitely people—are classified as trivial or nontrivial. It's his way of distinguishing between what and who matters and what and who doesn't.

"Your explication seems vague to me," the persistent Raoul objected. "A theorem is obvious if it's easy for *whom* to see?"

"For God and Himmel," someone said.

Noam laughed. "Make that Himmel and God."

"I'm sorry, that wasn't really an evening together, was it?" Noam said as we walked back to the Graduate College in soft silk air smelling of spring. Can't he even take my hand? I was thinking. "Unfortunately, I have a dinner party tomorrow night. But why don't we have dinner on Friday? This time I'll pay, I promise. It will have to be quite late, though. I won't be free until after nine."

We had our late dinner that Friday night, and a long lunch on Saturday, lunch on Sunday, and dinner again on Wednesday. Through all this Noam's vivid gaze and conversation were the only things that held me. I hadn't had such a chaste romantic relationship with a man since high school. (I was fairly certain it was romantic.) I began to realize, as I had on the sidewalk outside Lahiere's, that I would have to take the initiative if we were going to do more than eat and talk.

That Thursday was a glorious, blooming day. When we met for lunch, I suggested that we just buy some strawberries at Davidson's and a bottle of Beaujolais at Nassau Liquors and go have them over on the other side of Lake Carnegie.

"I'll show you where the wild asparagus grow."

And I did.

There's been so much serious discussion devoted to the profound question of the vaginal vs. the clitoral orgasm. Why doesn't anyone speak about the mental orgasm? It's what's going on in your head that can make the difference, not which and how many of your nerve endings are being rubbed. Judged on the quantitative neurological scale, our lovemaking wasn't memorable. It's other details I remember:

Noam downed more than his share of the wine, according to his characteristic style of mechanically finishing off whatever he's given, saving himself from having to deliberate over what and how much to eat. I watched him in pleased (get 'em drunk) astonishment as he gulped the wine down like a bottle of Coca-Cola.

He lay back, positioning his face in the shade of my body, looking up at me. He was quiet for once. Was it the wine or the sight of me with the sun pouring down on my head? I had a very sharp impression—now transformed into an equally vivid memory—of how I must have appeared to him, lit up against the brilliant blue sky.

"Like sunlight made tangible," he said, tentatively touching my hair.

Our first kiss was hebetatically clumsy, for I took him by surprise. I took him by surprise a good part of the way. At each early stage of our very linear progress from first kiss to final gasp he searched my face, all his features asking: "You don't mean to . . . ? I couldn't possibly . . . could I?" and then expressing their pleasure at the answer they found in my look. This catechism of facial expressions only once broke out into speech:

"Could we be arrested?" he asked before entering me.

And I remember too the intensity of my pleasure, which wasn't at all physical, as he shuddered within me while inside my head sang the triumphant thought: I am making love to this man . . . to Noam Himmel . . . the genius.

Erica Jong

"En Route to the Congress of Dreams or the Zipless Fuck"

from *Fear of Flying*

There were 117 psychoanalysts on the Pan Am flight to Vienna and I'd been treated by at least six of them. And married a seventh. God knows it was a tribute either to the shrinks' ineptitude or my own glorious unanalyzability that I was now, if anything, more scared of flying than when I began my analytic adventures some thirteen years earlier.

My husband grabbed my hand therapeutically at the moment of take-off.

"Christ—it's like ice," he said. He ought to know the symptoms by now since he's held my hand on lots of other flights. My fingers (and toes) turn to ice, my stomach leaps upward into my rib cage, the temperature in the tip of my nose drops to the same level as the temperature in my fingers, my nipples stand up and salute the inside of my bra (or in this case, dress—since I'm not wearing a bra), and for one screaming minute my heart and the engines correspond as we attempt to prove again that the laws of aerodynamics are not the flimsy superstitions which, in my heart of hearts, I *know* they are. Never mind the diabolical INFORMATION TO PASSENGERS, I happen to be convinced that only my own concentration (and that of my mother—who always seems to *expect* her children to die in a plane crash) keeps this bird aloft. I congratulate myself on every successful takeoff, but not too enthusiastically because it's also part of my personal religion that the minute you grow overconfident and really *relax* about the flight, the plane crashes instantly. Constant vigilance, that's my motto. A mood of cautious optimism should prevail. But actually my mood is better described as cautious pessimism. OK, I tell myself, we *seem* to be off the ground and into the clouds but the danger isn't past. This is, in fact, the most perilous patch of air. Right here over Jamaica Bay where the plane banks and turns and the "No Smoking" sign goes off. This may well be where we go screaming down in thousands of flaming pieces. So I keep concentrating very hard, helping the pilot (a reassuringly midwestern voice named Donnelly) fly the 250-passenger motherfucker. Thank God for his crew cut and middle-America diction. New Yorker that I am, I would never trust a pilot with a New York accent.

As soon as the seat-belt sign goes off and people begin moving about the cabin, I glance around nervously to see who's on board. There's a big-breasted mama-analyst named Rose Schwamm-Lipkin with whom I recently had a consultation about whether or not I should leave my current analyst (who isn't, mercifully, in evidence). There's Dr. Thomas Frommer, the harshly Teutonic expert on *Anorexia Nervosa,* who was my husband's first analyst. There's kindly, rotund Dr. Arthur Feet, Jr., who was the third (and last) analyst of my friend Pia. There's compulsive little Dr. Raymond Schrift who is hailing a blond stewardess (named "Nanci") as if she were a taxi. (I saw Dr. Schrift for one memorable year when I was fourteen and starving myself to death in penance for having finger-fucked on my parents' living-room couch. He kept insisting that the horse I was dreaming about was my father and that my periods would return if only I would "ackzept being a vohman.") There's smiling, bald Dr. Harvey Smucker whom I saw in consultation when my first husband decided he was Jesus Christ and began threatening to walk on the water in Central Park Lake. There's foppish, hand-tailored Dr. Ernest Klumpner, the supposedly "brilliant theoretician" whose latest book is a psychoanalytic study of John Knox. There's black-bearded Dr. Stanton Rappoport-Rosen who recently gained notoriety in New York analytic circles when he moved to Denver and branched out into something called "Cross-Country Group Ski-Therapy." There's Dr. Arnold Aaronson pretending to play chess on a magnetic board with his new wife (who was his patient until last year), the singer Judy Rose. Both of them are surreptitiously looking around to see who is looking at them—and for one moment, my eyes and Judy Rose's meet. Judy Rose became famous in the fifties for recording a series of satirical ballads about pseudointellectual life in New York. In a whiny and deliberately unmusical voice, she sang the saga of a Jewish girl who takes courses at the New School, reads the Bible for its prose, discusses Martin Buber in bed, and falls in love with her analyst. She has now become one with the role she created.

Besides the analysts, their wives, the crew, and a few poor outnumbered laymen, there were some children of analysts who'd come along for the ride. Their sons were mostly sullen-faced adolescents in bell bottoms and shoulder-length hair who looked at their parents with a degree of cynicism and scorn which was almost palpable. I remembered myself traveling abroad with my parents as a teen-ager and always trying to pretend they weren't with me. I tried to lose them in the Louvre! To avoid them in the Uffizi! To moon alone over a Coke in a Paris café and pretend that those loud people at the next table were not—though clearly they were—my parents. (I was pretending, you see, to be a Lost Generation exile with my parents sitting three feet away.) And here I was back in my own past, or in a bad dream or a bad movie: *Analyst* and *Son of Analyst*. A planeload of shrinks and my adolescence all around me. Stranded in midair over the Atlantic with 117 analysts many of whom had heard my long, sad story and none of whom remembered it. An ideal beginning for the nightmare the trip was going to become.

We were bound for Vienna and the occasion was historic. Centuries ago, wars ago, in 1938, Freud fled his famous consulting room on the Berggasse when the Nazis threatened his family. During the years of the Third Reich any mention of his name was banned in Germany, and analysts were expelled (if they were lucky) or gassed (if they were not). Now, with great ceremony, Vienna was welcoming the analysts back. They were even opening a museum to Freud in his old consulting room. The mayor of Vienna was going to greet them and a reception was to be held in Vienna's pseudo-Gothic Rathaus. The enticements included free food, free *Schnaps*, cruises on the Danube, excursions to vineyards, singing, dancing, shenanigans, learned papers and speeches and a tax-deductible trip to Europe. Most of all, there was to be lots of good old Austrian *Gemütlichkeit*. The people who invented *scmaltz* (and crematoria) were going to show the analysts how welcome back they were.

Welcome back! Welcome back! At least those of you who survived Auschwitz, Belsen, the London Blitz and the co-optation of America. *Willkommen!* Austrians are nothing if not charming.

Holding the Congress in Vienna had been a hotly debated issue for years, and many of the analysts had come only reluctantly. Anti-Semitism was part of the problem, but there was also the possibility that radical students at the University of Vienna would decide to stage demonstrations. Psychoanalysis was out of favor with New Left members for being "too individualistic." It did nothing, they said, to further "the worldwide struggle toward communism."

I had been asked by a new magazine to observe all the fun and games of the Congress closely and to do a satirical article on it. I began my research by approaching Dr. Smucker near the galley, where he was being served coffee by one of the stewardesses. He looked at me with barely a glimmer of recognition.

"How do you feel about psychoanalysis returning to Vienna?" I asked in my most cheerful lady-interviewer voice. Dr. Smucker seemed taken aback by the shocking intimacy of the question. He looked at me long and searchingly.

"I'm writing an article for a new magazine called *Voyeur*," I said. I figured he'd at least have to crack a smile at the name.

"Well then," Smucker said stolidly, "how do *you* feel about it?" And he waddled off toward his short bleached-blond wife in the blue knit dress with a tiny green alligator above her (blue) right breast.

I should have known. Why do analysts always answer a question with a question? And why should this night be different from any other night—despite the fact that we are flying in a 747 and eating unkosher food?

"The Jewish science," as anti-Semites call it. Turn every question upside down and shove it up the asker's ass. Analysts all seem to be Talmudists who flunked out of seminary in the first year. I was reminded of one of my grandfather's favorite gags:

Q: "Why does a Jew always answer a question with a question?"

A: "And why should a Jew *not* answer a question with a question?"

Ultimately though, it was the unimaginativeness of most analysts which got me down. OK, I'd been helped a lot by my first one—the German who was going to give a paper in Vienna—but he was a rare breed: witty, self-mocking, unpretentious. He had none of the flat-footed literal-mindedness which makes even the most brilliant psychoanalysts sound so pompous. But the others I'd gone to—they were so astonishingly literal-minded. The horse you are dreaming about is your father. The kitchen stove you are dreaming about is your mother. The piles of bullshit you are dreaming about are, in reality, your analyst. This is called the *transference*. No?

You dream about breaking your leg on the ski slope. You have, in fact, just broken your leg on the ski slope and you are lying on the couch wearing a ten-pound plaster cast which has had you housebound for weeks, but has also given you a beautiful new appreciation of your toes and the civil rights of paraplegics. But the broken leg in the dream represents your own "mutilated genital." You always wanted to have a penis and now you feel guilty that you have *deliberately* broken your leg so that you can have the pleasure of the cast, no?

No!

OK, let's put the "mutilated genital" question aside. It's a dead horse, anyway. And forget about your mother the oven and your analyst the pile of shit. What do we have left except the smell? I'm not talking about the first years of analysis when you're hard at work discovering your own craziness so that you can get some work done instead of devoting your *entire* life to your neurosis. I'm talking about when both you and your husband have been in analysis as long as you can remember and it's gotten to the point where no decision, no matter how small, can be made without both analysts having an imaginary caucus on a cloud above your head. You feel rather like the Trojan warriors in the *Iliad* with Zeus and Hera fighting above them. I'm talking about the time when your marriage has become a *menage à quatre*. You, him, your analyst, his analyst. Four in a bed. This picture is definitely rated X.

We had been in this state for at least the past year. Every decision was referred to the shrink, or the shrinking process. Should we move into a bigger apartment? "Better see what's going on first." (Bennett's euphemism for: back to the couch.) Should we have a baby? "Better work things through first." Should we join a new tennis club? "Better see what's going on first." Should we get a divorce? "Better work through the *unconscious meaning* of divorce first."

Because the fact was that we'd reached that crucial time in a marriage (five years and the sheets you got as wedding presents have just about worn thin) when it's time to decide whether to buy new sheets, have a baby perhaps, and live with each other's lunacy ever after—or else give up the ghost of the marriage (throw out the sheets) and start playing musical beds all over again.

The decision was, of course, further complicated by analysis—the basic assumption of analysis being (and never mind all the evidence to the contrary) that you're getting better all the time. The refrain goes something like this:

"Oh-I-was-self-destructive-when-I-married-you-baby-but-I'm-so-much-more-healthy-now-ow-ow-ow."

(Implying that you might just choose someone better, sweeter, handsomer, smarter, and maybe even luckier in the stock market.)

To which he might reply:

"Oh-I-hated-all-women-when-I-fell-for-you-baby-but-I'm-so-much-more-healthy-now-ow-ow-ow."

(Implying that *he* might just find someone sweeter, prettier, smarter, a better cook, and maybe even due to inherit piles of bread from her father.)

"Wise up Bennett, old boy," I'd say—(whenever I suspected him of thinking those thoughts), "you'd probably marry someone even more phallic, castrating, and narcissistic than I am." (First technique of being a shrink's wife is knowing how to hurl all their jargon back at them, at carefully chosen moments.)

But I was having those thoughts myself and if Bennett knew, he didn't let on. Something seemed very wrong in our marriage. Our lives ran parallel like railroad tracks. Bennett spent the day at his office, his hospital, his analyst, and then evenings at his office again, usually until nine or ten. I taught a couple of days a week and wrote the rest of the time. My teaching schedule was light, the writing was exhausting, and by the time Bennett came home, I was ready to go out and break loose. I had had plenty of solitude, plenty of long hours alone with my typewriter and my fantasies. And I seemed to meet men everywhere. The world seemed crammed with available, interesting men in a way it never had been before I was married.

What *was* it about marriage anyway? Even if you loved your husband, there came that inevitable year when fucking him turned as bland as Velveeta cheese: filling, fattening even, but no thrill to the taste buds, no bittersweet edge, no danger. And you longed for an overripe Camembert, a rare goat cheese: luscious, creamy, cloven-hoofed.

I was not against marriage. I believed in it in fact. It was necessary to have one best friend in a hostile world, one person you'd be loyal to no matter what, one person who'd always be loyal to you. But what about all those other longings which after a while marriage did nothing much to appease? The restlessness, the hunger, the thump in the gut, the thump in the cunt, the longing to be filled up, to be fucked through every hole, the yearning for dry champagne and wet kisses, for the smell of peonies in a penthouse on a June night, for the light at the end of the pier in *Gatsby*. . . . Not those *things* really—because you knew that the very rich were duller than you and me—but what those things *evoked*. The sardonic, bittersweet vocabulary of Cole Porter love songs, the sad sentimental Rogers and Hart lyrics, all the romantic nonsense you yearned for with half your heart and mocked bitterly with the other half.

Growing up female in America. What a liability! You grew up with your ears full of cosmetic ads, love songs, advice columns, whoreoscopes, Hollywood gossip, and moral dilemmas on the level of TV soap operas. What litanies the advertisers of the good life chanted at you! What curious catechisms!

"Be kind to your behind." "Blush like you mean it." "Love your hair." "Want a better body? We'll rearrange the one you've got." "That shine on your face should come from him, not from your skin." "You've come a long way, baby." "How to score with every male in the zodiac." "The stars and sensual you." "To a man they say Cutty Sark." "A diamond is forever." "If you're concerned about douching . . ." "Length and coolness come together." "How I solved my intimate odor problem." "Lady be cool." "Every woman alive loves Chanel No. 5." "What makes a shy girl get intimate?" "*Femme*, we named it after you."

What all the ads and all the whoreoscopes seemed to imply was that if only you were narcissistic *enough*, if only you took proper care of your smells, your hair, your boobs, your eyelashes, your armpits, your crotch, your stars, your scars, and your choice of Scotch in bars—you would meet a beautiful, powerful, potent, and rich man who would satisfy every longing, fill every hole, make your heart skip a beat (or stand still), make you misty, and fly you to the moon (preferably on gossamer wings), where you would live totally satisfied forever.

And the crazy part of it was that even if you were *clever*, even if you spent your adolescence reading John Donne and Shaw, even if you studied history or zoology or physics and hoped to spend your life pursuing some difficult and challenging career—you *still* had a mind full of all the soupy longings that every high-school girl was awash in. It didn't matter, you see, whether you had an IQ of 170 or an IQ of 70, you were brainwashed all the same. Only the surface trappings were different. Only the *talk* was a little more sophisticated. Underneath it all, you longed to be annihilated by love, to be swept off your feet, to be filled up by a giant prick spouting sperm, soapsuds, silks and satins, and of course, money. Nobody bothered to tell you what marriage was really about. You weren't even provided, like European girls, with a philosophy of cynicism and practicality. You expected *not* to desire any other men after marriage. And you expected your husband not to desire any other women. Then the desires came and you were thrown into a panic of self-hatred. What an evil woman you were! How could you keep being infatuated with strange men? How could you study their bulging trousers like that? How could you sit at a meeting imagining how every man in the room would screw? How could you sit on a train fucking total strangers with your eyes? How could you *do* that to your husband? Did anyone ever tell you that maybe it had nothing whatever to do with your husband?

And what about those other longings which marriage stifled? Those longings to hit the open road from time to time, to discover whether you could still live alone inside your own head, to discover whether you could manage to survive in a cabin in the woods without going mad; to discover, in short, whether you were still whole after so many years of being half of something (like the back two legs of a horse outfit on the vaudeville stage).

Five years of marriage had made me itchy for all those things: itchy for men, and itchy for solitude. Itchy for sex and itchy for the life of a recluse. I knew my itches were contradictory—and that made things even worse. I knew my itches were un-American—and that made things *still* worse. It is heresy in America to embrace any way of life except as half of a couple. Solitude is un-American. It may be condoned in a man—especially if he is a "glamorous bachelor" who "dates starlets" during a brief interval between marriages. But a woman is always presumed to be alone as a result of abandonment, not choice. And she is treated that way: as a pariah. There is simply no dignified way for a woman to live alone. Oh, she can get along financially perhaps (though not nearly as well as a man), but emotionally she is never left in peace. Her friends, her family, her fellow workers never let her forget that her husbandlessness, her childlessness—her *selfishness*, in short—is a reproach to the American way of life.

Even more to the point: the woman (unhappy though she knows her married friends to be) can never let *herself* alone. She lives as if she were constantly on the brink of some great fulfillment. As if she were waiting for Prince Charming to take her away "from all this." All what? The solitude of living inside her own soul? The certainty of being herself instead of half of something else?

My response to all this was not (not yet) to have an affair and not (not yet) to hit the open road, but to evolve my fantasy of the Zipless Fuck. The zipless fuck was more than a fuck. It was a platonic ideal. Zipless because when you came together zippers fell away like rose petals, underwear blew off in one breath like dandelion fluff. Tongues intertwined and turned liquid. Your whole soul flowed out through your tongue and into the mouth of your lover.

For the true, ultimate zipless A-1 fuck, it was necessary that you never get to know the man very well. I had noticed, for example, how all my infatuations dissolved as soon as I really became friends with a man, became sympathetic to his problems, listened to him *kvetch* about his wife, or ex-wives, his mother, his children. After that I would like him, perhaps even love him—but without passion. And it was passion that I wanted. I had also learned that a sure way to exorcise an infatuation was to write about someone, to observe his tics and twitches, to anatomize his personality in type. After that he was an insect on a pin, a newspaper clipping laminated in plastic. I might enjoy his company, even admire him at moments, but he no longer had the power to make me wake up trembling in the middle of the night. I no longer dreamed about him. He had a face.

So another condition for the zipless fuck was brevity. And anonymity made it even better.

During the time I lived in Heidelberg I commuted to Frankfurt four times a week to see my analyst. The ride took an hour each way and trains became an important part of my fantasy life. I kept meeting beautiful men on the train, men who scarcely spoke English, men whose clichés and banalities were hidden by my ignorance of French, or Italian, or even German. Much as I hate to admit it, there are *some* beautiful men in Germany.

One scenario of the zipless fuck was perhaps inspired by an Italian movie I saw years ago. As time went by, I embellished it to suit my head. It used to play over and over again as I shuttled back and forth from Heidelberg to Frankfurt, from Frankfurt to Heidelberg:

A grimy European train compartment (Second Class). The seats are leatherette and hard. There is a sliding door to the corridor outside. Olive trees rush by the window. Two Sicilian peasant women sit together on one side with a child between them. They appear to be mother and grandmother and granddaughter. Both women vie with each other to stuff the little girl's mouth with food. Across the way (in the window seat) is a pretty young widow in a heavy black veil and tight black dress which reveals her voluptuous figure. She is sweating profusely and her eyes are puffy. The middle seat is empty. The corridor seat is occupied by an enormously fat woman with a moustache. Her huge haunches cause her to occupy almost half of the vacant center seat. She is reading a pulp romance in which the characters are photographed models and the dialogue appears in little puffs of smoke above their heads.

This fivesome bounces along for a while, the widow and the fat woman keeping silent, the mother and grandmother talking to the child and each other about the food. And then the train screeches to a halt in a town called (perhaps) CORLEONE. A tall languid-looking soldier, unshaven, but with a beautiful mop of hair, a cleft chin, and somewhat devilish, lazy eyes, enters the compartment, looks insolently around, sees the empty halfseat between the fat woman and the widow, and, with many flirtatious apologies, sits down. He is sweaty and disheveled but basically a gorgeous hunk of flesh, only slightly rancid from the heat. The train screeches out of the station.

Then we become aware only of the bouncing of the train and the rhythmic way the soldier's thighs are rubbing against the thighs of the widow. Of course, he is also rubbing against the haunches of the fat lady—and she is trying to move away from him—which is quite unnecessary because he is unaware of her haunches. He is watching the large gold cross between the widow's breasts swing back and forth in her deep cleavage. Bump. Pause. Bump. It hits one moist breast and then the other. It seems to hesitate in between as if paralyzed between two repelling magnets. The pit and the pendulum. He is hypnotized. She stares out the window, looking at each olive tree as if she had never seen olive trees before. He rises awkwardly, half-bows to the ladies, and struggles to open the window. When he sits down again his arm accidentally grazes the widow's belly. She appears not to notice. He rests his left hand on the seat between his thigh and hers and begins to wind rubber fingers around and under the soft flesh of her thigh. She continues staring at each olive tree as if she were God and had just made them and were wondering what to call them.

Meanwhile the enormously fat lady is packing away her pulp romance in an iridescent green plastic string bag full of smelly cheeses and blackening bananas. And the grandmother is rolling ends of salami in greasy newspaper. The mother is putting on the little girl's sweater and wiping her face with a handkerchief, lovingly moistened with maternal spittle. The train screeches to a stop in a town called (perhaps) PRIZZI, and the fat lady, the mother, the grandmother, and the little girl leave the compartment. Then the train begins to move again. The gold cross begins to bump, pause, bump between the widow's moist breasts, the fingers begin to curl under the widow's thighs, the widow continues to stare at the olive trees. Then the fingers are sliding between her thighs and they are parting her thighs, and they are moving upward into the fleshy gap between her heavy black stockings and her garters, and they are sliding up under her garters into the damp unpantied place between her legs.

The train enters a *galleria*, or tunnel, and in the semidarkness the symbolism is consummated.

There is the soldier's boot in the air and the dark walls of the tunnel and the hypnotic rocking of the train and the long high whistle as it finally emerges.

Wordlessly, she gets off at a town called, perhaps, BIVONA. She crosses the tracks, stepping carefully over them in her narrow black shoes and heavy black stockings. He stares after her as if he were Adam wondering what to name her. Then he jumps up and dashes out of the train in pursuit of her. At that very moment a long freight train pulls through the parallel track obscuring his view and blocking his way. Twenty-five freight cars later, she has vanished forever.

One scenario of the zipless fuck.

Zipless, you see, *not* because European men have button-flies rather than zipper-flies, and not because the participants are so devastatingly attractive, but because the incident has all the swift compression of a dream and is seemingly free of all remorse and guilt; because there is no talk of her late husband or of his fiancée; because there is no rationalizing; because there is no talk at *all*. The zipless fuck is absolutely pure. It is free of ulterior motives. There is no power game. The man is not "taking" and the woman is not "giving." No one is attempting to cuckold a husband or humiliate a wife. No one is trying to prove anything or get anything out of anyone. The zipless fuck is the purest thing there is. And it is rarer than the unicorn. And I have never had one. Whenever it seemed I was close, I discovered a horse with a papier-mâché horn, or two clowns in a unicorn suit. Alessandro, my Florentine friend, came close. But he was, after all, one clown in a unicorn suit.

Consider this tapestry, my life.

Binnie Kirshenbaum

"Jews Have No Business Being Enamored of Germans"

from *A Disturbance in One Place*

The multimedia artist has clogs on his feet, a fashion blunder I thought even the Swedes had gotten over. He also wears paint-splattered blue jeans and an insignia sweatshirt. I squint to make out the gothic lettering: *Universität Heidelberg*.

"Heidelberg?" I raise one eyebrow.

"Yes," he says. "I got this the last time I was there. Do you like it?"

"No," I tell him. "I don't like it."

He visits Germany regularly, often going to Berlin. Berlin is where it's happening, a forefront of a place, the artist's Mecca. He has many German friends.

"It doesn't bother you? Make you uneasy?" I scout for an ashtray. You'd think he'd have put one out, knowing I was coming over.

"It's a new generation," he excuses them, the Germans. "Besides, my friends are all artists and academics, scholars." He makes it sound as if only butchers and saloon keepers were responsible.

His affection for Germans confirms some suspicions I have about the multimedia artist: 1) he has a short and convenient view of history, and 2) he is cheap, tight with a dollar. Only cheap people can put up with the Germans, tolerate their stingy ways. The only things Germans do with largesse is plop potatoes on a plate and gas people.

The multimedia artist is taken with Aryan intellectualism. He's impressed by Heidegger, by Wittgenstein, by Kant. Logic, reason, ideas of the mind that get you nowhere.

"Did you know," I ask, "Kant was a virgin? His whole life and he never got laid?"

"Of course I know that. Everyone knows that. But what of it? The man was brilliant."

"He couldn't have been too brilliant," I remark. "Couldn't even figure out how to get some pussy."

"He had a higher calling," the multimedia artist defends his idol.

Jews really shouldn't have Germans for idols. Not that the multimedia artist is all that Jewish, although a German wouldn't have made such a distinction. That the multimedia artist was Jewish at all did come as a surprise to me. That he and I have exchanged intimacies, bodily fluids, is a case of mistaken identity on both our parts.

When I first met him, he looked familiar. He does look familiar. He looks like me. Of him I could say: We are of the same place. His features, too, are from no one land but from everywhere. He shares my coloring, although he wears his black hair in a ponytail. When I'd asked him, "Where are you from?" he said, "Minnesota." There are places in the world I never imagine having Jewish populations: China, Honduras, Bali, Minnesota. I thought American Jews were pretty much confined to New York, California, with a smattering of us—having conked out halfway across the country—in Chicago.

I hadn't a clue the multimedia artist was Jewish until he brought the subject up, asking me, "What's your ethnic background?"

"Jewish," I said.

"You're kidding?" He was even more distressed than when he'd learned I was married. "I never get involved with Jewish women."

"Why?" I asked. "What are you?"

"Jewish," he said.

"From Minnesota?" My mind was reeling from the anachronism. "Were you the only one?"

"No," he said. "There were a lot of us. Not that being Jewish meant anything. We were all very assimilated," he said, as if the Jews of Minnesota had come over on the Mayflower, had Jews been allowed aboard the Mayflower. Then, as if I were supposed to say thank you, he said, "Well, you don't look at all Jewish."

"You're a new experience for me, too," I assured him. As a rule, I steer clear of Jewish men. As a rule, perhaps, but the love of my life is a Jew, although that's a feature of his I have to remind myself of because he, too, has forsaken it. "Your husband's not Jewish?" the multimedia artist asked.

"Anglo-Saxon," I said.

"And the other one?"

With all its implications, I intoned, "Sicilian."

It is the foreigners, the others, the outsiders, who find me exotic, rare, a wonder to behold. Such men do not point to my painted fingernails and cry, "JAP!" Only Jews have such contempt for their own, the kind of contempt that results in becoming enamored of Germans.

Jews have no business being enamored of Germans. We ought not to tangle with them. I know this from history and from experience.

I was fifteen years old, staying in a Youth Hostel in Amsterdam because I was on a Teen Tour and had no choice of accommodations. On this Teen Tour, I buddied around with a robust blond girl from Maine. We were a good team. Two pretty girls, but of such different styles, different tastes, that neither stepped on the other's toes.

Our last night in Amsterdam I had every intention of going to sleep early, but the blond girl from Maine came to me and said, "There's a handsome man in the Common Room. I want to meet him." The Common Room was what passed for a lobby in a Youth Hostel. She begged me to accompany her, to bolster her confidence. "Then you can go to bed," she promised.

He had shoulder-length hair. His fingernails needed cutting. He was twenty-nine years old, a biochemist, and was staying at a Youth Hostel instead of a nice hotel because he was a chintzy German.

When I woke up briefly at two in the morning, the blond girl's bed was empty. Good for her, I thought, although it was beyond me what she saw in some old hippie who wore clogs on his feet.

At breakfast, our packs leaning against our chairs for imminent departure, the blond girl from Maine said, "There he is. Come with me to say good-bye."

He wrote down her address in a worn leather book. "Und you?" He asked for my address too. Europeans, particularly Northern and Central Europeans, stress address exchanges. Spend ten minutes on a train with one, chat for two seconds in a café, and they'll whip out the address book. I used to think this was their way of being friendly. Later I learned it's because, should they wind up in your part of the world, they've got a place to freeload.

When my Teen Tour ended, I arrived home to find four letters waiting for me. Letters from someone with a goofy name—Fritz, Ralph, Kraut, Krupp—a name you might give a dog. He wrote of his travels and how the Scottish Highlands—dark, mysterious, haunting—reminded him of me, and I wondered, "Who the fuck is this guy?"

Perhaps the blond girl from Maine could solve the riddle, so I called her. "Yes," she knew. "The one I was with in Amsterdam."

"He must've mixed us up," I said. "Write to him and set him straight, would you?" I had no desire to receive another skeevy letter.

The fifth skeevy letter explained: No, he hadn't mixed us up. My friend, the blond Christian girl, was very nice, but he wanted the Jewess.

I tore his letter into a lot of pieces before throwing it in the trash. A month went by, when he called me on the telephone. He was at Kennedy Airport, en route to California for a conference, and wanted to spend the weekend in New York, at my house.

"I don't live in New York City," I said. "I live in a suburb. It's not at all like the city. You can't see anything from where I live."

"I wish only to see you," he told me.

"Hang on. I have to ask my mother."

My mother's response was a shock, a cold betrayal. "Of course he can stay here." She said we'd be happy to welcome him as our guest.

My mother and stepfather thought he was a fine young man. They liked his Ph.D., his manners. So polite. He complimented my mother on her cooking, which only a German could do—rave over meatloaf seasoned with onion soup mix.

"And what do your parents do for a living?" my stepfather asked the fine young German man.

"My mother," he said, "is a librarian. My father is deceased. He was executed by the Russians for war crimes before I was born."

I choked on a Tater Tot.

He excused himself from the dinner table to go to the toilet. That's how he phrased it—the toilet—which was disgusting, and I apologized to my mother for bringing Nazi offspring to the house. "I had no idea," I said.

"Don't blame the son for the father's sins," my stepfather admonished me.

"Oh, none of that concerned us," my mother waved off the Holocaust and a world war.

Very shortly after my mother and her husband went to sleep, the son of the Nazi came after me, sneaking into my bedroom. Although he didn't have a bayonet, he did have an erection that he pressed against me.

I pushed him off. "Beat it," I said.

"Excuse me?" His English wasn't all that great. The idiom wasn't in his vocabulary. To make myself understood, I had to shove him, hard, from my bed.

He landed on the floor, and rose up, but only to his knees. Kneeling, he reached out to touch me. "I am zorry," he whispered. "Please. Accept forgiveness. I am zo zorry."

Pity I was too young to appreciate the potential, the possibilities such an affair held open. A dominatrix daydream, and I didn't take advantage. Instead I said, "Get the fuck out of my room, creep."

He walked to the door and, before leaving, said lovingly, "Jew bitch."

Now, in front of me, the multimedia artist folds, neatly, his *Universität Heidelberg* sweatshirt and places it on a chair. I am fully clothed, and I step back to study him, his nakedness, his obliviousness to the situation: a naked Jewish man enamored of Germans.

Jerzy Kosinski

From *Steps*

She never knew I was her lover although we had worked together for a long time in the same office. Our desks were in the same room, and often at lunchtime we sat beside one another in the cafeteria.

It was almost a year now since I had stopped inviting her to dinner or to the theater or to the other functions that she was never willing to attend. I tried to pry some information about her from our fellow workers, but they knew less than I. She had never been close to anyone at the office. One of the men told me he had heard she had been divorced a few years ago, and that her only child was living with its father somewhere in the south.

I began following her. Once I spent an entire Saturday skulking in a doorway across from the building in which she lived. That afternoon she left her apartment and returned at about seven. Before eight she went out again and strolled toward the main thoroughfare. I followed her until she reached the square, where she hailed a taxi. I walked back to my observation post.

Standing in the shallow doorway opposite her house, I waited as the drizzle turned into a persistent rain, drenching my coat. Past midnight a cab stopped in front of the door; she got out alone.

I brooded over my obsession and the absurd vigils it had led me to.

Since I seemed to have no chance of becoming her lover, I decided to forge an indirect link through which I could learn more about her. I got hold of one of my friends who I supposed would be able to make contact with her, and confided in him. My friend was prepared for the undertaking, and we immediately began to devise a feasible plan.

He would begin by establishing business dealings between his firm and my employer's. Then he would inquire about certain products that were handled by the department in which the woman worked. Two days later he informed me that he had made a business appointment for the next day and thought it likely he would negotiate directly with her.

As I saw him enter the office I grew tense. Without looking at me, he walked over to the section manager. Then I heard him speaking with the girl.

That afternoon he informed me that all had gone well and a further meeting had been arranged. It was after this second meeting that she accepted his invitation to dinner.

Within the week she became his mistress. He described her as devoted and ready to do anything for him: she had become his instrument, and if I was ready to possess her, he could arrange it. He added that he had already required of her that she submit one day to another man as proof of her love and loyalty to him. He had assured her that she would never know the stranger's identity, because her eyes would be blindfolded. At first she was indignant, claiming she was being humiliated and insulted. Then, he said, she agreed.

The following evening I left my apartment and took a cab to his house. I arrived too early and had to walk slowly around the neighborhood. Finally I waited silently outside his door, listening. I heard nothing, and rang the bell; the door opened and my friend calmly gestured me in.

A circular white wool rug covered the center of the bedroom floor. A lamp cast its shaded light on the naked woman who lay there, a wide black blindfold covering half her face from the forehead to the base of her nose. My friend knelt down beside her, stroking her with his hands. He beckoned to me. I approached. A melancholy ballad was drifting up from a phonograph; the girl lay still, seemingly unaware of the third presence in the room.

I watched his fingers slide loosely over her skin. As she half rose toward him, seeking him with her hands, he whispered something to her. She dejectedly fell back on the rug, turning her face away from him, her back arched and her hands crossed as though for protection. I hesitated.

Patiently he stroked her again. The cords in her neck softened, her fingers unclenched, but she did not yield any access. My friend rose, and picking up his dressing gown, walked to the door. I heard him turn on the television in the library.

Remembering that I must not speak, I gazed at her tousled hair, her neatly curving thighs, the rounded flesh of her shoulders. I was aware that to her I was no more than a whim of the man she loved, a mere extension of his body, his touch, his love, his contempt. I felt my craving grow as I stood over her, but the consciousness of my role prevailed over my desire to possess her. To overcome this I tried to recall those images of her which had so often aroused me in the office: an underarm glimpsed through the armhole of her sleeveless blouse, the motion of her hips within the confines of her skirt.

I moved closer; she resisted but did not pull away. I began to touch her mouth, her hair, her breasts, her belly, stroking her flesh until she moaned and raised her arms in what could have meant either rejection or appeal. I drew myself up to take her, my eyes closed to shut out her nakedness, my face brushing the smooth blindfold.

I entered her abruptly: she did not resist. With a movement at first timorous and now almost impassioned, her hands gathered me in, pressing my face to her breast. Her loosened hair was spreading around her head, her body tautened, her lips parted in voiceless amazement. Our bodies shuddered; I slid down at her side.

She lay rigid, her hands folded piously on her breast like the medieval effigy of a saint. She was cold and stiff and quiet; only her twisted face had not yet surrendered to the lull which held her body. Her blindfold was stained with the sweat falling from between her drawn brows.

I went to the bathroom, signaling to my host on the way. I dressed and left the apartment. At home I flung myself on the bed. Instantly my image of her divided: the woman in the office, clothed, indifferent, crossing the room; and the naked blindfolded girl, giving herself at another man's command. Both images were clear and sharp—but they refused to merge. For hours each displaced and supplanted the other.

I woke several times during the night, unable to recall the shape or movement of her body, but vividly remembering the smallest details of her clothes. It was as though I were forever undressing her, forever held back by mounds of blouses, skirts, girdles, stockings, coats, and shoes.

If I could become one of them, if I could only part with my language, my manner, my belongings.

I was in a bar in a run-down section of the city beyond the covered bazaar. Without hesitating I walked over to the bartender. As he leaned forward I began my deaf-mute charade, signaling for a glass of water. The barman waved me away impatiently, but I stood my ground and repeated my pantomime. I could feel the stares of the people in the bar. When I jerked my shoulders and flapped my ear like a spastic they scrutinized me closely, and I sensed that to some of them I had suddenly become an object of interest. I knew I had to be very careful of their suspicions, of any attempt to find out who I was or where I had come from.

Two men and a woman edged nearer, and touched me. At first I ignored their overtures, giving the woman, the boldest and most silent, a chance to elbow the others aside.

I continued to motion for water. A man came forward to order a drink for me, but I refused, grimacing my disgust for arrack and gesturing apologies for my refusal. A couple drew closer. They beckoned me to leave with them. I did not understand what they were saying, and making a show of being attracted to the bright jewelry they wore, I turned and slowly looked into their faces. Their gaze bore down on me.

There was a store I entered several times. Nothing distinguished it from the others of the neighborhood. Most of the shops and bars in the vicinity had some connection with illegal activities—the blackmarket, stolen goods, or traffic in young country girls. Often I hung around the shop until closing time, and watched the patrons wandering out the back door to the barn in the yard. As a silent, gesturing spastic I was not a threat to the callers—I could be given a task, a few coins, and then be dismissed. Eventually I followed them, but was pushed back into the shop and out into the street. The final time I stayed late and tried to join the men. No one stopped me, but at the barn door a woman motioned me to stand guard.

From my vantage point I peered into the barn. I saw a great circle of naked men lying on their backs, their feet joined at the center like the spokes of a wheel. A woman was standing at their feet, pulling off her ragged dress. She was gross and heavy, her skin moist and hairy. She was splashing water from a wooden bucket over her belly and legs. And as she washed herself and the water spattered on the ground, the men fidgeted, their hands playing at their thighs or their arms shifting behind their heads. It was as though she had become the healer of these broken men, and at the sound of the water a momentary surge went through these petty thieves and weary pimps. She plodded across to one of them, squatting over him. For a moment he grunted, cried out hoarsely, half rose, and then fell heavily back. The woman stepped away from him and passed on to his neighbor, picking her way like a bloated toad over the worn stones of a mudhole. One by one she served them; those she had not yet reached twitched in their efforts to restrain the energy that urged through their loins. One by one they fell back, like corpses laid out in shallow coffins. Now the barn looked as if it had been pressed into service for the dead and the dying from a derailed train. As she rose and walked around the silent men, the woman resembled a nurse checking the victims. She bathed, and again the water splashed. Now there was no answering sound, no movement.

At times my disguise became a hazard. One day, wandering about longer than usual, I decided to have a meal before finding a place to sleep. I went into a place that I knew was usually crowded. The bar itself was almost empty that night. But I spotted several familiar faces—a group of manual workers in the front of the room and two or three of the local bosses, their heads together, at the private tables in the back.

A surly peasant stood at the counter, mumbling as he drank. Away by the wall, half lost in the shadows, a man was slumped over his glass.

Suddenly the street door blew open and a dozen policemen rushed in. Some stationed themselves between the door and the crowd; others followed a kitchen boy to the man drooping at the bar.

The police first sat the man up, then pulled him off the stool. As his body swung around I caught sight of the knife that stuck out from his ribs. There was a bloodstain on the wall. The crowd broke into a frenzy of talk. Only then did I realize that I was the likeliest suspect of them all. There could be no explanation for my dress, my acts, or my presence.

If I continued to be a deaf-mute, I would be accused of this crime, the senseless act of a defective. My mask would trap me further. But if I were to bolt through the police cordon, I would risk a bullet. I realized that within a few seconds I would be led away with the others. Turning toward the bar I picked up the bartender's rag, and seizing a tray of dirty coffee cups, trotted into the kitchen.

Occasionally I would attempt to get part-time jobs. One night, employed as a handyman in a neighborhood restaurant, I noticed the proprietor sitting and talking with the last customers—three men and a woman.

There had been a short circuit downstairs; I approached the table, motioning to the proprietor. I met the woman's startled, uncertain glance and instantly exaggerated my role: I slapped my right ear several times as the men guffawed. She blushed; as if ashamed of her companions, but she continued to watch me.

The woman returned several days later accompanied by a man I had not seen before. It was late and most of the tables were empty. Since the proprietor was away, I went to the two as soon as they were seated. The woman's left hand lay palm down on the tablecloth, and she was attentively rubbing her cuticles with her right forefinger. I emptied the ashtray and adjusted the napkins and cutlery. The man asked for something, and when I shrugged meekly, the woman spoke, perhaps explaining that she had seen me before and that I could neither hear nor speak. The man scrutinized me coldly, then relaxed as I brushed an invisible speck of dust from the tablecloth. The woman nervously crumpled her handkerchief, obviously conscious of my proximity. I withdrew without turning around and again slapped my ears.

Next day I was summoned by the proprietor, who explained in gestures that I had to do a different job. An hour later one of the waiters led me to a tall apartment house, where we took an elevator to the top floor. The door was opened by the woman I had seen in the restaurant.

I was hired to clean her apartment after the large parties she regularly gave. The parties, catered by the restaurant where I had worked, were often attended by the underworld. I was careful not to wander too close to the rooms with locked doors. I knew of too many people who had vanished from that quarter of the city because of their curiosity. After several days my presence and the hum of my vacuum cleaner went as unnoticed as the familiar creaking of the floorboards or the intermittent rattle of the steam pipes.

While dusting the furniture I covertly watched the woman's face reflected in mirrors: her image split into fragments as she rearranged her hair. I would smile politely when I caught her hesitant glance.

I worked undisturbed because my duties were simple and I needed no instruction. I noticed that when my new employer wanted to tell me something she became self-conscious and was upset by my violent ear-slappings.

Several times she tested me. Once when I was dusting, she silently approached the piano and struck a chord. Another time, as I was putting away the wine glasses, she came from behind and suddenly shouted. I managed to restrain even the smallest twitch. One evening, without looking at me, she motioned for me to follow her.

She forgot herself completely as she stretched under me, her eyes straining toward the headboard. Her whole body became involved in drawing breath, driven by tides and currents flowing and ebbing in rapid surges. Swaying like a clump of weed in the sea, she quivered, a rushing stream of words broke over her lips like foam. It was as if I were the master of all this fluid passion, and her tumbling words its final wave.

In her last outpouring she broke into a language I could understand, and spoke of herself as a zealot entering a church built long ago from the ruins of pagan temples, a novice in the inner sanctum of the church, not knowing at whose altar she knelt, to which god she prayed.

Her voice grew rough and hoarse as she writhed on the bed, thrashing from side to side. I held her arms and shook her, diving into her with all my weight. Like a joyous mare in its solitary stall, she cried out again and again, as though trying to detach into speech what had been fused with her flesh. She whispered that she veered toward the sun, which would melt her with its heat. Her sentences poured and broke, and she muttered that the sun left only the glow of stars brushing close to each other. Slowly her lips grew parched—she slept.

Michael Lowenthal

"Infinity of Angles"

from *The Same Embrace*

I t had been less than two years, but already the trip to Germany had lodged in the myth-space of Jacob's mind, as though it were history, a parable, not his own recent adventure. In the way of most memories, it was at once etched with diamond clarity and blurred like a view of the world through tears.

The Common Press was feeling flush in the fall of '91. The Mellon grant had come through, and the mystery novel Chantelle had acquired on a whim proved a surprise bestseller. This year they could afford to send someone to the Frankfurt Book Fair.

The trip turned out to be too full of business to allow much pleasure. Jacob worked the noisy exhibit hall, pitching the mystery at booth after booth in hopes of clinching translation deals. In the evenings, after meetings with distributors, he was too exhausted to do anything but sleep in the hotel's stiff bed.

But the last night, knowing he'd never forgive himself otherwise, Jacob mustered the energy to go out. He studied the listings in his *Spartacus Guide*, ruling out half a dozen clubs with names like Blue Angels and Construction 5 as American wannabes. Finally, he picked one by its German name and its unglamorous address, in a small alley off the Alte Gasse.

• • •

Bierstube Funzel was a dingy corridor of a room, with a bar along one wall and orange vinyl booths along the other. The place didn't resemble a nightclub so much as a railroad-car diner. Jacob half expected to smell the smoky perfume of sizzling bacon.

He ordered a draft—pushing a wad of marks to the bartender and trusting he'd receive correct change—then claimed a seat in an empty booth. At the room's far end was a tiny dance floor, ten feet wide and five deep, mottled with weakly colored lights. Nobody danced. Jacob almost spat up his beer when he heard the song whimpering through the toaster-sized speakers: *Boogie oogie boogie woogie dancin' shoes, keep me dancin' all night. Boogie oogie boogie woogie dancin' shoes, make me queen of the night.*

The oddest thing was that the walls were covered with a sheer reflective material—something between tin foil and aluminized mylar—so from his seat Jacob enjoyed a multitude of views of every spot in the bar. It was like sitting in the barber's chair when he held the mirror behind your head, and you saw yourself from an infinity of angles.

Unsettled by the voyeuristic decor, Jacob lowered his eyes to the wheaty froth of his beer.

"Yes, it is strange."

The hot force of the words accosted Jacob's neck. He looked up to find a man crouched beside him, shockingly close. He wore a black mesh T-shirt tucked into pristine, pressed white jeans.

"It is strange," the man repeated in a light German accent, "but think of the advantages for cruising. Normally, you see somebody across the crowd, you think he is good-looking, you approach. But when you see him from the front, you discover he is hideous. Here, this is eliminated. For example, I knew before I walked over that you were handsome from every side."

Too startled to acknowledge the compliment, Jacob merely motioned for the man to sit. He was baffled and somewhat ashamed that everyone in Frankfurt spoke to him immediately in English. He had dressed in what he thought was the Euro uniform—black shoes, jeans, button-down shirt—and had even slicked some gel into his hair, but still they were able to pick him out.

The stranger stared. His squat face followed the outline of a battle-ship's hull, jawbones angling sharply to the keel of his chin. His straw-blond hair flopped in symmetrical crests from a neat center part. The cut reminded Jacob of the men in his antique photographs, painfully sincere as they posed for the slow camera.

"I haven't introduced myself," the man said. "My name is Hannes."

Jacob shook his hand, bony but firm. "I'm Jacob."

"Jacob. Beautiful name. In German we would say 'Ya-cob.' "

"Actually," Jacob said, "I *am* kind of German. My grandparents."

Hannes scanned Jacob's face the way a grocery shopper might scrutinize produce. "Jewish?" he asked.

"I was raised Jewish," Jacob qualified.

"Yes. Yes, I could tell."

"You could tell? I don't know, that sounds a little scary."

"Oh no. Please. Don't mistake me." Hannes encircled Jacob's wrist with gentle fingertips. "I love Jews. Judaism. In fact, that's what I study at university. American Jewish literature."

"Seriously?"

"Yes, yes. Saul Bellow, Philip Roth. Singer. Malamud. Potok. I read them all. It's going to be my dissertation."

"Wow," Jacob said. "You're more Jewish than me. I saw the movie of *The Chosen*. Does that count?"

Hannes tightened his grip on Jacob's wrist. Below the table, he wedged his knee between Jacob's two. "You have to *read* Potok. He is very subtle."

In America, Hannes's brazenness would be too much, a wrecking ball of a come-on. But here Jacob accepted it. "How did you get into all of this?" he asked, placing his own hand on top of Hannes's, constructing a stack of flesh on the beer-sticky table.

"It's the most dynamic strain of American writing, don't you think? So many issues. I just finished Wiesel's *Night* again, maybe the fifth time. It never stops fascinating. The whole question of how to believe in God after Auschwitz."

Jacob chuckled. "It's never been that big a dilemma for me. I mean, I don't think God was too convincing *before* Auschwitz."

Hannes's pale lips opened a divot in his face. "No, you can't be serious. Please tell me you are joking."

"Oh, sorry. Are you religious or something?"

"No, but you should be," Hannes said, squeezing Jacob's arm with frightening force on the *you*. "You are part of such a beautiful tradition. Don't you feel lucky to be Jewish?"

Jacob shrugged. "I guess the grass is always greener."

Hannes's eyebrows collapsed into an adorable curving V, like a child's crayon rendition of a bird, all wings. "I do not know what this means," he said.

"The grass is greener? You've never heard that? I'm surprised. Your English is really good. It means, um, that things never look as good from the inside as they do from the outside."

Hannes seemed to swish the idiom around his mouth as though it were expensive wine. Then he moved his face next to Jacob's, so close that the tiny hairs on Jacob's earlobes stood on end. He whispered, "I would like you to see me from the inside."

The words tickled like mild electricity, a thrilling, almost painful sting on Jacob's skin. He opened his mouth to laugh, but the sound was muffled by Hannes's tongue. He choked for a second, then thrust back with his own tongue, testing the sharpness of Hannes's rear teeth.

A moment later he froze, certain he was being watched. He retreated his tongue partway and looked up: Three more of himself mimed the gesture in the reflective wall paneling. He was kissing this broad stranger, and kissing him, and kissing him again.

Jacob gazed into the foily reflections, expecting the sudden clarity of revelation. But the paneling was dull and dented in spots. He saw only a blurry, generic figure staring back.

Hannes's apartment was on the fifth floor of a concrete block building. Climbing the steep stairs, Jacob felt a tackiness of sweat between his shirt collar and his neck, like the gummy lip of glue on an envelope. He could smell the yeasty warmth of his own underarms. He hadn't tried this in far too long.

The place was tiny. A single bed was pushed into the corner, its frame rusted as a summer-camp cot. An overturned cardboard box bowed with the weight of library books. Everything wore the sallow dinginess of the lone light bulb that dangled from the ceiling, a tiny upside-down skull casting more shadow than light.

"This is it," Hannes said, crouching to avoid knocking his head on the hanging bulb.

The long climb had squeezed Jacob's bladder; the need to pee radioed from his abdomen in urgent waves. "Is there a bathroom?" he asked.

"Over here." Hannes ushered him inside and flipped the light, then backed out and closed the door.

Jacob drained himself with a forceful stream, and as his chest regained room for air, space freed also in his mind to consider the best approach. He wanted to connect this time, to achieve more than a rote physical release. How could he take the encounter to a deeper level?

When he came out of the bathroom, Hannes was standing naked at the foot of the bed, holding five strands of thin black rope.

"Tie me," he demanded.

Jacob's stomach lurched with fear and excitement. Okay, he thought. Fair enough. Maybe Hannes was the one with a plan.

Hannes's body was as spare as his apartment. The satin skin of his chest was interrupted only by a tiny heart of hair between the gum-colored nipples. A whorled stub of bellybutton jutted from his flat stomach, as if he were so skinny that there was no room for this extra piece of flesh.

"Tie me," he said again. He tossed the ropes.

Jacob caught the strands in one fist. With the other hand he began unbuttoning his shirt to catch up with Hannes's nakedness.

"No," Hannes said. "Tie me first."

He lay on the bed, his arms and legs flung to the corners of the frame. Now Jacob allowed himself to examine Hannes's dick. The shaft appeared smooth, devoid of the usual veins, as if made of plastic. A snorkel of foreskin hung compliantly from the tip.

Hannes's chest heaved in the studied, serious breaths of a weightlifter preparing to lift the bar. Jacob hovered over him, fumbling with the ropes. The positioning was awkward. There wasn't room to stand.

"Here," Hannes instructed. "On top."

Jacob climbed on the sunken mattress. His shoes were still on. He worried about hurting Hannes, about soiling the sheets. He looped one black strand through the bedframe's rusty pipes, then wound the rope around Hannes's wrist. When he pulled the knot, his balance slipped. He lunged, catching his entire weight with one desperate knee. The knee thudded directly on Hannes's sternum.

Hannes gasped in a convulsing reflex. Jacob tried to right himself, to alleviate the crushing load. But looking down, he saw the pain had torqued a dreamy smile onto Hannes's face.

The smile injected a roller-coaster thrill into the walls of Jacob's gut. He shifted his full weight back onto Hannes, rolling his knee pestle-like in the hollow of his ribs. He hadn't known this drive since he and Jonathan were kids and staged brawls in the leaf-strewn backyard—this desire to see how much he could get away with.

He fixed the first knot, then tied the other wrist, not consciously inflicting pain, but not caring if he did. He bound both ankles, then found the fifth rope and zeroed in on the crotch.

By now Hannes was fully hard. His balls rose and fell with his excited breath, shifting beneath the pink wrinkled scrotum like some elusive undersea creature. Jacob wound the rope twice around the entire package, then a third time, jerking the strand upward the way a cowboy snugs his lasso's noose.

"Tight enough?" he asked.

Hannes's response was high-voiced and shivery, as if his throat were the thing being squeezed. "Tighter."

"Like this?" Jacob yanked once more and secured a final knot. Now the veins showed in the skin of Hannes's dick, a blue-red reticulation as intricate as an autumn leaf's underside.

Jacob's own dick surged as well, levering his underwear's elastic band. He stood and stripped his shirt.

He climbed back onto the bed and knelt between Hannes's legs. Bending, he licked Hannes's chest with tiny paintbrush strokes. He lapped around the swatch of hair, then up to the neck, over the chin's peak to the mouth.

Hannes jerked his head away. "No," he said. "No kissing."

The injunction startled Jacob. It was confusing to be in control but not. He snaked down Hannes's body, grazing the skin with his incisors. He sucked a nipple into his mouth and nibbled gingerly. Hannes arched his back, pushing the flesh further between Jacob's teeth. The nipple was tough but stretchy; it was like chewing a rubber band.

Hannes's breath quickened. "Go on," he said. "Go ahead."

Jacob moved to the other nipple, but Hannes shook his head. "No. Not that. Aren't you going to hit?"

Jacob had never hit anybody. He had play-spanked a guy once, but nothing for real. Now he took an experimental swipe at Hannes's chest. The sound was flat as a fake movie slap.

"Don't hold back," Hannes coached. "I want you to hurt."

Jacob recalled Hannes's zombie smile when he had kneed him in the chest, and he wanted that power again. He wanted to punch the expression back onto Hannes's face. His hand cut the air in a blurry arc. This time the apartment echoed with a fleshy thud.

Jacob slapped again, lower this time, on Hannes's stomach. The clean *pop* thrilled his ears. He whipped down another time. A pink impression of his hand stained the skin. It was intoxicating: the clap of flesh, Hannes's gasping twitch, the dangerous burn on his palm.

Then he grabbed the shaft. He'd only had sex with one uncut guy before, and that just a fumble in the dark. He had never had the chance for close study. There wasn't much play left, because of the binding rope, but Jacob tugged the clam's foot of skin until the dick seemed to consume itself, a turtle retracting into its shell.

"*Ja,*" Hannes moaned. "*Ja.* That's good."

Jacob pinched, digging his fingernails in the silky skin.

"Hit me," Hannes said, lifting his hips. "Hit me there."

Jacob was paralyzed. Some instinctive empathy would not permit his arms to move.

"Come on," Hannes said. "Do it." His voice was now a breathy rasp. "I know you've thought of it. You must be full of hate. After all the things we did to you."

Now Jacob flinched with understanding. And suddenly he did want to hit Hannes. He wanted to knock these crazy thoughts back inside him, far away, out of reach.

His hand flashed down, smacking the tight globe of flesh. Hannes spasmed against the blow, but Jacob did it again. He allowed himself to forget the damage he could do.

A bead of liquid leaked from the German's cock. Jacob could tell he was close. "The dresser," Hannes said. "Top drawer."

Jacob leapt from the bed, breathing hard. It was the same place he kept condoms in his own apartment. The drawer was filled with underwear and neatly balled socks. He rifled through, searching for the familiar shiny foil packages. Then, probing in the corner, his fingers bumped something hard and cold. He appraised its perilous weight as he pulled it out. The knife was locked in its open position, the four-inch blade exposed like naked flesh.

"Here," Hannes called. "Bring it here." His voice was distant and strangely liquid.

Jacob followed the command. His brain felt swollen, pressing his skull the way it did in an airplane descending too rapidly.

Now Hannes was crying, heaving wet gulps of air. "Please. Take revenge. Use the knife."

Jacob's fist clenched the burnished handle. Ripples of nausea pulsed from a sour spot at his stomach's bottom.

The German writhed in his restraints. His erection had lost some of its stiffness. The loosening foreskin bunched around the head like kissed lips.

"Cut it," Hannes said. "Like yours. Make me like you."

Jacob was not his body, not his legs or his arms. He bent over Hannes, pointing the knife in front of him the way he would aim a flashlight to penetrate darkness.

Then he sliced. A single swiping motion.

He cut the right wrist free so Hannes would be able to untie the other. He dropped the knife, kicked it far under the bed. Then he grabbed his shirt and ran for the door.

Bernard Malamud

"Still Life"

Months after vainly seeking a studio on the Via Margutta, del Babuino, della Croce, and elsewhere in that neighborhood, Arthur Fidelman settled for part of a crowded, windowy, attic-like atelier on a cobblestone street in the Trastevere, strung high with sheets and underwear. He had, a week before, in "personal notices" in the American-language newspaper in Rome, read: "Studio to share, cheap, many advantages, etc., A. Oliovino," and after much serious anguish (the curt advertisement having recalled dreams he had dreamed were dead), many indecisions, enunciations, and renunciations, Fidelman had, one very cold late-December morning, hurried to the address given, a worn four-story building with a yellowish façade stained brown along the edges. On the top floor, in a thickly cluttered artist's studio smelling aromatically of turpentine and oil paints, the inspiring sight of an easel lit in unwavering light from the three large windows setting the former art student on fire once more to paint, he had dealt not with a pittore, as expected, but with a pittrice, Annamaria Oliovino.

The pittrice, a thin, almost gaunt, high-voiced, restless type, with short black uncombed hair, violet mouth, distracted eyes and tense neck, a woman with narrow buttocks and piercing breasts, was in her way attractive if not in truth beautiful. She had on a thick black woolen sweater, eroded black velveteen culottes, black socks, and leather sandals spotted with drops of paint. Fidelman and she eyed each other stealthily and he realized at once she was, as a woman, indifferent to him or his type, who or which made no difference. But after ten minutes, despite the turmoil she exuded even as she dispassionately answered his hesitant questions, the art student, ever a sucker for strange beauty and all sorts of experiences, felt himself involved with and falling for her. Not my deep dish, he warned himself, aware of all the dangers to him and his renewed desire to create art; yet he was already half in love with her. It can't be, he thought in desperation; but it could. It had happened to him before. In her presence he tightly shut both eyes and wholeheartedly wished against what might be. Really he trembled, and though he labored to extricate his fate from hers, he was already a plucked bird, greased, and ready for frying. Fidelman protested within—cried out severely against the weak self, called himself ferocious names but could do not much, a victim of his familiar response, a too passionate fondness for strangers. So Annamaria, who had advertised a twenty-thousand-lire monthly rental, in the end doubled the sum, and Fidelman paid through both nostrils, cash for first and last months (should he attempt to fly by night) plus a deposit of ten thousand for possible damages. An hour later he moved in with his imitation-leather suitcase. This happened in the dead of winter. Below the cold sunlit windows stood two frozen umbrella pines and beyond, in the near distance, sparkled the icy Tiber.

The studio was well heated, Annamaria had insisted, but the cold leaked in through the wide windows. It was more a blast; the art student shivered but was kept warm by his hidden love for the pittrice. It took him most of a day to clear himself a space to work, about a third of the studio was as much as he could manage. He stacked her canvases five deep against her portion of the walls, curious to examine them, but Annamaria watched his every move (he noticed several self-portraits) although she was at the same time painting a monumental natura morta of a loaf of bread with two garlic bulbs ("Pane ed Aglii"). He moved stacks of *Oggi*, piles of postcards and yellowed letters, and a bundle of calendars going back to many years ago; also a Perugina candy box full of broken pieces of Etruscan pottery, one of small sea shells, and a third of medallions of various saints and of the Virgin, which she warned him to handle with care. He had uncovered a sagging cot by a dripping stone sink in his corner of the studio and there he slept. She furnished an old chafing dish and a broken table, and he bought a few household things he needed. Annamaria rented the art student an easel for a thousand lire a month. Her quarters were private, a room at the other end of the studio whose door she kept locked, handing him the key when he had to use the toilet. The wall was thin and the instrument noisy. He could hear the whistle and rush of her water, and though he tried to be quiet, because of the plumbing the bowl was always brimful and the pour of his stream embarrassed him. At night, if there was need, although he was tempted to use the sink, he fished out the yellowed, sedimented pot under his bed; once or twice, as he was using it in the thick of night, he had the impression she was awake and listening.

They painted in their overcoats, Annamaria wearing a black babushka, Fidelman a green wool hat pulled down over his frozen ears. She kept a pan of hot coals at her feet and every so often lifted a sandaled foot to toast it. The marble floor of the studio was sheer thick ice; Fidelman wore two pairs of tennis socks his sister, Bessie, had recently sent him from the States. Annamaria, a lefty, painted with a smeared leather glove on her hand, and theoretically his easel had been arranged so that he couldn't see what she was doing but he often sneaked looks at her work. The pittrice, to his surprise, painted with flicks of her fingers and wrists, peering at her performance with almost shut eyes. He noticed she alternated still lifes with huge lyric abstractions—massive whorls of red and gold exploding in all directions, these built on, entwined with, and ultimately concealing a small black religious cross, her first two brushstrokes on every abstract canvas. Once when Fidelman gathered the nerve to ask her why the cross, she answered it was the symbol that gave the painting its meaning.

He was eager to know more but she was impatient. "Eh," she shrugged, "who can explain art."

Though her response to his various attempts to become better acquainted were as a rule curt, and her voluntary attention to him, shorter still—she was able, apparently, to pretend he wasn't there—Fidelman's feeling for Annamaria grew, and he was as unhappy in love as he had ever been.

But he was patient, a persistent virtue, served her often in various capacities, for instance carrying down four flights of stairs her two bags of garbage shortly after supper—the portinaia was crippled and the portiere never around—sweeping the studio clean each morning, even running to retrieve a brush or paint tube when she happened to drop one—offering any service any time, you name it. She accepted these small favors without giving them notice.

One morning after reading a many-paged letter she had just got in the mail, Annamaria was sad, sullen, unable to work; she paced around restlessly, it troubled him. But after feverishly painting a widening purple spiral that continued off the canvas, she regained a measure of repose. This heightened her beauty, lent it somehow a youthful quality it didn't ordinarily have—he guessed her to be no older than twenty-seven or -eight; so Fidelman, inspired by the change in her, hoping it might foretoken better luck for him, approached Annamaria, removed his hat, and suggested since she went out infrequently why not lunch for a change at the trattoria at the corner, Guido's, where workmen assembled and the veal and white wine were delicious? She, to his surprise, after darting an uneasy glance out of the window at the tops of the motionless umbrella pines, abruptly assented. They ate well and conversed like human beings, although she mostly limited herself to answering his modest questions. She informed Fidelman she had come from Naples to Rome two years ago, although it seemed much longer, and he told her he was from the United States. Being so physically close to her, able to inhale the odor of her body—like salted flowers—and intimately eating together, excited Fidelman, and he sat very still, not to rock the boat and spill a drop of what was so precious to him. Annamaria ate hungrily, her eyes usually lowered. Once she looked at him with a shade of a smile and he felt beatitude; the art student contemplated many such meals though he could ill afford them, every cent he spent saved and sent by Bessie.

After zuppa inglese and a peeled apple she patted her lips with a napkin and, still in good humor, suggested they take the bus to the Piazza del Popolo and visit some painter friends of hers.

"I'll introduce you to Alberto Moravia."

"With pleasure," Fidelman said, bowing.

But when they stepped into the street and were walking to the bus stop near the river a cold wind blew up and Annamaria turned pale.

"Something wrong?" Fidelman inquired.

"The East Wind," she answered testily.

"What wind?"

"The Evil Eye," she said with irritation. "Malocchio."

He had heard something of the sort. They returned quickly to the studio, their heads lowered against the noisy wind, the pittrice from time to time furtively crossing herself. A black-habited old nun passed them at the trattoria corner, from whom Annamaria turned in torment, muttering, "Jettatura! Porca miseria!" When they were upstairs in the studio she insisted Fidelman touch his testicles three times to undo or dispel who knows what witchcraft, and he modestly obliged. Her request had inflamed him although he cautioned himself to remember it was, in purpose and essence, theological.

Later she received a visitor, a man who came to see her on Monday and Friday afternoons after his work in a government bureau. Her visitors, always men, whispered with her a minute, then left restlessly; most of them, excepting also Giancarlo Balducci, a cross-eyed illustrator—Fidelman never saw again. But the one who came oftenest stayed longest, a solemn gray-haired gent, Augusto Ottogalli, with watery blue eyes and missing side teeth, old enough to be her father for sure. He wore a slanted black fedora, and a shabby gray overcoat too large for him, greeted Fidelman vacantly, and made him inordinately jealous. When Augusto arrived in the afternoon the pittrice usually dropped anything she was doing and they retired to her room, at once locked and bolted. The art student wandered alone in the studio for dreadful hours. When Augusto ultimately emerged, looking disheveled, and if successful, defeated, Fidelman turned his back on him and the old man hastily let himself out of the door. After his visits, and only his, Annamaria did not appear in the studio for the rest of the day. Once when Fidelman knocked on her door to invite her out to supper, she told him to use the pot because she had a headache and was sound asleep. On another occasion when Augusto was locked long in her room with her, after a tormenting two hours Fidelman tiptoed over and put his jealous ear to the door. All he could hear was the buzz and sigh of their whispering. Peeking through the keyhole he saw them both in their overcoats, sitting on her bed, Augusto tightly clasping her hands, whispering passionately, his nose empurpled with emotion, Annamaria's white face averted. When the art student checked an hour afterwards, they were still at it, the old man imploring, the pittrice weeping. The next time, Augusto came with a priest, a portly, heavy-breathing man with a doubtful face. But as soon as they appeared in the studio Annamaria, enraged to fury, despite the impassioned entreatments of Augusto, began to throw at them anything of hers or Fidelman's she could lay hands on.

"Bloodsuckers!" she shouted, "scorpions! parasites!" until they had hastily retreated. Yet when Augusto, worn and harried, returned alone, without complaint she retired to her room with him.

2

Fidelman's work, despite the effort and despair he gave it, was going poorly. Every time he looked at unpainted canvas he saw harlequins, whores, tragic kings, fragmented musicians, the sick and the dread. Still, tradition was tradition and what if he should want to make more? Since he had always loved art history he considered embarking on a "Mother and Child," but was afraid her image would come out too much Bessie— after all, fifteen years between them. Or maybe a moving "Pietà," the dead son's body held like a broken wave in mama's frail arms? A curse on art history—he fought the fully prefigured picture though some of his former best paintings had jumped in every detail to the mind. Yet if so, where's true engagement? Sometimes I'd like to forget every picture I've seen, Fidelman thought. Almost in panic he sketched in charcoal a coat-tailed "Figure of a Jew Fleeing" and quickly hid it away. After that, ideas, prefigured or not, were scarce. "Astonish me," he muttered to himself, wondering whether to return to surrealism. He also considered a series of "Relations to Place and Space," constructions in squares and circles, the pleasures of tri-dimensional geometry of linear abstraction, only he had little heart for it. The furthest abstraction, Fidelman thought, is the blank canvas. A moment later he asked himself, if painting shows who you are, why should not painting?

After the incident with the priest Annamaria was despondent for a week, stayed in her room sometimes bitterly crying, Fidelman often standing helplessly by her door. However this was a prelude to a burst of creativity by the pittrice. Works by the dozens leaped from her brush and stylus. She continued her lyric abstractions based on the theme of a hidden cross and spent hours with a long black candle, burning holes in heavy white paper ("Buchi Spontanei"). Having mixed coffee grounds, sparkling bits of crushed mirror, and ground-up sea shells, she blew the dust on mucilaged paper ("Velo nella Nebbia"). She composed collages of rags and toilet tissue. After a dozen linear studies ("Linee Discendenti"), she experimented with gold leaf sprayed with umber, the whole while wet combed in long undulations with a fine comb. She framed this in a black frame and hung it on end like a diamond ("Luce di Candela"). Annamaria worked intently, her brow furrowed, violet mouth tightly pursed, eyes lit, nostrils palpitating in creative excitement. And when she had temporarily run out of new ideas she did a mythological bull in red clay ("La Donna Toro"), afterwards returning to nature morte with bunches of bananas; then self-portraits.

The pittrice occasionally took time out to see what Fidelman was up to, although not much, and then editing his efforts. She changed lines and altered figures, or swabbed paint over whole compositions that didn't appeal to her. There was not much that did, but Fidelman was grateful for any attention she gave his work, and even kept at it to incite her criticism. He could feel his heart beat in his teeth whenever she stood close to him modifying his work, he deeply breathing her intimate smell of sweating flowers. She used perfume only when Augusto came and it disappointed Fidelman that the old man should evoke the use of bottled fragrance; yet he was cheered that her natural odor, which he, so to say, got for free, was so much more exciting than the stuff she doused herself with for her decrepit Romeo. He had noticed she had a bit of soft belly but he loved the pliant roundness and often daydreamed of it. Thinking it might please her, for he pleased her rarely (he reveried how it would be once she understood the true depth of his love for her), the art student experimented with some of the things Annamaria had done—the spontaneous holes, for instance, several studies of "Lines Ascending," and two lyrical abstract expressionistic pieces based on, interwoven with, and ultimately concealing a Star of David, although for these attempts he soon discovered he had earned, instead of her good will, an increased measure of scorn.

However, Annamaria continued to eat lunch with him at Guido's, and more often than not, supper, although she said practically nothing during meals and afterwards let her eye roam over the faces of the men at the other tables. But there were times after they had eaten when she would agree to go for a short walk with Fidelman, if there was no serious wind; and once in a while they entered a movie in the Trastevere, for she hated to cross any of the bridges of the Tiber, and then only in a bus, sitting stiffly, staring ahead. As they were once riding, Fidelman seized the opportunity to hold her tense fist in his, but as soon as they were across the river she tore it out of his grasp. He was by now giving her presents—tubes of paints, the best brushes, a few yards of Belgian linen, which she accepted without comment; she also borrowed small sums from him, nothing startling—a hundred lire today, five hundred tomorrow. And she announced one morning that he would thereafter, since he used so much of both, have to pay additional for water and electricity—he already paid extra for the heatless heat. Fidelman, though continually worried about money, assented. He would have given his last lira to lie on her soft belly, but she offered niente, not so much as a caress; until one day, he was permitted to look on as she sketched herself nude in his presence. Since it was bitter cold the pittrice did this in two stages. First she removed her sweater and brassiere and, viewing herself in a long, faded mirror, quickly sketched the upper half of her body before it turned blue. He was dizzily enamored of her form and flesh. Hastily fastening the brassiere and pulling on her sweater, Annamaria stepped out of her sandals and peeled off her culottes, and white panties torn at the crotch, then drew the rest of herself down to her toes. The art student begged permission to sketch along with her but the pittrice denied it, so he had, as best one can, to commit to memory her lovely treasures—the hard, piercing breasts, narrow shapely buttocks, vine-hidden labia, the font and sweet beginning of time. After she had drawn herself and dressed, and when Augusto appeared and they had retired behind her bolted door, Fidelman sat motionless on his high stool before the glittering blue-skied windows, slowly turning to ice to faint strains of Bach.

3

The art student increased his services to Annamaria, her increase was scorn, or so it seemed. This severely bruised his spirit. What have I done to deserve such treatment? That I pay my plenty of rent on time? That I buy her all sorts of presents, not to mention two full meals a day? That

I live in flaming hot and freezing cold? That I passionately adore each sweet-and-sour bit of her? He figured it bored her to see so much of him. For a week Fidelman disappeared during the day, sat in cold libraries or stood around in frosty museums. He tried painting after midnight and into the early-morning hours but the pittrice found out and unscrewed the bulbs before she went to bed. "Don't waste my electricity, this isn't America." He screwed in a dim blue bulb and worked silently from 1 A.M. to 5. At dawn he discovered he had painted a blue picture. Fidelman wandered in the streets of the city. At night he slept in the studio and could hear her sleeping in her room. She slept restlessly, dreamed badly, and often moaned. He dreamed he had three eyes.

For two weeks he spoke to no one but a dumpy four-and-a-half-foot female on the third floor, and to her usually to say no. Fidelman, having often heard the music of Bach drifting up from below, had tried to picture the lady piano player, imagining a quiet blonde with a slender body, a woman of grace and beauty. It had turned out to be Clelia Montemaggio, a middle-aged old-maid music teacher, who sat at an old upright piano, her apartment door open to let out the cooking smells, particularly fried fish on Friday. Once when coming up from bringing down the garbage, Fidelman had paused to listen to part of a partita at her door and she had lassoed him in for an espresso and pastry. He ate and listened to Bach, her plump bottom moving spryly on the bench as she played not badly. "Lo spirito," she called to him raptly over her shoulder, "Parchitettura!" Fidelman nodded. Thereafter whenever she spied him in the hall she attempted to entice him with cream-filled pastries and J.S.B., whom she played apparently exclusively.

"Come een," she called in English, "I weel play for you. We weel talk. There is no use for too much solitude." But the art student, burdened by his, spurned hers.

Unable to work, he wandered in the streets in a desolate mood, his spirit dusty in a city of fountains and leaky water taps. Water, water everywhere, spouting, flowing, dripping, whispering secrets, love love love, but not for him. If Rome's so sexy, where's mine? Fidelman's Rome-less Rome. It belonged least to those who yearned most for it. With slow steps he climbed the Pincio, if possible to raise his spirits gazing down at the rooftops of the city, spires, cupolas, towers, monuments, compounded history, and past time. It was in sight, possessable, all but its elusive spirit;

after so long he was still straniero. He was then struck by a thought: if you could paint this sight, give it its quality in yours, the spirit belonged to you. History become aesthetic! Fidelman's scalp thickened. A wild rush of things he might paint swept sweetly through him: saints in good and bad health, whole or maimed, in gold and red; nude gray rabbis at Auschwitz, black or white Negroes—what not when *any* color dripped from your brush? And if these, so also ANNAMARIA ES PULCHRA. He all but cheered. What more intimate possession of a woman! He would paint her, whether she permitted or not, posed or not—she was his to paint, he could with eyes shut. Maybe something will come after all of my love for her. His spirits elevated, Fidelman ran most of the way home.

It took him eight days, a labor of love. He tried her as nude and, although able to imagine every inch of her, could not commit it to canvas. Then he suffered until it occurred to him to paint her as "Virgin with Child." The idea astonished and elated him. Fidelman went feverishly to work and caught an immediate likeness in paint. Annamaria, saintly beautiful, held in her arms the infant resembling his little nephew Georgie. The pittrice, aware, of course, of his continuous activity, cast curious glances his way, but Fidelman, painting in the corner by the stone sink, kept the easel turned away from her. She pretended unconcern. Done for the day he covered the painting and carefully guarded it. The art student was painting Annamaria in a passion of tenderness for the infant at her breast, her face responsive to its innocence. When, on the ninth day, in trepidation Fidelman revealed his work, the pittrice's eyes clouded and her underlip curled. He was about to grab the canvas and smash it up all over the place when her expression fell apart. The art student postponed all movement but visible trembling. She seemed at first appalled, a darkness descended on her, she was undone. She wailed wordlessly, then sobbed, "You have seen my soul." They embraced tempestuously, her breasts stabbing him, Annamaria bawling on his shoulder. Fidelman kissed her wet face and salted lips, she murmuring as he fooled with the hook of her brassiere under her sweater, "Aspetta, aspetta, caro, Augusto viene." He was mad with expectation and suspense.

Augusto, who usually arrived punctually at four, did not appear that Friday afternoon. Uneasy as the hour approached, Annamaria seemed relieved as the streets grew dark. She had worked badly after viewing Fidelman's painting, sighed frequently, gazed at him with sweet-sad smiles. At six she gave in to his urging and they retired to her room, his un-framed "Virgin with Child" already hanging above her bed, replacing a gaunt self-portrait. He was curiously disappointed in the picture—surfacy thin—and made a mental note to borrow it back in the morning to work on it more. But the conception, at least, deserved the reward. Annamaria cooked supper. She cut his meat for him and fed him forkfuls. She peeled Fidelman's orange and stirred sugar in his coffee. Afterwards, at his nod, she locked and bolted the studio and bedroom doors and they undressed and slipped under her blankets. How good to be for a change on this side of the locked door, Fidelman thought, relaxing marvelously. Annamaria, however, seemed tensely alert to the noises of the old building, includ-ing a parrot screeching, some shouting kids running up the stairs, a so-prano singing "Ritorna, vincitor!" But she calmed down and then hotly embraced Fidelman. In the middle of a passionate kiss the doorbell rang.

Annamaria stiffened in his arms. "Diavolo! Augusto!"

"He'll go away," Fidelman advised. "Both doors locked."

But she was at once out of bed, drawing on her culottes. "Get dressed," she said.

He hopped up and hastily got into his pants.

Annamaria unlocked and unbolted the inner door and then the outer one. It was the postman waiting to collect ten lire for an overweight let-ter from Naples.

After she had read the long letter and wiped away a tear they un-dressed and got back into bed.

"Who is he to you?" Fidelman asked.

"Who?"

"Augusto."

"An old friend. Like a father. We went through much together."

"Were you lovers?"

"Look, if you want me, take me. If you want to ask questions, go back to school."

He determined to mind his business.

"Warm me," she said, "I'm freezing."

Fidelman stroked her slowly. After ten minutes she said, " 'Gioco di mano, gioco di villano.' Use your imagination."

He used his imagination and she responded with excitement. "Dolce tesoro," she whispered, flicking the tip of her tongue into his ear, then with little bites biting his earlobe.

The doorbell rang loudly.

"For Christ's sake, don't answer," Fidelman groaned. He tried to hold her down but she was already up, hunting her robe.

"Put on your pants," she hissed.

He had thoughts of waiting for her in bed but it ended with his dressing fully. She sent him to the door. It was the crippled portinaia, the art student having neglected to take down the garbage.

Annamaria furiously got the two bags and handed them to her.

In bed she was so cold her teeth chattered.

Tense with desire Fidelman warmed her.

"Angelo mio," she murmured. "Amore, possess me."

He was about to when she rose in a hurry. "The cursed door again!"

Fidelman gnashed his teeth. "I heard nothing."

In her torn yellow silk robe she hurried to the front door, opened and shut it, quickly locked and bolted it, did the same in her room, and slid into bed.

"You were right, it was nobody."

She embraced him, her hairy armpits perfumed. He responded with postponed passion.

"Enough of antipasto," Annamaria said. She reached for his member.

Overwrought, Fidelman, though fighting himself not to, spent himself in her hand. Although he mightily willed resurrection, his wilted flower bit the dust.

She furiously shoved him out of bed, into the studio, flinging his clothes after him.

"Pig, beast, onanist!"

4

At least she lets me love her. Daily Fidelman shopped, cooked, and cleaned for her. Every morning he took her shopping sack off the hook, went to the street market, and returned with the bag stuffed full of greens, pasta, eggs, meat, cheese, wine, bread. Annamaria insisted on three hearty meals a day although she had once told him she no longer enjoyed eating. Twice he had seen her throw up her supper. What she enjoyed he didn't know except it wasn't Fidelman. After he had served her at her table he was allowed to eat alone in the studio. At two every afternoon she took her siesta, and though it was forbidden to make noise, he was allowed to wash the dishes, dust and clean her room, swab the toilet bowl. She called, Fatso, and in he trotted to get her anything she had run out of—drawing pencils, sanitary belt, safety pins. After she waked from her nap, rain or shine, snow or hail, he was now compelled to leave the studio so she could work in peace and quiet. He wandered, in the tramontana, from one cold two-bit movie to another. At seven he was back to prepare her supper, and twice a week Augusto's, who sported a new black hat and spiffy overcoat, and pitied the art student with both wet blue eyes but wouldn't look at him. After supper, another load of dishes, the garbage downstairs, and when Fidelman returned, with or without Augusto Annamaria was already closeted behind her bolted door. He checked through the keyhole on Mondays and Fridays but she and the old gent were always fully clothed. Fidelman had more than once complained to her that his punishment exceeded his crime, but the pittrice said he was a type she would never have any use for. In fact he did not exist for her. Not existing how could he paint, although he told himself he must? He couldn't. He aimlessly froze wherever he went, a mean cold that seared his lungs, although under his overcoat he wore a new thick sweater Bessie had knitted for him, and two woolen scarves around his neck. Since the night Annamaria had kicked him out of bed he had not been warm; yet he often dreamed of ultimate victory. Once when he was on his lonely way out of the house—a night she was giving a party for some painter friends, Fidelman, a drooping butt in the corner of his mouth, carrying the garbage bags, met Clelia Montemaggio coming up the stairs.

"You look like a frozen board," she said. "Come in and enjoy the warmth and a little Bach."

Unable to unfreeze enough to say no, he continued down with the garbage.

"Every man gets the woman he deserves," she called after him.

"Who got," Fidelman muttered. "Who gets."

He considered jumping into the Tiber but it was full of ice that winter.

One night at the end of February, Annamaria, to Fidelman's astonishment—it deeply affected him—said he might go with her to a party at Giancarlo Balducci's studio on the Via dell'Oca; she needed somebody to accompany her in the bus across the bridge and Augusto was flat on his back with the Asian flu. The party was lively—painters, sculptors, some writers, two diplomats, a prince and a visiting Hindu sociologist, their ladies, and three hotsy-totsy, scantily dressed, unattached girls. One of them, a shapely beauty with orange hair, bright eyes, and warm ways became interested in Fidelman, except that he was dazed by Annamaria, seeing her in a dress for the first time, a ravishing, rich, ruby-colored affair. The cross-eyed host had provided simply a huge cut-glass bowl of spiced mulled wine, and the guests dipped ceramic glasses into it, and guzzled away. Everyone but the art student seemed to be enjoying himself. One or two of the men disappeared into other rooms with female friends or acquaintances and Annamaria, in a gay mood, did a fast shimmy to rhythmic hand-clapping. She was drinking steadily and, when she wanted her glass filled, politely called him "Arturo." He began to have mild thoughts of possibly possessing her.

The party bloomed, at least forty, and turned wildish. Practical jokes were played. Fidelman realized his left shoe had been smeared with mustard. Balducci's black cat mewed at a fat lady's behind, a slice of sausage pinned to her dress. Before midnight there were two fist-fights, Fidelman enjoying both but not getting involved, though once he was socked on the neck by a sculptor who had aimed at a painter. The girl with the orange hair, still interested in the art student, invited him to join her in Balducci's bedroom, but he continued to be devoted to Annamaria, his eyes tied to her every move. He was jealous of the illustrator who, whenever near her, nipped her bottom.

One of the sculptors, Orazio Pinello, a slender man with a darkish face, heavy black brows, and bleached blond hair, approached Fidelman. "Haven't we met before, caro?"

"Maybe," the art student said, perspiring lightly. "I'm Arthur Fidelman, an American painter."

"You don't say? Action painter?"

"Always active."

"I refer of course to Abstract Expressionism."

"Of course. Well, sort of. On and off."

"Haven't I seen some of your work around? Galleria Schneider? Some symmetric, hard-edge, biomorphic forms? Not bad as I remember."

Fidelman thanked him, in full blush.

"Who are you here with?" Orazio Pinello asked.

"Annamaria Oliovino."

"Her?" said the sculptor. "But she's a fake."

"Is she?" Fidelman said with a sigh.

"Have you looked at her work?"

"With one eye. Her art is bad but I find her irresistible."

"Peccato." The sculptor shrugged and drifted away.

A minute later there was another fistfight, during which the bright-eyed orange head conked Fidelman with a Chinese vase. He went out cold, and when he came to, Annamaria and Balducci were undressing him in the illustrator's bedroom. Fidelman experienced an almost overwhelming pleasure, then Balducci explained that the art student had been chosen to pose in the nude for drawings both he and the pittrice would do of him. He explained there had been a discussion as to which of them did male nudes best and they had decided to settle it in a short contest. Two easels had been wheeled to the center of the studio; a half hour was allotted to the contestants, and the guests would judge who had done the better job. Though he at first objected because it was a cold night, Fidelman nevertheless felt warmish from wine so he agreed to pose; besides he was proud of his muscles and maybe if she sketched him nude it might arouse her interest for a tussle later. And if he wasn't painting he was at least being painted.

So the pittrice and Giancarlo Balducci, in paint-smeared smocks, worked for thirty minutes by the clock, the whole party silently looking on, with the exception of the orange-haired tart, who sat in the corner eating a prosciutto sandwich. Annamaria, her brow furrowed, lips pursed, drew intensely with crayon; Balducci worked calmly in colored chalk. The guests were absorbed, although after ten minutes the Hindu went home. A journalist locked himself in the painter's bedroom with orange head and would not admit his wife, who pounded on the door. Fidelman, standing barefoot on a bathmat, was eager to see what Annamaria was accomplishing but had to be patient. When the half hour was up he was permitted to look. Balducci had drawn a flock of green and black abstract testiculate circles. Fidelman shuddered. But Annamaria's drawing was representational, not Fidelman although of course inspired by him: a gigantic funereal phallus that resembled a broken-backed snake. The blond sculptor inspected it with half-closed eyes, then yawned and left. By now the party was over, the guests departed, lights out except for a few dripping white candles. Balducci was collecting his ceramic glasses and emptying ashtrays, and Annamaria had thrown up. The art student afterwards heard her begging the illustrator to sleep with her but Balducci complained of fatigue.

"I will if he won't," Fidelman offered.

Annamaria, enraged, spat on her picture of his unhappy phallus.

"Don't dare come near me," she cried. "Malocchio! Jettatura!"

5

The next morning he awoke sneezing, a nasty cold. How can I go on? Annamaria, showing no signs of pity or remorse, continued shrilly to berate him. "You've brought me nothing but bad luck since you came here. I'm letting you stay because you pay well but I warn you to keep out of my sight."

"But how—" he asked hoarsely.

"That doesn't concern me."

"—how will I paint?"

"Who cares? Paint at night."

"Without light—"

"Paint in the dark. I'll buy you a can of black paint."

"How can you be so cruel to a man who loves—"

"I'll scream," she said.

He left in anguish. Later while she was at her siesta he came back, got some of his things, and tried to paint in the hall. No dice. Fidelman wandered in the rain. He sat for hours on the Spanish Steps. Then he returned to the house and went slowly up the stairs. The door was locked. "Annamaria," he hoarsely called. Nobody answered. In the street he stood at the river wall, watching the dome of St. Peter's in the distance. Maybe a potion, Fidelman thought, or an amulet? He doubted either would work. How do you go about hanging yourself? In the late afternoon he went back to the house—would say he was sick, needed rest, possibly a doctor. He felt feverish. She could hardly refuse.

But she did, although explaining she felt bad herself. He held on to the banister as he went down the stairs. Clelia Montemaggio's door was open. Fidelman paused, then continued down, but she had seen him. "Come een, come een."

He went reluctantly in. She fed him camomile tea and panettone. He ate in a wolfish hurry as she seated herself at the piano.

"No Bach, please, my head aches from various troubles."

"Where's your dignity?" she asked.

"Try Chopin, that's lighter."

"Respect yourself, please."

Fidelman removed his hat as she began to play a Bach prelude, her bottom rhythmic on the bench. Though his cold oppressed him and he could hardly breathe, tonight the spirit, the architecture, moved him. He felt his face to see if he was crying but only his nose was wet. On the top of the piano Clelia had placed a bowl of white carnations in full bloom. Each white petal seemed a white flower. If I could paint those gorgeous flowers, Fidelman thought. If I could paint something. By Jesus, if I could paint myself, that'd show them! Astonished by the thought he ran out of the house.

The art student hastened to a costume shop and settled on a cassock and fuzzy black soup-bowl biretta, envisaging another Rembrandt: "Portrait of the Artist as Priest." He hurried with his bulky package back to the house. Annamaria was handing the garbage to the portinaia as Fidelman thrust his way into the studio. He quickly changed into the priest's vestments. The pittrice came in wildly to tell him where he got off, but when she saw Fidelman already painting himself as priest, with a moan she rushed into her room. He worked with smoking intensity and in no time created an amazing likeness. Annamaria, after stealthily re-entering the studio, with heaving bosom and agitated eyes closely followed his progress. At last, with a cry she threw herself at his feet.

"Forgive me, Father, for I have sinned—"

Dripping brush in hand, he stared down at her. "Please, I—"

"Oh, Father, if you knew how I have sinned. I've been a whore—"

After a moment's thought, Fidelman said, "If so, I absolve you."

"Not without penance. First listen to the rest. I've had no luck with men. They're all bastards. Or else I jinx them. If you want the truth I am an Evil Eye myself. Anybody who loves me is cursed."

He listened, fascinated.

"Augusto is really my uncle. After many others he became my lover. At least he's gentle. My father found out and swore he'd kill us both. When I got pregnant I was scared to death. A sin can go too far. Augusto told me to have the baby and leave it at an orphanage, but the night it was born I was confused and threw it into the Tiber. I was afraid it was an idiot."

She was sobbing. He drew back.

"Wait," she wept. "The next time in bed Augusto was impotent. Since then he's been imploring me to confess so he can get back his powers. But every time I step into the confessional my tongue turns to bone. The priest can't tear a word out of me. That's how it's been all my life, don't ask me why because I don't know."

She grabbed his knees. "Help me, Father, for Christ's sake."

Fidelman, after a short tormented time, said in a quavering voice, "I forgive you, my child."

"The penance," she wailed, "first the penance."

After reflecting, he replied, "Say one hundred times each, Our Father and Hail Mary."

"More," Annamaria wept. "More, more. Much more."

Gripping his knees so hard they shook she burrowed her head into his black-buttoned lap. He felt the surprised beginnings of an erection.

"In that case," Fidelman said, shuddering a little, "better undress."

"Only," Annamaria said, "if you keep your vestments on."

"Not the cassock, too clumsy."

"At least the biretta."

He agreed to that.

Annamaria undressed in a swoop. Her body was extraordinarily lovely, the flesh glowing. In her bed they tightly embraced. She clasped his buttocks, he cupped hers. Pumping slowly he nailed her to her cross.

Leonard Michaels

"Murderers"

When my uncle Moe dropped dead of a heart attack I became expert in the subway system. With a nickel I'd get to Queens, twist and zoom to Coney Island, twist again toward the George Washington Bridge—beyond which was darkness. I wanted proximity to darkness, strangeness. Who doesn't? The poor in spirit, the ignorant and frightened. My family came from Poland, then never went any place until they had heart attacks. The consummation of years in one neighborhood: a black Cadillac, corpse inside. We should have buried Uncle Moe where he shuffled away his life, in the kitchen or toilet, under the linoleum, near the coffee pot. Anyhow, they were dropping on Henry Street and Cherry Street. Blue lips. The previous winter it was cousin Charlie, forty-five years old. Moe, Charlie, Sam, Adele—family meant a punch in the chest, fire in the arm. I didn't want to wait for it. I went to Harlem, the Polo Grounds, Far Rockaway, thousands of miles on nickels, mainly underground. Tenements watched me go, day after day, fingering nickels. One afternoon I stopped to grind my heel against the curb. Melvin and Arnold Bloom appeared, then Harold Cohen. Melvin said, "You step in dog shit?" Grinding was my answer. Harold Cohen said, "The rabbi is home. I saw him on Market Street. He was walking fast." Oily Arnold, eleven years old, began to urge: "Let's go up to our roof."

The decision waited for me. I considered the roof, the view of industrial Brooklyn, the Battery, ships in the river, bridges, towers, and the rabbi's apartment. "All right," I said. We didn't giggle or look to one another for moral signals. We were running.

The blinds were up and curtains pulled, giving sunlight, wind, birds to the rabbi's apartment—a magnificent metropolitan view. The rabbi and his wife never took it, but in the light and air of summer afternoons, in the eye of gull and pigeon, they were joyous. A bearded young man, and his young pink wife, sacramentally bald. Beard and Baldy, with everything to see, looked at each other. From a water tank on the opposite roof, higher than their windows, we looked at them. In psychoanalysis this is "The Primal Scene." To achieve the primal scene we crossed a ledge six inches wide. A half-inch indentation in the brick gave us fingerholds. We dragged bellies and groins against the brick face to a steel ladder. It went up the side of the building, bolted into brick, and up the side of the water tank to a slanted tin roof which caught the afternoon sun. We sat on that roof like angels, shot through with light, derealized in brilliance. Our sneakers sucked hot slanted metal. Palms and fingers pressed to bone on nailheads.

The Brooklyn Navy Yard with destroyers and aircraft carriers, the Statue of Liberty putting the sky to the torch, the dull remote skyscrapers of Wall Street, and the Empire State Building were among the wonders we dominated. Our view of the holy man and his wife, on their living-room couch and floor, on the bed in their bedroom, could not be improved. Unless we got closer. But fifty feet across the air was right. We heard their phonograph and watched them dancing. We couldn't hear the gratifications or see pimples. We smelled nothing. We didn't want to touch.

For a while I watched them. Then I gazed beyond into shimmering nullity, gray, blue, and green murmuring over rooftops and towers. I had watched them before. I could tantalize myself with this brief ocular perversion, the general cleansing nihil of a view. This was the beginning of philosophy. I indulged in ambience, in space like eons. So what if my uncle Moe was dead? I was philosophical and luxurious. I didn't even have to look at the rabbi and his wife. After all, how many times had we dissolved stickball games when the rabbi came home? How many times had we risked shameful discovery, scrambling up the ladder, exposed to their windows—if they looked. We risked life itself to achieve this eminence. I looked at the rabbi and his wife.

Today she was a blonde. Bald didn't mean no wigs. She had ten wigs, ten colors, fifty styles. She looked different, the same, and very good. A human theme in which nothing begat anything and was gorgeous. To me she was the world's lesson. Aryan yellow slipped through pins about her ears. An olive complexion mediated yellow hair and Arabic black eyes. Could one care what she really looked like? What was *really*? The minute you wondered, she looked like something else, in another wig, another style. Without the wigs she was a baldy-bean lady. Today she was a blonde. Not blonde. A blonde. The phonograph blared and her deep loops flowed Tommy Dorsey, Benny Goodman, and then the thing itself, Choo-Choo Lopez. Rumba! One, two-three. One, two-three. The rabbi stepped away to delight in blond imagination. Twirling and individual, he stepped away snapping fingers, going high and light on his toes. A short bearded man, balls afling, cock shuddering like a springboard. Rumba! One, two-three. *Olé! Vaya*, Choo-Choo!

> I was on my way to spend some time in Cuba.
> Stopped off at Miami Beach, la-la.
> Oh, what a rumba they teach, la-la.
> Way down in Miami Beach,
> Oh, what a chroombah they teach, la-la.
> Way-down-in-Miami-Beach.

She, on the other hand, was somewhat reserved. A shift in one lush hip was total rumba. He was Mr. Life. She was dancing. He was a naked man. She was what she was in the garment of her soft, essential self. He was snapping, clapping, hopping to the beat. The beat lived in her visible music, her lovely self. Except for the wig. Also a watchband that desecrated her wrist. But it gave her a bit of the whorish. She never took it off.

Harold Cohen began a cocktail-mixer motion, masturbating with two fists. Seeing him at such hard futile work, braced only by sneakers, was terrifying. But I grinned. Out of terror, I twisted an encouraging face. Melvin Bloom kept one hand on the tin. The other knuckled the rumba numbers into the back of my head. Nodding like a defective, little

Arnold Bloom chewed his lip and squealed as the rabbi and his wife smacked together. The rabbi clapped her buttocks, fingers buried in the cleft. They stood only on his legs. His back arched, knees bent, thighs thick with thrust, up, up, up. Her legs wrapped his hips, ankles crossed, hooked for construction. "Oi, oi, oi," she cried, wig flashing left, right, tossing the Brooklyn Navy Yard, the Statue of Liberty, and the Empire State Building to hell. Arnold squealed oi, squealing rubber. His sneaker heels stabbed tin to stop his slide. Melvin said, "Idiot." Arnold's ring hooked a nailhead and the ring and ring finger remained. The hand, the arm, the rest of him, were gone.

We rumbled down the ladder. "Oi, oi, oi," she yelled. In a freak of ecstasy her eyes had rolled and caught us. The rabbi drilled to her quick and she had us. "*OI, OI,*" she yelled above congas going clop, doom-doom, clop, doom-doom on the way to Cuba. The rabbi flew to the window, a red mouth opening in his beard: "Murderers." He couldn't know what he said. Melvin Bloom was crying. My fingers were tearing, bleeding into brick. Harold Cohen, like an adding machine, gibbered the name of God. We moved down the ledge quickly as we dared. Bongos went tocka-ti-tocka, tocka-ti-tocka. The rabbi screamed, "MELVIN BLOOM, PHILLIP LIEBOWITZ, HAROLD COHEN, MELVIN BLOOM," as if our names, screamed this way, naming us where we hung, smashed us into brick.

Nothing was discussed.

The rabbi used his connections, arrangements were made. We were sent to a camp in New Jersey. We hiked and played volleyball. One day, apropos of nothing, Melvin came to me and said little Arnold had been made of gold and he, Melvin, of shit. I appreciated the sentiment, but to my mind they were both made of shit. Harold Cohen never again spoke to either of us. The counselors in the camp were World War II veterans, introspective men. Some carried shrapnel in their bodies. One had a metal plate in his head. Whatever you said to them they seemed to be thinking of something else, even when they answered. But step out of line and a plastic lanyard whistled burning notice across your ass.

At night, lying in the bunkhouse, I listened to owls. I'd never before heard that sound, the sound of darkness, blooming, opening inside you like a mouth.

Cynthia Ozick

"The Pagan Rabbi"

> Rabbi Jacob said: "He who is walking along and studying, but then breaks off to remark, 'How lovely is that tree!' or 'How beautiful is that fallow field!'—Scripture regards such a one as having hurt his own being."
>
> —*from* THE ETHICS OF THE FATHERS

When I heard that Isaac Kornfeld, a man of piety and brains, had hanged himself in the public park, I put a token in the subway stile and journeyed out to see the tree.

We had been classmates in the rabbinical seminary. Our fathers were both rabbis. They were also friends, but only in a loose way of speaking: in actuality our fathers were enemies. They vied with one another in demonstrations of charitableness, in the captious glitter of their scholia, in the number of their adherents. Of the two, Isaac's father was the milder. I was afraid of my father; he had a certain disease of the larynx, and if he even uttered something so trivial as "Bring the tea" to my mother, it came out splintered, clamorous, and vindictive.

Neither man was philosophical in the slightest. It was the one thing they agreed on. "Philosophy is an abomination," Isaac's father used to say. "The Greeks were philosophers, but they remained children playing with their dolls. Even Socrates, a monotheist, nevertheless sent money down to the temple to pay for incense to their doll."

"Idolatry is the abomination," Isaac argued, "not philosophy."

"The latter is the corridor to the former," his father said.

My own father claimed that if not for philosophy I would never have been brought to the atheism which finally led me to withdraw, in my second year, from the seminary. The trouble was not philosophy—I had none of Isaac's talent: his teachers later said of him that his imagination was so remarkable he could concoct holiness out of the fine line of a serif. On the day of his funeral the president of his college was criticized for having commented that although a suicide could not be buried in consecrated earth, whatever earth enclosed Isaac Kornfeld was ipso factor consecrated. It should be noted that Isaac hanged himself several weeks short of his thirty-sixth birthday; he was then at the peak of his renown; and the president, of course, did not know the whole story. He judged by Isaac's reputation, which was at no time more impressive than just before his death.

I judged by the same, and marveled that all that holy genius and intellectual surprise should in the end be raised no higher than the next-to-lowest limb of a delicate young oak, with burly roots like the toes of a gryphon exposed in the wet ground.

The tree was almost alone in a long rough meadow, which sloped down to a bay filled with sickly clams and a bad smell. The place was called Trilham's Inlet, and I knew what the smell meant: that cold brown water covered half the city's turds.

On the day I came to see the tree the air was bleary with fog. The weather was well into autumn and, though it was Sunday, the walks were empty. There was something historical about the park just then, with its rusting grasses and deserted monuments. In front of a soldiers' cenotaph a plastic wreath left behind months before by some civic parade stood propped against a stone frieze of identical marchers in the costume of an old war. A banner across the wreath's belly explained that the purpose of war is peace. At the margins of the park they were building a gigantic highway. I felt I was making my way across a battlefield silenced by the victory of the peace machines. The bulldozers had bitten far into the park, and the rolled carcasses of the sacrificed trees were already cut up into logs. There were dozens of felled maples, elms, and oaks. Their moist inner wheels breathed out a fragrance of barns, countryside, decay.

In the bottommost meadow fringing the water I recognized the tree which had caused Isaac to sin against his own life. It looked curiously like a photograph—not only like that newspaper photograph I carried warmly in my pocket, which showed the field and its markers—the drinking-fountain a few yards off, the ruined brick wall of an old estate behind. The caption-writer had particularly remarked on the "rope." But the rope was no longer there; the widow had claimed it. It was his own prayer shawl that Isaac, a short man, had thrown over the comely neck of the next-to-lowest limb. A Jew is buried in his prayer shawl; the police had handed it over to Sheindel. I observed that the bark was rubbed at that spot. The tree lay back against the sky like a licked postage stamp. Rain began to beat it flatter yet. A stench of sewage came up like a veil in the nostril. It seemed to me I was a man in a photograph standing next to a gray blur of tree. I would stand through eternity beside Isaac's guilt if I did not run, so I ran that night to Sheindel herself.

I loved her at once. I am speaking now of the first time I saw her, though I don't exclude the last. The last—the last together with Isaac—was soon after my divorce; at one stroke I left my wife and my cousin's fur business to the small upstate city in which both had repined. Suddenly Isaac and Sheindel and two babies appeared in the lobby of my hotel—they were passing through: Isaac had a lecture engagement in Canada. We sat under scarlet neon and Isaac told how my father could now not speak at all.

"He keeps his vow," I said.

"No, no, he's a sick man," Isaac said. "An obstruction in the throat."

"I'm the obstruction. You know what he said when I left the seminary. He meant it, never mind how many years it is. He's never addressed a word to me since."

"We were reading together. He blamed the reading, who can blame *him*? Fathers like ours don't know how to love. They live too much indoors."

It was an odd remark, though I was too much preoccupied with my own resentments to notice. "It wasn't what we read," I objected. "Torah tells that an illustrious man doesn't have an illustrious son. Otherwise he wouldn't be humble like other people. This much scholarly stuffing I retain. Well, so my father always believed he was more illustrious than anybody, especially more than your father. *Therefore,*" I delivered in Talmudic cadence, "what chance did I have? A nincompoop and no *sitzfleish*. Now you, you could answer questions that weren't even invented yet. Then you invented them."

"Torah isn't a spade," Isaac said. "A man should have a livelihood. You had yours."

"The pelt of a dead animal isn't a living either, it's an indecency."

All the while Sheindel was sitting perfectly still; the babies, female infants in long stockings, were asleep in her arms. She wore a dark thick woolen hat—it was July—that covered every part of her hair. But I had once seen it in all its streaming black shine.

"And Jane?" Isaac asked finally.

"Speaking of dead animals. Tell my father—he won't answer a letter, he won't come to the telephone—that in the matter of the marriage he was right, but for the wrong reason. If you share a bed with a Puritan you'll come into it cold and you'll go out of it cold. Listen, Isaac, my father calls me an atheist, but between the conjugal sheets every Jew is a believer in miracles, even the lapsed."

He said nothing then. He knew I envied him his Sheindel and his luck. Unlike our fathers, Isaac had never condemned me for my marriage, which his father regarded as his private triumph over my father, and which my father, in his public defeat, took as an occasion for declaring me as one dead. He rent his clothing and sat on a stool for eight days, while Isaac's father came to watch him mourn, secretly satisfied, though aloud he grieved for all apostates. Isaac did not like my wife. He called her a tall yellow straw. After we were married he never said a word against her, but he kept away.

I went with my wife to his wedding. We took the early train down especially, but when we arrived the feast was well under way, and the guests far into the dancing.

"Look, look, they don't dance together," Jane said.

"Who?"

"The men and the women. The bride and the groom."

"Count the babies," I advised. "The Jews are also Puritans, but only in public."

The bride was enclosed all by herself on a straight chair in the center of a spinning ring of young men. The floor heaved under their whirl. They stamped, the chandeliers shuddered, the guests cried out, the young men with linked arms spiraled and their skullcaps came flying off like centrifugal balloons. Isaac, a mist of black suit, a stamping foot, was lost in the planet's wake of black suits and emphatic feet. The dancing young men shouted bridal songs, the floor leaned like a plate, the whole room teetered.

Isaac had told me something of Sheindel. Before now I had never seen her. Her birth was in a concentration camp, and they were about to throw her against the electrified fence when an army mobbed the gate; the current vanished from the terrible wires, and she had nothing to show for it afterward but a mark on her cheek like an asterisk, cut by a barb. The asterisk pointed to certain dry footnotes: she had no mother to show, she had no father to show, but she had, extraordinarily, God to show—she was known to be, for her age and sex, astonishingly learned. She was only seventeen.

"What pretty hair she has," Jane said.

Now Sheindel was dancing with Isaac's mother. All the ladies made a fence, and the bride, twirling with her mother-in-law, lost a shoe and fell against the long laughing row. The ladies lifted their glistering breasts in their lacy dresses and laughed; the young men, stamping two by two, went on shouting their wedding songs. Sheindel danced without her shoe, and the black river of her hair followed her.

"After today she'll have to hide it all," I explained.

Jane asked why.

"So as not to be a temptation to men," I told her, and covertly looked for my father. There he was, in a shadow, apart. My eyes discovered his eyes. He turned his back and gripped his throat.

"It's a very anthropological experience," Jane said.

"A wedding is a wedding," I answered her, "among us even more so."

"Is that your father over there, that little scowly man?"

To Jane all Jews were little. "My father the man of the cloth. Yes."

"A wedding is not a wedding," said Jane: we had had only a license and a judge with bad breath.

"Everybody marries for the same reason."

"No," said my wife. "Some for love and some for spite."

"And everybody for bed."

"Some for spite," she insisted.

"I was never cut out for a man of the cloth," I said. "My poor father doesn't see that."

"He doesn't speak to you."

"A technicality. He's losing his voice."

"Well, he's not like you. He doesn't do it for spite," Jane said.

"You don't know him," I said.

He lost it altogether the very week Isaac published his first remarkable collection of responsa. Isaac's father crowed like a passionate rooster, and packed his wife and himself off to the Holy Land to boast on the holy soil. Isaac was a little relieved; he had just been made Professor of Mishnaic History, and his father's whims and pretenses and foolish rivalries were an embarrassment. It is easy to honor a father from afar, but bitter to honor one who is dead. A surgeon cut out my father's voice, and he died without a word.

Isaac and I no longer met. Our ways were too disparate. Isaac was famous, if not in the world, certainly in the kingdom of jurists and scholars. By this time I had acquired a partnership in a small book store in a basement. My partner sold me his share, and I put up a new sign: "The Book Cellar"; for reasons more obscure than filial (all the same I wished my father could have seen it) I established a department devoted especially to not-quite-rare theological works, chiefly in Hebrew and Aramaic, though I carried some Latin and Greek. When Isaac's second volume reached my shelves (I had now expanded to street level), I wrote him to congratulate him, and after that we corresponded, not with any regularity. He took to ordering all his books from me, and we exchanged awkward little jokes. "I'm still in the jacket business," I told him, "but now I feel I'm where I belong. Last time I went too fur." "Sheindel is well, and Naomi and Esther have a sister," he wrote. And later: "Naomi, Esther, and Miriam have a sister." And still later: "Naomi, Esther, Miriam, and Ophra have a sister." It went on until there were seven girls. "There's nothing in Torah that prevents an illustrious man from having illustrious daughters," I wrote him when he said he had given up hope of another rabbi in the family. "But where do you find seven illustrious husbands?" he asked. Every order brought another quip, and we bantered back and forth in this way for some years.

I noticed that he read everything. Long ago he had inflamed my taste, but I could never keep up. No sooner did I catch his joy in Saadia Gaon than he had already sprung ahead to Yehudah Halevi. One day he was weeping with Dostoyevski and the next leaping in the air over Thomas

Mann. He introduced me to Hegel and Nietzsche while our fathers wailed. His mature reading was no more peaceable than those frenzies of his youth, when I would come upon him in an abandoned classroom at dusk, his stocking feet on the windowsill, the light already washed from the lowest city clouds, wearing the look of a man half-sotted with print.

But when the widow asked me—covering a certain excess of alertness or irritation—whether to my knowledge Isaac had lately been ordering any books on horticulture, I was astonished.

"He bought so much," I demurred.

"Yes, yes, yes," she said. "How could you remember?"

She poured the tea and then, with a discreetness of gesture, lifted my dripping raincoat from the chair where I had thrown it and took it out of the room. It was a crowded apartment, not very neat, far from slovenly, cluttered with dolls and tiny dishes and an array of tricycles. The dining table was as large as a desert. An old-fashioned crocheted lace runner divided it into two nations, and on the end of this, in the neutral zone, so to speak, Sheindel had placed my cup. There was no physical relic of Isaac: not even a book.

She returned. "My girls are all asleep, we can talk. What an ordeal for you, weather like this and going out so far to that place."

It was impossible to tell whether she was angry or not. I had rushed in on her like the rainfall itself, scattering drops, my shoes stuck all over with leaves.

"I comprehend exactly why you went out there. The impulse of a detective," she said. Her voice contained an irony that surprised me. It was brilliantly and unmistakably accented, and because of this jaggedly precise. It was as if every word emitted a quick white thread of great purity, like hard silk, which she was then obliged to bite cleanly off. "You went to find something? An atmosphere? The sadness itself?"

"There was nothing to see," I said, and thought I was lunatic to have put myself in her way.

"Did you dig in the ground? He might have buried a note for goodbye."

"Was there a note?" I asked, startled.

"He left nothing behind for ordinary humanity like yourself."

I saw she was playing with me. "Rebbetzin Kornfeld," I said, standing up, "forgive me. My coat, please, and I'll go."

"Sit," she commanded. "Isaac read less lately, did you notice that?"

I gave her a civil smile. "All the same he was buying more and more."

"Think," she said. "I depend on you. You're just the one who might know. I had forgotten this. God sent you perhaps."

"Rebbetzin Kornfeld, I'm only a bookseller."

"God in his judgment sent me a bookseller. For such a long time Isaac never read at home. Think! Agronomy?"

"I don't remember anything like that. What would a Professor of Mishnaic History want with agronomy?"

"If he had a new book under his arm he would take it straight to the seminary and hide it in his office."

"I mailed to his office. If you like I can look up some of the titles—"

"You were in the park and you saw nothing?"

"Nothing." Then I was ashamed. "I saw the tree."

"And what is that? A tree is nothing."

"Rebbetzin Kornfeld," I pleaded, "it's a stupidity that I came here. I don't know myself why I came, I beg your pardon, I had no idea—"

"You came to learn why Isaac took his life. Botany? Or even, please listen, even mycology? He never asked you to send something on mushrooms? Or having to do with herbs? Manure? Flowers? A certain kind of agricultural poetry? A book about gardening? Forestry? Vegetables? Cereal growing?"

"Nothing, nothing like that," I said excitedly. "Rebbetzin Kornfeld, your husband was a rabbi!"

"I know what my husband was. Something to do with vines? Arbors? Rice? Think, think, think! Anything to do with land—meadows—goats—a farm, hay—anything at all, anything rustic or lunar—"

"Lunar! My God! Was he a teacher or a nurseryman? Goats! Was he a furrier? Sheindel, are you crazy? *I* was the furrier! What do you want from the dead?"

Without a word she replenished my cup, though it was more than half full, and sat down opposite me, on the other side of the lace boundary line. She leaned her face into her palms, but I saw her eyes. She kept them wide.

"Rebbetzin Kornfeld," I said, collecting myself, "with a tragedy like this—"

"You imagine I blame the books. I don't blame the books, whatever they were. If he had been faithful to his books he would have lived."

"He lived," I cried, "in books, what else?"

"No," said the widow.

"A scholar. A rabbi. A remarkable Jew!"

At this she spilled a furious laugh. "Tell me, I have always been very interested and shy to inquire. Tell me about your wife."

I intervened: "I haven't had a wife in years."

"What are they like, those people?"

"They're exactly like us, if you can think what we would be if we were like them."

"We are not like them. Their bodies are more to them than ours are to us. Our books are holy, to them their bodies are holy."

"Jane's was so holy she hardly ever let me get near it," I muttered to myself.

"Isaac used to run in the park, but he lost his breath too quickly. Instead he read in a book about runners with hats made of leaves."

"Sheindel, Sheindel, what did you expect of him? He was a student, he sat and he thought, he was a Jew."

She thrust her hands flat. "He was not."

I could not reply. I looked at her merely. She was thinner now than in her early young-womanhood, and her face had an in-between cast, poignant still at the mouth and jaw, beginning to grow coarse on either side of the nose.

"I think he was never a Jew," she said.

I wondered whether Isaac's suicide had unbalanced her.

"I'll tell you a story," she resumed. "A story about stories. These were the bedtime stories Isaac told Naomi and Esther: about mice that danced and children who laughed. When Miriam came he invented a speaking cloud. With Ophra it was a turtle that married a blade of withered grass. By Leah's time the stones had tears for their leglessness. Rebecca cried because of a tree that turned into a girl and could never grow colors again in autumn. Shiphrah, the littlest, believes that a pig has a soul."

"My own father used to drill me every night in sacred recitation. It was a terrible childhood."

"He insisted on picnics. Each time we went farther and farther into the country. It was a madness. Isaac never troubled to learn to drive a car, and there was always a clumsiness of baskets to carry and a clutter of buses and trains and seven exhausted wild girls. And he would look for special places—we couldn't settle just here or there, there had to be a brook or such-and-such a slope or else a little grove. And then, though he said it was all for the children's pleasure, he would leave them and go off alone and never come back until sunset, when everything was spilled and the air freezing and the babies crying."

"I was a grown man before I had the chance to go on a picnic," I admitted.

"I'm speaking of the beginning," said the widow. "Like you, wasn't I fooled? I was fooled, I was charmed. Going home with our baskets of berries and flowers we were a romantic huddle. Isaac's stories on those nights were full of dark invention. May God preserve me, I even begged him to write them down. Then suddenly he joined a club, and Sunday mornings he was up and away before dawn."

"A club? So early? What library opens at that hour?" I said, stunned that a man like Isaac should ally himself with anything so doubtful.

"Ah, you don't follow, you don't follow. It was a hiking club, they met under the moon. I thought it was a pity, the whole week Isaac was so inward, he needed air for the mind. He used to come home too fatigued to stand. He said he went for the landscape. I was like you, I took what I heard, I heard it all and never followed. He resigned from the hikers finally, and I believed all that strangeness was finished. He told me it was absurd to walk at such a pace, he was a teacher and not an athlete. Then he began to write."

"But he always wrote," I objected.

"Not this way. What he wrote was only fairy tales. He kept at it and for a while he neglected everything else. It was the strangeness in another form. The stories surprised me, they were so poor and dull. They were a little like the ideas he used to scare the girls with, but choked all over with notes, appendices, prefaces. It struck me then he didn't seem to understand he was only doing fairy tales. Yet they were really very ordinary—full of sprites, nymphs, gods, everything ordinary and old."

"Will you let me see them?"

"Burned, all burned."

"Isaac burned them?"

"You don't think I did! I see what you think."

It was true that I was marveling at her hatred. I supposed she was one of those born to dread imagination. I was overtaken by a coldness for her, though the sight of her small hands with their tremulous staves of fingers turning and turning in front of her face like a gate on a hinge reminded me of where she was born and who she was. She was an orphan and had been saved by magic and had a terror of it. The coldness fled. "Why should you be bothered by little stories?" I inquired. "It wasn't the stories that killed him."

"No, no, not the stories," she said. "Stupid corrupt things. I was glad when he gave them up. He piled them in the bathtub and lit them with a match. Then he put a notebook in his coat pocket and said he would walk in the park. Week after week he tried all the parks in the city. I didn't dream what he could be after. One day he took the subway and rode to the end of the line, and this was the right park at last. He went every day after class. An hour going, an hour back. Two, three in the morning he came home. 'Is it exercise?' I said. I thought he might be running again. He used to shiver with the chill of night and the dew. 'No, I sit quite still,' he said. 'Is it more stories you do out there?' 'No, I only jot down what I think.' 'A man should meditate in his own house, not by night near bad water,' I said. Six, seven in the morning he came home. I asked him if he meant to find his grave in that place."

She broke off with a cough, half artifice and half resignation, so loud that it made her crane toward the bedrooms to see if she had awakened a child. "I don't sleep any more," she told me. "Look around you. Look, look everywhere, look on the windowsills. Do you see any plants, any common house plants? I went down one evening and gave them to the garbage collector. I couldn't sleep in the same space with plants. They are like little trees. Am I deranged? Take Isaac's notebook and bring it back when you can."

I obeyed. In my own room, a sparse place, with no ornaments but a few pretty stalks in pots, I did not delay and seized the notebook. It was a tiny affair, three inches by five, with ruled pages that opened on a coiled wire. I read searchingly, hoping for something not easily evident. Sheindel by her melancholy innuendo had made me believe that in these few sheets Isaac had revealed the reason for his suicide. But it was all a disappointment. There was not a word of any importance. After a while I concluded that, whatever her motives, Sheindel was playing with me again. She meant to punish me for asking the unaskable. My inquisitiveness offended her; she had given me Isaac's notebook not to enlighten but to rebuke. The handwriting was recognizable yet oddly formed, shaky and even senile, like that of a man outdoors and deskless who scribbles in his palm or on his lifted knee or leaning on a bit of bark; and there was no doubt that the wrinkled leaves, with their ragged corners, had been in and out of someone's pocket. So I did not mistrust Sheindel's mad anecdote; this much was true: a park, Isaac, a notebook, all at once, but signifying no more than that a professor with a literary turn of mind had gone for a walk. There was even a green stain straight across one of the quotations, as if the pad had slipped grassward and been trod on.

I have forgotten to mention that the notebook, though scantily filled, was in three languages. The Greek I could not read at all, but it had the shape of verse. The Hebrew was simply a miscellany, drawn mostly from Leviticus and Deuteronomy. Among these I found the following extracts, transcribed not quite verbatim:

Ye shall utterly destroy all the places of the gods, upon the high mountains, and upon the hills, and under every green tree.

And the soul that turneth after familiar spirits to go a-whoring after them, I will cut him off from among his people.

These, of course, were ordinary unadorned notes, such as any classroom lecturer might commonly make to remind himself of the text, with a phrase cut out here and there for the sake of speeding his hand. Or I thought it possible that Isaac might at that time have been preparing a paper on the Talmudic commentaries for these passages. Whatever the case, the remaining quotations, chiefly from English poetry, interested me only slightly more. They were the elegiac favorites of a closeted Romantic. I was repelled by Isaac's Nature: it wore a capital letter, and smelled like my own Book Cellar. It was plain to me that he had lately grown painfully academic: he could not see a weed's tassel without finding a classical reference for it. He had put down a snatch of Byron, a smudge of Keats (like his Scriptural copyings, these too were quick and fragmented), a pair of truncated lines from Tennyson, and this unmarked and clumsy quatrain:

> *And yet all is not taken. Still one Dryad*
> *Flits through the wood, one Oread skims the hill;*
> *White in the whispering stream still gleams a Naiad;*
> *The beauty of the earth is haunted still.*

All of this was so cloying and mooning and ridiculous, and so pedantic besides, that I felt ashamed for him. And yet there was almost nothing else, nothing to redeem him and nothing personal, only a sentence or two in his rigid self-controlled scholar's style, not unlike the starched little jokes of our correspondence. "I am writing at dusk sitting on a stone in Trilham's Inlet Park, within sight of Trilham's Inlet, a bay to the north of the city, and within two yards of a slender tree, *Quercus velutina*, the age of which, should one desire to measure it, can be ascertained by (God forbid) cutting the bole and counting the rings. The man writing is thirty-five years old and aging too rapidly, which may be ascertained by counting the rings under his poor myopic eyes." Below this, deliberate and readily more legible than the rest, appeared three curious words:

Great Pan lives.

That was all. In a day or so I returned the notebook to Sheindel. I told myself that she had seven orphans to worry over, and repressed my anger at having been cheated.

She was waiting for me. "I am so sorry, there was a letter in the notebook, it had fallen out. I found it on the carpet after you left."

"Thank you, no," I said. "I've read enough out of Isaac's pockets."

"Then why did you come to see me to begin with?"

"I came," I said, "just to see you."

"You came for Isaac." But she was more mocking than distraught. "I gave you everything you needed to see what happened and still you don't follow. Here." She held out a large law-sized paper. "Read the letter."

"I've read his notebook. If everything I need to fathom Isaac is in the notebook I don't need the letter."

"It's a letter he wrote to explain himself," she persisted.

"You told me Isaac left you no notes."

"It was not written to me."

I sat down on one of the dining room chairs and Sheindel put the page before me on the table. It lay face up on the lace divider. I did not look at it.

"It's a love letter," Sheindel whispered. "When they cut him down they found the notebook in one pocket and the letter in the other."

I did not know what to say.

"The police gave me everything," Sheindel said. "Everything to keep."

"A love letter?" I repeated.

"That is what such letters are commonly called."

"And the police—they gave it to you, and that was the first you realized what"—I floundered after the inconceivable—"what could be occupying him?"

"What could be occupying him," she mimicked. "Yes. Not until they took the letter and the notebook out of his pocket."

"My God. His habit of life, his mind . . . I can't imagine it. You never guessed?"

"No."

"These trips to the park—"

"He had become aberrant in many ways. I have described them to you."

"But the park! Going off like that, alone—you didn't think he might be meeting a woman?"

"It was not a woman."

Disgust like a powder clotted my nose. "Sheindel, you're crazy."

"I'm crazy, is that it? Read his confession! Read it! How long can I be the only one to know this thing? Do you want my brain to melt? Be my confidant," she entreated so unexpectedly that I held my breath.

"You've said nothing to anyone?"

"Would they have recited such eulogies if I had? Read the letter!"

"I have no interest in the abnormal," I said coldly.

She raised her eyes and watched me for the smallest space. Without any change in the posture of her suppliant head her laughter began; I have never since heard sounds like those—almost mouselike in density for fear of waking her sleeping daughters, but so rational in intent that it was like listening to astonished sanity rendered into a cackling fugue. She kept it up for a minute and then calmed herself. "Please sit where you are. Please pay attention. I will read the letter to you myself."

She plucked the page from the table with an orderly gesture. I saw tha this letter had been scrupulously prepared; it was closely written. Her tone was cleansed by scorn.

" 'My ancestors were led out of Egypt by the hand of God,' " she read.

"Is this how a love letter starts out?"

She moved on resolutely. "We were guilty of so-called abominations well-described elsewhere. Other peoples have been nourished on their mythologies. For aeons we have been weaned from all traces of the same."

I felt myself becoming impatient. The fact was I had returned with a single idea: I meant to marry Isaac's widow when enough time had passed to make it seemly. It was my intention to court her with great subtlety at first, so that I would not appear to be presuming on her sorrow. But she was possessed. "Sheindel, why do you want to inflict this treatise on me? Give it to the seminary, contribute it to a symposium of professors."

"I would sooner die."

At this I began to attend in earnest.

" 'I will leave aside the wholly plausible position of so-called animism within the concept of the One God. I will omit a historical illumination of its continuous but covert expression even within the Fence of the Law. Creature, I leave these aside—' "

"What?" I yelped.

" 'Creature,' " she repeated, spreading her nostrils. " 'What is human history? What is our philosophy? What is our religion? None of these teaches us poor human ones that we are alone in the universe, and even without them we would know that we are not. At a very young age I understood that a foolish man would not believe in a fish had he not had one enter his experience. Innumerable forms exist and have come to our eyes, and to the still deeper eye of the lens of our instruments; from this minute perception of what already is, it is easy to conclude that further forms are possible, that all forms are probable. God created the world not for Himself alone, or I would not now possess this consciousness with which I am enabled to address thee, Loveliness.' "

"Thee," I echoed, and swallowed a sad bewilderment.

"You must let me go on," Sheindel said, and grimly went on. " 'It is false history, false philosophy, and false religion which declare to us human ones that we live among Things. The arts of physics and chemistry begin to teach us differently, but their way of compassion is new, and finds few to carry fidelity to its logical and beautiful end. The molecules dance inside all forms, and within the molecules dance the atoms, and within the atoms dance still profounder sources of divine vitality. There is nothing that is Dead. There is no Non-life. Holy life subsists even in the stone, even in the bones of dead dogs and dead men. Hence in God's fecundating Creation there is no possibility of Idolatry, and therefore no possibility of committing this so-called abomination.' "

"My God, my God," I wailed. "Enough, Sheindel, it's more than enough, no more—"

"There is more," she said.

"I don't want to hear it."

"He stains his character for you? A spot, do you think? You will hear." She took up in a voice which all at once reminded me of my father's: it was unforgiving. " 'Creature, I rehearse these matters though all our language is as breath to thee; as baubles for the juggler. Where we struggle to understand from day to day, and contemplate the grave for its riddle, the other breeds are born fulfilled in wisdom. Animal races conduct themselves without self-investigations; instinct is a higher and not a lower thing. Alas that we human ones—but for certain pitifully primitive approximations in those few reflexes and involuntary actions left to our bodies—are born bare of instinct! All that we unfortunates must resort to through science, art, philosophy, religion, all our imaginings and tormented strivings, all our meditations and vain questionings, all!—are expressed naturally and rightly in the beasts, the plants, the rivers, the stones. The reason is simple, it is our tragedy: our soul is included in us, it inhabits us, we contain it, when we seek our soul we must seek in ourselves. To see the soul, to confront it—that is divine wisdom. Yet how can we see into our dark selves? With the other races of being it is differently ordered. The soul of the plant does not reside in the chlorophyll, it may roam if it wishes, it may choose whatever form or shape it pleases. Hence the other breeds, being largely free of their soul and able to witness it, can live in peace. To see one's soul is to know all, to know all is to own the peace our philosophies futilely envisage. Earth displays two categories of soul: the free and the indwelling. We human ones are cursed with the indwelling—' "

"Stop!" I cried.

"I will not," said the widow.

"Please, you told me he burned his fairy tales."

"Did I lie to you? Will you say I lied?"

"Then for Isaac's sake why didn't you? If this isn't a fairy tale what do you want me to think it could be?"

"Think what you like."

"Sheindel," I said, "I beg you, don't destroy a dead man's honor. Don't look at this thing again, tear it to pieces, don't continue with it."

"I don't destroy his honor. He had none."

"Please! Listen to yourself! My God, who was the man? Rabbi Isaac Kornfeld! Talk of honor! Wasn't he a teacher? Wasn't he a scholar?"

"He was a pagan."

Her eyes returned without hesitation to their task. She commenced: " 'All these truths I learned only gradually, against my will and desire. Our teacher Moses did not speak of them; much may be said under this head. It was not out of ignorance that Moses failed to teach about those souls that are free. If I have learned what Moses knew, is this not because we are both men? He was a man, but God addressed him; it was God's will that our ancestors should no longer be slaves. Yet our ancestors, being stiff-necked, would not have abandoned their slavery in Egypt had they been taught of the free souls. They would have said: "Let us stay, our bodies will remain enslaved in Egypt, but our souls will wander at their pleasure in Zion. If the cactus-plant stays rooted while its soul roams, why not also a man?" And if Moses had replied that only the world of Nature has the gift of the free soul, while man is chained to his, and that a man, to free his soul, must also free the body that is its vessel, they would have scoffed. "How is it that men, and men alone, are different from the world of Nature? If this is so, then the condition of men is evil and unjust, and if this condition of ours is evil and unjust in general, what does it matter whether we are slaves in Egypt or citizens in Zion?" And they would not have done God's will and abandoned their slavery. Therefore Moses never spoke to them of the free souls, lest the people not do God's will and go out from Egypt.' "

In an instant a sensation broke in me—it was entirely obscure, there was nothing I could compare it with, and yet I was certain I recognized it. And then I did. It hurtled me into childhood—it was the crisis of insight one experiences when one has just read out, for the first time, that conglomeration of figurines which makes a word. In that moment I penetrated beyond Isaac's alphabet into his language. I saw that he was on the side of possibility: he was both sane and inspired. His intention was not to accumulate mystery but to dispel it.

"All that part is brilliant," I burst out.

Sheindel meanwhile had gone to the sideboard to take a sip of cold tea that was standing there. "In a minute," she said, and pursued her thirst. "I have heard of drawings surpassing Rembrandt daubed by madmen who when released from the fit couldn't hold the chalk. What follows is beautiful, I warn you."

"The man was a genius."

"Yes."

"Go on," I urged.

She produced for me her clownish jeering smile. She read: " 'Sometimes in the desert journey on the way they would come to a watering place, and some quick spry boy would happen to glimpse the soul of the spring (which the wild Greeks afterward called naiad), but not knowing of the existence of the free souls he would suppose only that the moon had cast a momentary beam across the water. Loveliness, with the same innocence of accident I discovered thee. Loveliness, Loveliness.' "

She stopped.

"Is that all?"

"There is more."

"Read it."

"The rest is the love letter."

"Is it hard for you?" But I asked with more eagerness than pity.

"I was that man's wife, he scaled the Fence of the Law. For this God preserved me from the electric fence. Read it for yourself."

Incontinently I snatched the crowded page.

" 'Loveliness, in thee the joy, substantiation, and supernal succor of my theorem. How many hours through how many years I walked over the cilia-forests of our enormous aspiring vegetable-star, this light rootless seed that crawls in its single furrow, this shaggy mazy unimplanted cabbage-head of our earth!—never, all that time, all those days of un-fulfillment, a white space like a desert thirst, never, never to grasp. I thought myself abandoned to the intrigue of my folly. At dawn, on a hillock, what seemed the very shape and seizing of the mound's nature—what was it? Only the haze of the sunball growing great through hoarfrost. The oread slipped from me, leaving her illusion; or was never there at all; or was there but for an instant, and ran away. What sly ones the free souls are! They have a comedy we human ones cannot dream: the laughing drunkard feels in himself the shadow of the shadow of the shadow of their wit, and only because he has made himself a vessel, as the two banks and the bed of a rivulet are the naiad's vessel. A naiad I may indeed have viewed whole: all seven of my daughters were once wading in a stream in a compact but beautiful park, of which I had much hope. The youngest being not yet two, and fretful, the older ones were told to keep her always by the hand, but they did not obey. I, having passed some way into the woods behind, all at once heard a scream and noise of splashes, and caught sight of a tiny body flying down into the water. Running back through the trees I could see the others bunched to-gether, afraid, as the baby dived helplessly, all these little girls frozen in a garland—when suddenly one of them (it was too quick a movement for me to recognize which) darted to the struggler, who was now underwa-ter, and pulled her up, and put an arm around her to soothe her. The arm was blue—blue. As blue as a lake. And fiercely, from my spot on the bank, panting, I began to count the little girls. I counted eight, thought myself not mad but delivered, again counted, counted seven, knew I had counted well before, knew I counted well even now. A blue-armed girl had come to wade among them. Which is to say the shape of a girl. I questioned my daughters: each in her fright believed one of the others had gone to pluck up the tiresome baby. None wore a dress with blue sleeves.' "

"Proofs," said the widow. "Isaac was meticulous, he used to account for all his proofs always."

"How?" My hand in tremor rustled Isaac's letter; the paper bleated as though whipped.

"By eventually finding a principle to cover them," she finished mali-ciously. "Well, don't rest even for me, you don't oblige me. You have a long story to go, long enough to make a fever."

"Tea," I said hoarsely.

She brought me her own cup from the sideboard, and I believed as I drank that I swallowed some of her mockery and gall.

"Sheindel, for a woman so pious you're a great skeptic." And now the tremor had command of my throat.

"An atheist's statement," she rejoined. "The more piety, the more skepticism. A religious man comprehends this. Superfluity, excess of custom, and superstition would climb like a choking vine on the Fence of the Law if skepticism did not continually hack them away to make freedom for purity."

I then thought her fully worthy of Isaac. Whether I was worthy of her I evaded putting to myself; instead I gargled some tea and returned to the letter.

" 'It pains me to confess,' " I read, " 'how after that I moved from clarity to doubt and back again. I had no trust in my conclusions because all my experiences were evanescent. Everything certain I attributed to some other cause less certain. Every voice out of the moss I blamed on rabbits and squirrels. Every motion among leaves I called a bird, though there positively was no bird. My first sight of the Little People struck me as no more than a shudder of literary delusion, and I determined they could only be an instantaneous crop of mushrooms. But one night, a little after ten o'clock at the crux of summer—the sky still showed strings of light—I was wandering in this place, this place where they will find my corpse—' "

"Not for my sake," said Sheindel when I hesitated.

"It's terrible," I croaked, "terrible."

"Withered like a shell," she said, as though speaking of the cosmos; and I understood from her manner that she had a fanatic's acquaintance with this letter, and knew it nearly by heart. She appeared to be thinking the words faster than I could bring them out, and for some reason I was constrained to hurry the pace of my reading.

" '—where they will find my corpse withered like the shell of an insect,' " I rushed on. " 'The smell of putrefaction lifted clearly from the bay. I began to speculate about my own body after I was dead—whether the soul would be set free immediately after the departure of life; or whether only gradually, as decomposition proceeded and more and more of the indwelling soul was released to freedom. But when I considered how a man's body is no better than a clay pot, a fact which none of our sages has ever contradicted, it seemed to me then that an indwelling soul by its own nature would be obliged to cling to its bit of pottery until the last crumb and grain had vanished into earth. I walked through the ditches of that black meadow grieving and swollen with self-pity. It came to me that while my poor bones went on decaying at their ease, my soul would have to linger inside them, waiting, despairing, longing to join the free ones. I cursed it for its gravity-despoiled, slow, interminably languishing purse of flesh; better to be encased in vapor, in wind, in a hair of a coconut! Who knows how long it takes the body of a man to shrink into gravel, and the gravel into sand, and the sand into vitamin? A hundred years? Two hundred, three hundred? A thousand perhaps! Is it not true that bones nearly intact are constantly being dug up by the paleontologists two million years after burial?'—Sheindel," I interrupted, "this is death, not love. Where's the love letter to be afraid of here? I don't find it."

"Continue," she ordered. And then: "You see I'm not afraid."

"Not of love?"

"No. But you recite much too slowly. Your mouth is shaking. Are you afraid of death?"

I did not reply.

"Continue," she said again. "Go rapidly. The next sentence begins with an extraordinary thought."

" 'An extraordinary thought emerged in me. It was luminous, profound, and practical. More than that, it had innumerable precedents; the mythologies had documented it a dozen dozen times over. I recalled all those mortals reputed to have coupled with gods (a collective word, showing much common sense, signifying what our philosophies more abstrusely call Shekhina), and all that poignant miscegenation represented by centaurs, satyrs, mermaids, fauns, and so forth, not to speak of that even more famous mingling in Genesis, whereby the sons of God took the daughters of men for brides, producing giants and possibly also those abortions, leviathan and behemoth, of which we read in Job, along with unicorns and other chimeras and monsters abundant in Scripture, hence far from fanciful. There existed also the example of the succubus Lilith, who was often known to couple in the mediaeval ghetto even with prepubescent boys. By all these evidences I was emboldened in my confidence that I was surely not the first man to conceive such a desire in the history of our earth. Creature, the thought that took hold of me was this: if only I could couple with one of the free souls, the strength of the connection would likely wrest my own soul from my body—seize it, as if by a tongs, draw it out, so to say, to its own freedom. The intensity and force of my desire to capture one of these beings now became prodigious. I avoided my wife—' "

Here the widow heard me falter.

"Please," she commanded, and I saw creeping in her face the completed turn of a sneer.

" '—lest I be depleted of potency at that moment (which might occur in any interval, even, I assumed, in my own bedroom) when I should encounter one of the free souls. I was borne back again and again to the fetid viscosities of the Inlet, borne there as if on the rising stink of my own enduring and tedious putrefaction, the idea of which I could no longer shake off—I envisaged my soul as trapped in my last granule, and that last granule itself perhaps petrified, never to dissolve, and my soul condemned to minister to it throughout eternity! It seemed to me my soul must be released at once or be lost to sweet air forever. In a gleamless dark, struggling with this singular panic, I stumbled from ditch to ditch, strained like a blind dog for the support of solid verticality; and smacked my palm against bark. I looked up and in the black could not fathom the size of the tree—my head lolled forward, my brow met the trunk with all its gravings. I busied my fingers in the interstices of the bark's cuneiform. Then with forehead flat on the tree, I embraced it with both arms to measure it. My hands united on the other side. It was a young narrow weed, I did not know of what family. I reached to the lowest branch and plucked a leaf and made my tongue travel meditatively along its periphery to assess its shape: oak. The taste was sticky and exaltingly bitter. A jubilation lightly carpeted my groin. I then placed one hand (the other I kept around the tree's waist, as it were) in the bifurcation (disgustingly termed crotch) of that lowest limb and the elegant and devoutly firm torso, and caressed that miraculous juncture with a certain languor, which gradually changed to vigor. I was all at once savagely alert and deeply daring: I chose that single tree together with the ground near it for an enemy which in two senses would not yield: it would neither give nor give in. "Come, come," I called aloud to Nature. A wind blew out a braid of excremental malodor into the heated air. "Come," I called, "couple with me, as thou didst with Cadmus, Rhoecus, Tithonus, Endymion, and that king Numa Pompilius to whom thou didst give secrets. As Lilith comes without a sign, so come thou. As the sons of God came to copulate with women, so now let a daughter of Shekhina the Emanation reveal herself to me. Nymph, come now, come now."

" 'Without warning I was flung to the ground. My face smashed into earth, and a flaky clump of dirt lodged in my open mouth. For the rest, I was on my knees, pressing down on my hands, with the fingernails clutching dirt. A superb ache lined my haunch. I began to weep because I was certain I had been ravished by some sinewy animal. I vomited the earth I had swallowed and believed I was defiled, as it is written: "Neither shalt thou lie with any beast." I lay sunk in the grass, afraid to lift my head to see if the animal still lurked. Through some curious means I had been fully positioned and aroused and exquisitely sated, all in half a second, in a fashion impossible to explain, in which, though I performed as with my own wife, I felt as if a preternatural rapine had been committed upon me. I continued prone, listening for the animal's breathing. Meanwhile, though every tissue of my flesh was gratified in its inmost awareness, a marvelous voluptuousness did not leave my body; sensual exultations of a wholly supreme and paradisal order, unlike anything our poets have ever defined, both flared and were intensely satisfied in the same moment. This salubrious and delightful perceptiveness excited my being for some time: a conjoining not dissimilar (in metaphor only; in actuality it cannot be described) from the magical contradiction of the tree and its issuance-of-branch at the point of bifurcation. In me were linked, *in the same instant*, appetite and fulfillment, delicacy and power, mastery and submissiveness, and other paradoxes of entirely remarkable emotional import.

" 'Then I heard what I took to be the animal treading through the grass quite near my head, all cunningly; it withheld its breathing, then snored it out in a cautious and wisp-like whirr that resembled a light wind through rushes. With a huge energy (my muscular force seemed to have increased) I leaped up in fear of my life; I had nothing to use for a weapon but—oh, laughable!—the pen I had been writing with in a little notebook I always carried about with me in those days (and still keep on my person as a self-shaming souvenir of my insipidness, my bookishness, my pitiable conjecture and wishfulness in a time when, not yet knowing thee, I knew nothing). What I saw was not an animal but a girl no older than my oldest daughter, who was then fourteen. Her skin was as perfect as an eggplant's and nearly of that color. In height she was half as tall as I was. The second and third fingers of her hands—this I noticed at once—were peculiarly fused, one slotted into the other, like the ligula of a leaf. She was entirely bald and had no ears but rather a type of gill or envelope, one only, on the left side. Her toes displayed the same oddity I had observed in her fingers. She was neither naked nor clothed—that is to say, even though a part of her body, from hip to just below the breasts (each of which appeared to be a kind of velvety colorless pear, suspended from a very short, almost invisible stem), was luxuriantly covered with a flossy or spore-like material, this was a natural efflorescence in the manner of, with us, hair. All her sexual portion was wholly visible, as in any field flower. Aside from these express deviations, she was commandingly human in aspect, if unmistakably flowerlike. She was, in fact, the reverse of our hackneyed euphuism, as when we say a young girl blooms like a flower—she, on the contrary, seemed a flower transfigured into the shape of the most stupendously lovely child I had ever seen. Under the smallest push of wind she bent at her superlative waist; this, I recognized, and not the exhalations of some lecherous beast, was the breathlike sound that had alarmed me at her approach: these motions of hers made the blades of grass collide. (She herself, having no lungs, did not "breathe.") She stood bobbing joyfully before me, with a face as tender as a morning-glory, strangely phosphorescent: she shed her own light, in effect, and I had no difficulty in confronting her beauty.

" 'Moreover, by experiment I soon learned that she was not only capable of language, but that she delighted in playing with it. This she literally could do—if I had distinguished her hands before anything else, it was because she had held them out to catch my first cry of awe. She either caught my words like balls or let them roll, or caught them and then darted off to throw them into the Inlet. I discovered that whenever I spoke I more or less pelted her; but she liked this, and told me ordinary human speech only tickled and amused, whereas laughter, being highly plosive, was something of an assault. I then took care to pretend much solemnity, though I was lightheaded with rapture. Her own "voice" I apprehended rather than heard—which she, unable to imagine how we human ones are prisoned in sensory perception, found hard to conceive. Her sentences came to me not as a series of differentiated frequencies but (impossible to develop this idea in language) as a diffused cloud of field fragrances; yet to say that I assimilated her thought through the olfactory nerve would be a pedestrian distortion. All the same it was clear that whatever she said reached me in a shimmer of pellucid perfumes, and I understood her meaning with an immediacy of glee and with none of the ambiguities and suspiciousness of motive that surround our human communication.

" 'Through this medium she explained that she was a dryad and that her name was Iripomoňoéià (as nearly as I can render it in our narrowly limited orthography, and in this dunce's alphabet of ours which is notoriously impervious to odoriferous categories). She told me what I had already seized: that she had given me her love in response to my call.

" ' "Wilt thou come to any man who calls?" I asked.

" ' "All men call, whether realizing it or not. I and my sisters sometimes come to those who do not realize. Almost never, unless for sport, do we come to that man who calls knowingly—he wishes only to inhabit us out of perversity or boastfulness or to indulge a dreamed-of disgust."

" ' "Scripture does not forbid sodomy with the plants," I exclaimed, but she did not comprehend any of this and lowered her hands so that my words would fly past her uncaught. "I too called thee knowingly, not for perversity but for love of Nature."

" ' "I have caught men's words before as they talked of Nature, you are not the first. It is not Nature they love so much as Death they fear. So CoryĬyĬyb my cousin received it in a season not long ago coupling in a harbor with one of your kind, one called Spinoza, one that had catarrh of the lung. I am of Nature and immortal and so I cannot pity your deaths. But return tomorrow and say Iripomoňoéià." Then she chased my last word to where she had kicked it, behind the tree. She did not come back. I ran to the tree and circled it diligently but she was lost for that night.

" 'Loveliness, all the foregoing, telling of my life and meditations until now, I have never before recounted to thee or any other. The rest is beyond mean telling: those rejoicings from midnight to dawn, when the greater phosphorescence of the whole shouting sky frightened thee home! How in a trance of happiness we coupled in the ditches, in the long grasses, behind a fountain, under a broken wall, once recklessly on the very pavement, with a bench for roof and trellis! How I was taught by natural arts to influence certain chemistries engendering explicit marvels, blisses, and transports no man has slaked himself with since Father

Adam pressed out the forbidden chlorophyll of Eden! Loveliness, Loveliness, none like thee. No brow so sleek, no elbow-crook so fine, no eye so green, no waist so pliant, no limbs so pleasant and acute. None like immortal Iripomoňoéià.

" 'Creature, the moon filled and starved twice, and there was still no end to the glorious archaic newness of Iripomoňoéià.

" 'Then last night. Last night! I will record all with simplicity.

" 'We entered a shallow ditch. In a sweet-smelling voice of extraordinary redolence—so intense in its sweetness that even the barbaric stinks and wind-lifted farts of the Inlet were overpowered by it—Iripomoňoéià inquired of me how I felt without my soul. I replied that I did not know this was my condition. "Oh yes, your body is now an empty packet, that is why it is so light. Spring." I sprang in air and rose effortlessly. "You have spoiled yourself, spoiled yourself with confusions," she complained, "now by morning your body will be crumpled and withered and ugly, like a leaf in its sere hour, and never again after tonight will this place see you." "Nymph!" I roared, amazed by levitation. "Oh, oh, that damaged," she cried, "you hit my eye with that noise," and she wafted a deeper aroma, a leeklike mist, one that stung the mucous membranes. A white bruise disfigured her petally lid. I was repentant and sighed terribly for her injury. "Beauty marred is for our kind what physical hurt is for yours," she reproved me. "Where you have pain, we have ugliness. Where you profane yourselves by immorality, we are profaned by ugliness. Your soul has taken leave of you and spoils our pretty game." "Nymph!" I whispered, "heart, treasure, if my soul is separated how is it I am unaware?"

" ' "Poor man," she answered, "you have only to look and you will see the thing." Her speech had now turned as acrid as an herb, and all that place reeked bitterly. "You know I am a spirit. You know I must flash and dart. All my sisters flash and dart. Of all races we are the quickest. Our very religion is all-of-a-sudden. No one can hinder us, no one may delay us. But yesterday you undertook to detain me in your embrace, you stretched your kisses into years, you called me your treasure and your heart endlessly, your soul in its slow greed kept me close and captive, all the while knowing well how a spirit cannot stay and will not be fixed. I made to leap from you, but your obstinate soul held on until it was snatched straight from your frame and escaped with me. I saw it hurled out onto the pavement, the blue beginning of day was already seeping down, so I ran away and could say nothing until this moment."

" ' "My soul is free? Free entirely? And can be seen?"

" ' "Free. If I could pity any living thing under the sky I would pity you for the sight of your soul. I do not like it, it conjures against me."

" ' "My soul loves thee," I urged in all my triumph, "it is freed from the thousand-year grave!" I jumped out of the ditch like a frog, my legs had no weight; but the dryad sulked in the ground, stroking her ugly violated eye. "Iripomoňoéià, my soul will follow thee with thankfulness into eternity."

" ' "I would sooner be followed by the dirty fog. I do not like that soul of yours. It conjures against me. It denies me, it denies every spirit and all my sisters and every nereid of the harbor, it denies all our multiplicity, and all gods diversiform, it spites even Lord Pan, it is an enemy, and you, poor man, do not know your own soul. Go, look at it, there it is on the road."

" 'I scudded back and forth under the moon.

" ' "Nothing, only a dusty old man trudging up there."

" ' "A quite ugly old man?"

" ' "Yes, that is all. My soul is not there."

" ' "With a matted beard and great fierce eyebrows?"

" ' "Yes, yes, one like that is walking on the road. He is half bent over under the burden of a dusty old bag. The bag is stuffed with books—I can see their raveled bindings sticking out."

" ' "And he reads as he goes?"

" ' "Yes, he reads as he goes."

" ' "What is it he reads?"

" ' "Some huge and terrifying volume, heavy as a stone." I peered forward in the moonlight. "A Tractate. A Tractate of the Mishnah. Its leaves are so worn they break as he turns them, but he does not turn them often because there is much matter on a single page. He is so sad! Such antique weariness broods in his face! His throat is striped from the whip. His cheeks are folded like ancient flags, he reads the Law and breathes the dust."

" ' "And are there flowers on either side of the road?"

" ' "Incredible flowers! Of every color! And noble shrubs like mounds of green moss! And the cricket crackling in the field. He passes indifferent through the beauty of the field. His nostrils sniff his book as if flowers lay on the clotted page, but the flowers lick his feet. His feet are bandaged, his notched toenails gore the path. His prayer shawl droops on his studious back. He reads the Law and breathes the dust and doesn't see the flowers and won't heed the cricket spitting in the field."

" ' "That," said the dryad, "is your soul." And was gone with all her odors.

" 'My body sailed up to the road in a single hop. I alighted near the shape of the old man and demanded whether he were indeed the soul of Rabbi Isaac Kornfeld. He trembled but confessed. I asked if he intended to go with his books through the whole future without change, always with his Tractate in his hand, and he answered that he could do nothing else.

" ' "Nothing else! You, who I thought yearned for the earth! You, an immortal, free, and caring only to be bound to the Law!"

" 'He held a dry arm fearfully before his face, and with the other arm hitched up his merciless bag on his shoulder. "Sir," he said, still quavering, "didn't you wish to see me with your own eyes?"

" ' "I know your figure!" I shrieked. "Haven't I seen that figure a hundred times before? On a hundred roads? It is not mine! I will not have it be mine!"

" ' "If you had not contrived to be rid of me, I would have stayed with you till the end. The dryad, who does not exist, lies. It was not I who clung to her but you, my body. Sir, all that has no real existence lies. In your grave beside you I would have sung you David's songs, I would have moaned Solomon's voice to your last grain of bone. But you expelled me, your ribs exile me from their fate, and I will walk here alone always, in my garden"—he scratched on his page—"with my precious birds"—he scratched at the letters—"and my darling trees"—he scratched at the tall side-column of commentary.

" 'He was so impudent in his bravery—for I was all fleshliness and he all floppy wraith—that I seized him by the collar and shook him up and down, while the books on his back made a vast rubbing one on the other, and bits of shredding leather flew out like a rain.

" ' "The sound of the Law," he said, "is more beautiful than the crickets. The smell of the Law is more radiant than the moss. The taste of the Law exceeds clear water."

" 'At this nervy provocation—he more than any other knew my despair—I grabbed his prayer shawl by its tassels and whirled around him once or twice until I had unwrapped it from him altogether, and wound it on my own neck and in one bound came to the tree.

" ' "Nymph!" I called to it. "Spirit and saint! Iripomoňoéià, come! None like thee, no brow so sleek, no elbow-crook so fine, no eye so green, no waist so pliant, no limbs so pleasant and acute. For pity of me, come, come."

" 'But she does not come.

" ' "Loveliness, come."

" 'She does not come.

" 'Creature, see how I am coiled in the snail of this shawl as if in a leaf. I crouch to write my words. Let soul call thee lie, but body . . .

" ' . . . body . . .

" ' . . . fingers twist, knuckles dark as wood, tongue dries like grass, deeper now into silk . . .

" ' . . . silk of pod of shawl, knees wilt, knuckles wither, neck . . .' "

Here the letter suddenly ended.

"You see? A pagan!" said Sheindel, and kept her spiteful smile. It was thick with audacity.

"You don't pity him," I said, watching the contempt that glittered in her teeth.

"Even now you don't see? You can't follow?"

"Pity him," I said.

"He who takes his own life does an abomination."

For a long moment I considered her. "You don't pity him? You don't pity him at all?"

"Let the world pity me."

"Goodbye," I said to the widow.

"You won't come back?"

I gave what amounted to a little bow of regret.

"I told you you came just for Isaac! But Isaac"—I was in terror of her cough, which was unmistakably laughter—"Isaac disappoints. 'A scholar. A rabbi. A remarkable Jew!' Ha! He disappoints you?"

"He was always an astonishing man."

"But not what you thought," she insisted. "An illusion."

"Only the pitiless are illusory. Go back to that park, Rebbetzin," I advised her.

"And what would you like me to do there? Dance around a tree and call Greek names to the weeds?"

"Your husband's soul is in that park. Consult it." But her low derisive cough accompanied me home: whereupon I remembered her earlier words and dropped three green house plants down the toilet; after a journey of some miles through conduits they straightway entered Trilham's Inlet, where they decayed amid the civic excrement.

Francine Prose

From "Three Pigs in Five Days"

It had never been cold or bitter when Nina was here with Leo. The rain had fallen in warm oily drops and thoughtful cooling showers. But this time, Leo had warned her a few days before she left: "The weather could be beastly. But even if it's freezing and wet, better Paris than here!"

Nina had nodded. Yes, of course. By then she'd spent two weeks on the edge of tears that welled up and spilled over whenever she thought about asking Leo if they were really breaking up. Even if it was freezing and wet, better Paris than here. Nina could hardly disagree with that incon-testable statement. Everyone loved Paris, rain or shine. With Leo or without him.

With Leo or without him. The most idiotic thing would be to let that bogus distinction warp her whole time in Paris. The Luxembourg Gar-dens with Leo vs. the gardens without, boulevards she'd walked with him vs. the same avenues alone, the Mona Lisa smiling at Leo or, less mysteriously, at Nina. The narrow lanes it was best to avoid for fear of suddenly coming upon a bistro she had eaten in with Leo, or had been too nervous to eat in, too busy looking at him. With Leo or without him. How small that difference was compared with other, more major differences. For example, the weather.

The air here had always felt sweet on her skin, even when it was gritty and polluted. But now the rain fell in cold needles, and the damp breath of the stones was the secret slow revenge of all that historic beauty. No one liked being outside, and people got it over with quickly, slipping into doorways as if on secret missions.

Last May Nina kept catching glimpses of the city as it must have looked once—and still looked in Doisneau and Brassaï photos of Paris in the '40s and '50s. Girls in pretty dresses, lovers embracing on the street, *La Vie de Bohème* with a fashion makeover involving nose rings, fishnet, and dreadlocks. But Paris in November seemed much closer to New York: Everyone wore the same winter clothes, the same harried expressions, as if all of them were late for jobs they were already in danger of losing.

Nina wandered for a while, vaguely toward the river. It was not unpleasant except for the problem of not knowing where she was going or how she would know when she got there and could give up and go back to the hotel. Having no destination made her unsure and self-conscious, as if someone were observing all the confusions and worries that showed plainly on her face.

The first time they'd walked in Paris, Leo talked about Rimbaud and the demonic marathon walks that left holes in his shoes and his feet. Nina had known about Rimbaud's walks, but she smiled and let Leo tell her. For all she knew, Leo was planning a walk just as frenzied and manic for them.

Leo was a fast walker, no maps, no red lights, no split-second hesitations; there was never any doubt that he would decide the route they would take. But then he would put his arm around her, and they'd begin to walk very close, their hips and upper thighs rubbing beneath Leo's jeans and Nina's thin dress. Pedestrians moved over. It must have been very clear that Leo and Nina should get off the streets and go directly back to bed.

Nina would visit the Louvre. That was a destination. She imagined telling Leo she'd been to a show of one of his favorite painters, Tintoretto or Carpaccio, the largest canvases, the biggest collection assembled anywhere ever. But wait! The second most idiotic thing would be to fill her time in Paris like an empty sack with glittery things to catch

Leo's interest. What about *her* favorite artists? She'd always liked the French Orientalists: Géricault and Gérôme. But now it seemed depressing to go to the Orsay and stare at pictures of naked Moorish girls being bathed and perfumed for some pasha.

She stopped in front of a window in which exquisite shoes were arranged at angles that made them appear to be taking off or landing. Her eyes tracked to a pair of red suede high heels so elegant and graceful they could afford to flirt with an edge of the cartoonish and the Minnie Mouse.

She and Leo often window-shopped but never really went shopping in Paris. What would be the point? Shopping was about the future: a sweater to wear tomorrow, a bowl in which to put apples at home. But they'd had no reason to want anything beyond the present moment. And of course the future was banned as a subject for thought or discussion.

Did *this* count as shopping: That last trip, they'd gone to a Monoprix for the graph-paper notebooks Leo bought by the dozen. They'd passed racks of dresses and skirts, intriguing French cosmetics, packs of hosiery spouting puffs of beige net and black Lycra. They were walking through the underwear department when Leo stopped and gave Nina a questioning look. And she'd shrugged, embarrassed, but not saying no. Leo wandered off and meditatively browsed the cheap pretty bras and panties.

She watched him from a distance. It was such a tired cliché, guys and their underwear fetish. But Leo's rapt concentration drew her in, and she realized with surprise that his intensity was fixed on her, on her body and what they would do, until gradually her clear view was heated and blurred by desire, and she looked around uneasily to see if strangers were watching.

That was the trouble with sexual drift: Such thoughts could function like radar, sending out loud, deceptive, misreadable signals to the rest of the population. Now, for example, her erotic reverie about Leo seemed to have attracted a man to the shoe store window, a nice-looking guy in a leather jacket who took in the whole window and then—she could see this from the corner of her eye—focused on the red suede shoes she'd been gazing at all this time.

He looked at the shoes, he looked at Nina. At the shoes, at Nina. Was he about to offer to buy her the shoes in return for some sexual service so degrading and baroque that even this handsome Frenchman couldn't get a woman to do it for free?

"*Quels beaux souliers rouges,*" he said.

Nina smiled and nodded as he spoke to her in French. The man who'd brought her breakfast had spoken English, as had Madame Cordier, so this was almost the first French she'd heard, not counting announcements at the airport, the taxi driver who drove her into town, and the TV narrators with their monotonous play-by-plays of happy peasants slaughtering pigs. Nina understood nearly everything people said, but was shy about speaking. Leo's French was fluent, so she always let him talk.

Eventually she realized that the man was saying something about "The Red Shoes," the Hans Christian Andersen story, and then *The Red Shoes*, the Michael Powell film about a ballet based on the Hans Christian Andersen story.

What an amazing coincidence! *The Red Shoes* was Nina's favorite film, that is, the favorite film of her childhood. Nina gasped with surprise, an intake of breath that must have sounded like horror.

She turned and hurried away from him, her heart pounding with shame and regret. Why am I running? Nina thought. Let's be objective here. The guy was better looking than Leo. He liked her favorite childhood movie. (What was it that she had liked so much? The romance? The ballet? Another story, like *Anna Karenina*, about a woman so jacked around by men that the only sensible solution was to fling herself in front of a train?) She and this Frenchman could fall in love. Her whole life could change. He probably had a spacious attractive apartment into which she could move. She could shop in the markets, buy flowers, breads, cheeses . . . and then what? In her luxurious Paris flat, in the gathering dusk, she could pine away for Leo.

Oh, none of this would be happening if she were here with Leo! Passion gave lovers license not to engage with the world as they coasted through it in their little cocoon-made-for-two. But the world lay in wait for them. And as soon as they were alone—on their own—it got them back with a vengeance. It was so risky, being shut off in some little love capsule, losing contact with the truth, losing your faculties, your judgment. It was dangerous, like joining a cult or a fascist army of two.

Crossing the intersection, Nina saw that she had somehow landed directly outside La Coupole. It could have been an accident, or some masochistic homing instinct. She stared into the enclosed porch of the bright café, at morose couples cradling tiny cups and gazing out at the street, and at others who'd chosen to be inside, to be warm and look at each other.

Nina thought of Simone de Beauvoir hanging out in this very café, writing or talking or reading amid a smoky blue haze of ideas, black coffee, and Gauloises. She saw de Beauvoir trying her hardest not to think about Jean-Paul Sartre, off somewhere with a beautiful, much younger, female philosophy student.

This was one of the problems with love! It could narrow your field of vision and limit your intelligence to the point at which you were insulting everyone else's. Imagine, reducing Simone de Beauvoir to a country-and-western torch song, the existentialist Tammy Wynette standing by her Sartre! All right, de Beauvoir's affair with Sartre was a little . . . problematic. But what about her writing? Her books? Her international reputation? Nina thought of Billie Holiday. *Hush now, don't explain.* Those four words, the first line of the existentialist national anthem.

Not long ago, Leo had told Nina that Simone de Beauvoir's grave had become a shrine for young French feminists who left flowers and handwritten notes on her tomb, asking her for advice and favors. Maybe that's what Nina should do. Go search for Simone de Beauvoir's grave. She was in the mood for something like that, some pilgrimage or symbolic act or oracular consultation. But she couldn't imagine what she would write in a note to leave on Simone de Beauvoir's grave. *Please send Leo back to me.* Nina would be ashamed! She'd always thought of herself as a feminist. It was something a woman just naturally was, if she had any brains. But what kind of feminist was Nina, unable to think of anything to ask this saint of women's rights except to intervene and, please, oh please, make her boyfriend love her again? De Beauvoir would have understood. She knew all about patience, about men who disappeared, about waiting for them, believing in them . . . outlasting the competition.

Nina walked into the café and ordered black coffee to keep up the buzz from the coffee she'd drunk with Madame Cordier. Several times this morning she'd had to pause on her walk while a frolicky hiccough interrupted her heartbeat. She hoped it was a caffeine overdose and didn't mean that she was dying.

Nina eased off her coat and looked around, but got no farther than a young couple nearby who were causing quite a scene. A pale girl in black with orange hair and dark roots shouldered a video camera trained on her Arab boyfriend. As she talked into the microphone, Nina understood her so easily that for a moment she thought her French had improved until she realized that the girl was American, speaking English.

"Tuesday morning," she said. "Eleven A.M. Achmed is eating breakfast. Achmed has ordered coffee. He's about to take his first sip. Let's go in for a close-up. Monsieur Achmed, please. Look at the camera."

Achmed raised one weary shoulder and half-hid his regal face, slouching down in his chair till his long legs reached across the aisle and under the next empty table. Nina was openly staring now, but Achmed didn't return her gaze, though he was aware of her watching. His lidded eyes were like half-lowered shades covering the windows while the house's owner waited inside for guests to arrive and adore him.

Of all the people in Paris these two had been ordered up and sent here expressly for Nina. This girl on her junior year abroad videotaping her boyfriend reminded Nina of herself, taking notes on Hemingway's sink and Oscar Wilde's bathtub. After Achmed was long gone, the poor girl could watch the tape, just as Nina—at especially self-tormenting moments—could reread her piece on historic hotels in a back issue of *Allo!*

Simone de Beauvoir, Billie Holiday, and now this girl in the café. Next it would be Jean Seberg, Héloïse, Maria Callas, Piaf, every woman who'd ever gotten famous for suffering over men. But wasn't it always like that? The world showed you what you were looking for, what you were tuned in to see. Once Nina had had a redheaded boyfriend, and for that time and long after, she was shocked to find the streets of New York crowded—teeming—with redheads. This morning a man with copper-colored hair had brought her coffee. But it was no longer a message, just the color of someone's hair.

Nina signaled for the check. Wait. She didn't have French francs. Her legs went weak, even after she recalled that she'd changed fifty dollars at the airport. What did she think they would do to her if she didn't have cash? Surely the café took credit cards. Probably traveler's checks, too.

She paid the bill, left the café, and walked on with no idea where she was going and only intermittent clues about where she actually was. She wandered into crooked lanes lined with yellow restaurant signs and placards picturing platters of couscous or glossy Vietnamese stir-fry, a deserted side street of dusty shops with vintage printing presses, a block of bland concrete apartment houses. At last she rounded a corner and found herself in the place de la Contrescarpe.

Getting her bearings encouraged her, as did the lovely square. Hey, this wasn't so bad—being in Paris by herself without a care in the world! And let's hear it for magical thinking! Once more, it was as if her thoughts affected her surroundings, as if the improvement in her mood had managed to conjure up this curving street of bookstores, this shop window full of glossy volumes on Flemish painting, these bins of wispy botanical drawings in crackling cellophane slips. The rain had stopped. From time to time there were even coy hints that the sun might break through.

Nina walked on and got lost again and at last had a panicky moment when she came out of a dark narrow street and into an open square and looked up and saw the Eiffel Tower looming above her like Godzilla. All right! She knew where she was now! Not where she wanted to be! In the wrong direction completely and much farther than she'd intended.

But what was she so scared of? At any point she could find the nearest metro station and take the subway back to the hotel. What stop *was* nearest the hotel? That was something Leo would know, one of the many travel facts he would have on file in his mind. Probably he would also know where exactly the hotel was. *This* was scary, Nina saw now, how quickly one could surrender charge of the most basic information.

Once she'd got lost with Leo. Even Leo was lost. They'd come out on a grimy boulevard jammed with buses emitting black smoke. Leo sent her to look at the street sign, and when she came back and told him the name, he gritted his teeth and snapped, "Spell it!"

An elderly gentleman stopped and helped them, a pleasant man who seemed to Nina still to be living in Paris in the '50s, a city of lovers so wrapped up in each other they often wound up lost and had to be set back on course. He beamed and warmly grasped Leo's elbow, and soon Leo and Nina forgot their quarrel and were grinning at each other and at the old man, whom they kept turning around to wave at.

Now, reaching a corner, Nina looked down a street of pale dignified houses. It was the neighborhood—the street—on which she'd stayed with Leo. Halfway down that block was the hotel in which Edith Wharton entertained Morton Fullerton while waiting for the plasterers and parquet-polishers and stained-glass installers to finish work on her home. Now the hotel seemed magnetic, drawing Nina to it. And for what? To gaze in at the lobby with a lump in her throat?

Nina remembered Leo pointing down the street and noting that the Rodin Museum was just a few blocks over. He said they had to go there, but they hadn't gone anywhere. They'd stayed in their room and joked about Nina writing a piece for which she didn't have to get out of bed. They never went outside—not once—except to move to the next hotel. So the neighborhood was harmless enough if Nina steered clear of that one building.

She would go to the Rodin Museum. And she would try, she would really try not to get suckered into thinking about the tragic life and death of Camille Claudel.

Leo loved the story of Camille Claudel having been Rodin's student, his mistress, then his colleague, a gifted sculptor, then going mad because he wouldn't leave his wife. Just before they put her away in the mental ward forever, she destroyed her own work, trashed her entire studio and her most brilliant sculptures.

Nina liked the story considerably less than Leo did, yet now the thought of Camille Claudel made Nina feel reassuringly in control. She was still a long way from going certifiably insane over Leo! Were there Claudels in the Rodin Museum? Nina couldn't remember. But she wanted to find out. It was similar to, but better than, a pilgrimage to Simone de Beauvoir's grave. If this was what Paris was giving her, Nina might as well be gracious and take it. De Beauvoir, Claudel, Madame Cordier, Achmed's girlfriend, Nina—sisters under the skin, in this city of women who love too much, Paris, city of broken hearts!

She walked around the block to avoid the Edith Wharton hotel and was afraid she was lost again when she took a turn—the wrong one, surely—and found herself alongside the smooth cement wall that bordered Rodin's gardens. This experience of being lost and lost and then suddenly found had happened to her in Venice but never before in Paris.

Somehow she'd found the Rodin Museum! But the heavy doors were half shut. The ticket booth was empty. Was the museum closed? Nina might have turned away, but at that moment a chill autumn sun burst through the clouds, which (thinking magically, again) she took as a message of personal encouragement.

Several people were in the garden, too far away for Nina to see if they were museumgoers or workers. On the opposite side of the building was the famous statue of Balzac in his voluminous robe, staggering beneath the prodigious weight of his own genitalia. From a sagging rope connecting two trees hung scallops of tri-color bunting and a banner announcing the hundred and fiftieth *anniversaire* of the *naissance* of Auguste Rodin.

Nina ventured up the walk between the plane trees, up the steps, through the doors, and into the huge foyer. The wintry light streaming onto the parquet floors and the scrolling staircase was refracted at crisp brilliant angles by the antique glass in the tall windows.

A young man was sitting at a desk. After a while he looked up. He was desolated to tell Nina that the museum was *fermé*.

"*Pourquoi?*" said Nina.

"*Une fête,*" he explained. "*L'anniversaire de l'artiste.*"

"Ah, *oui! D'accord!*" said Nina. She felt she should seem more happy about the great sculptor's birthday than disappointed for her own selfish reasons, being shut out of the museum. But why hadn't they posted a sign outside or closed the gate completely? Why had they lured her in so this young man could reject her in person?

Just then a door opened, and an elderly woman ran out and shook Nina's hand.

"Welcome! Welcome! *Enchantée!*"

Obviously, she was mistaking Nina for someone else. But in the rush of the moment Nina couldn't say so. First there was the challenge of putting it in French. And something about the woman's age made Nina hesitant, lest the woman assume her mistake was a sign of decrepitude and decline. Or was Nina the decrepit one? Her own self-doubt was so intense that for a moment she wondered: Maybe they *did* know each other, and Nina had just forgotten. Lately she often found herself greeting strangers warmly or failing to recognize people who seemed to have known her for years. She often believed and trusted the other person more than she trusted herself, and had had many friendly bewildered chats on the phone before the caller inquired if she might like to sit on his face. All this had set her up for Leo's telling her what to think, all the more so because she thought of herself as having a mind of her own.

"*Je suis Madame Arlette Martin,*" the old woman said.

Nina smiled and inclined her head. There was no need for her to say her name—that is, whatever name was supposed to be hers.

Madame Martin addressed the young man in French, too fast for Nina to catch it. Like Madame Cordier, the old woman was wearing a suit, but hers was a severe dark blue. A tiny medal winked from her right lapel. Another little sparrow, the same species as Madame Cordier, a different breed from the peasant women who slaughtered the nightly pig.

A silk paisley scarf was tucked artfully under the collar of her jacket. Her penciled eyebrows were sketched in with a feathery hint of surprise repeated in the bright blue eyes that widened as she said, "*Parlez-vous français?*"

"*Je comprends,*" said Nina. "*Mais je ne parle pas.*"

Madame Martin smiled ruefully. She understood why Nina might not want to speak: shyness combined with an understandable respect for the beauties of the French language.

"*Je suis désolée! Je ne parle pas anglais.*" Well then, it was settled. She could just speak French to Nina and not have to listen to what Nina said.

And Nina might not have to reveal that she wasn't whoever this woman thought. Because by now Madame Martin had taken Nina's coat and they were rapidly passing the point at which Nina could gracefully bail out. And what if she didn't? At parties, everyone pretended to recognize people they couldn't place and watched helplessly as the last moment for a confession sped by. Obviously, whomever Nina had been mistaken for was entitled to be welcomed and given a private tour of the museum that was closed to Nina. And as Leo used to say: Whom was it going to hurt?

Had Nina had a good flight? Madame Martin began in a French that sounded as if she herself were learning it phonetically.

"*Oui*," said Nina. "*Très confortable.*"

Madame touched her heart and said, It is his birthday. Already her speech had been slightly sped up by an influx of emotion.

It occurred to Nina that she could write a piece for *Allo!* on the centenary and a half of August Rodin's birth. *Allo!* readers adored that sort of thing, invitations to make their own pilgrimages to honor the first appearance or demise of romantic cultural figures.

Madame Martin stepped back so Nina could precede her into the museum. And now it was definitely too late to find out who she thought Nina was. Probably some American art historian or curator or writer. Writer? Had Leo alerted her, too? Relax, Nina reminded herself. He couldn't have known she'd come here.

Nina drifted into a gleaming salon, then stopped so abruptly that the old woman almost stepped on her heels and gave a stifled yelp of alarm. A moment later, Nina paused before a marble sculpture of a crouched woman, leaning forward, spilling her long hair onto a rock. Her white marble back was smoother than skin. The hollows at the base of her spine made Nina's hand ache to touch them.

Last summer, Nina rode up in the elevator at *Allo!* with a man who had a beautiful tattoo, an elaborate apple tree dropping an apple that reappeared twice as it rolled down the length of his suntanned arm. Nina could hardly stop herself from reaching out to press the apple with the tip of her finger. The man wore black short shorts, a leather cap, a leather lace-up vest. He probably wouldn't have minded. Leo would have misunderstood; he would have thought her wanting to touch the man's arm was about sex. But it was more about childhood, when the world had a sexual buzz, the air, the sun, the bees, earthworms, dogshit, and you wanted to touch it all, before you learned that you shouldn't.

An old girlfriend of Leo's had joined a cult and now wrote him letters saying that she was experiencing nonstop sex with plants and rocks and trees. Leo told Nina, and they'd had a good laugh about that. They knew what real sex was. It wasn't about vibrations from rocks or about the vegetable kingdom. Nor was it those women shrieking behind every French hotel room door!

He loved women, someone said in French. Madame Martin had come up behind Nina.

Madame spoke faster and faster, and soon Nina was losing crucial connectives. Sometimes she would follow whole sentences and then miss one critical word. What made it even harder was the talking and stopping, talking and stopping, the peculiar rhythms of speech while walking through a museum. Half the time Nina's back was turned as she moved from one work to another, in this case from naked body to naked body or group of naked bodies, lovely smooth athletic torsos, one sex sculpture after another, here a couple embracing, tipped back on their knees, his face buried in her breast, there a young man with his robe open to just above his groin.

The gist of what Madame Martin was saying was what a genius Rodin was, his work was entirely original, entirely new, like the cave paintings at Lascaux, like the Renaissance, Leonardo. Never in art history did the human body have the life that Rodin gave it. How sad it was, how long it took for the world to recognize his gifts. First they accused him of casting from life, and then called his work obscene. Madame threw up her hands and shrugged. Then she said something Nina didn't quite get, something about people, Paris, rumors accusing Rodin of being Nijinsky's lover. . . . Was Rodin Nijinsky's lover? The next few sentences streamed past in a current that Nina could only observe until the word *Rilke* leaped out like a gleaming silver trout.

"Yes, Rilke!" Nina said. *"Son secrétaire."*

You didn't have to be a psychologist to understand that Madame Martin was madly in love with Rodin. Well, who wouldn't adore this genius who so worshiped the female body? There were photographs on the walls that Nina and Madame Martin studied together: Rodin, incredibly handsome at every stage of his life.

In one photo he sat on a park bench. He'd grown stout and looked very much the Artist in his bushy white beard, long morning coat, and straw hat. He was sketching a Thai or Cambodian dancer, a lovely girl of about eleven, in costume, with her toes turned out, her delicate hands curled like temple spires. In the background, two policemen looked on, fascinated. Leo would have loved this photo with its graphic representation of Eros on the periphery of the domain of Law and Order.

It was sad, Madame Martin was saying. Fame ignored Rodin in his youth; old age cut him down in his prime. His mind went, he was not himself, and just before his death he finally married Rose Beuret, who had been his mistress for forty years and bore him a son, and in the beginning wet down his maquettes so that the clay wouldn't harden. Madame Martin doused one of the sculptures with imaginary water: a naked woman crouched like a cat on the chest of a naked man.

"Madame Rodin," Nina said. "*Sa femme. Après quarante ans.*"

Was Nina's French so unintelligible? The old woman looked bewildered. At last, she nodded vigorously. Ah, yes, Madame Rodin, the old shoe worn for forty years and married mostly for comfort, the good fit of the broken-in. Madame Rodin posed no threat; she was no one Madame Martin had to contend with.

They reached a group of figures in bronze, and perhaps Nina already knew whose work it was because she leaned over and checked the caption though she hadn't, with the others. Of course, it was Camille Claudel's, this trio of tragic figures, a man trudging forward, suffering, refusing to be consoled or dissuaded, though a nude kneeling woman pulled at his arm, begging him to stay. He forged onward into the protective and smothering embrace of a monstrous old hag with wings, a witch pretending to be an angel.

Maturity, the piece was called.

"Give me a break," said Nina.

"*Pardon?*" said Madame Martin.

The sculpture was technically excellent. But not nearly so good, not half so good as the worst piece by Rodin. But of course. His work was all about sex, and this one was all about grief. Who would choose this sculpture over a Rodin, except perhaps for a melancholic, suicidal adolescent?

But that was unfair to Camille Claudel! Her life was so much harder than Rodin's, as she progressed through the frustrating stages from student to apprentice to famous artist's mistress. A childish voice whined in Nina's head: At least she had Rodin! Nina remembered Leo saying how they'd found Claudel in her studio standing amid the shards of clay and chunks of broken marble. Maybe she overlooked this sculpture or wanted it to survive: her wrenching transparent comment on losing Rodin to his wife.

"*C'est triste,*" Madame Martin said.

"*Oui, c'est triste,*" said Nina. And now she felt bitterly sorry for poor

Camille Claudel, dead and buried in the ground while they patronized her with their pity, Nina and this old woman who loved Rodin herself and was secretly glad that her major rival was out of the way for good. Wasn't this just another version of the jealous unspoken competition that had made for such a lively breakfast this morning with Madame Cordier?

As if Claudel's grief were contagious, Nina felt tired and chilled, and her guide wasn't nearly so frisky as she'd been a short while before. But then Madame Martin had a happy idea.

"*Venez, venez,*" she said. Nina trotted after her, outside, across the garden and into an adjacent building.

"*Son atelier,*" Madame announced, and now it was Nina who touched her heart.

"His studio," she translated for herself.

"*Oui,*" said Madame Martin.

Elegant track lighting spotlit selected parts of a long dark room with a central island partitioned into segments—not unlike a salad bar. But this salad bar held clay body parts, thousands of thumb-sized legs, knees, shoulders, tiny forearms and tinier noses. They reminded Nina of *milagros*, those silver cutouts of feet, heads, and eyes that, in Latin countries, the faithful left on their altars to let the saints know which organs were in need of miraculous cures. In his office Leo had a giant wooden cross encrusted with *milagros*—practically his favorite possession. He said one reason he loved it was because he was Jewish. But unlike *milagros*, those icons of damage and disease, these arms and legs were healthy. In fact they were in motion, wriggling around in their cases, seeking their lost living bodies.

"*Toujours, toujours,*" said Madame Martin. She held out her hand and flexed her fingers as if kneading clay, and she and Nina stood there watching her knead the air. Always Rodin had clay in his hand, always he was making something: a body out of nothing.

Nina walked along the cases and stopped at a tray of breasts, the shape and size of gooseberries, walnuts, grapes, or cherries, each one different from the next, every one of them pretty. The old woman noticed where Nina had stopped.

He loved the body, she said.

And now she was nearing a part of her story that she so much wanted Nina to hear that for the first time she acknowledged that Nina might not be following every word. She slowed down and repeated everything several different ways.

It seemed that Rodin often made love to his models in his studio. And when he did, he put a sign on his door that said: ABSENT, VISITING CATHEDRALS.

She looked at Nina, expectantly.

"*Quel homme,*" said Nina, shaking her head.

"*Quel homme,*" Madame Martin agreed.

Still speaking deliberately, she made sure Nina understood that cathedrals were important to Rodin. He wrote a book on cathedrals, he believed that the body was a cathedral, that the great cathedrals were constructed on the principles of the body.

Absent. Visiting Cathedrals. Whose heart wouldn't be won forever? Still, Nina wondered sourly if he had one Absent, Visiting Cathedrals sign that he recycled for different women, or if he bothered making a new sign for each new model he made love to, or if by that point Rodin and his model were in such a fever of desire that she preferred him to use an old sign rather than take time to scribble a new one.

"*Venez,*" the old woman said, and graced Nina with a puckish grin. She groped along a dark wall.

"*Et voilà!*" she exclaimed. She pushed a button, and a hidden door in the wall swung open. Then she ushered Nina into a long narrow room, surgically clean and bare but for a row of sliding compartments on each side and perpendicular to each wall.

Madame Martin slid out a heavy vertical flat. Nina started to help her, but Madame waved her away. Nina stepped up to look at the sketch on the flat, a drawing in soft pencil of a masturbating woman, shown only from the tops of her breasts to the middle of her thighs, her long torso arched diagonally across the heavy paper.

"Oh, my goodness!" said Nina.

"*C'est beau, non?*" said Madame Martin.

"*C'est beau. Oui,*" Nina said.

Why had the old woman brought her here? Why was she showing this to Nina? Or really, to whomever she thought Nina was? That probably explained it. She had mistaken Nina for some curator who warranted the cellar-to-attic tour: the sculptures, the photos, the atelier, and now the dirty pictures.

Nina had known these drawings were here. In fact she'd been thinking about them—expecting to see them—when Madame Martin opened the door in the wall. Leo had spoken of Rodin's erotic drawings locked away in the museum. Maybe he'd even mentioned it when he'd pointed out the museum from a distance. And now Nina was getting to see them. Wait till she told Leo!

The old woman stood on her toes and strained as she pulled out the flats, each of which contained one drawing: women on their backs with their legs spread, their hands behind their heads, two naked women, face-to-face, one on the other's lap.

It could hardly have been weirder, being here in total silence except for the creaking of the flats, with this genteel, proper Frenchwoman and these intensely erotic drawings. The only way to deal with it was to have the out-of-body experience that was learned behavior for looking at art in museums. Asexual, clinically detached, like going to the doctor's. As if the naked people on canvas weren't naked people, as if what Rodin put on paper had had nothing to do with sex. Nina and Leo used to talk about this. What was wrong with those poor critics and art historians who had such a stake in denying that certain artists loved the body? Some problem with *their* own bodies, perhaps? No problem with Leo's and Nina's!

The drawings were spectacular, and again there was no mistaking that the man who had drawn them was madly in love with every curve and fold, every inch of the flesh that he so tenderly translated from three dimensions into two. Probably there were critics who saw the story of Camille Claudel as the case history of a misogynist: clinical evidence that Rodin secretly hated women. Let them take a good look at these drawings and see if they still believed that! But no doubt they'd already seen them and remained unpersuaded.

Given the drawings' subject matter, it was not at all surprising when Madame Martin reverted to her dearest subject: how much Rodin loved the body. He wanted to be God, she said, making Adam and Eve out of clay.

Gradually, Nina understood what Madame Martin was doing: She was showing Nina what she had, how much she'd been given to live with. Like a house-proud wife or widow taking guests on tour of her magnificent home: Look at what my man bought for me, look at what he left me. As if Rodin had meant these drawings for Madame Martin to hoard in this museum. Not for Camille Claudel, not for his wife—and certainly not for Nina. He'd done all this for Madame Martin to cherish and use as she pleased.

Finally they rolled back the last flat. They both felt a little drained. Madame Martin walked Nina out through the atelier and back onto the wide path lined with plane trees. She invited her to stroll through the gardens, spend as long as she liked, go through the museum again if she needed more for her essay.

Her essay! Nina nodded. She could agree to that—with genuine conviction and an easy conscience. She would write an essay for *Allo!* But not the essay Madame meant. She could hardly tell *Allo!* readers about the erotic drawings, fill their heads with envious dreams of what they would never see. She thanked Madame Martin, who smiled briskly and gave her head a sparrowlike shake and mimed that she was shivering and hurried back indoors.

Nina had gotten away with it. She'd been taken around the museum without being found out as someone other than the person whom she was supposed to be.

A moment later Madame Martin reappeared. Nina's heart skipped a beat, assisted by the black coffee and the fear that the woman she'd been mistaken for had arrived in their absence, or else a phone call had come in, and Nina's game was up.

But Madame Martin had merely remembered that she still had Nina's coat. She ran, with the coat stretched across her arms, the way war victims on the TV news ran with wounded children. Nina hurried toward her, to spare her a trip across the garden. It was all very awkward, getting her coat back. Nina thanked her even more warmly. They said good-bye several times more.

Nina felt as if she were being watched by someone who might be offended if she turned and left. She walked beneath a bare pergola down the length of the garden. The lawns and flower beds were undergoing major excavation. Huge areas were dug up and roped off with neon-orange plastic net, and the ripe smell of sewers and wet cement hung thickly in the air. Shouldn't they have finished before the sculptor's birthday? They'd be done by spring or summer, when the tourists came back.

After a decent interval, Nina left the grounds and returned to the deserted street. She looked around. Where to? What now? Leo would know where to go.

But what made Leo so special? Who was Leo compared with Rodin? And what was sleeping with Leo beside what she'd just experienced, the orgy she'd taken part in, the lustful entwining of bodies and limbs that Rodin set in motion: ecstatic, blissful, unsatisfied still, all these years after his death?

Thane Rosenbaum

"Romancing the *Yohrzeit* Light"

The sizzle from an ignited match always revived the same memory.

With her face bathed softly in light, Esther would rotate the fire with two steady, benevolent hands, blessing the end of yet another week, and the beginning of Shabbat.

She was a short woman, with dark hair and light skin. He remembered how her small frame appeared to be a liability before each Friday night benediction. But she was resourceful, a survivor of the Holocaust; a tall table and long candles were no match for her. She would prop herself on her toes for the actual kindling, then drop down again.

Pressing her palms gently over her closed eyelids, she would then entrust the soul with the task of sight. A beige, embroidered veil, which had concealed her features, by now was raised and folded over her hair. She would stare off into some dark, spiritual galaxy. Her lips trembled, and from her mouth came a melody of ancient Hebrew hymns, delivered in a faint, garbled whisper, so that even God would have trouble hearing.

Then, with eyes still closed, she would cast out her arms in some confused abandon, the performance of some modified breaststroke that brought the flames closer together. The lights from the candles would dance joyously on her face, shining upon her in some angelic way, transcending the mere commencement of the Sabbath.

All this, and the haunting vision of the memory it produced, caused a deep lament in Adam on the first anniversary of his mother's death. The mettle of a loving son was about to be measured by the flick of his own wrist, as the faithful alchemy of fire and wax passed on to the next generation.

By Jewish law, each year, on the same day that she died, he was required to light one candle in her memory. The *yohrzeit*, Jews call it. It was to be no ordinary candle, either, but rather one capable of burning for twenty-four hours without interruption.

Despite his deep affection for his mother, Adam was bereft of her spiritual wisdom; he had inherited none of Esther's ability to commune with Friday's flames. On the day marking Esther's first *yohrzeit*, it became sadly apparent how the obligations and rituals of his faith competed—all too unsuccessfully—against the blasphemy to which he had grown accustomed.

Adam's relationship with his mother had never been easy when she was alive; now, after her death, her candle wasn't about to cooperate, either.

At first he wasn't sure about the correct date on which this all was to take place. According to the Christian calendar, Esther had died on October 16, but for Jews there was some altogether different configuration of sun and moon that fashioned the days and months of the year. The Hebrew date was bound to be different, perhaps by a week or maybe more—in any direction, no less. Adam was at a complete loss as to how to arrive at some symmetry between these competing calendars. In the absence of user-friendly conversion charts, he simply resigned himself to performing his rite of Jewish remembrance according to the only days of the year that he knew.

As midnight approached on October 16, Adam frantically realized that he did not own a *yohrzeit* candle.

"Just great," he muttered, flipping through a kitchen drawer filled with wires, playing cards, and assorted rubber bands. "I've got these birthday candles, but they won't last for a whole day, even if I stand here and light them one at a time," he thought.

He eyed a cupboard that had been relegated to storing the odds and ends that never got used in his life, or art. Standing on the counter like a child searching for an advance on the evening's cookie allowance, he found a long, opaque cylinder filled with equal layers of kaleidoscopic wax—the kind of mood maker that might service a temporary power outage quite well.

"This might last for a whole day," he said quizzically, "but I need something that rabbis would approve of—something with a kosher U on it, or a circle with a pig's face exxed out right on the front. What else is in here?" He fumbled nervously with all sorts of unmeltable objects, slamming cabinets and clanging anything that happened to get in his way.

But the candles were the least of his problems. He lived among so many unkosher influences both in and out of his apartment, that the lighting of the *yohrzeit* candle—albeit a solid gesture and a good beginning—would not have redressed the multitude of sins he committed daily. He could no longer be redeemed. After a lifetime of going too far it wasn't even clear whether his god, or his people, even wanted him back.

Esther had raised him in an Americanized kosher home—observance within the threshold, nutritional anarchy outside. But he had slackened the already compromised routine well beyond the acceptable limits. He ate all manner of spineless fish, and the commingled flesh of unhoofed animals. His hot dogs didn't answer to a higher authority other than his own whim of which sidewalk peddler to patronize.

His neighborhood on the Upper West Side was filled with synagogues, but Adam acted as though they were virtual leper colonies—cursed concrete structures set in between the familiar brownstones, to be avoided at all cost. He never celebrated Rosh Hashanah (actually, he couldn't tell you exactly what time of the year it even was). During the fall, when fashionably dressed Jewish families all over Manhattan rushed to services, Adam blankly assumed the coincidence of various nearby, midweek weddings. Instead, he welcomed the New Year on January 1, in Central Park at the stroke of twelve, jogging soberly in the Midnight Run, his body aglow under mushroom clouds of bursting fireworks.

Recently he had fallen in love with yet another in an unending series of Gentile women. All were very beautiful, taller than Adam, and from parts of the world that he had never visited. The conversations were brief, the relationships even shorter. Misbegotten romances guided by primal, rather than tribal, considerations.

If Adam's taste in women wanted to conform to the preferences of his people—or the hopes of his mother—a nice Jewish girl could easily have been found; but it wasn't as though Jewish girls were much interested in him, either. They looked upon him as though he were a *sheygets*, often surprised to learn that he was Jewish at all.

Adam had the rugged look of a Nordic caveman. To locate the physical attributes of *his* species, he would have had more luck at the Museum of Natural History than any other place on the West Side. For one thing, his arms were well out of proportion with the rest of his body. They were long, and seemed to hang down to the ground from his five-eight frame. He had long blond hair that was thick and uncombed, and a grayish beard that couldn't decide what purpose to play on his face. His eyes were large and blue, overwhelming a pair of round, small-framed glasses that looked as though he had just picked them off the street. His nose was small and impractical. Generally speaking, a far cry from the more typical Hebrew violinist or plastic surgeon.

What's more, professionally, he was a painter—an abstract expressionist, no less. Although he was a successful downtown artist, represented by one of the more tony Soho galleries, that was not quite enough for the Daughters of Jerusalem. Naturally, they would want a more stable lifestyle, seeking the comforts of a West End Avenue co-op, a summer house on the Island, and a standing smoked fish order from Zabar's.

Gentile women from foreign countries, on the other hand, appreciated something in Adam that the women of his own tribe had missed. Adam had that threatening, reckless quality that draws people to New York in the first place. He lived on the top floor of a five-floor walk-up, with no doorman. He rode a motorcycle. His fingernails were polished with either black greasepaint or some other dark acrylic. His hands perpetually smelled as though they had just been lathered in turpentine.

Adam offered himself to these women as their first great American fling; a nice way to be introduced to the mania of New York. After that, they would be gone, and he would be in search of still another romantic traveler.

Now there was Tasha Haglund, newly arrived from Malmö and working in New York as a fashion model for the Ford Agency. The first time he met her Adam felt that something was different—not just in her, but in him as well. The setting itself was a change of pace. It wasn't at one of those phantom Manhattan parties, arranged by the roving downtown elite. Adam knew them well, the kind of inbred gathering that would be suffocating to anyone except those with the airy ambitions of the casually hip. Tasha he met at Barnes & Noble, uptown. She was reading Günter Grass; he was staring at compositions in a book that contained the paintings of Anselm Kiefer.

"I very much like Kiefer," she said, as a way of introduction. Adam had been sitting on the floor; Tasha kneeled down beside him. "I saw one of his shows in Berlin. His paintings are so filled with modern despair. What do you think?"

He couldn't think. Who was she? Where does such a person come from? She was a typical-looking Swede: the blond hair, the blue eyes, the robust smile, the velvety skin tone. Modeling agencies scout these women zealously, then import them to America like ski equipment.

But here again Tasha was different. In a curious way, she looked a little like Adam; their hair and skin color almost matched, although Adam was always in a need of a shampoo and a shave. She even had long arms, just like his.

"I miss home. I feel lost in New York."

"So do I."

"But isn't this where you are from?"

Hopelessly aware of Adam's fidelity to a certain species of flesh, Esther never hesitated to offer her own wishes for his romantic future. "You need to find someone who knows who you are and understands where you come from."

"I think it's a little late for that, don't you think?" he would say, not very reassuringly. "I'm not even sure who I am, or where I come from."

Whenever speaking with Esther about such matters, he always tried to paint right through the experience. At that moment in the conversation, he was splashing paint around liberally, embellishing a pulverized Coke can that he had tarred right onto the canvas.

"*Ach*, ever since your father died—one rebellion after another. Running away from who you are. Pretending to be someone else. Who do you think you are fooling?"

"Pretty much everybody but you. You're a tough one."

"I didn't survive the camps so you could walk around looking and acting like a camp guard. Look at you. Nothing Jewish that I can see."

"We've talked about this enough. I can't change. I can't be who you want. You want to live through me. You'll need to find someone else."

"Thank God your father has been dead all these years—because *this*," she said, raising an open palm up and down, "would have killed him." She then sighed, and watched paint splatter and suffuse with other materials. Her manic son was now sweating, the veins in his wrist pulsing, the rhythm of each stroke urgent—threatening to knock the entire canvas over.

An hour before midnight. Cabs roamed the near-empty avenues, searching for fares. A few homeless men were bickering on the corner. Spanish music pounded against a closed window, muffled but still able to be heard from the street.

Adam feared that his break from his people and his infidelity to Esther's memory were about to be tested once more. But where could he find an official *yohrzeit* candle at this late hour? Regretably, even in New York, there are no all-night Judaica convenience shops for the modern Jew on the run.

Hurriedly, he grabbed his coat and left the apartment in search of a *yohrzeit* candle. It was a chilly, luminous Manhattan night. Checkerboard windows, hanging from a brick-infested sky, signed on and off, revealing the habits of those who slept within. A cascade of unseasonable snowflakes gradually made their way down to the side streets. Adam lifted his collar and turned the corner, heading toward the Korean market on Broadway and Eighty-fifth Street. Perhaps a convenience store that housed all that emergency juice, milk, and eggs might also carry the essentials for the neglectful Jew.

As he approached the man working the counter—a short, hunched-over fellow with a round face—Adam wondered whether there was a Korean word for *yohrzeit*, something that would make his improbable request somewhat easier to reject. He inched closer to the man, as though he was going to drop the word right into his ear, not wanting anything to get lost in transmission.

"Do you have any *yohrzeit* candles?"

The man, standing behind a display of Snickers bars, blondies, and sugarless chewing gum, was guarding a computerized cash register. An elderly woman was in the back, sorting through a display of cat food. A reward for her pet, the one other breathing entity in her apartment that separated her from virtual isolation.

Much to Adam's surprise, the Korean on the late shift nodded effusively, as if some common language had been discovered. He walked out from behind the counter, grabbed hold of Adam's arm and escorted him past the tofu and the yucca, over to a shelf brimming with crackers and low-fat oatmeal cookies. At the very bottom of the shelf, seemingly tiny and humbled, and arranged neatly so as not to offend, stood a few wax-filled glasses—a wick in each, secured to the bottom by a metal clasp. A cheap gummy label was stamped decorously right on the front of each one, bearing the reverential Hebrew word YOHRZEIT.

"Wow, you have a lot of them, I see," Adam exclaimed.

The Korean, this time less enthusiastically, nodded once more.

"A lot of dead Jews around here, I guess, or just their relatives."

The Korean agreed, just as a large cat emerged from the end of the aisle.

Adam paid for the candle and left, thinking that he should have bought more—for next year, and the year after that, perhaps. But this was his first voyage of remembrance. No need to stockpile, at least not just yet. The experience might prove too painful. He could end up feeling foolish, or worse, more empty than usual. It was just a candle, after all. Wasn't there some other way to honor the dead, something that might—at the same time—help him find his way own way back, too?

With only minutes to spare before midnight, he stood in front of the dinner table, which was flush against the window, facing the back of a ten-story apartment building. Late-night neighbors, taking a break from *Letterman*, could see Adam slicing away at the side panel of a matchbox, with no result. With each thrust of his hand, his frustration grew.

"Come on, come on," he implored, as though trying to reason with this souvenir from Indochine.

One wooden match after another struck the flinted side panel, and then split in two. Finally, one match crackled and sustained a blaze, then suffocated in his hand. The next attempt took hold and remained steady, but the wick to the *yohrzeit* candle, although surrounded by the flame, refused the offering. The *yohrzeit* would not light.

"Ouch!" The flame consumed the match and reached Adam's fingers.

"Am I going to need a torch for this thing?"

But then, on the very next try, all the elements for mourning cooperated—the match lit, the *yohrzeit* relented.

"Thank God." He sighed, exhausted and now nervously giddy.

With the flame now in front of him, he stared at its inaugural motions. "What now?" he thought. "Do I just stand around for twenty-four hours?"

Adam didn't know the prayers; the kaddish remained a mystery, like a foreign language. The Hebrew vowels and consonants just wouldn't come. He may have once known them, but no longer. Lost somewhere in some cavern of memory.

The candle, though bright, did not shine on Adam in the way he had remembered similar flames gravitating toward Esther. He checked his reflection in the window for some comforting radiance; all that he saw was a sketch of his own facial shadow, giving forth a quizzical, somber look. There was an uneasy silence in the room. He continued to search his memory for some Hebrew, any Hebrew—even a nice happy Hanukkah song would do in that moment of sanctified, stupefied remembrance.

The room was dark except for the candle, which cast a playful shadow against the wall. The flame seemed to dance. A *yohrzeit* with a sense of humor.

After Esther's death, Adam had lapsed into an ungovernable depression. The world around him seemed more dark and lifeless than usual. His art began to reflect these feelings, becoming even more spasmodic; the angry expressionistic images choking the canvas, and each other. The canvases themselves took on more monstrous apocalyptic shapes and physical dimensions. Some he couldn't even get out of his studio the usual way—through the elevator or main door. They had to be lowered from the window of his downtown loft. And the representational images, well . . . they depicted burnings, famines, sicknesses, nightmares—devastations of one sort or another. The urban litter that he normally assimilated into his paintings acquired a more raw and violent form—a selection that better reflected the madness of New York. Crack vials, used condoms, a doll missing its arms, a discarded pair of underwear.

Sheinman, his gallery dealer, always said about Adam's work, "What is it with you and garbage? What do you have against throwing things out? Don't get me wrong, I love the commissions, but why not try using just paint next time?"

Esther used to put it another way: "Why not paint something Jewish,

Adam? If you're not going to be a doctor or a lawyer, at least let me have a Chagall for a son."

"I can't paint a cow upside down, Mom," Adam would reply. "It's just not what I do. I know nothing about the shtetls. Never been to that part of the world. Don't really care to go."

"So paint me a nice Posner window, then," she would say, with a sigh, realizing that reaching her son—either the artist or the spiritual anarchist—was well beyond her grasp.

And it wasn't just his art that had incorporated his mood. Adam had resigned himself to a silent type of mourning. He lost weight. He couldn't sleep. The nighttime calculation of barn animals didn't seem to help, either. He stared at the ceiling, admiring the abstract contours of chipped paint, searching for some comfort beyond a roof over his head. He found himself lost, no matter where he turned.

The depression continued until the day, less than a month before, when Tasha appeared suddenly—urgently almost—at Barnes & Noble.

"Are you always this sad?" she asked at the bookstore.

He stood up, giving him—for the moment, at least—a height advantage that would be lost once she did the same. "It's been a bad year. My mother died only a few months ago."

"I'm sorry to hear that," she said, "how sad. I think I now understand. . . ." But she also seemed somewhat surprised by what may have been a uniquely American custom of sharing bereavement with even the most remote of strangers.

From that maudlin beginning, a relationship grew—but not completely to Adam's satisfaction. There was a missing sexual component to their love, which Adam, as hard as he tried, could not seem to ignore. Tasha was ruled entirely by the Swedish way of subdued emotions, even among intimates. All those inviting looks, yet faultlessly decorous and self-consciously prim. And there was the understandable cynicism too. She hadn't gotten this far unmindful of how her face seduced men and intimidated women. New in the country and suspicious of its various solicitations, Tasha refused to sleep with any man until firmly convinced that she would not awake as a spoil of carnal conquest.

"Are you a virgin?" he wanted to know after a few dates ended with nothing more intimate than his face pressed up against Tasha's closed front door.

"Of course not."

"Well then, how long am I going to have to wait? We've been seeing each other for weeks now."

"When the mood hits me, you'll be the first to know," she assured him, stroking his face gently.

Accustomed as Adam was to dating Gentiles of unsurpassable beauty—some who thought little of giving over their bodies to his craven desires—he was surprised by Tasha's resolve, and his own stamina.

But desperation often reveals itself in dramatic ways. While Adam's sex life remained on hold, waiting for Tasha's trust and desire to materialize, his art did not. He had transformed his mourning over his mother, and his yet unconsummated love for Tasha, into a reservoir of artistic output, which surprisingly began to take on a new aesthetic. He started to work in warm, bright colors, turning away from the various shades of gloomy charcoal that defined his usual work. He painted a few portraits: one of Esther, sitting in one of her favorite chairs, matronly and refined; there was another of Tasha, alone in a lush green field, the sky behind her a hazy blue; and one of himself, straddling a motorcycle, the George Washington Bridge off in the horizon.

He painted feverishly, all through the nights, and then—without almost any sleep—he continued unrelievedly, the next day.

"We've got enough here for three shows," Sheinman said. "I think you need to rest up a bit. You planning on dying?"

But the pace continued. He moved from one project to the next. His eyes took on a burning, deep-red glow. Bathing became an afterthought. He had hardly eaten, or changed his clothes, for days. Dried blotches of paint, like lesions, were everywhere—on his face, on his shirts, on his jeans, all over his apartment and studio.

It was within this cloud of mania and deprivation that the lighting of the candle took place. Filled with a desire to mourn, and tormented by sexual frustration, Adam lit the *yohrzeit* candle. Now silenced, with nothing to say, he walked away from the vigil, hoping that further immersion in his work would deflect his thoughts from the kaddish. He once more began to paint, but soon thereafter, while wiping off a brush, a knock at the door again changed the course of the evening.

Keys jingled and fumbled at the other end. Tasha, wearing blue jeans, a white shirt, and black blazer, came in on her own.

"Sorry, I couldn't wait for you to open the door," she announced to an empty room. Burdened with suitcases and bags, she added, "I thought you might be asleep."

Tasha wasn't easily given to unannounced visits. Adam had given her a set of keys the month before, but she had yet to avail herself of this privilege, fearing that the exercise of such liberties might give rise to a misleading impression. Now, suddenly, it was precisely that impression she wanted to convey.

"Where are you?"

"Over here," Adam answered, making his way back into the living room. "What are you doing in town? Aren't you supposed to be in Miami Beach, shooting for that German catalogue I can never pronounce?"

"The shoot was over early. I decided to rush back to see you." After a pause, she observed: "Boy, you smell. What's happened?"

Normally excited to see Tasha, Adam was now disappointed by her unexpected appearance.

"Thanks for the tip. I'll shower."

"You don't seem at all excited to see me," she remarked curiously. "I came back because of you. I think it's time. The wait is over."

Adam's lustful mind sensed something different. "The wait is over," he thought. Yet this sudden stirring didn't feel quite right.

"Tonight?" he asked. "All of a sudden? What's in the drinking water down in South Beach these days?"

"I don't know. It was a gorgeous day—sunny, cool, the water as blue as a Swedish summer sky. What can I say. I got in the mood, and you have suffered enough," she said wistfully. "Let's make it a romantic evening. I stopped and bought some polenta and teriyaki chicken from the gourmet deli on my way over. I also got candles."

She looked around the room, dropping her suitcase near the couch. On the table she saw the candle, already lit. "Oh, super, you were on the same wavelength, I see. My horoscope said this would happen. Hey, wait a minute, were you expecting me, or someone else?"

"Like who?" he countered, and looked around. It was merely a *yohrzeit* light, not a candle for a seance, he thought.

"You've got a romantic candle all ready for someone," she said. "Who is it for, if not for me?"

"Romantic? You call that thing *romantic?*" But then, Adam's mind switched gears, as if the flame on the table had taken offense, and was now suddenly receding.

"Don't be silly, it's you, of course," he said, holding out his arms to Tasha, enveloping her in a hug. With her face safely camouflaged in his neck, he sneaked a peak at the *yohrzeit* not wanting to provoke any jealous rivalry between these two seemingly competitive flames.

Once secure that there was no other woman in Adam's life for whom the candle burned, Tasha cautiously moved closer to the *yohrzeit* flame. It seemed to grow hotter and stronger with her guarded advance; with each step it gained renewed strength, a fiery explosion of minute sparks, as if anticipating some strange battle that needed to be waged. With twenty-two hours still to go, the flame suddenly grew in intensity, lighting up the room with a furious incandescent swagger.

"This is such a strange candle," she noted. "Not very romantic at all, actually. I've never seen anything like this—certainly not in Sweden. It's just a block of wax in a cheap glass."

"Well, it lasts longer," Adam said unconvincingly. "When a romantic evening goes on well into the night, those dainty candles die too soon. This kind is much more economical."

"I thought Americans were wasteful."

"Not with candles. We have a special thrift about them."

"Okay, let's forget about the candle for a minute. Adam, I had a few screwdrivers on the plane," Tasha announced, "and I've missed you, I've really missed you."

He wanted to tell her that this was not the time. There were vital religious issues to consider here. She wouldn't understand at first, but he would try to explain. After all, she was an intelligent, modern European. Surely she would respect the traditions of his people—once he announced that he had a people. He would reason with her. Tomorrow would do just as well. The mood could be recaptured—he hoped. Yes, this was the day he was anticipating so anxiously. And yes, the wait had required the patience of one of Adam's biblical forebears. But even he—an all-American in Jewish irreverence—knew not to tamper with the *yohrzeit* candle. He owed something to Esther's memory; staying celibate on the anniversary of his mother's death was the least he could do.

But he wasn't crazy, either.

"Let's do it here, right here," she suggested.

"Where?"

"On the table. We'll just move the candle."

"We can't move the candle," Adam said, his eyes glancing toward the flickering *yohrzeit*. The flame seemed to bend disapprovingly, with a cool diffidence.

"Sure, why not," she said, a bit befuddled. "The table seems safe and sturdy." A hiccup, brought on by airline booze, jarred the momentary stillness. Then her head tilted back in sensual amusement.

"Because . . ." Adam stammered. But there was no completion of the thought, at least not one that was obvious. He felt anguish over Esther's botched remembrance, yet, at the same time, arousal from Tasha's advances.

"Because . . ."

"I think it will be fun. What a memory we'll have," she said. "I've never done it before on a table," she confessed, as she looked on adventurously toward the butcher block. "Have you?"

Adam faltered. "Ah . . . why no . . . at least not like this." A pause, and then, "How about we do this on another night, maybe even somewhere else?"

"What?" Tasha cried out. "You've been hanging around me for weeks. Cajoling me. Seducing me. Enticing me. Telling me how unnatural my attitude was; how much it reflected my lack of trust. So now, I race all the way back from Miami to be with you, to end our wait—and *your* suffering—and you're no longer interested! The time is now, Adam. Here, let me help you with your belt."

The Swede wanted her Jewish painter, now. On the table, no less, in front of Mom. She grabbed at Adam's fly at the same time as she threw off her blazer, dropped her jeans, and nearly ripped the T-shirt that clung stiffly to her body. While sliding on the table, she pulled Adam upon her with one hand, and she shifted the *yohrzeit* candle over a few feet with the other. Adam's eyes watched the flame gasp for life. His heart, pulsing with sexual anticipation, raced just to keep up.

Adam knew enough about the imperatives of his people to know that the *yohrzeit* flame was to remain undisturbed. As the candle shifted locations, he called out, "Esther!"

"Who's Esther?" Tasha asked.

With pants crumpled around his ankles like an accordion of denim, Adam announced nervously, "My mother."

"Do you always call out your mother's name before you make love?" she said, lying on the table, a model wearing nothing but her underwear and a curiosity about Adam's yet-unexplored sexual technique.

"Not usually," he said, panting away, concerned that such unfathomable foreplay had scared Tasha away. A confession was bound to change the already tense, awkward mood under which the lovers labored, as they danced on Esther's portable grave.

"I think that's cute," Tasha said, "thinking of your mother at a time like this. Maybe Freud was right about little boys and their mothers."

As Tasha pulled Adam upon herself again, tugging him alternately from his shoulder and shirt collar, she leaned over to her left and exhaled forcefully, her breath aimed at the *yohrzeit* candle.

"Good night, Mom," Tasha said. "You really shouldn't watch what I'm about to do to your son."

Adam closed his eyes and grimaced.

But the flame surged even more demonstrably. Tasha tried again, with the same result—the table remained illuminated by the small, stubborn candle.

"That's funny," Tasha remarked in a half pant, "the damn thing won't go out. What kind of candle is this, one of those trick ones?"

Adam realized that he wasn't going to educate this Gentile about the ways of Jewish remembrance. Not now, perhaps never. He was unequivocally caught between two worlds—sandwiched between two competing desires. A small blond table had served up two irreconcilable courses on this most emotional of evenings: a Swedish smorgasbord of temptation, juxtaposed with a paltry three ounces of scrupulous wax.

As Tasha was fast discovering, the candle appeared to be supernaturally endowed. Perhaps a Jewish mother, even one no longer of this world, is never too far away from protecting her son. Both the flame and the most excitable part of Adam's anatomy remained erect. One would have to wither.

"I'm getting tired of this," she said, craning her neck, her face growing red, her body tired from all the respiratory exertions. "There will be nothing left of me when the fun starts." Tasha puffed away at the candle as if it were a birthday cake resistant to childhood wishes.

With frustration growing, Tasha grabbed a coffee saucer and placed it over the *yohrzeit*, suffocating it irrevocably.

Once the candle went out, Adam permitted himself to relax. What was he to do, after all? The *yohrzeit* flame had met a premature demise. Not such a big tragedy in this world. It was a false start; his period of mourning ended suddenly. Adam's need for Tasha's body had abbreviated the anniversary of his mother's death. Esther would have to wait until next year. Maybe there is no return from the dead.

Suddenly, Adam's sexual technique seemed more adroit then before. Sexual restraint went the same way of spiritual observance. A butcher-block table was transformed into a palace of divine passion. Human legs dangled beside wooden ones, Tasha and Adam's limbs kicking wildly into the air; animal noises, grunts and groans, screamed from a now shadowless room.

Three weeks later Tasha formally moved into Adam's apartment. The aborted *yohrzeit* candle had by now become an indistinct memory, but the evidence of its ruin would remain forever with him. Using a small spatula, Adam had removed the unused wax, then pulverized the glass into crystal shards, which he slapped upon a canvas that he intended to paint entirely in black. It was to be a celestial scene of bright stars amidst a universal void. He had returned to his old melancholy, but familiar, form.

Christmas was approaching, Tasha's first in America. Manhattan was cooperating for the occasion. Central Park was covered with a light layer of snow. Holiday smells muscled their way into the grimy air. Shoppers slammed into one another on the streets and in the stores with few of their customary snarls—a New Yorker's way of demonstrating peace on earth and goodwill toward fellow men.

Tasha brought home a handsome evergreen—a Douglas fir to be exact—Adam's first Christmas tree.

"We can do this, right?" she asked.

"Why not?"

"I don't know what happens to Jewish boys on their first Christmas."

"Well, we'll just find out."

Adam watched Tasha's excited face as she carefully unpacked a box of dainty decorations that she had brought over with her from Malmö. As she unwrapped them, she lifted them up one by one, and guided by some ornamental instinct, attached each of them to the tree. An angel. A gingerbread man. A Christmas ram made of straw. A reindeer. A Swedish Santa—the *juletomte*, also dressed in red. Hand-carved wooden hearts. There were a few gremlins and a grimacing troll. And an entire assortment of woven baskets, filled with homemade candies and caramels wrapped in holiday paper, which weighed down the branches with a colorful harvest.

"This is always my favorite season," she confessed, searching each limb for a desirable resting place. "Back home in Sweden, my whole family would love it when Father would hoist up that great big tree we had every year."

"Sounds nice," Adam would say, cheerily, repeating to himself *she's so gorgeous*, in rhapsodic justification.

She had prepared a traditional Swedish Christmas eve smorgasbord of smoked ham, dried white codfish, and for dessert, *julgrot*, which, he was to learn, was a porridge of cooked rice.

"You know, there is an almond in the *julgrot*. Back in Sweden, the person who gets the almond in their portion is said to be the first to get married."

"There's only two of us here. I guess we can't lose."

"This makes me feel so at home. Now, where's that angel?"

Adam smiled, the sides of his mouth turning slightly upwards. But where was *his* home, he wondered quietly?

The Swedish Christmas carol, *"Nu Ar Det Jul Igen,"* resonated throughout the apartment, played on a CD that her sister had sent in a holiday care package. The melody was upbeat, but the lyrics seemed harsh. Of course, Adam didn't understand any Swedish, yet. So he simply let the music transport him wherever it wanted. He lay beside the tree, shifting already-wrapped presents around in tidy arrangement. Tasha's face reflected a swelling of Yuletide anticipation that he had never known.

She found her angel, lodged in the bottom of the box, preserved carefully in tissue paper. This angel was silver, with a big holder on the top of one of the wings for a candle. She stepped on a chair, then arched on her toes for that extra boost, rising above the highest point of the tree, and added the final touch. The angel stood poised at the summit like a saintly crown. A match sizzled, and she lit the candle, placing it gently inside the angel. Adam watched silently as Tasha remained on the chair, crying blissfully, her face a splendid glow, resurrecting her childhood here on West Eighty-seventh Street in Manhattan. As the night wore on, Adam fell asleep beside the Christmas tree, curled up like an unwrapped present, a lifeless ornament, the keeper of the flame.

Henry Roth

From A *Diving Rock* on the Hudson

So there he was, Ira at the beginning of November 1922, the later part of his sixteenth year, and technically a junior at DeWitt Clinton, though not quite, Ira sauntering through 119th Street homeward toward the gray trestle on Park Avenue. And with not a worry in the world, not an overt worry in the world. With a canker in the soul, yes, but then he kept that under control by buying a little tin of two condoms now and then, because most of the time Sundays had become his again. Pop had shifted from evening banquets to regular breakfast communion "extras" in Rockaway Beach. He earned a little less than he did at the evening banquets in Coney Island. But he hated the stairs in the Coney Island banquet hall. The Rockaway dining room had no stairs between it and the kitchen. That was worth a dollar, a dollar and a half less. So Sunday mornings, in the fall and winter, Ira could lie abed, usually awake, lurking, wait till Mom took her black oilcloth shopping bag, and went shopping for the week among the pushcarts under the Cut.

"Minnie. Okay?"

She said all kinds of dirty words at first; where did she learn them? After he showed her how different it was, "Fuck me, fuck me good!" He wished she wouldn't, though he liked it. He wished she wouldn't, because it incited him, spurred him on too much. He wished she wouldn't, though he grinned about it afterward: so *prust*, as they would say in Yiddish, so coarse: "Fuck me, fuck me good." It made him come before he wanted to, though he knew he ought to come fast to be safe, but not so fast as her dirty words made him, that and her crying out, "Ah, ah, oooh wah, ooowah!" Still, it made him feel proud too, and even prouder when she almost whooped with rapture, "Oooh, you're a good fucker. Oooh, don't get off yet!" But he had to, right away quick, as soon as it was over, quick and into his own bed, or start dressing. And he hardly had to coax anymore. She was ready as soon as he snapped the lock; a minute after Mom left, he pressed the little brass of the lock down: tink-tunk. Everything with celerity, everything coordinated. Nearly. She slid out of her folding cot, and into Mom and Pop's double bed beside it; while he dug for the little tin of Trojans in his pants pocket, little aluminum pod at two for a quarter. And then she watched him, strict and serious, her face on the fat pillow, her hazel eyes, myopic and close together—like Pop's—watched him roll a condom on his hard-on, readying her pussy while he hurried toward her, opening her flower to him when he reached the bed. What dirty words she greeted him with: "Fuck me like a hoor. No, no kisses. I don't want no kisses. Just fuck me good."

"All right. All right."

"That rubber all right? I don't want that white stuff in me—"

"No, no. I just bought 'em. Okay. A-a-h."

"O-oh. They're like the ones before?"

"Yeah. Real Trojans. Yeah. Come on."

"O-oh. So you can give me a dollar, too."

"All right. Later. Later."

Afterward she might even haggle with him for more than a dollar. "You worked in Madison Square Garden last night. I want a new sash on me; I want to get a wide sash with a bow."

"How much d'you think I made yesterday? Two dollars and a half! You made some money yourself working in the five and ten Saturday."

"Mama doesn't give me anything. Everything is for you. For you and for her Persian lamb coat—I don't count."

"Aw, come on." He had to get things settled fast, because you never knew when Mom would be back. If you argued too long, and delayed until after Mom returned, he'd have to sneak the money to Minnie anyway, but she would look sulky, cheated. And that was bad. Hearing them disputing once, Mom had looked puzzled. "All right, all right. I'll give you the dollar and a half. Only don't make a fuss. Jesus!"

—Oh, horror, horror.

That's right, Ecclesias. That's why I turned to you. As a buffer against my demon, my dybbuk, my nemesis—haven't I changed? O me, Angnel, come ti muti!

—Your pseudo-recondite self.

But I have changed, haven't I? Still, for all that, I could sit back this very moment, and raise my eyes to the window, the curtained window above the word processor, above imaginary you, Ecclesias, and wish myself fervently never to have been.

—And well you might. But what good does your fervent wishing do? Evidently something blocks the act itself. What is it?

I have an illusion I owe something to the species, as a specimen.

—Your offering may be of value. There's no telling. In any case, since you've chosen this mode of oblation, chosen to live, to scrive, then there's no undoing the done. There's only the outwearing it, the outwearying it, the attenuating of remorse, and guilt. That's all you can do, as far as you personally are concerned. And of course, there's always room for enhanced comprehension. How deep can one delve into platitude? As to your wish never to have been, that will soon be granted, if that's any comfort.

It isn't; it isn't the same thing at all.

—There's no expunging of the been, of the past, if that's what you mean. How can you expunge that which has ceased to be? Carry on, as the British say. What else is left? At worst—what is it at worst? Senescent erotic fantasy. At best, you've breached a mighty barrier within yourself, and done so, witting or unwitting, for the benefit of others. If in your own lifetime you've achieved an accession of reality—to give it a name, and a clumsy one—a long-belated transformation of view that conforms more closely with the actual, that's all the consolation available to you at this stage of the game.

Was grinsest du mir, heilige Schädel? said Goethe, said Faust (said Ira?) to the skull on the table.

—Did Faust say that? But I still don't know why you're quoting Goethe.

Yes, contented was he, and why not, when everything was under control. It was like a sneaky mini-family, a tabooed one, and discovered by him, by cunning exploitation of accident, to seal off a little enclave within, utterly unspeakable, vicious, yes, near brutally wicked, oh, wicked was too insipid, all the evil consummate, rolled up, concentrate, essence, wild, and made him feel so depraved that anything went, anything he could think of, rending all the enclosures: Mephisto wrapped in a bed-sheet in front of a mirror, the pier glass mirror, in a moment of playfulness: "Look at that, Minnie. I'm a Roman in a Roman toga, sticking out with a rubber Trojan."

And she giggled, but only enough not to delay proceedings. "Don't fool around. Hurry up."

Wasn't he lucky though?

Even at this late hour, and yours truly a man near eighty; for these things are like to one who has sniffed the coocoo, and never lost the beatitude; that was the worst of it, the ambivalence of sin, if you call it that, of depravity, the amphi-balance of it, the Escher fugue, the optical illusion, the Jekyll-Hyde slide, the fleur du mal.

Lucky, supremely lucky, the luck of having Pop a waiter, on a Sunday morning again, and long gone to Rockaway Beach to wait on table on a breakfast "benket." Well, it got so actually it wasn't limited to Sunday mornings. Hell, no. At sixteen going on seventeen, and lusty, and Minnie at fourteen plus, and now in Julia Richmond High School. And she was dating boys, and going out a bit, and to dances, and someone must have broken her cherry already, and he was the one reaping the full benefit, because there was never any blood, though she would never let him inside before. Maybe the guy had hurt her. "No, just between. I don't want that white stuff in me."

And then she finally surrendered, after he told her about Theodora, and how it was done, how it had to be done, for her to get the real thrill he got out of it, not her way, and how it was safe, it was safe, too.

She knew about it. "So you got one o' those?" she asked.

"Yeah." His head began to reel.

She knew. She knew. "So is it a good one?" White-and-pink cheeks had she, somewhat a severe face, cold, unresponsive, even for a fourteen-year-old kid, translucent hazel eyes. She wrinkled her nose skeptically under wavy red bangs. "Is it brand-new? It's clean?"

"Brand-new," he protested, and more vehemently, "What d'you think? I'll use a secondhand one? I'll show it to you. Look."

And almost as if against her will, but consumed with need, want, heat, his pitiless aphrodisiac wheedling, she stood up, from homework table, green-oilcloth-covered—she made for the closed bedroom door, closed, now that the other rooms were cold, and only the kitchen gas-heated. "So come on."

What delirium, surprise and dividend, even though she was so peremptory, serious; yet the green-painted blistery kitchen walls did a jig, a veritable jig—still, *she* didn't notice anything, he everything: the walls dimpled, the walls jigged, they rippled to and fro as the little brass nipple loosed the tongue-plunk of the lock, close sesame, magic-charm plunk that freed the walls from being walls, changed them to shimmering, rich green drapes. Freed them and him and everybody, liberated, when you were really going to do it to her, sink it inside your sister, really into Minnie. She was letting him into her. What luck he'd bought the little tin, after—after Theodora. Yip silently with joy. Yip, yip, yahoo. Look at those walls doing a Highland fling in ecstasy, a lilt in kilts. Yippee.

Delirious he, so prosaic she, as if begrudging a needed item, a staple of oestrus. But what the hell, begrudging or not, his, his to have, to have, to fuck her on edge of bed, his bed, first bedroom, on his bed athwart, just two feet away hardly from airshaft window, and the cold no longer felt. Don't lose a second before Mom came home. For a minute into Minnie, sink it in her, sin it in her. Quick, go. O-o-oh, look at her: carmine between lifted thighs. Quick! Roll it on, pale sheath over fiery shaft.

"Okay?" Ira asked when they came back out of the bedroom into the kitchen. He'd been super-lucky: the second time this week. The first time was in Mom and Pop's bed Sunday—that was good. He had used his last condom, but was it ever good! She made so much noise he was nearly afraid. So early in the morning. And on Sunday. All the neighbors home. Jesus, if they ever guessed he was doing it to his own sister. He fucks his sister, the micks would say. Hey. How about us gittin' a piece of her ass, too? He knew them.

"Okay?" Ira repeated when Minnie didn't answer—though he suspected it wasn't.

"Oh, don't ask me. It was all right." She sounded none too ravished, as she followed him into the kitchen. "Sometimes you get bigger at the end," she complained. She yanked at her stocking.

"I had to hurry," he conciliated. Actually, he felt sheepish, because the surprising opportunity had caught him unprepared. It had overaroused his ardor with wild, evil greed of transgression, the dire joy of perpetration. The flood of the heinous had been too much for him to withstand. He had barely synchronized with her. "You wanna try again?" he offered belatedly. "I can wash the rubber again."

"No, I don't wanna." She cut off further allusion sharply. "Don't wash it again. Don't do me no favors—" She halted abruptly. "What d'you mean, again? Wasn't it a new one? You said it was brand-new."

"Oh, sure, sure," he lied vehemently. He had washed it once.

"Then I don't wanna talk about it."

"Yeah? So okay. Okay," he snapped at her. Hell with her. Main concern was to get back to the kitchen table speedily. Roll back the tongue of the lock fast. Compose everything back to normal. Get to the toilet with the squishy condom. . . . He opened the toilet door, exited from the kitchen, dropped the rubber in round mini-whirlpool, flushed it down in noisy maelstrom, out of sight of the dingy white enamel.

And back in the kitchen again, he sat down to his textbooks, features engrossed, maybe even hostile, as he often was, when she asked him a question in English, and he shook her off or derided her. Easy to be surly this time, complemented by her glowering. Gave authenticity to what they were ostensibly engrossed in doing: studying high school homework, ignoring each other. So it wasn't so good. So she didn't plead, Fuck me, fuck me good. So she didn't animal-yearn, O-o-wah, o-owah. He had laid her. Got his. Settle down now. Safe.

"Is it all right?" she asked, guarded, darkly.

"What?"

"When you went in the toilet."

"Oh, sure," he blustered, then contemptuously, "Jesus! What d'ye think?"

"Aw, you stink," she said.

"Oh, yeah? Just because of this once." She was belittling his prowess. He could tell she meant he had gotten more out of it than she had. "I told you I was in a hurry."

"No more! That's all. If it's such a hurry."

"But Sunday in the morning was—"

"Not even Sunday. No more."

"All right, no more," he agreed cynically. He could get around that one—next time.

"*Briderl*. You stink, if you wanna know."

"Aw, go to hell. Waddaye want? So once I got too excited." And then it suddenly occurred to him that he might have cause for concern. "Oh, Jesus!"

"Whatsa matter?"

He stood up. Had he pulled that chain long enough? Swirled the damned thing down? Really down for good, not just out of sight? He stepped hastily toward the bathroom door.

"I hear Mom," said Minnie.

Flop down again, or else Mom might think—might think he was dodging. Flop down to chair, bend over book.

And in came Mom, bringing fresh, cold air with her, as if in the container of her coat, breathless from the climb, her short, heavy self toting handbag; and at once, down on the table with it—and right for the bathroom!

Oh, Jesus Christ, oh, Jesus Christ. If he didn't, if he didn't! Minnie was right: never again, never again! Go to Theo, Theodora, Theotorah, Theowhorah. Anything. He still knew the way. Go to anybody, take a chance, get a dose, anything—Ira shut his eyes, waited. No. No. The toilet flushed and gurgled. No. No. It was all right. Got away with it. Of course. What the hell was he so scared about?

Mom came back into the kitchen. "*Noo, kinderlekh.* You must be hungry by now. No? When Mamie goes to buy a corset, she's a worse *kushenirke* than even I am. What am I? I'm a lady by comparison. If she didn't torture that shopkeeper on 116th Street to prostration with 'Ah, it's so dear; you make too much money on it, it's outrageous, it's exorbitant. What is it? Is it made of gold? It's only a corset. From cloth, from bone.' She has a nerve of brass."

"Oh, is that where you were?" Minnie asked. "I wondered. So did she buy it?"

"Indeed. Finally. '*Ai, vey, vey*,' the shopkeeper said. '*Frau*, you should wear it in good health. To earn what I have just earned cost me a parcel of health.' 'One has to look well about you before loosening purse strings,' she said. 'Heh, heh, heh,' he laughed. A clever Jew he was. 'Look well about you. That's a shred of comfort. About you indeed. May you rejoice in the wearing of it about you too.' Then I hurried home as fast as I could. A little coffee and milk and a bulkie?"

Philip Roth

From *The Counterlife*

Food had been laid out by a local caterer under the patio awning while the mourners were still at the synagogue, and scattered around the downstairs rooms were folding chairs rented from the funeral parlor. The girls from Ruth's softball team, who had taken the afternoon off from school to help out the Zuckermans, were clearing away the used paper plates and replenishing the serving platters from the reserves in the kitchen. And Zuckerman went looking for Wendy.

It was Wendy actually—when she'd become frightened that Henry was beginning to lose his mind—who had first suggested Nathan as a confidant. Carol, assuming that Nathan hadn't the slightest authority over his brother any longer, had urged Henry to talk to a psychotherapist in town. And for an hour each Saturday morning—until that horrendous Saturday expedition to New York—he had done it, gone off and spoken with great candor about his passion for Wendy, pretending to the therapist, however, that the passion was for Carol, that it was she whom he was describing as the most playful, inventive sexual partner any man could ever hope to have. This resulted in long, thoughtful discussions of a marriage that seemed to interest the therapist enormously but depressed Henry even further because it was such a cruel parody of his own. As far as Carol knew, not until she'd phoned to tell Nathan that

Henry was dead had he even been aware of his brother's illness. Scrupulously following Henry's wishes, Zuckerman played dumb on the telephone, an absurd act that only compounded the shock and made clear to him how incapable Henry had been of reaching *any* decision rationally once the ordeal had begun. Out at the cemetery, while Henry's children stood at the graveside struggling to speak, Zuckerman had finally understood that the reason to have stopped him was that he had wanted to be stopped. The last thing Henry must have imagined was that Nathan would sit there and accept with a straight face, as justification for such a dangerous operation, the single-minded urging of that maniac-making lust that he had himself depicted so farcically in *Carnovsky*. Henry had expected Nathan to *laugh*. Of course! He had driven over from Jersey to confess to the mocking author the ridiculous absurdity of his dilemma, and instead he had been indulged by a solicitous brother who was unable any longer to give either advice or offense. He had come over to Nathan's apartment to be told how utterly meaningless was Wendy's mouth beside the ordered enterprise of a mature man's life, and instead the sexual satirist had sat there and seriously listened. Impotence, Zuckerman had been thinking, has cut him off from the simplest form of distance from his predictable life. As long as he was potent he could challenge and threaten, if only in sport, the solidity of the domestic relationship; as long as he was potent there was some give in his life between what was routine and what is taboo. But without the potency he feels condemned to an ironclad life wherein all issues are settled.

Nothing could have made this clearer than how Henry had described to him becoming Wendy's lover. Apparently from the instant she'd come into the office for the interview and he'd closed the door behind her, virtually every word they exchanged had goaded him on. "Hi," he'd said, shaking her hand, "I heard such marvelous things about you from Dr. Wexler. And now that I look at you, I think you're almost too good. You're going to be so distracting, you're so pretty."

"Uh-oh," she said, laughing. "Maybe I should go then."

What had delighted Henry was not only the speed with which he'd put her at ease but having put himself at ease as well. It wasn't always like that. Despite his well-known rapport with his patients, he could still be ridiculously formal with people he didn't know, men no less than women, and sometimes, say, when interviewing someone for a job in his own office, seem to himself as though *he* were the person being interviewed. But something vulnerable in this young woman's appearance—something particularly tempting about her tiny breasts—had emboldened him, though precisely at a moment when being emboldened might not be such a great idea. Both at home and in the office everything was going so well that an extraneous adventure with a woman was the *last* thing he needed. And yet, because everything *was* going well, he could not rein in that robust, manly confidence that he could tell was knocking her for a loop already. It was just one of those days when he felt like a movie star, acting out some grandiose whatever-it-was. Why suppress it? There were enough days when he felt like a twerp.

"Sit down," he said. "Tell me about yourself and what you want to do."

"What I want to do?" Someone must have advised her to repeat the doctor's question if she needed time to think up the right answer or to remember the one she'd prepared. "I want to do a lot of things. My first exposure to a dental practice was with Dr. Wexler. And he's wonderful—a true gentleman."

"He's a nice guy," Henry said, thinking, altogether involuntarily, out of this damn excess of confidence and strength, that before it was over he'd show her what wonderful was.

"I learned a lot in his office of what's going on in dentistry."

He encouraged her gently. "Tell me what you know."

"What do I know? I know that a dentist has to make a choice of what kind of practice he wants. It's a business, you have to choose a market, and yet you're dealing with something that's very intimate. People's mouths, how they feel about them, how they feel about their smiles."

Mouths *were* his business, of course—hers too—and yet talking about them like this—at the end of the day, with the door closed, and the slight, young blonde petitioning for a job—was turning out to be awfully stimulating. He remembered the sound of Maria's voice telling him all about how wonderful his cock was—"I put my hand into your trousers, and it astonishes me, it's so big and round and hard." "Your control," she would say to him, "the way you make it last, there's no one like you, Henry." If Wendy were to get up and come over to the desk and put her hand in his pants, she'd find out what Maria was talking about.

"The mouth," Wendy was saying, "is really the most personal thing that a doctor can deal with."

"You're one of the few people who's ever said that," Henry told her. "Do you realize that?"

When he saw the flattery raise the color in her face, he pushed the conversation in a more ambiguous direction, knowing, however, that no one overhearing them could legitimately have charged him with talking to her about anything other than her qualifications for the job. Not that anyone could possibly overhear them.

"Did you take *your* mouth for granted a year ago?" he asked.

"Compared to what I think of it now, yes. Of course, I always cared for my teeth, cared about my smile—"

"You cared about *yourself*," Henry put in approvingly.

Smiling—and it *was* a good smile, the badge of utterly innocent, childish abandon—she happily picked up the cue. "I care about me, yes, sure, but I didn't realize that there was so much psychology involved in dentistry."

Was she saying that to get him to slow down, was she asking him politely to please back off about *her* mouth? Maybe she wasn't as innocent as she looked—but that was even *more* exciting. "Tell me a bit about that," Henry said.

"Well, what I said before—how you feel about your smile is a reflection of how you feel about yourself and what you present to other people. I think that whole personalities may develop, not only about your teeth, but everything else that goes with it. You're dealing in a dental office with the whole person, even if it just looks like you're dealing with the mouth. How do I satisfy the whole person, including the mouth? And when you talk about cosmetic dentistry, that's *real* psychology. We had some problems in Dr. Wexler's office with people who were having crowns done, and they wanted white-white teeth, which didn't go with their own teeth, with their coloring. You have to get them to understand what natural-looking teeth are. You tell them, 'You're going to have the smile that's perfect for you, but you can't go through and just pick out *the* perfect smile and have it put in your mouth.' "

"And have the mouth," Henry added, helping her out, "that looks like it belongs to you."

"Absolutely."

"I want you to work with me."

"Oh, great."

"I think we can make it," Henry said, but before *that* took on too much meaning, he moved quickly to present to his new assistant his own ideas, as though by being dead serious about dentistry he could somehow stop himself before he got grossly suggestive. He was wrong. "Most people, as you must know by now, don't even think that their mouth is part of the body. Or teeth are part of the body. Not consciously they don't. The mouth is a hollow, the mouth is nothing. Most people, unlike you, will never tell you what their mouth means. If they're frightened of dental work it's sometimes because of some frightening experience early on, but primarily it's because of what the mouth means. Anyone touching it is either an invader or a helper. To get them from thinking that someone working on them is invading them, to the idea that you are helping them on to something good, is almost like having a sexual experience. For most people, the mouth is secret, it's their hiding place. Just *like* the genitals. You have to remember that embryologically the mouth is related to the genitals."

"I studied that."

"Did you? Good. Then you realize that people want you to be very tender with their mouths. Gentleness is the most important consideration. With all types. And surprisingly enough, men are more vulnerable, particularly if they've lost teeth. Because losing teeth for a man is a strong experience. A tooth for a man is a mini-penis."

"I hadn't realized that," she said, but didn't seem affronted in any way.

"Well, what do *you* think of the sexual prowess of a toothless man? What do you think he thinks? I had a guy here who was very prominent. He had lost all his teeth and he had a young girlfriend. He didn't want her to know he had dentures, because that would mean he was an old man, and she was a young girl. About your age. Twenty-one?"

"Twenty-two."

"She was twenty-one. So I did implants for him, instead of dentures, and he was happy, and she was happy."

"Dr. Wexler always says that the most satisfaction comes from the greatest challenge, which is usually a disaster case."

Had Wexler fucked her? Henry had never as yet gone beyond the usual flirtation with any assistant of any age—it wasn't only unprofessional but hopelessly distracting in a busy practice, and could well lead to the *dentist's* becoming the disaster case. He realized then that he ought never to have hired her; he had been entirely too impulsive, and was now making things even worse by all this talk about mini-penises that was giving him an enormous hard-on. Yet with everything that was combining these days to make him feel so bold, he couldn't stop. What's the worst that could happen to him? Feeling so bold, he had no idea. "The mouth, you mustn't forget, is the primary organ of experience . . ." On he went, looking unblinkingly and boldly at hers.

Nonetheless, a full six weeks passed before he overcame his doubts, not only about crossing the line further than he had at the interview but about keeping her on in the office at all, despite the excellent job she was doing. Everything he'd been saying about her to Carol happened to be true, even if to him it sounded like the most transparent rationalization for why she was there. "She's bright and alert, she's cute and people like her, she can relate to them, and she helps me enormously—because of her, when I walk in, I can get right to it. This girl," he told Carol, and more often than he needed to during those early weeks, "is saving me two, three hours a day."

Then one evening after work, as Wendy was cleaning his tray and he was routinely washing up, he turned to her and, because there simply seemed no way around it any longer, he began to laugh. "Look," he said, "let's pretend. You're the assistant and I'm the dentist." "But I *am* the assistant," Wendy said. "I know," he replied, "and I'm the dentist—but pretend anyway." "And so," Henry had told Nathan, "that's what we did." "You played Dentist," Zuckerman said. "I guess so," Henry said, "—she pretended she was called 'Wendy,' and I pretended I was called 'Dr. Zuckerman,' and we pretended we were in my dental office. And then we pretended to fuck—and we fucked." "Sounds interesting," Zuckerman said. "It was, it was wild, it made us crazy—it was the strangest thing I'd ever done. We did it for weeks, pretended like that, and she kept saying, 'Why is it so exciting when all we're pretending to be is what we are?' God, was it great! Was she hot!"

Well, that larky, hot stuff was over now, no more mischievously turning what-was into what-wasn't or what-might-be into what-was—there was only the deadly earnest this-is-it of what-is. Nothing a successful, busy, energetic man likes more than a little Wendy on the side, and nothing a Wendy could more enjoy than calling her lover "Doctor Z."— she's young, she's game, she's in his office, he's the boss, she sees him in his white coat being adored by everyone, sees his wife chauffeuring the children and turning gray while she doesn't think twice about her twenty-inch waist . . . heavenly all around. Yes, his sessions with Wendy had been Henry's art; his dental office, after hours, his atelier; and his impotence, thought Zuckerman, like an artist's artistic life drying up for good. He'd been reassigned the art of the responsible—unfortunately by then precisely the hackwork from which he needed longer and longer vacations in order to survive. He'd been thrown back on his talent for the prosaic, precisely what he'd been boxed in by all his life. Zuckerman had felt for him terribly, and so, stupidly, stupidly, did nothing to stop him.

Helen Schulman

"P. S."

It had been a long time between drinks of water for Louise Brown. It was an early spring outside her office window, and if she craned her neck between the stacks of applications and the stacks of folders that hemmed her windowsill, she could see that beyond her little cubicle the world was full of boys.

Shaggy boys with bandannas leapt through the air like eager golden retrievers to catch a Frisbee with an open jaw of a palm. There were boys without their shirts on. Boys smoking pot and boys flirting and hundreds of boys, it seemed, leaning into hundreds of lank, skinny girls, with lank, skinny hair, in lank, skinny skirts; all these couples hanging out on the great, grand limestone steps of the central library of the university. They were half Louise's age, the boys were, and they all looked like they were getting plenty. What had happened to her life?

She turned to the application in her lap. This particular young man wanted to be a sculptor, he wanted to be a Master of Fine Arts, and he wanted this divine transformation to occur at the very fine institution where she was now acting admissions coordinator. Louise sighed heavily and reached for a cigarette, knocking over another pile of folders with a roughened elbow, an elbow that years ago her ex-husband, Alan, used to massage after her bath with cream. The folders slid to the floor,

spilling all those forms covered with sloppy pen and ink that had ex-
plicitly stated in bold print: TO BE TYPED ONLY. The floor was a mess.
Fighting back the urge to weep, she leaned over, started straightening up.
Warshofsky, Evans, Aguado—she'd re-alphabetize all of them in record
time. Louise picked up another folder. Turetsky, Scott.

Scott fucking Turetsky.

And for a moment, her heart stopped. It did that now and again, a little mitral-valve-prolapse action, a familiar suspension of her most vital
organ, like a dancer's leap, she and her life supports hanging in the air,
bridging two moments in time. Then came the crash in her chest, the
heavy beating of a desperate bird's wings, the poor thing (her heart)
banging up against the sliding glass doors of a patio.

Louise caught her breath. Scott Turetsky. She petted the outside of his
folder.

There had been a Scott Turetsky when she was a girl growing up in
Larchmont. Her Scott Turetsky had been a painter and a printmaker (a
printmaker!), and she'd loved him from afar from the moment she first
saw him, which was registration day freshman year of high school. He
had a girlfriend then—Scott Turetsky always had a girlfriend—a beautiful hippie chick, Roberta Goldman, with long, flowing red gold hair
and long, flowing Indian skirts and toe rings and earrings and bracelets
around her upper arms, one bejeweled job gracing her left ankle. When
the two of them, Scott and Berta, as he called her, walked into the school
gym arm in arm that morning, the seas parted, and they skipped to the
head of the line, directly in front of Louise. Scott's hair was long then,
too. It was thick and black with silver gray streaks, like a smattering of
frost had wafted down and graced it; and it was unbrushed and matted
in a long, loose ponytail that was tied with a rubber band.

Three years later, after Berta had been replaced by Trisha the dancer,
and Trisha had been replaced by Theresea Longo, the dark-eyed daughter of the proprietor of the lone Italian restaurant in Larchmont, and
after Theresea had been dallied with and sent back to the kitchen, he
was hers. Scott Turetsky was hers. They dated hot and heavy the summer before her senior year. Scott had just returned home from several
months in Italy; his parents and his grandmother had refused to continue
wiring him advances on his inheritance, so he had come back from Europe to work off his coming art-school expenses in a local food emporium

called Cheeze Bazaar. Louise would wait for him to sweep and close up shop, and then they'd ride around for hours in his beat-up old red truck. He was full of Italian phrases and romantic stories, and she spent hours listening to him while brushing out his long salt-and-pepper locks. They broke up just weeks before he was to drive up to Rhode Island to go to art school. "It's only fair to you," Scott said, one afternoon in the truck, *after* she had given him a blow job. "I don't want to hold you back; I want you to have a wild and adventurous life." Louise. Wild and adventurous.

It was the drive to Rhode Island that killed him.

He'd never even gotten to school, never got to test his mettle as an artist, never had time to regret his decision, to come to his senses, go crawling back to Louise, to grovel in the dirt. He'd never even had a chance to miss her.

Nor was she granted the booby prize, the status of being his girlfriend at the time of his death. In fact, Scott Turetsky had just started up a little end-of-summer thing with her best friend, Missy, so Louise had none of the dignity of widowhood, which Missy dined out on for years.

Now she looked down at the folder. Dare she peek inside?

Turetsky, F. Scott.

F. Scott? The name was written in at the top of the application in a tight and even hand. Not typed, of course, but in a rich black ink, perhaps a fountain pen—which her Scott Turetsky had favored, the wealth and elegance, the gravitas of oily ink. The letters had nice full curves to them before they feathered away into nothing. She glanced further down the paragraph. His address was left blank. A post-office box. A post-office box in Mamaroneck. Mamaroneck, the sister city to her native Larchmont.

She read on. Date of birth: August 28, 1973.

Her Scott Turetsky (not an F. Scott Turetsky) had been born August 28, 1961. She knew this because he also had died on August 28—August 28, 1981—a fact that a lot of people in her town had valued as having some mystical if useless significance but that she had only found creepy and fitting and somehow round: a kid dying the moment he turned twenty, just as he became a man.

More, there was more. This Scott Turetsky, F. Scott Turetsky, was about to graduate from the Rhode Island School of Design. He was a painter and a printmaker. He favored large, oblong canvases, like her

Scott Turetsky had, and he painted only in oils, too, although unlike her guy, he liked to layer the paint with linseed oil until the colors melted slightly under its weight, "like brown sugar burning," said his essay. He liked to "caramelize" the "hues." F. Scott Turetsky had also spent a year in Italy, where he spent most of his time "eating gelati, drinking wine and looking at art, sitting in churches, spending my Bar Mitzvah money." There was an ironic edge to his essay; it was gently self-mocking but full of self-love as well. "I believe in myself. I guess you could say I believe in myself totally. I want to live wildly and adventurously, which might be interpreted as hubris but is honestly the way I feel about myself."

F. Scott Turetsky had three recommendation letters, two from the high priest and priestess of RISD and one from Louise's very own high school art teacher, Ms. Cipriani. "While I don't normally approve of high school students painting nudes from living models, Scott's portrait of his girlfriend is reminiscent of one of Matisse's cruder odalisques."

Louise was reeling. Berta, Trisha, Theresea Longo, all of his exes, captured in full flower, their finest hour, at the art show of the senior class. It was a town scandal, Rabbi and Mrs. Turetsky loyally at their son's side, holding their heads high; the girls aflutter, instant celebrities. Her Scott Turetsky had never immortalized her own naked, nubile image—he'd promised but had never gotten around to it. He'd rather (his words) make love to her than reduce her to a work of art.

She looked down at F. Scott Turetsky's application. A phone number: (401). Without hesitating, she picked up the phone and dialed. The phone rang one time, two times, three; exhausted, she almost rested the receiver in its cradle. But she hung in there. Four rings, five rings, six rings. On the seventh, someone picked up.

"Hey," said a mysterious young man.

"Hey yourself," said Louise.

Why on earth did she say that?

"Baby," he said.

"This is Louise Brown," Louise said. "From Columbia, School of the Arts, admissions."

"So you're not my baby," the young man laughed.

No. Apparently not.

"Is this F. Scott Turetsky?" she asked, all business.

"Yeah," he said. "Sure." And then, "Louise Brown from the Admissions Department, you're not going to believe me, but I was just about to pick up the phone. I forgot to send in my slides. This must be some weird psychic phenomenon, you know?"

"You're telling me," Louise said.

It was a Wednesday, the day of F. Scott Turetsky's trumped-up interview. Louise had scheduled him at the end of the day. This way she could spend the better part of the morning in Emporio Armani trying to find a skirt that looked like one she had bought in the House of Shalimar in 1979. Nineteen seventy-nine. Six years after F. Scott Turetsky was born. She finally settled on a gauzy eight-tiered swirl that flirted about her ankles. After she paid up—a small down payment on an apartment— Louise slipped into a local coffee shop, made her way into the bathroom and changed, shoving her jeans into the wastebasket in the corner. She looked at herself hard in the mirror—how rough her skin seemed, how large her pores were—and then took her long brown hair (hair she had blown dry straight for the first time in seventeen years that morning) out of its clip and fastened it in a silky loose braid. Another look he'd liked.

Back at the office, F. Scott Turetsky was late by three-quarters of an hour. Louise was prepared for this. He'd always been late before. She'd taken to telling him that the movies started half an hour earlier than they actually began. *Midnight Express.* How hard she'd grabbed his right hand when the hero bit out his fellow prisoner's tongue. So hard, Scott Turetsky's left hand fell from its working position on her breast.

It was 5:48 exactly. Louise, practically apoplectic, knew this, for she was staring at the clock when F. Scott Turetsky knocked on her office door, which she'd left an inviting halfway open.

"Hey," he said.

"Hey yourself," said Louise, a little too jovially, before turning around. "Come on in."

She sounded like an admissions officer.

F. Scott Turetsky came in. Louise swiveled in her chair and sized him up. He was the right height (five feet ten inches), the right weight (155). Actually, he looked a little thicker, but he was four years older, four years older than when she'd last laid eyes upon him. His eyes were the same flawed cobalt blue (brown specks). F. Scott Turetsky wore baggy jeans and a big, striped baggy polo shirt; his dark hair was shaved close to his pretty head. It was shaved in patterns in the back, the New York skyline, but among the darker patches of his stubble, Louise thought she could see a smattering of silver frost.

So it was him. A little older, perhaps, a little more handily equipped with a set of laugh lines. But it was him. Or some fascimile—a clone perhaps, a ghost. It was him.

That or his identical nephew.

It was him, now with a tattoo braceleting his wrist, crawling up his arm. When he turned to close the door, she could see a blue-and-green serpent inked across his neck.

It was him, but a variation.

F. Scott Turetsky was sitting in her office.

God.

Louise began to talk. She appeared to herself to be reciting the entire course catalog in a bureaucratic drone. But inside, inside! "Hey," she wanted to call out, "it's me, it's me—it's me inside this grown-up body. Under the aerobicized muscles, the thickening skin, under the permanent tan line on my left ring finger, under the scars—inflicted by life, by disappointment, by my weaknesses and jealousies and flaws, inflicted by you!—it's me, it's me, your Sugar Magnolia, your Cinnamon Girl!"

She wanted to crawl across the floor, unzip his pants and suck on his cock.

Instead she went on and on about School of the Arts course offerings while she drank him in.

He was slow, flirty, a little shy, asking questions and then answering them himself, as had always been his way.

"I mean, hey, you know, I'm like a rube, raised in the burbs. Providence ain't much of a city. . . . Will I get eaten alive here? I mean, hey, Ms. Louise Brown, is there any hope in the Big Apple for a small-town loser like me?" He flashed her a killer smile.

"Sure, there's hope," he said, answering himself. He was really smiling now. "There's always hope—right, Louise, you're thinking that there's hope for me. I can tell. I can tell what you're thinking, and it's hopeful. I can read your mind."

At an outdoor café on Upper Broadway, they ate burritos and drank margaritas, letting the sheer force and volume of the begging, amputated homeless drive them inside. And so it was a piece of cake getting him back up to her apartment, with both of them already three sheets to the wind.

Ha. She'd wrangled a beautiful young boy into her home, one she prayed was still in possession of a pair of muscular ridges that rode the knobby track of his spine, of a hairless back, of an abdomen that she remembered came in sections. How long had it been since she'd slept with a body that didn't slide?

How long had it been, honestly, since she'd slept with anyone?

Louise needed this night! So she finagled F. Scott Turetsky upstairs, pushing away the fear that her own age might prove a deterrent. Somewhere deep in his abnormally young psyche, F. Scott Turetsky might also remember their other life and miss her nubile image, but then again the Scott Turetsky that she knew had been less than appreciative of her corporeal gifts. She had been so waiflike and slight back then. It had been hard, when she was dressed, to distinguish her breasts from her ribs. Once, after sex, Scott Turetsky had insisted on lying on his side on his bed—his penis now a little kickstand—and examining her naked. He had Louise parade back and forth like a model—an embarrassed, awkward and shy model, with hunched-over shoulders and hands that fluttered about in a weak little fan dance to hide herself. After ten agonizing minutes, Scott declared her pretty OK—which made Louise's head feel light and her cheeks flush hot—if only her butt were a little higher. Then he jumped up from the bed, cupped it in his hands and lifted to prove his point.

Too bad Scott Turetsky didn't live long enough to fall victim to a slow metabolism, a balding head and a thickening gut like the rest of the male members of their high school class. Too bad some heartless woman somewhere didn't get to pinch his love handles and giggle when he was striking out as an artist in New York and most needed her support. Too bad someone in as good shape as Louise was right then didn't suggest he take up jogging while, dressed only in socks and a blue striped button-down and totally vulnerable, he was getting ready to go to work at his uncle's car dealership in New Jersey.

Too bad that, unlike the rest of them, Scott Turetsky got to die when he was perfect.

But with F. Scott Turetsky, Louise had the hometown advantage. She knew F. Scott Turetsky would have a penchant for older women. She remembered Scott Turetsky telling her this himself when they were lying naked in Manor Park one night seventeen years before on a blanket made up of their cutoff shorts and black concert T-shirts, her lacy white bra curled like a kitten at his ankles.

It was ex post facto, and over before she knew it, and she was antsy and he was spent, and they were lying a foot apart and not touching on the hot, moist lawn that led up to the little local beach, a tiny pathetic spit of sand—his words punctuated by the obscene wet slap of the sound.

In order to get a conversation going—it was embarrassing, lying apart and naked like that, her thighs squid white in the moonlight; it was embarrassing, to have been as dry as a desert and not to have come and not to have had the time to properly fake it—Louise was bemoaning the fact that she was getting older. A senior. Used goods. When so many pretty skinny little freshman girls were dying to take her place.

She reached out her hand to his.

She didn't want to lose him. No matter how self-centered he was, no matter that he was a lousy lover. She was seventeen. What did she know but lousy lovers? None of that mattered, not the strange pungent mix of his "natural" deodorant and his body odor, his silly affectations, his incredible self-love.

"Not to worry," said Scott Turetsky. "I really dig older women. I mean really old, like thirty-four or thirty-five. As long as they're still in shape. Strong girls. That's when they're at their sexual height. For a guy, it's nineteen. So you're lucky. You're catching me at my peak."

Then he rolled over and mounted her again.

But in her apartment, as an adult, making out on her couch with an older but still young F. Scott Turetsky, Louise changed her tune. I'm lucky, she thought, I'm so very lucky to be here now with him. And it seemed like in the four intervening years—four years F. Scott Turetsky time—he had picked up some pointers. He was passionate, kissing up and down her neck. He was passionate, worrying at her earlobe. His body was familiar. So boyish and so beautiful. When he pulled his shirt off over the back of his head, his once hairless chest now sported curly black spirals around the nipples, and farther down, in the bottom quadrants of his stomach, it got curlier and thicker still, leading a woolly path to his groin.

Louise thought, I can't believe how lucky I am. To have a second chance.

"Wait a minute," said F. Scott Turetsky. "Don't you want to talk?"

Talk?

"You know, get to know each other a little, before, before you and I make love." Here he reached out his hand, took hers in his dry palm.

Make love?

When was the last time anyone had seduced her just by putting her off?

Scott Turetsky. He'd done the same thing their first time in the back of his truck. He'd gotten her going until she was crazy, and then he'd stopped short, so that Louise was so loose and trembly she felt that if someone were to pull a secret thread she would unravel and fall apart. He'd stopped her, because he was the sensitive one and she the over-eager, anxious slut. He'd stopped her, even though he'd done it with Berta and Trisha and Theresea Longo and probably half of Rome, while this was Louise's first anything. The experienced Scott Turetsky had Louise Brown the virgin begging for it.

Now she was older, wiser.

"OK, F. Scott," she said. "Let's talk."

F. Scott combed his fingers through her fingers. "You're hands are so beautiful—they look like Georgia O'Keeffe's. Are you an artist?"

"No," said Louise. "I'm the School of the Arts acting admissions co-ordinator."

"I know that, Louise Brown." He smiled at her shyly. "But what are you in your heart?"

In her heart, that wobbly, faltering muscle, that generator of panic and fear? What was she in her heart but lonely?

"I don't know," said Louise softly. She hated him.

F. Scott Turetsky's right index finger grazed her collarbone.

"Everyone's an artist in their heart."

She didn't have time for this. But F. Scott Turetsky was going on. See, his parents were willing to spring for his tuition. He knew he should probably just move out to Williamsburg, get a day job and paint his ass off, but he'd never really been out of school before, and he guessed—his finger exploring the hollows above her breasts—he was a little scared. Of the real world.

Oh God, thought Louise. I'm not seventeen anymore—I don't have to listen to this.

She decided to take matters into her own hands. Literally.

"Hey, this is all right," F. Scott Turetsky said.

In a minute, they were both naked and on the floor, existential crises now mercifully forgotten.

He stopped for just a moment to pull his wallet out of his jeans. He plucked out a condom, a fluorescent yellow lubricated Sheik, and said, "Is this all right? I mean, I wouldn't want you to do anything you didn't want to."

That same old Scott Turetsky line.

"It's fine," said Louise, "it's good." And when he fumbled a little with the rubber, she said under her breath, "Come on."

Once cloaked, F. Scott Turetsky stuck out in front of himself like a luminous yellow wand.

He rolled on top of her, so Louise turned the tables this time, and she rolled on top of him. "Mmmm," said F. Scott Turetsky, "whatever the hell you want."

Who was this guy, this cute young guy, this M.F.A. applicant that Louise was now fucking? Was he really her beloved Scott Turetsky, her old lost love reincarnate? Or was he just some kid whom she'd practically picked up from the street?

What did it matter, now that she was finally getting a piece of what she wanted? Weren't there always going to be Scott Turetskys and F. Scott Turetskys, a new crop every generation, coming off the sexy-bad-boyfriend assembly line?

She'd met more than a few of them since her divorce. Producers, war correspondents, videographers. After thirty they grew their hair long again; they wore it in ponytails. And these guys were always off somewhere, Bali or Morocco or Bhutan, and they were always hopelessly in love with some Peace Corps gal or an Iranian photographer or a gorgeous mixed-race actress who just got cast in an upscale miniseries; some woman who jerked and jerked and jerked them around, who jerked them around so much they couldn't help jerking you around, too, these Scott and F. Scott Turetskys. It was the trickle-down theory of romance.

But now Louise was on top. She was on top and liking it. This F. Scott Turetsky had melted into a blissful and helpless puddle between her hips.

Every few seconds, he would arch up or thrust or twitch or something, a little weak smile teasing at his lips, but at best his rhythm was syncopated and close to annoying; so, soon, through caresses and a careful squeezing of her inner organs, Louise seized control of the situation, F. Scott Turetsky giving up.

When they were young, Louise and Scott Turetsky, the summer nights in Larchmont were thick with the scent of pollen and perfume, the smell of gasoline, of pot, of cigarettes, of bug spray and his deodorant. Their young naked bodies were softened by the filmy haze of suburban starlight; they were as blurry and unreal as if a cinematographer were viewing them through a layer of shimmery gauze. When they were young, Louise would spread her legs and let Scott Turetsky enter her, whether she was ready or not, whether it hurt her or not, and she'd say, "I love you, Scott; I love you, honey," in intervals of about seventy-five seconds. She counted. She counted the intervals between her words of encouragement and the moments until it was over. Sometimes, sometimes it felt like his fucking her went on forever; then other times it was over before she knew it.

But when it was over, when he had come, when he had finished, he would completely collapse, sinking down on Louise, his hipbone grinding into her pelvis; the weight of his body flattening out her lungs, making it hard to breathe; the soft, tender tissue of her vagina aflame and burning—so much so that after a couple of rounds of this, when she peed later, even in the shower, it would sting. And she'd think, Someday I will find someone who loves me; someday I'll get married and have a husband; someday sex will be something I like, I love—it will be something good.

Now, in her apartment with F. Scott Turetsky, it was Louise who was keeping it going, getting him to the brink, then pulling back, then getting him to the brink again. The poor kid was all shiver and moan.

"Oh God," he said, "thank you. Thank you, God, a lot."

With a slow in and out she pleased him.

Only when he gave up the ghost did she finally allow herself to come. And then they slid away from each other in a loose knot, on her living-room floor, F. Scott Turetsky's right arm slung haphazardly across her waist as he lightly, lightly began to snore, while Louise tried to even out her own breathing, to calm her racing heart.

Now she was lying half-clothed—for she still had her T-shirt on—on her floor with a boy half her age, dead asleep, in her arms, with a boy she didn't know. His mouth was open, and a little spit bubble breathed in and out of the corner. She smelled his buzzed head; it was as sweaty and sweet as a baby's. What had she done? She could lose her job for this. Now that he'd slept with her, maybe this strange kid thought he could gain admission to the graduate program of his choice. Or worse yet, he just might fall in love.

She wriggled out from under his arm. She covered him with one of her sofa throws. Then she got up and went into the kitchen, looking for a cigarette. In the cookie jar was her emergency pack. She tapped one out and lit up. Smoking, she went back into the living room. A beautiful naked boy was sleeping on her rug.

She'd fucked him.

When they were young, when they were done, Louise would trace the words "I love you" across Scott Turetsky's still-panting moist back with the tip of her right forefinger—employing the same hope and delicacy with which she might have traced those heartfelt words on a steamed-up backseat window. And she'd say, "That was great, Scott—I really love you," which was true. The second part was true: She really did; she really did love him. She loved him and she loved him and she loved him, and she was never going to get over him, no matter what anybody had to say about puppy love and life experience. No, Louise never was going to get over the stupid dead boy she loved with all her heart when she was so ridiculously, improbably young that it should have been against the law.

It should have been against the law back then to have been as young as Louise Brown once was.

And now, at last, she's old.

Gerald Shapiro

"Worst-Case Scenarios"

Spivak leaned forward in his chair, ready to pounce. "Let me give you a for-instance," he said, and reached for the telephone that sat in front of him on the polished rosewood conference table. A group of elderly women sat across from him, some of them tapping their fingers on the tabletop, others holding their purses in front of them like shields. The air in the conference room was lush with the scent of perfume. "Now, let's just say that you're home alone," Spivak began. "It's nighttime. Very late—one, two in the morning." He punched some buttons on the phone. "Okay—the telephone rings."

And it did. The ring blasted into the conference room, and the group of elderly women flinched at the sound. Spivak leaned over and adjusted the volume on the side of the phone. He looked intently across the table at a tall, buxom woman in a navy blue dress. Her silver hair was thick and piled high off her head, and a broad streak of white shot straight up through the middle of it, rising off her forehead like a runway.

"What should you do?" he asked her. "Should you answer it?"

The phone rang again, just as she was about to speak. "I'd be in bed," she said. "My husband would answer it. The phone's on his side."

The phone rang again. "He isn't there," Spivak snapped.

"He's not?" the woman asked, smiling. "Where is he?"

"Let's say he's dead," Spivak said, and watched her face fall. The phone rang again. "You're all alone," Spivak continued. "I told you that."

"That's a despicable thing to say," the woman said.

Spivak bit his lip and reconsidered. "Wait a second," he said in a conciliatory tone of voice. "He's not dead, he's just away." The phone rang again. "Yeah, there you go—he's out of town, on business. And it's very, very late," he reminded her. "Should you answer it? It might be one of your children."

The phone rang again, and again the women across the table flinched.

"Of course it might be someone calling to see if anyone's home," Spivak said. "Someone wanting to break in, let's say. Rapists, thieves."

"My children wouldn't call that late," the woman in the blue dress said. "They're very considerate." She brought a tissue out of her purse and wiped at her forehead with it. Again the phone rang; it seemed to be getting louder.

"They might," Spivak said. "They might need help. It could be an emergency. One of your grandchildren, maybe." He turned to another of the women seated around the table, this one thin and fidgety, wearing a red sweat suit. Her white hair was bound up in a matching bandanna. "What about you?" he asked her.

The phone rang again. It was definitely getting louder.

"I'll admit it—I'd be a little nervous," the woman said, and laughed nervously, running a hand rapidly up and down the loose flesh of her neck as if to make sure she was still there.

"Of course you'd be nervous," Spivak said. The phone rang again. "Let's face it—you'd be terrified." He pushed the telephone across the polished rosewood toward the woman in the navy blue dress. "Pick it up. Go ahead," he told her. "Say hello."

The woman gazed down at the phone tentatively, as though it might be a firecracker. It rang again, and finally she picked it up. "Hello?" she said. Amazingly, her voice rang out in the room as though she'd spoken into a microphone. Even more amazingly, it wasn't her voice at all. It was a man's voice, deep and authoritative. It sounded eerily like Gregory Peck in *To Kill a Mockingbird*.

"Oh, my goodness!" the woman exclaimed into the phone's receiver, and again her words poured out loud and clear for all the women in the room to hear.

Spivak reached under the table and fiddled with a device hidden out of sight. "Now say hello again," he instructed the woman, and this time when she spoke into the phone it was her own voice, tremulous and plaintive, that came flooding out.

He adjusted the knot in his necktie as he settled back in his chair, then he crossed one leg over the other under the table and smiled. He sat there like that for a moment, smoothing the crease in his slacks, letting the silence build just a bit before he spoke. "I'd like you to meet the Flaxman Voice Transformer Deluxe," he said. "The single woman's friend par excellence." He lifted a small black box from beneath the conference table and held it in his palm like a ruby. "The 620, our best seller—six men's registers to pick from, basso profundo to an Irish tenor, plus the incessant bark of a Rottweiler, for those tough-to-get-rid-of prank callers." Spivak reached for another phone and picked up the receiver. As he spoke into it, he rotated a dial on the voice transformer. "Hello, hello, hello," he said, and it sounded like the rising pitch at the start of an old Three Stooges comedy. "One end plugs into the handset, the other end into any standard wall jack," he said as he hung up the phone. "A child can operate it. What do you think?" He gazed across the table at the woman in the blue dress, who still held the phone receiver in her hand. "You can hang it up now," he suggested to her gently, and she did.

"While I have your attention, ladies," he said, "let me give you another for-instance. Call it a worst-case scenario if you like. Let's say, just for the fun of it, that you're on vacation. You're in Europe. Why not! Live it up! You're in Venice, you're on the Grand Canal, you're in a gondola, somebody's singing "O Sole Mio" in the background. You took every precaution before you left—locked every window, every door, made sure the gas was turned off on the stove, stopped the paper, had a neighbor come over and collect your mail every day. You've got light timers on in every room. You've hired a boy down the street to keep the lawn mowed. Cute little kid. You've thought of everything. Unfortunately for you, so have a couple of tattooed ignoramuses who are in your backyard just about now—and they're going to break into your house in about two seconds flat."

At first Spivak had worked on everything. He'd done fine work in focus groups on breakfast cereals, women's fashions, perfume, cruise offers, packaged noodle dinners, mail-order fruit, book clubs, and a variety of diet plans. For nearly six months he'd navigated through some pretty tricky market research for a spray-on spaghetti sauce called Pasta-Magic. He'd done focus groups for both Democrats and Republicans, for the Humane Society and the National Rifle Association. He'd even done one for the Unitarian Church.

But then, five years ago, after the unpleasantness with the Instant Pot-o-Stew account, just when things had started to look truly bleak for him at the marketing agency, out of the blue his unit suddenly inherited the Flaxman account. Oh, of course at first he'd belittled the Flaxman line of products. Who wouldn't have? "God, look at this pathetic crap," he'd joked to his co-workers, leafing through the crudely produced catalogue of Flaxman gadgets. "Get a load of this: a pencil that tests the lead content in your tap water? Special socks that retard plantar warts? Be still my heart!"

"This is career death," he told his creative director, a pimply boy named Berenson. "Putting me on this account—this is the kind of thing that ruins a guy's career. This is the kind of thing that happened to Pinsker, isn't it?" he asked, referring to a drooling seventy-year-old art director who sat in a small, airless cubicle far away from any windows, doodling logos for powdered toothpaste on large sketch pads all day.

"What happened to Pinsker is that somebody invented television," Berenson said. "The Korean War ended. Women started having sex. Anyway, don't worry about him, Leo. Worry about yourself. Pinsker owns stock in the agency, the creep. I can't fire him. I'd love to fire him—he reminds me of my grandfather, who used to pinch me and poke me whenever my parents weren't looking. But that's all behind me now." Berenson stood up and leaned over his desk, splaying his fingers out in front of him. "You don't own any stock in the agency yet, do you?" he asked.

"No," Spivak said.

"You're a lot older than me, aren't you?"

"Quite a few years," Spivak said. He started edging toward the door of Berenson's office.

"Was there anything else you wanted to talk about?" Berenson asked.

"No, I guess not."

In the first months after he'd begun to work on the Flaxman account, Spivak gradually came to the sickening realization that his focus group work had never been so sharp. Something amazing happened to him when he was talking to groups of women about Flaxman products. For a time he desperately denied the obvious—who, after all, would want to admit that this kind of thing was his calling?—but after a few months there was no longer any way to deny the rush of adrenalin he felt when he began a pitch. "Let's say, just for the sake of argument," he'd begin, "that you've got radon in your home." And then he'd be off to the races. "Radon—you can't smell it, you can't see it. Sure, the Environmental Protection Agency tells you they're not *positive* that radon is harmful. Hello? Come again? Not *positive?* Here's a worst-case scenario for you: it's killing your kids. You heard me: killing your children, silently, slowly, inch by inch, as you sit here today." And then he'd whip out the Flaxman Radon Detector Deluxe, a little tube that looked like it might contain nasal spray.

Within eight months, over sixty Flaxman products were being focus-grouped in cities around the country, and sales were climbing steadily. Spivak found himself, after fifteen years in marketing, suddenly in the chips at last. At marketing conventions, total strangers would approach him and ask for tips. "Do that worst-case scenario stuff for me," they'd say. "Give me one—just an example." And Spivak, feeling a bit sheepish, would do it. The truth was, as awful as it was to admit it, he could do that kind of thing in his sleep. In fact, he often did.

Spivak stopped for lunch at one-thirty; after all, there was only so much terror he could strike into the hearts of elderly women on two cups of coffee and a bagel with cream cheese. He calculated the morning's results: a solid B, more or less. He'd done better, he'd done worse. You learned to take the bad with the good in Spivak's line. Not everything lit them up like the Flaxman Voice Transformer. That one was definitely a keeper, he told himself. Maybe it was the Gregory Peck voice that got them. What the hell—*he* wanted to sound like Gregory Peck, why shouldn't the average housewife? Now he sat slumped in his chair at the rosewood conference table. A turkey sandwich someone had ordered in from a nearby deli sat untouched on the table next to the telephone. Spivak wasn't in any mood to touch it: who knew what was in that thing, anyway? Turkey, mayo, tomato, lettuce—it was all a breeding ground for filth and disease. Flaxman should come out with a bacterial detection system. Carry it with you to foreign countries! Works just as well here at home! He saw it suddenly—it looked like one of those gizmos that takes your temperature in your ear. Here's the demo: stick it in a burrito down south of the border and watch the needle jump! Make a note, he told himself, but he simply didn't have the energy at the moment to whip out his miniature tape recorder.

After he'd tossed the sandwich into a wastebasket (a simple turn-around jumper, though he thought he'd executed it with genuine grace), he stopped a moment to figure the two-hour time difference in his head, and then called Chicago to catch his daughter, Elena, in the midst of her Friday after-school rapture. It was one of the rare moments during the course of a week when she'd be reasonably willing to talk to him.

"Daddy," Elena gushed, her voice soft and girlish—the same voice he'd heard her use with her new boyfriend, Todd, the one with the Italian motor scooter. Spivak imagined her crouched down in a ball, her back against the knotty pine paneling in the family room, the phone cradled in the crook of her neck, hugging her jawbone as if glued there. He saw her fingers entwined in a long, curly black strand of her hair. Where had all that hair come from, he wondered. Spivak's wife, Rachel, had an unruly strawberry blond mop, and his own hair, what there was of it, was a shy, retiring shade of mousy brown. Maybe good hair skipped a generation, like Huntington's chorea.

Lately, though, maybe the past year, two years, he'd begun to feel that the real mystery wasn't Elena's hair; it was Elena, period, the entire package. Her voice on the phone unnerved him, as it always did these days, and made him think of her legs, which in the last year and a half had lost their baby fat and had developed long, sensuous curves unlike any he'd ever seen when he was her age. What the hell had been going on with puberty these past few years? Was it something in the water? Had girls been this pretty when *he* was in the ninth grade? Had they seemed so grown-up, so terrifyingly *aware* of themselves?

"Hey," he said to her. "How's life? How's school?"

"Stupid," she said in a tone that suggested that the question, too, had been stupid. "Totally. Beyond belief."

"And your mother?"

"Let's not talk about it. Let's be kind. Let's talk about you," Elena purred.

"Since when do you call your mother *it?*"

There was a long pause. "How's it going, Daddy? I miss you."

"You doing your homework?"

"Yeah. I'm doing it."

"You know the deal—you pull a B-plus average this semester—"

"We're all going to Florida this summer," she said, mimicking his voice. "Walt Disney World, the whole *cucaracha*. I know. That's a bribe, Daddy. Mom says it's—"

"Hey, the world works on a series of bribes. One bribe after another. It's what makes the world go round. Tell that to your mother. Tell her Professor Spivak has spoken."

"When'll you be home?"

"Another couple of days. We just have one or two more of these focus groups to do, then I'm on that plane. What's it doing back there?"

"Snowing. The dry kind—you can't even make snowballs out of it," Elena moaned. "It just flies around and gets in your eyes. Boring, boring, boring."

"It sounds pretty to me," he said in a slightly aggrieved tone of voice. "Like one of those paperweights. What do you want me to bring back from San Francisco? How about some sourdough bread?"

"Yuck. I'm on a diet," Elena said.

"Diet? My little girl?"

"Daddy," she complained. And then her low voice purred mischievously again: "I'm not so little anymore." He heard her intake of breath, as though she'd surprised herself by saying it.

My God, he thought, she was fourteen years old: where in the name of God had she gotten a voice like that?

There was still the matter of lunch. At a Guatemalan diner on Twenty-Fourth Street, Spivak sat at a table by the window so he could watch the parade of passersby. Sunlight striped into the diner through the window blinds, reminding him of Elena, and of the snow falling in Chicago. Two thousand miles away snow was falling; Lake Michigan was frozen from shore to shore. Thinking of it, looking through the window blinds at the sunny winter afternoon, he felt suddenly displaced, as though he'd been evicted from his life and was tumbling through the ether, through nothingness. This was what children were for, Spivak told himself: sooner or later, they made you think you'd stepped off a ledge into thin air. He sipped a Calistoga water and ate an order of cheese pupusas and pastalitos accompanied by a sharp, vinegary cabbage salad. A group of Hispanic female impersonators merengued down the sidewalk past his window; a woman carrying an infant on each hip walked by, followed by two more children attached to her waist with short lengths of rope; traffic slowed to accommodate a funeral procession, complete with large placards bearing sepia-toned photographs of the deceased and a marching band full of doleful trumpets and tubas; a burly brown-skinned fruit peddler rambled through the crowd on the sidewalk, hawking bananas, mangoes, plantains, and papayas. He happened to catch Spivak's gaze for a moment, and held up a banana in what Spivak assumed was an obscene gesture.

And then, just as he was eating the last of his pupusas, a woman walked by, her pace quick and determined. Middling height, browning-blonde hair, square shoulders, and a thoughtful, resolute cast to her features. A lavender blouse and what looked like a floral-patterned batik skirt. She wasn't in Spivak's line of sight for more than a second, but he knew her instantly: Betsy Ingraham, the girl he'd never had a snowball's chance in hell of dating in high school—twenty-five years since they'd last seen one another and now here she was, walking down a street in San Francisco, half a continent away from De Lesseps High in Kansas City, Missouri. He realized in that instant that she'd never really been out of his thoughts, her face never far from his mind's gaze these past twenty-five years.

Spivak was out of his chair in the next breath, racing for the diner's door. "Betsy!" he yelled out.

"Excuse me!" the cafe's proprietor cried from behind the cash register. Spivak hastily whipped out his wallet and threw a few bills on a nearby table. Then he raced down the street, dodging through pedestrian traffic.

"Betsy," he cried again. And this time, the woman with the resolute features stopped and turned around.

"Betsy," he said again, this time in a panting voice. He tried to smile at her, but the utter lack of recognition in her face wiped the attempt off his lips immediately.

"Do I know you?" she asked.

"Yes! Leo Spivak! De Lesseps High, class of '68!" he said. "I mean, no, we didn't know each other." He gulped for air. What the hell, they were so far away from that world, cut free of it in time and space. He felt utterly free now, not just older but actually reborn. "I knew *you*. I was in love with you," he said. "I mean absolutely mad for you. It was pathetic."

She looked at him intently then, holding a hand up to shield her eyes as though they were standing in bright sunlight, though in fact they were in deep shade under the awning of a video store. "Leo?" she said.

"Spivak. We were in Advanced Placement English together. Mrs. Menotti's class, senior year. My paper was on F. Scott Fitzgerald."

Still she looked at him without a spark. "Leo Spivak," she said. Then she shrugged, just a small gesture, a flick of her shoulders. "Hello. Do you live here now?"

"No, no, I live in Chicago. I'm just here on business. You?"

"In the Sunset district—it's out by the ocean. I've lived here since college. What kind of business?"

"Oh, nothing very exciting. Marketing and advertising, that kind of thing." He always hated it when people asked him what he did for a living. If he'd only been able to say something like, "Oh, I run a non-profit organization devoted to saving starving African war orphans," or something like that, he might have had some chance to feel good about himself. As it was, what was he going to say? I scare elderly women to death? That's my job?

Betsy lowered her hand from her eyes. "Oh, advertising. That must be very exciting," she said, and smiled at him. She was still gorgeous, her skin smooth and lightly tanned, her eyes bright blue. Her eyebrows were dark and heavy, unplucked, and this feature, which he'd never noticed in high school, somehow made her even more beautiful to him now.

"It's a living. And what about you?" he asked her.

"I'm a lawyer—legal aid for the homeless, mostly."

There it was—one of those starving African orphan jobs! He should have known; in high school Betsy Ingraham had worn her hair long and straight like Joan Baez and played the guitar in the yearly variety show; one year she sang "Kumba Ya," another year "Blowin' in the Wind." She wasn't just beautiful, she was noble, too. Spivak could hardly stand it. He bit his lip. "That's very admirable," he said.

"I hate it, actually," she said. "Homeless people are pretty depressing.

Most of them are crazy. I spend a lot of time talking to people who think that God talks to them through the toilet—that kind of thing." She shifted her weight and adjusted the jute bag that was slung over one of her shoulders.

My God, she's even amusing, Spivak said to himself. I never knew she was amusing. Who could have known such a thing? A moment of silence went by, and with alarm he felt the thread between them begin to slacken. "This is sure wild, isn't it?" he said, and mopped his brow with the back of one hand. "I mean seeing each other here after all these years."

"Oh, it's not so wild. Two years ago I was in Chinatown to buy fish for dinner and I saw Brad Pettybone. I hadn't seen him since senior prom. Remember Brad?"

Remember Brad! Who was she kidding? Brad Pettybone, class salutatorian; Brad Pettybone, all-state wrestler; Brad Pettybone, the lead in *The Music Man*, the senior class musical—the only guy in school to have a noticeable cleft in his chin. Spivak was amazed that the name still conjured up such a wave of longing and envy and regret. Brad Pettybone had probably groped Betsy Ingraham big-time, back when groping was as good as it got. Spivak's imagination fastened itself on the image of the two of them, Brad and Betsy, somewhere quiet and dark in Kansas City, some glade in the forest primeval, a few crickets providing the only background noise to cover their slurping adolescent kisses in the front seat of something like a T-bird. God, what it must have been like!

"Leo?" she said. Passersby jostled them on the sidewalk, and they moved closer to the video store's windows to get out of the mainstream of traffic.

"Oh, yes. Brad," Spivak said. "Sure I remember him."

"Coincidences aren't that rare, really. It's a small world."

"Tiny," Spivak agreed.

"Well," Betsy said, and looked at her watch. "Well, it was awfully nice to see you."

"Are you married?" he asked suddenly.

"Yes, yes I am. Two children, a boy and a girl," she said. Her eyes wandered away from him, and again he felt the moment pulling apart, going dead on him like an overfed goldfish. What the hell was he doing? What did he want?

"I am, too. One daughter," he said. "My wife's a CPA."

"Congratulations," Betsy said, and smiled. "That must make it nice at income tax time." She looked at her watch again.

"Betsy Ingraham," he said, nodding his head like a dummy. "Betsy Ingraham. This is amazing. So tell me, what's your name now? Your married name, I mean."

Betsy seemed to be nibbling on something inside her mouth. She looked away. "You're not going to call me or anything, are you?"

"No, no, I just want to know!" he said. He laughed gently to show the innocence of his intent, and shook his head as if to say, What a loony idea! "Hey, that was high school, okay?" he said.

"Wexler," she said. "My husband's name is Arthur. He works at a science museum here in the city. Look, I really ought to be heading off. This is my one free afternoon all week, and I've got a ton of errands. It was great to see you." She looked flustered for a moment, as if she might be running through a short list of conversational closers: See you soon, Keep in touch, Have a nice day. None of them seemed appropriate, so she said, "Well—so long." There was a split second, just before she walked away, when it seemed likely that they might touch: shake hands, if nothing else, or perhaps exchange air-kisses, maybe even—could it be?—hug one another briefly. But he hesitated, waiting for her to make the move (he, after all, had already leaped past the bounds of propriety with that idiotic declaration of high-school infatuation, hadn't he?), and the moment passed.

For a moment, a breath or two, Spivak stood watching the back of her head as it disappeared amidst the bustle of foot traffic. Then he ran after her again, caught her half a block down the street and whirled her around by an elbow, feeling the soft washed silk of her lavender blouse. "Okay, look," he panted. "I said I was in love with you all the way through high school. It wasn't love, exactly. I mean, maybe it was love, but it was something else, too. I wanted to fuck you—I didn't even know the word *fuck* at the time, but I wanted to *blah-blah* you in the worst way possible. I'm talking about explosive sex, lots of it, the kind that breaks furniture. The kind where you look at your watch and it's Tuesday all of a sudden. The kind that makes you feel like something has *happened* to you, for God's sake. Call me crazy, but *that's* what I'm talking about."

The stream of pedestrian traffic parted around them like water around a rock. They stood there, the two of them. Spivak heard the echo of what he'd just said, as though a tape delay inside his head was playing it back for him. What was he thinking of? What was happening to him? He was afraid to look at her, afraid she'd be looking at her watch again.

"Where's your hotel?" she asked after a moment of silence.

He couldn't help himself; he knew it was tacky, but he simply had to know. "So how was it?" he asked. Betsy lay face down on the bed, her head underneath a pillow. She said something, but the words were muffled. After a moment he lifted the pillow and said, "Would you repeat that?"

"I said it was nice. You talk dirty a lot."

"I've never done that before in my life. Did you like it?"

"It was okay."

"Which part? I mean which—what?"

"*I'm* not going to say any of that."

He leaned down to the pillow. "How about 'I'm gonna suck your tits.' " Silence. "How was that? How about 'Ride me, Baby, ride me.' "

"Stop it." She pulled her head out from under the pillow and sat up, facing away from him. "I've got to go," she said, talking to her watch.

"Wait a second—wait," Spivak said. "Hold it. We've just spent twenty minutes here. Twenty minutes. I've been waiting twenty-five years for this—it's like a dream come true for me. It can't be over in twenty minutes."

Betsy turned to him and put a hand on his arm. "Look, it may be a dream to you, but I've got errands to run," she said. "It's no joke—I really do."

"Just give me ten more minutes. And for God's sake, whatever you do, don't put on any clothes."

She sighed. "Can I go to the bathroom, please?"

"Of course you can. Call me Leo, will you? That's a particular turn-on for me, don't ask me why."

"I'll be right back, Leo," she said, and walked to the bathroom. He watched her backside as she covered the ten feet or so to the door, the sway of her legs and her ass, the dimples behind her knees. The bed was a mess—they'd really had at it. Wow, this was something. His eyes ranged over the bedclothes, the crumpled sheets, the lavender blouse and batik skirt in a small heap on the carpet. Room service—that was it. He'd call and order up some champagne—what the hell! He'd pay for it in cash, that way it wouldn't show up on the hotel bill, Rachel wouldn't ever have to know.

My God, he thought. What am I doing? Rachel's face was before him suddenly, fragile and luminous and forgiving. What are you doing, Leo? she asked him. What kind of a putz are you being? He sank back against the headboard of the bed, put a hand over his eyes, and took several deep breaths. Okay, he told himself. This is pretty bad. This is definitely the worst thing I've ever done in my marriage. This is a lot worse than lying about the dented fender on the Oldsmobile. This is worse than what I did with Suzy Chudnow under the table at the company Christmas party two years ago, because then I was stone-drunk, for crissake, and anyway, we were just kidding around. It was also worse, he realized, than that time in Florida at the convention, because that time *nothing went on*, it was a little hanky-panky above the waist, a little slappy-hands below the waist, and a couple of kisses that threatened to pull his lips right off his face, but other than that *nothing went on*. Yes, this one was really bad, no doubt about it.

But it could have been worse. He could have fucked one of Rachel's best friends, for instance. He could have fucked her sister, for that matter, he told himself, and believe me, she'd do it, too. That sister of hers—don't get me started on her sister. Talk about predators. Or Rachel could have been in the hospital, let's say, for an operation, and he could have fucked her night nurse—now that would have been unforgivable. That would have been beyond the pale. Or he could have fucked somebody at home, in his own bed, under his own sheets, somebody—oh my God—somebody from down the street, one of those women from the neighborhood watch committee. That was off the map, a sin of unthinkable proportion. Don't even talk about it. A felony, a capital crime. This was bad, all right, but it wasn't *that* bad.

Betsy came out of the bathroom wrapped in a towel. "Take that thing off, will you?" he said, and miraculously she dropped the towel to the floor. "Stop right there!" he cried. "Just stand there a minute! Don't move." She stood still. "You're gorgeous," he told her.

"Thank you," she said, and bit her lip. "Can I move now?"

"Yes."

She moved toward the bed, her skin glowing in the lamplight. "Listen: I want to meet your husband," Spivak told her as she lay down beside him. "I want to meet Arthur."

"You what? You're kidding."

"I want to meet your whole family, in fact."

"Absolutely not," Betsy said, and got up. "Where are my panties?"

"Absolutely not, *Leo*," he reminded her.

"Leo, look, help me find my panties, will you." She flung the crumpled sheets off the bed. "What am I doing? Goddamnit, where are they?" She quickly slipped on her bra, then her blouse and her skirt. At each stage of the process, Spivak uttered soft little yelps of protest, but Betsy seemed not to be listening. When she was dressed she got down on her hands and knees and peered under the bed. "Help me out here, will you?" she asked him. "I've got to find my panties."

"We could all have dinner together. You pick the restaurant."

"Are you kidding?" Betsy said, her voice muffled by the mattress. "You're crazy, you know that? Goddamnit, they have to be here somewhere."

"Listen. Just listen to me. Do this one thing for me and I'll never bother you again," he said. "I won't call you, I won't even think about you. I'm not kidding."

She stood up straight and looked down at him. "I should never have done this. I must be crazy. I don't even know you." She sighed deeply, put a hand to her forehead, and looked around the room again, though this time her movements were slower, and her shoulders slumped. "They walked off—my panties just skipped town," she said, more to herself than to Spivak. "They're smarter than I am; they knew better than to stick around."

"See, that's just what I mean. You're funny—I didn't know you were funny," Spivak said in an admiring voice. "I love that. I mean, that's better than 'I want to suck your tits,' as far as I'm concerned. Now here's what I have in mind: just a simple dinner, something Chinese, maybe. We can order family style. Moo goo gai pan, that kind of thing."

Betsy stared at him as if he might be on fire. "Why would I do that?" she asked. "What could that possibly accomplish? Are you out of your mind?"

"Just this one little thing? And then I'm gone, I'm out of your life for good."

"Listen, I'm sorry—"

"Listen, *Leo.*"

"Leo," she said, mimicking his voice, "you're not *in* my life. We just did something, it's the stupidest thing I've ever done in my life, and it's over. Don't ask me why I did it. I don't *know* why I did it. As far as I'm concerned, it didn't happen. This is just a bad dream, and I'm waking up. You didn't stop me on the street, we didn't come up to your hotel room, I didn't take off my *clothes*, my God, my God!" she said, and smacked herself in the forehead as if killing a mosquito that had landed there. "We didn't—we didn't have sex, we didn't do *anything*," she continued with her eyes closed. "We weren't even in Advanced Placement English together—and we're not having this conversation." She put on her shoes and walked toward the door. "My God, I'm not wearing any underpants," she murmured in a soft, bewildered voice. She stopped at the door and turned back to look at him. "Look," she said, "no hard feelings, okay? I hope you worked it through, whatever it was. Maybe you're not crazy. I don't know. But you're very strange. I've got to get out of here, I've got to get home." She shook her head wearily and looked at her watch again. "Don't get up. And don't say anything."

"Don't say anything, *Leo*," he reminded her as she walked out the door.

At seven o'clock that evening, Spivak's cab pulled up in front of an impressive cream-colored stucco house near the University of California Medical Center. It was a bungalow in the craftsman style, with wide overhanging eaves and a generous front porch covered with potted plants. As Spivak stepped out onto the sidewalk, he sniffed a salty tang riding the breeze; it was foggy here, and the air was considerably cooler than it had been downtown. He checked the address once more on the scrap of paper in his palm and then bounded up the flight of red brick steps to the front door and rang the bell.

A tall, nondescript, balding man Spivak's age answered the door. He held a newspaper, and his face wore a look of sullen confusion. "Yes?" he asked Spivak.

"I know this sounds odd," Spivak began, "but your wife left this pair of panties in my hotel room this afternoon." He held out the panties, which were of pale pink satin. "She couldn't find them when she left," he went on. "I was lying on top of them all the time. What a goofball!"

"Excuse me?" the man at the door asked. He adjusted his glasses and stared at the panties Spivak held out to him. Tentatively, he reached for them, then drew his hand back and looked at Spivak intently. "Did you say what your name was?" he asked.

"Leo Spivak. Call me Leo. You're Arthur, aren't you? Betsy didn't tell me much about you. You do museum work, don't you?"

Arthur stared at him a moment longer, then opened the door wider and stepped aside, a gesture Spivak interpreted as an invitation to come inside. He thrust the panties into Arthur's hand and walked into the house.

"This is beautiful," he said, sweeping his gaze around the polished hardwood floors, the Persian rugs, the beautifully framed artwork dotting the walls of the living room. "This is like something out of a magazine, I'm not kidding you. What *taste!*" He put his hands in his pockets and uttered a long, low whistle of approval. "I like it—no, wait, scratch that! I *love* it."

Arthur shut the door quietly and turned toward Spivak. He held the newspaper to his chest and deposited the panties carefully on a small table in the entryway. "What did you say your name was?" he asked.

"Leo Spivak. Betsy and I went to high school together in Kansas City. De Lesseps High. You know—Ferdinand De Lesseps? A man, a plan, a canal: Panama. That's a palindrome. I guess you probably knew that, though. You spell it the same, backwards or forwards. Actually De Lesseps didn't complete the Panama Canal."

"And you're telling me—"

"That was Goethals, another guy—another high school altogether."

"You're saying this afternoon, you and Betsy. . . ."

"Fairmont Hotel, room fourteen-sixty. It was all my idea. I was having lunch at a little Guatemalan place in the Mission. Can I sit down?"

Arthur nodded, and Spivak sat down on a long white sofa. "I called my daughter this afternoon. She's fourteen. Do you know what they're like when they get that age?"

"No," Arthur said. He stood by the bay windows and tapped his newspaper against the panes of glass. "You and Betsy? This afternoon?" he asked again.

"It was a long-distance call—we live in Chicago. We talked awhile. We didn't say anything. I mean we said some things, but we didn't really say anything. Anyway, I hung up and I thought to myself—I don't know what I thought." He wrung his hands. "It's like she's been kidnapped by aliens or something. She calls her mother *it*. What am I supposed to think about that?"

"And you're telling me she left her panties? She just left them? You expect me to believe Betsy left her panties at the Fairmont Hotel and now you've come to deliver them?" Arthur said. He was tapping the newspaper in one palm now, like a riding crop.

"She was in a hurry to leave," Spivak said. "She was upset."

"Who *are* you?" Arthur demanded.

"Leo Spivak. De Lesseps High. Maybe it's not Elena at all. I don't know. I've been doing this work—you don't want to know about it, believe me. I'm in marketing, in Chicago. Did I mention that yet? This one account, it's like it's become my whole career—my entire life, in fact. Sometimes I think I spend all my time making up these things. Worst-case scenarios, I call them. I mean, that's my job. But you don't want to hear about any of that," he said, noting the waning intensity in Arthur's gaze. "You want to hear about me and Betsy, I guess," Spivak continued. "I spent four years slobbering over her back in high school. I mean I was insane over her. I never told anyone. I was a secret slobberer. Who was I going to tell? Mr. Langford, the counselor? Why would I tell him? He always had his fly half open. For all I knew, he was worse off than I was. Anyway, I haven't seen her since graduation. I always thought about her, though—wondered what she might be doing, where she was, all of that. I never even let myself *imagine* having sex with her. Well, okay, I imagined it, but I didn't *linger* on it, if you know what I mean. Then today, this afternoon, out of the blue—Wow! Whoa! Amazing! Talk about delayed gratification!"

Arthur took a running leap at Spivak and landed on his upper body. The two of them cracked hard into the back of the sofa and Spivak's glasses broke in two at the bridge against Arthur's chin. "Sonuvabitch," Arthur muttered through clenched teeth. He didn't seem to know any more about fighting than Spivak did, but that didn't matter because he was on top; he grabbed Spivak's thinning hair and wrenched it, flailed with his fists against Spivak's upper chest and shoulders, slapped Spivak hard a couple of times in the face, then lifted a book off the coffee table, a heavy volume on Impressionist Art, and dropped it on Spivak's nose.

After a moment they separated, and Arthur slumped back against one of the arms of the sofa, winded. He put his knuckles over his eyes and breathed heavily.

"Arthur? What was that sound?" Betsy's voice called from upstairs, and in a moment she came down in a white terry-cloth robe, combing out her wet hair.

"Don't come in here," Arthur said in a weak voice. He rose from the sofa on unsteady legs.

Betsy walked into the living room. She looked first at Arthur, then down at Spivak, who sat crumpled at the far end of the sofa, holding both hands over his nose. For a long moment she didn't speak. Then she said, "Oh, my God."

Late that night—his watch was broken, so he didn't really have any idea of the time—Spivak managed to unlock the door to his hotel room and totter inside. "Sonuvabitch. Suck my tits," he muttered, then he shut his eyes, flipped on the overhead light, and groped his way toward the disheveled bed.

First he'd had quite a bit to drink in the Rainbow Room downstairs, and then when they asked him to leave, he'd gone to another bar around the corner, someplace small and dark where the music was sad and no one wondered about the dried blood on his chin. He felt his nose gingerly: it wasn't throbbing anymore, just aching sharply. Worse than his nose—worse, in fact, than the shooting pain in his left shoulder, and the bruises on his chest, and the pounding headache that felt like an awl had been driven partway into his right eardrum—was the fact that the two halves of his eyeglasses had been taped together so ineptly that, unless he squinted grotesquely, the entire world seemed to be coming at him from two wildly different angles.

Then Spivak opened his eyes and peered through slits, taking in the room. His lips spread into a wan smile. There, on the desk by the minibar, was his heavy, squarish black sample case. He pushed himself off the bed, stumbled his way to the sample case, and clawed at the latches until they popped open. For a moment he tried to sort through the contents of the case, but then, gasping for air, he upended the thing and watched Flaxman gadgets cascade to the floor, one after another, hitting and bouncing helter-skelter.

Spivak sank to his knees and grabbed the Flaxman Voice Transformer Deluxe, then he scooted across the floor to the night stand by the bed, and in a moment he had hooked the device to the phone. "Hello. Suck my tits," he said into the receiver, and the words came back to him in Gregory Peck's voice, a deep mutter choked with integrity—Atticus Finch arguing for the life of his client. "Sonuvabitch," Spivak said.

He dragged the phone up onto the bed and lay back against the pillows, exhausted. After a moment, when he'd gathered enough stamina, he dialed a long-distance number and listened to his breathing as the connection clicked into place. Then he counted the rings—eight, nine, ten, eleven, then twelve—before finally, just as he was about to hang up, he heard someone pick up the phone on the other end, and Rachel's soft, puzzled, sleepy voice came fuzzily on the line. "Hello?" she whispered.

Spivak shut his eyes and felt the receiver hot against his ear. "Hi," he said.

"Hello?" she repeated. "Who is this?"

"I'm calling to apologize," he said. The baritone decency of the voice shocked him; it sounded so much more genuine than anything he'd ever said before. "It's the only thing I can do."

"Who is this?" Her voice was sharper now.

"I've done something pretty bad this time," he said again, and this time, mixed in with Gregory Peck's voice, Spivak heard the wet hint of his own tears.

"If you call this number again, I'll contact the police."

"It could have been worse—don't get me wrong. But this was bad. This was bad. This is definitely worse than that Suzy Chudnow business. It's worse than that convention in Florida, too," Spivak continued, though he knew she'd already hung up.

Enid Shomer

"The Problem with Yosi"

Naomi's eyes swept the crowd in the kibbutz meeting hall to make sure everyone was listening. Her head moved deliberately, like a gun turret searching out a moving target.

"Then, he reached over and touched my breast," she said.

A unanimous "oy" rose from the members.

"What does Zalman say?" a woman asked.

The kibbutz doctor, seated beside Naomi at the table on the dais, leaned forward on his arms. "Other than his weight, he's in excellent health for a man of thirty-two. He's got some appetite."

The crowd mumbled. Naomi stood to get their attention, her silvery hair and freckled face shining in a beam from the overhead lamp. "What about a psychiatrist?" she asked. "Maybe we should send him down to Haifa to see Dr. Morganstern. She helped little Dafna that time. Remember?" she prodded them. "When Dafna pulled her eyebrows out?"

"Yes," the doctor said, "but that was what we call a neurotic compulsion. Yosi isn't sick. He's just lonely."

"No one ever wanted to marry him," a man called out. "I remember when he tried. Seemed like he asked nearly everyone."

"Last night on the path he touched my breast," Naomi repeated. "This is not a good omen. Something must be done."

268

Heads nodded agreement. The members—the *chaverim*—began to brainstorm, leaning forward and back in their folding chairs. "Order!" the leader, Lev, cried. "Let's take a break and have our tea." The *chaverim* aligned themselves at the back of the room near the samovar, their voices swelling and quickening. The name "Yosi" moved up and down the line like a password.

In the cow shed, Yosi was settling the milk cows for the night and cleaning the stalls. Sharon was helping him.

"You are liking the smell of the hay?" he asked, handing down a bale from the loft.

"Yes," she answered in her careful, American-accented Hebrew. "I like the smell of the hay." They had agreed to have bilingual conversations so that each could practice the other one's language. "You like the cows, don't you?" Sharon led the oldest dairy cow, Tsiporet, into her stall.

"Oh, yes. I'm liking them very much."

"Better than Ton-and-a-Half?"

"No, not better," he said. "Just different. Like two different animals, like a cat and a dog."

"But they're all the same, cows—"

"No," Yosi interrupted. "No, the girls are cows. The boy cow is . . . is . . . I don't know the word in English, is *shor.*"

"A bull. *Shor* is the Hebrew?"

"*Shor,* yes. He is a bull. He is different."

"Is he mean?" she asked, leading the last cow in from the outdoor pen.

"Oh no. He's a good bull. He always does his job."

"I know." Sharon lined up the water pails to be disinfected. She had seen Ton-and-a-Half do his job. He was a prize bull from America whose sperm was used all over Israel to improve the breeding stock. Yosi was the one who collected the specimen each week. Two months before, she had seen the bull pumping into the warm receptacle built into the "breeding wall." It was her second day on the kibbutz. Yosi had run back and forth, leading the "teaser" away just in time to turn the bull's attention to the surrogate opening. This had been Yosi's job for years, in addition to caring for the ten dairy cows the members kept for their own supply of sweet milk and cream.

"Ton-and-a-Half is very happy. So he's not mean. I think he knows what I'm doing. He doesn't mind. He never gets the heifer. Once in a while I bring him a real cow like Tsiporet to make fresh her milk."

Sharon scrubbed and hosed out the buckets. "How did you get your job?"

"I've always been a *bakar*," he laughed. "Like Roy Rogers, like Hopalong."

"A cowboy?" Sharon studied the face set on the thick neck. A fringe of wispy blond hair glowed halolike around his bald head, giving him an expression of perpetual amazement. "You don't look like any cowboy I've ever seen," she said.

Yosi lowered his gaze to the floor as if he'd dropped something of value.

"Oh, but I think all that's missing, really, is the hat," Sharon added.

The meeting resumed. "Order!" Lev shouted, pounding the table with his hand. "Eli?"

A burly redhead rose. "Let's try to arrange a *shiduch* for him. My mother knows a matchmaker in Tel Aviv—"

"Yosi doesn't want to live in the city," Naomi objected. "A match with a city girl? They don't like the kibbutz life. They like their fancy clothes and their typewriters and their lipstick." Though Naomi had brought the complaint against Yosi, she had only his best interests at heart, she explained.

"How serious is it, Naomi?" Miriam asked.

"He put his hand on my breast."

"Yes, but you're old enough to be his mother. Do you think it could go farther than that? Do you think," she hesitated, "he might force himself on someone? Become violent?"

"Violent?" Naomi swatted the word away with her hand. "We're talking about Yosi. He's not a criminal. But it's so unpleasant having to push him away, treating him like a child. Yosi? I don't think he has violence in him. Still, we must do something. We can't have him hiding in the bushes waiting to touch women in the darkness."

"I think he was staring at me when I came out of the shower house the other day," another woman offered.

"So what's the harm in looking?" Lev joked. The women in the room groaned in unison.

"You want him looking at your wife, maybe?" It was Miriam.

"Pardon me," Lev said earnestly. "All right. Let's be practical. Who has an idea? Don't be shy, *chevrai*."

The room seemed to inflate like a balloon as they sighed deeply and pondered the question. Finally, Shimon spoke. "I was just remembering what my father did when I was seventeen. I mean, what he did to educate me about women."

The members waited as he groped for words, their eyes bright with anticipation. "He arranged for me a meeting in Tel Aviv."

"What does this have to do with Yosi?" Lev asked.

"A moment," Shimon continued. "He found a prostitute there, not an ordinary prostitute—"

"Tell me," Naomi chuckled, "what Israeli prostitute is an ordinary prostitute?"

"Order," Lev said calmly.

"She was very high-class. Superior in every way—gentle, kind—"

"And how did your father manage to find such a righteous whore?" Miriam asked.

The *chaverim* laughed. "A good qvestun!" shouted the old Russian, Samuel, from the last row.

"I don't know," Shimon confessed, his face red. "Anyway, it's not important—"

"To *you*, mebbe," Samuel countered. "But to your mother?"

"Order!" Lev repeated. "I think Shimon has an idea here."

"Thank you," Shimon said. "If Yosi is lonely and awkward with women, why not get him a prostitute—a very nice one, of course. A prostitute of his own, so to speak."

"Tel Aviv is too far away. I never noticed any in Haifa," Miriam worried. "I don't think there are any."

"You, mebbe, didn't notice," Samuel said. "You mebbe didn't notice World War I, but I assure you it happened."

Dr. Zalman took the floor, twisting the band of his wristwatch into a pretzel. "This idea sounds practical to me. And if it doesn't work, we'll know the problem goes deeper."

Again the *chaverim* buzzed and turned in their chairs, discussing the pros and cons. "Do I hear a motion?" Lev asked.

Shimon stood quickly to claim his idea. "I so move: that the kibbutz send Yosi to an appropriate prostitute—"

"How often?" someone asked. More buzzing. Shimon looked out over the faces in the room, watching their lips move, catching the emphatic phrase. "Once a week," he concluded.

"Everyone in agreement?" Lev polled them. Every hand went up. "Done! And who will tell him?"

"Let the doctor tell him," Naomi advised. "Say . . . that his hormones are building up and that it's healthy for a man to have sex on a regular basis. True?"

"True," the doctor agreed.

"And you, Samuel, you know-it-all. You find the prostitute."

"Mit pleasure."

Yosi studied the woman's calling card.

LEAH STAR (STROVOSKY)
18 MICHAEL
HAIFA, ISRAEL

A bright purple star exploded in the upper right-hand corner. The magenta letters were raised and seemed to flow like liquid under his calloused thumb as he touched them over and over.

Number 18 was the upstairs rear of a small apartment building overhung with bougainvillea, the orange blossoms bright against the white concrete. A small sign above the mailbox bore the same star as the calling card. In small script next to it were the words *Specialist in deep muscle massage*.

He had hardly pressed the buzzer when the door opened and a dark young woman took his hand, saying, "I'm so glad you could come."

"Thank you," he mumbled. His legs felt as if they were dissolving at the knees.

"Over here. Let's sit. I have made a small salad and we'll drink dry hock wine. You like hock, don't you?"

"Yes." He picked up a pillow decorated with metallic Yemenite embroidery and clutched it to his stomach.

"That was made by little deaf girls," she told him.

He looked around the room. "What was?"

"The pillow. The one in your lap. Would you like to eat now?"

"Yes." He was suddenly very hungry.

As he picked up his fork a large gray cat leapt onto the table. The utensil clattered to the floor.

"Oh Melech!" she chastised the cat. She removed him and set him gently on the floor, then came and stood behind Yosi as he leaned to retrieve the fork.

"Wait," she said, placing her hands on his shoulders. He froze. "You are very tense." Her fingers began to play his neck tendons like a keyboard. He let his head droop forward onto his chest.

"That feels good," he whispered.

She picked up the fork, letting her breasts graze his back as she leaned down. Then, with her arms around his neck, she wiped the fork with a napkin and pierced a tomato wedge.

"Open, please. Make big the tunnel for the choo-choo train." The fingers of her left hand stroked his lips. His mouth opened as if by reflex. She fed him the salad one piece at a time.

"That was delicious," he said, after she had wiped his mouth with the palm of her hand.

"Now it is my turn," she said, pretending to lift him from the chair.

"Your turn?" His eyes darted around the room.

"You feed me salad now," she explained. They traded places, and he imitated her perfectly. When he got to the last slice of cucumber he let the fork fall on purpose. She smiled, as if she knew what would happen next. The hard surface of his pants pressed against her arm as he straightened up and fed her the last morsel.

"And then what happened?" Sharon asked. She was standing in the barn doorway, a pail in one hand, the other hand on her waist.

"I'm embarrassed," Yosi admitted. "I know I promised, but . . ."

"What?"

"She is wonderful, my little Star. I am learning from her so much."

"Learning? Tell me."

He began to whistle and pull on Tsiporet's udder rhythmically. The cow's eyes looked waywardly at both of them as the fresh milk streamed into the bucket.

In the following weeks Yosi received letters every Sunday addressed in purple ink from Star. "Next time you come, bring me pictures from your childhood," the first letter requested. Another time she sent him green tea from Japan—a thin tissue-paper sack placed inside a note: "Steep this four minutes in boiling water," it instructed. "Next week kelp."

Yosi took a steamy shower every Thursday morning, shaved and readied himself like a bridegroom for his weekly visit with Leah. He had lost a few pounds, and his hair was slicked down now, leaving only a saucer-sized bald spot. Her insistence on touching his face convinced him that he was not as ugly as he had thought, that there was something exotic about his small gray eyes and fleshy ears.

Only Sharon knew what went on during his visits, and even she did not know everything. Nevertheless, she learned a great deal: the fourth week, Yosi had shaved Leah's legs for her; the sixth week he had licked honey from her breasts. She had given him a manicure and explained how the muscles in his arms worked. One Thursday morning, as Yosi left the dining hall in a cloud of hair tonic and cologne, Samuel had joked, "Look at him! A regular Mr. Hollywood!"

As Yosi pried the cow's mouth open, Sharon forced a large pill down her gullet. "You are not bored," he asked, "working with the cows?"

"No. Do you get bored with them?"

"They are like sisters," he said simply, replacing the lid on the bottle of capsules. "We must watch the next few days for the worms," he reminded her.

"Yosi, do you ever get bored with Star?"

He grabbed a shovel from its hook on the barn wall. "I am like Ton-and-a-Half, you know? Besides," he said, stabbing the shovel under a fresh pile of manure, "I love her."

Sharon carried a chair under each arm from the storage room to the main hall. "Where is everyone?" she asked Naomi, setting them down with a thud and a sigh.

"Outside, kibitzing."

"Looks like they're having their own meeting out there," Sharon observed.

"Yes." Naomi sat down at the end of an incomplete row. "It's about Yosi."

"But Yosi is in town. It's Thursday—"

"I know."

"Oh, I see." Sharon frowned.

"They're just jealous, of course. But they want to quit sending him to the prostitute. They say maybe he's rehabilitated by now, ready for a real girl."

The rising inflection of Naomi's voice made Sharon suddenly realize that this was a question.

"A real girl?"

"You know him well. He talks to you."

"You're not thinking of me with Yosi?"

Naomi patted Sharon's arm. "No, I don't mean you and Yosi. I meant he confides in you. Maybe he's told you something? Has he got his eye on someone here at the kibbutz?"

"I don't think so."

"I've known Yosi since he was a baby." Naomi wiped her neck with a handkerchief. "I only want what's best for him." She stared into Sharon's eyes, her forehead grooved with concern. "I don't want you to betray any confidences, exactly. Just tell me," she whispered loudly, "what's going on with him? What goes through his mind?"

"How good Leah is to him."

"The whore?"

"I don't think you ought to call her that."

"Aha!" Naomi exclaimed. "You've met her then?"

"Of course not. But Yosi's told me—"

"What?"

Sharon scrutinized Naomi. The freckles on her forehead, run together from the summer sun, suggested the shape of a land mass on a map. Asia, perhaps. "He loves her."

"I'm so glad for him." Naomi threw her arms around Sharon. Then her teeth bit into her lower lip, and she shook her head doubtfully. "We have a problem."

"We do?" Sharon followed Naomi's eyes to the doorway where a crowd of men had assembled. She could see their knobby legs as they shifted from one foot to the other and scuffed at the ground.

"The best defense is attack." Naomi held Sharon by the shoulders. "Are you willing to help?"

"Yes."

"Then here is what we will do." Naomi's eyebrows arched as she pulled Sharon closer. She unfolded a chair. The sound of its legs scraping the floor smothered her words as the hall began to fill.

Lev took up the usual business: first, a report on the grapefruit crop, a discussion of the new picking schedule. The allocation of money for a phonograph for the children's house was next. The poultry committee complained again about the unreliability of the itinerant chicken sexer and recommended employing one from nearby Kibbutz Shemesh in exchange for violin lessons with Samuel.

"Anything further?" Lev asked.

Shimon stood. "I wish to say I think it's enough, this sending Yosi to the prostitute. It's time for him to find someone on his own." The room remained quiet, so he continued. "I know practice makes perfect, but it isn't like he's going to make a career of it. We're not paying for him to become a concert violinist." The crowd fractured with laughter. Naomi's finger drummed on her ample thigh.

"Now?" Sharon asked her.

"Not yet."

"We never intended it as a permanent solution," Shimon went on.

"You can't cut a man's water off just like that!" Samuel objected, snapping his fingers for emphasis.

"We could wean him gradually . . . say, three more weeks," Shimon replied.

"That sounds reasonable," Doctor Zalman agreed. The *chaverim* buzzed briefly, an intermittent and unenthusiastic buzz, like the sound of a fly dying.

"Do I have a motion?" Lev asked.

"Now!" squeaked Naomi.

"*Rak rega echad!*" Sharon bellowed. "One minute please!" The *chaverim* were stunned first by the voice, then by the translation.

"Our newest member has the floor." Lev's voice was solemn.

"Thank you," Sharon said. Silence descended on the members like a sheet thrown over a bird cage. "The other night, when I was coming from the barn, he put his hand on my breast." Now the silence filled the room in heaps and drifts, engulfing her words. "And my leg," she added, "high up."

"Oh no," Miriam sighed.

"This sheds a different light," Doctor Zalman said, rubbing the side of his face as incredulity gave way to thought. Sharon glanced at Naomi, who was intently tracing the lines on her palm with a thumbnail.

"We could be the first kibbutz with a maniac on our hands," someone yelled.

"He could be working up to something bigger," the doctor said. "What did you do?"

"I told him," she cleared her throat with a low rumble, "that he must not do these things, because I don't feel romantic about him. I told him it was a serious matter. He was very ashamed." Naomi's plan was brilliant, but Sharon didn't quite know how much to embellish the story. She kept talking. "Actually, I felt he was trying to tell me something—"

"Exactly!" Naomi was on her feet. "Doctor, wouldn't you agree there is a pattern to his lapses?"

"A pattern?" the doctor echoed.

"First it was me," Naomi continued. "And who am I? Almost his mother, may she rest in peace. That's who I am. And now Sharon. And who is she?"

They looked at her blankly. Then, as if one candle after another were being lit, the room perceptibly brightened.

"Like a sister, perhaps?" Shimon ventured.

"Right. You see, he only does it to people he loves and trusts, people who would forgive him."

"Still—" Miriam objected.

"No. Listen, what does it mean?" Naomi raised her arms toward the ceiling. "He's sending us a message, *chevrai*—"

"Of course!" Samuel interrupted. "It's like the handwriting on the wall. But this time," his index finger wagged at them, "the handwriting is on, if you'll forgive me, the breast!"

"I know what the handwriting says." Naomi folded her arms and smiled broadly. An unspoken challenge radiated from her stout figure.

The buzz in the room was deafening, the sound of an airplane engine warming up.

"Would one of you prophets be so kind as to translate it then?" Lev asked, clapping his hands for order.

Naomi turned to stare at Shimon seated several rows behind her. He stood up slowly. "I, too, read the writing." He took a deep breath. "It says—" he watched Naomi as she wiggled two fingers alongside her ear, "it says that we should send him twice a week."

"And?" Lev prompted.

"I so move," Shimon said hurriedly, "that the kibbutz send Yosi to his appropriate prostitute twice a week—"

"Indefinitely," Naomi added.

A biblical "for eternity" from Sharon was muted by the enthusiastic clucking which filled the room.

The vote was again unanimous. At tea afterward, they congratulated themselves on the wisdom of their solution. Solomon himself could not have done better. In the barn, Tsiporet pulled hay from her rack and chewed it slowly as she waited for Yosi's hands.

Isaac Bashevis Singer

"Taibele and Her Demon"

Translated by Mirra Ginsburg

I

In the town of Lashnik, not far from Lublin, there lived a man and his
wife. His name was Chaim Nossen, hers Taibele. They had no children.
Not that the marriage was barren; Taibele had borne her husband a son
and two daughters, but all three had died in infancy—one of whooping
cough, one of scarlet fever, and one of diphtheria. After that Taibele's
womb closed up, and nothing availed: neither prayers, nor spells, nor po-
tions. Grief drove Chaim Nossen to withdraw from the world. He kept
apart from his wife, stopped eating meat and no longer slept at home, but
on a bench in the prayer house. Taibele owned a dry-goods store, inherited from her parents, and she sat there all day, with a yardstick on her
right, a pair of shears on her left, and the women's prayer book in Yiddish in front of her. Chaim Nossen, tall, lean, with black eyes and a
wedge of a beard, had always been a morose, silent man even at the best
of times. Taibele was small and fair, with blue eyes and a round face. Although punished by the Almighty, she still smiled easily, the dimples
playing on her cheeks. She had no one else to cook for now, but she lit
the stove or the tripod every day and cooked some porridge or soup for

279

herself. She also went on with her knitting—now a pair of stockings, now a vest; or else she would embroider something on canvas. It wasn't in her nature to rail at fate or cling to sorrow.

One day Chaim Nossen put his prayer shawl and phylacteries, a change of underwear, and a loaf of bread into a sack and left the house. Neighbors asked where he was going; he answered: "Wherever my eyes lead me."

When people told Taibele that her husband had left her, it was too late to catch up with him. He was already across the river. It was discovered that he had hired a cart to take him to Lublin. Taibele sent a messenger to seek him out, but neither her husband nor the messenger was ever seen again. At thirty-three, Taibele found herself a deserted wife.

After a period of searching, she realized that she had nothing more to hope for. God had taken both her children and her husband. She would never be able to marry again; from now on she would have to live alone. All she had left was her house, her store, and her belongings. The towns-people pitied her, for she was a quiet woman, kindhearted and honest in her business dealings. Everyone asked: how did she deserve such misfortunes? But God's ways are hidden from man.

Taibele had several friends among the town matrons whom she had known since childhood. In the daytime housewives are busy with their pots and pans, but in the evening Taibele's friends often dropped in for a chat. In the summer, they would sit on a bench outside the house, gossiping and telling each other stories.

One moonless summer evening when the town was as dark as Egypt, Taibele sat with her friends on the bench, telling them a tale she had read in a book bought from a peddler. It was about a young Jewish woman, and a demon who had ravished her and lived with her as man and wife. Taibele recounted the story in all its details. The women huddled closer together, joined hands, spat to ward off evil, and laughed the kind of laughter that comes from fear.

One of them asked: "Why didn't she exorcise him with an amulet?"

"Not every demon is frightened of amulets," answered Taibele.

"Why didn't she make a journey to a holy rabbi?"

"The demon warned her that he would choke her if she revealed the secret."

"Woe is me, may the Lord protect us, may no one know of such things!" a woman cried out.

"I'll be afraid to go home now," said another.

"I'll walk with you," a third one promised.

While they were talking, Alchonon, the teacher's helper who hoped one day to become a wedding jester, happened to be passing by. Alchonon, five years a widower, had the reputation of being a wag and a prankster, a man with a screw loose. His steps were silent because the soles of his shoes were worn through and he walked on his bare feet. When he heard Taibele telling the story, he halted to listen. The darkness was so thick, and the women so engrossed in the weird tale, that they did not see him. This Alchonon was a dissipated fellow, full of cunning goatish tricks. On the instant, he formed a mischievous plan.

After the women had gone, Alchonon stole into Taibele's yard. He hid behind a tree and watched through the window. When he saw Taibele go to bed and put out the candle, he slipped into the house. Taibele had not bolted the door; thieves were unheard of in that town. In the hallway, he took off his shabby caftan, his fringed garment, his trousers, and stood as naked as his mother bore him. Then he tiptoed to Taibele's bed. She was almost asleep, when suddenly she saw a figure looming in the dark. She was too terrified to utter a sound.

"Who is it?" she whispered, trembling.

Alchonon replied in a hollow voice: "Don't scream, Taibele. If you cry out, I will destroy you. I am the demon Hurmizah, ruler over darkness, rain, hail, thunder, and wild beasts. I am the evil spirit who espoused the young woman you spoke about tonight. And because you told the story with such relish, I heard your words from the abyss and was filled with lust for your body. Do not try to resist, for I drag away those who refuse to do my will beyond the Mountains of Darkness—to Mount Sair, into a wilderness where man's foot is unknown, where no beast dares to tread, where the earth is of iron and the sky of copper. And I roll them in thorns and in fire, among adders and scorpions, until every bone of their body is ground to dust, and they are lost for eternity in the nether depths. But if you comply with my wish, not a hair of your head will be harmed, and I will send you success in every undertaking . . ."

Hearing these words, Taibele lay motionless as in a swoon. Her heart fluttered and seemed to stop. She thought her end had come. After a while, she gathered courage and murmured: "What do you want of me? I am a married woman!"

"Your husband is dead. I followed in his funeral procession myself." The voice of the teacher's helper boomed out. "It is true that I cannot go to the rabbi to testify and free you to remarry, for the rabbis don't believe our kind. Besides, I don't dare step across the threshold of the rabbi's chamber—I fear the Holy Scrolls. But I am not lying. Your husband died in an epidemic, and the worms have already gnawed away his nose. And even were he alive, you would not be forbidden to lie with me, for the laws of the *Shulchan Aruch* do not apply to us."

Hurmizah the teacher's helper went on with his persuasions, some sweet, some threatening. He invoked the names of angels and devils, of demonic beasts and of vampires. He swore that Asmodeus, King of the Demons, was his step-uncle. He said that Lilith, Queen of the Evil Spirits, danced for him on one foot and did every manner of thing to please him. Shibtah, the she-devil who stole babies from women in childbed, baked poppyseed cakes for him in Hell's ovens and leavened them with the fat of wizards and black dogs. He argued so long, adducing such witty parables and proverbs, that Taibele was finally obliged to smile, in her extremity. Hurmizah vowed that he had loved Taibele for a long time. He described to her the dresses and shawls she had worn that year and the year before; he told her the secret thoughts that came to her as she kneaded dough, prepared her Sabbath meal, washed herself in the bath, and saw to her needs at the outhouse. He also reminded her of the morning when she had wakened with a black and blue mark on her breast. She had thought it was the pinch of a ghoul. But it was really the mark left by a kiss of Hurmizah's lips, he said.

After a while, the demon got into Taibele's bed and had his will of her. He told her that from then on he would visit her twice a week, on Wednesdays and on Sabbath evenings, for those were the nights when the unholy ones were abroad in the world. He warned her, though, not to divulge to anyone what had befallen her, or even hint at it, on pain of dire punishment: he would pluck out the hair from her skull, pierce her eyes, and bite out her navel. He would cast her into a desolate wilderness where bread was dung and water was blood, and where the wailing of Zalmaveth was heard all day and all night. He commanded Taibele to swear by the bones of her mother that she would keep the secret to her last day. Taibele saw that there was no escape for her. She put her hand on his thigh and swore an oath, and did all that the monster bade her.

Before Hurmizah left, he kissed her long and lustfully, and since he was a demon and not a man, Taibele returned his kisses and moistened his beard with her tears. Evil spirit though he was, he had treated her kindly . . .

When Hurmizah was gone, Taibele sobbed into her pillow until sunrise.

Hurmizah came every Wednesday night and every Sabbath night. Taibele was afraid that she might find herself with child and give birth to some monster with tail and horns—an imp or a mooncalf. But Hurmizah promised to protect her against shame. Taibele asked whether she need go to the ritual bath to cleanse herself after her impure days, but Hurmizah said that the laws concerning menstruation did not extend to those who consorted with the unclean host.

As the saying goes, may God preserve us from all that we can get accustomed to. And so it was with Taibele. In the beginning she had feared that her nocturnal visitant might do her harm, give her boils or elflocks, make her bark like a dog or drink urine, and bring disgrace upon her. But Hurmizah did not whip her or pinch her or spit on her. On the contrary, he caressed her, whispered endearments, made puns and rhymes for her. Sometimes he pulled such pranks and babbled such devil's nonsense, that she was forced to laugh. He tugged at the lobe of her ear and gave her love bites on the shoulder, and in the morning she found the marks of his teeth on her skin. He persuaded her to let her hair grow under her cap and he wove it into braids. He taught her charms and spells, told her about his night-brethren, the demons with whom he flew over ruins and fields of toadstools, over the salt marshes of Sodom, and the frozen wastes of the Sea of Ice. He did not deny that he had other wives, but they were all she-devils; Taibele was the only human wife he possessed. When Taibele asked him the names of his wives, he enumerated them: Namah, Machlath, Aff, Chuldah, Zluchah, Nafkah, and Cheimah. Seven altogether.

He told her that Namah was black as pitch and full of rage. When she quarreled with him, she spat venom and blew fire and smoke through her nostrils.

Machlath had the face of a leech, and those whom she touched with her tongue were forever branded.

Aff loved to adorn herself with silver, emeralds, and diamonds. Her braids were of spun gold. On her ankles she wore bells and bracelets; when she danced, all the deserts rang out with their chiming.

Chuldah had the shape of a cat. She meowed instead of speaking. Her eyes were green as gooseberries. When she copulated, she always chewed bear's liver.

Zluchah was the enemy of brides. She robbed bridegrooms of potency. If a bride stepped outside alone at night during the Seven Nuptial Benedictions, Zluchah danced up to her and the bride lost the power of speech or was taken by a seizure.

Nafkah was lecherous, always betraying him with other demons. She retained his affections only by her vile and insolent talk, which delighted his heart.

Cheimah should have, according to her name, been as vicious as Namah should have been mild, but the reverse was true: Cheimah was a she-devil without gall. She was forever doing charitable deeds, kneading dough for housewives when they were ill, or bringing bread to the homes of the poor.

Thus Hurmizah described his wives, and told Taibele how he disported himself with them, playing tag over roofs and engaging in all sorts of pranks. Ordinarily, a woman is jealous when a man consorts with other women, but how can a human be jealous of a female devil? Quite the contrary. Hurmizah's tales amused Taibele, and she was always plying him with questions. Sometimes he revealed to her mysteries no mortal may know—about God, his angels and seraphs, his heavenly mansions, and the seven heavens. He also told her how sinners, male and female, were tortured in barrels of pitch and caldrons of fiery coals, on beds studded with nails and in pits of snow, and how the Black Angels beat the bodies of the sinners with rods of fire.

The greatest punishment in Hell was tickling, Hurmizah said. There was a certain imp in Hell by the name of Lekish. When Lekish tickled an adulteress on her soles or under the arms, her tormented laughter echoed all the way to the island of Madagascar.

In this way, Hurmizah entertained Taibele all through the night, and soon it came about that she began to miss him when he was away. The summer nights seemed too short, for Hurmizah would leave soon after cockcrow. Even winter nights were not long enough. The truth was that she now loved Hurmizah, and though she knew a woman must not lust after a demon, she longed for him day and night.

II

Although Alchonon had been a widower for many years, matchmakers still tried to marry him off. The girls they proposed were from mean homes, widows and divorcees, for a teacher's helper was a poor provider, and Alchonon had besides the reputation of being a shiftless ne'er-do-well. Alchonon dismissed the offers on various pretexts: one woman was too ugly, the other had a foul tongue, the third was a slattern. The matchmakers wondered: how could a teacher's helper who earned nine groschen a week presume to be such a picker and chooser? And how long could a man live alone? But no one can be dragged by force to the wedding canopy.

Alchonon knocked around town—long, lean, tattered, with a red disheveled beard, in a crumpled shirt, with his pointed Adam's apple jumping up and down. He waited for the wedding jester Reb Zekele to die, so that he could take over his job. But Reb Zekele was in no hurry to die; he still enlivened weddings with an inexhaustible flow of quips and rhymes, as in his younger days. Alchonon tried to set up on his own as a teacher for beginners, but no householder would entrust his child to him. Mornings and evenings, he took the boys to and from the cheder. During the day he sat in Reb Itchele the teacher's courtyard, idly whittling wooden pointers, or cutting out paper decorations which were used only once a year, at Pentecost, or modeling figurines from clay. Not far from Taibele's store there was a well, and Alchonon came there many times a day, to draw a pail of water or to take a drink, spilling the water over his red beard. At these times, he would throw a quick glance at Taibele. Taibele pitied him: why was the man knocking about all by himself? And Alchonon would say to himself each time: "Woe, Taibele, if you knew the truth!"

Alchonon lived in a garret, in the house of an old widow who was deaf

and half-blind. The crone often chided him for not going to the synagogue to pray like other Jews. For as soon as Alchonon had taken the
children home, he said a hasty evening prayer and went to bed. Sometimes the old woman thought she heard the teacher's helper get up in the
middle of the night and go off somewhere. She asked him where he wandered at night, but Alchonon told her that she had been dreaming. The
women who sat on benches in the evenings, knitting socks and gossiping, spread the rumor that after midnight Alchonon turned into a were-
wolf. Some women said he was consorting with a succubus. Otherwise,
why should a man remain so many years without a wife? The rich men
would not trust their children to him any longer. He now escorted only
the children of the poor, and seldom ate a spoonful of hot food, but had
to content himself with dry crusts.

Alchonon became thinner and thinner, but his feet remained as nimble as ever. With his lanky legs, he seemed to stride down the street as
though on stilts. He must have suffered constant thirst, for he was always
coming down to the well. Sometimes he would merely help a dealer or
peasant to water his horse. One day, when Taibele noticed from the distance how his caftan was torn and ragged, she called him into her shop.
He threw a frightened glance and turned white.

"I see your caftan is torn," said Taibele. "If you wish, I will advance you
a few yards of cloth. You can pay it off later, five pennies a week."

"No."

"Why not?" Taibele asked in astonishment. "I won't haul you before
the rabbi if you fall behind. You'll pay when you can."

"No."

And he quickly walked out of the store, fearing she might recognize
his voice.

In summertime it was easy to visit Taibele in the middle of the night.
Alchonon made his way through back lanes, clutching his caftan around
his naked body. In winter, the dressing and undressing in Taibele's cold
hallway became increasingly painful. But worst of all were the nights
after a fresh snowfall. Alchonon was worried that Taibele or one of the
neighbors might notice his tracks. He caught cold and began to cough.
One night he got into Taibele's bed with his teeth chattering; he could
not warm up for a long time. Afraid that she might discover his hoax, he
invented explanations and excuses. But Taibele neither probed nor

wished to probe too closely. She had long discovered that a devil had all the habits and frailties of a man. Hurmizah perspired, sneezed, hiccuped, yawned. Sometimes his breath smelled of onion, sometimes of garlic. His body felt like the body of her husband, bony and hairy, with an Adam's apple and a navel. At times, Hurmizah was in a jocular mood, at other times a sigh broke from him. His feet were not goose feet, but human, with nails and frost blisters.

Once Taibele asked him the meaning of these things, and Hurmizah explained: "When one of us consorts with a human female, he assumes the shape of a man. Otherwise, she would die of fright."

Yes, Taibele got used to him and loved him. She was no longer terrified of him or his impish antics. His tales were inexhaustible, but Taibele often found contradictions in them. Like all liars, he had a short memory. He had told her at first that devils were immortal. But one night he asked: "What will you do if I die?"

"But devils don't die!"

"They are taken to the lowest abyss . . ."

That winter there was an epidemic in town. Foul winds came from the river, the woods, and the swamps. Not only children, but adults as well were brought down with the ague. It rained and it hailed. Floods broke the dam on the river. The storms blew off an arm of the windmill. On Wednesday night, when Hurmizah came into Taibele's bed, she noticed that his body was burning hot, but his feet were icy. He shivered and moaned. He tried to entertain her with talk of she-devils, of how they seduced young men, how they cavorted with other devils, splashed about in the ritual bath, tied elflocks in old men's beards, but he was weak and unable to possess her.

She had never seen him in such a wretched state. Her heart misgave her. She asked: "Shall I get you some raspberries with milk?"

Hurmizah replied: "Such remedies are not for our kind."

"What do you do when you get sick?"

"We itch and we scratch . . ."

He spoke little after that. When he kissed Taibele, his breath was sour. He always remained with her until cockcrow, but this time he left early. Taibele lay silent, listening to his movements in the hallway. He had sworn to her that he flew out of the window even when it was closed and sealed, but she heard the door creak. Taibele knew that it was sin-ful to pray for devils, that one must curse them and blot them from memory; yet she prayed to God for Hurmizah.

She cried out in anguish: "There are so many devils, let there be one more . . ."

On the following Sabbath, Taibele waited in vain for Hurmizah until dawn; he never came. She called him inwardly and muttered the spells he had taught her, but the hallway was silent. Taibele lay benumbed. Hurmizah had once boasted that he had danced for Tubal-cain and Enoch, that he had sat on the roof of Noah's Ark, licked the salt from the nose of Lot's wife, and plucked Ahasuerus by the beard. He had prophesied that she would be reincarnated after a hundred years as a princess, and that he, Hurmizah, would capture her, with the help of his slaves Chittim and Tachtim, and carry her off to the palace of Bashemath, the wife of Esau. But now he was probably lying somewhere ill, a helpless demon, a lonely orphan—without father or mother, without a faithful wife to care for him. Taibele recalled how his breath came rasping like a saw when he had been with her last; when he blew his nose, there was a whistling in his ear. From Sunday to Wednesday, Taibele went about as one in a dream. On Wednesday she could hardly wait until the clock struck midnight, but the night went, and Hurmizah did not appear. Taibele turned her face to the wall.

The day began, dark as evening. Fine snow dust was falling from the murky sky. The smoke could not rise from the chimneys; it spread over the roofs like ragged sheets. The rooks cawed harshly. Dogs barked. After the miserable night, Taibele had no strength to go to her store. Nevertheless, she dressed and went outside. She saw four pallbearers carrying a stretcher. From under the snow-swept coverlet protruded the blue feet of a corpse. Only the sexton followed the dead man.

Taibele asked who it was, and the sexton answered: "Alchonon, the teacher's helper."

A strange idea came to Taibele—to escort Alchonon, the feckless man who had lived alone and died alone, on his last journey. Who would come to the store today? And what did she care for business? Taibele had lost everything. At least, she would be doing a good deed. She followed the dead on the long road to the cemetery. There she waited while the gravedigger swept away the snow and dug a grave in the frozen earth.

They wrapped Alchonon the teacher's helper in a prayer shawl and a cowl, placed shards on his eyes, and stuck between his fingers a myrtle twig that he would use to dig his way to the Holy Land when the Messiah came. Then the grave was closed and the gravedigger recited the Kaddish. A cry broke from Taibele. This Alchonon had lived a lonely life, just as she did. Like her, he left no heir. Yes, Alchonon the teacher's helper had danced his last dance. From Hurmizah's tales, Taibele knew that the deceased did not go straight to Heaven. Every sin creates a devil, and these devils are a man's children after his death. They come to demand their share. They call the dead man Father and roll him through forest and wilderness until the measure of his punishment is filled and he is ready for purification in Hell.

From then on, Taibele remained alone, doubly deserted—by an ascetic and by a devil. She aged quickly. Nothing was left to her of the past except a secret that could never be told and would be believed by no one. There are secrets that the heart cannot reveal to the lips. They are carried to the grave. The willows murmur of them, the rooks caw about them, the gravestones converse about them silently, in the language of stone. The dead will awaken one day, but their secrets will abide with the Almighty and His judgment until the end of all generations.

Gilbert Sorrentino

"The Moon in Its Flight"

This was in 1948. A group of young people sitting on the darkened porch of a New Jersey summer cottage in a lake resort community. The host some Bernie wearing an Upsala College sweat shirt. The late June night so soft one can, in retrospect, forgive America for everything. There were perhaps eight or nine people there, two of them the people that this story sketches.

Bernie was talking about Sonny Stitt's alto on "That's Earl, Brother." As good as Bird, he said. Arnie said, bullshit: he was a very hip young man from Washington Heights, wore mirrored sunglasses. A bop drummer in his senior year at the High School of Performing Arts. Our young man, nineteen at this time, listened only to Rebecca, a girl of fifteen, remarkable in her New Look clothes. A long full skirt, black, snug tailored shirt of blue and white stripes with a high white collar and black velvet string tie, black kid Capezios. It is no wonder that lesbians like women.

At some point during the evening he walked Rebecca home. She lived on Lake Shore Drive, a wide road that skirted the beach and ran parallel to the small river that flowed into Lake Minnehaha. Lake Ramapo? Lake Tomahawk. Lake O-shi-wa-no? Lake Sunburst. Leaning against her father's powder-blue Buick convertible, lost, in the indigo night, the creamy stars, sound of crickets, they kissed. They fell in love.

One of the songs that summer was "For Heaven's Sake." Another, "It's Magic." Who remembers the clarity of Claude Thornhill and Sarah Vaughan, their exquisite irrelevance? They are gone where the useless chrome doughnuts on the Buick's hood have gone. That Valhalla of Amos 'n' Andy and guinea fruit peddlers with golden earrings. "Pleasa No Squeeze Da Banana." In 1948, the whole world seemed beautiful to young people of a certain milieu, or let me say, possible. Yes, it seemed a possible world. This idea persisted until 1950, at which time it died, along with many of the young people who had held it. In Korea, the Chinese played "Scrapple from the Apple" over loudspeakers pointed at the American lines. That savage and virile alto blue-clear on the sub-zero night. This is, of course, old news.

Rebecca was fair. She was fair. Lovely Jewish girl from the remote and exotic Bronx. To him, that vast borough seemed a Cythera—that it could house such fantastic creatures as she! He wanted to be Jewish. He was, instead, a Roman Catholic, awash in sin and redemption. What loathing he had for the Irish girls who went to eleven o'clock Mass, legions of blushing pink and lavender spring coats, flat white straw hats, the crinkly veils over their open faces. Church clothes, under which their inviolate crotches sweetly nestled in soft hair.

She had white and perfect teeth. Wide mouth. Creamy stars, pale nights. Dusty black roads out past the beach. The sunlight on the raft, moonlight on the lake. Sprinkle of freckles on her shoulders. Aromatic breeze.

Of course this was a summer romance, but bear with me and see with what banal literary irony it all turns out—or does not turn out at all. The country bowled and spoke of Truman's grit and spunk. How softly we had slid off the edge of civilization.

The liquid moonlight filling the small parking area outside the gates to the beach. Bass flopping softly in dark waters. What was the scent of the perfume she wore? The sound of a car radio in the cool nights, collective American memory. Her browned body, delicate hair bleached golden on her thighs. In the beach pavilion they danced and drank Cokes. Mel Tormé and the Mell-Tones. Dizzy Gillespie. "Too Soon To Know." In the mornings, the sun so crystal and lucent it seemed the very exhalation of the sky, he would swim alone to the raft and lie there, the beach empty, music from the pavilion attendant's radio coming to him in splinters. At such times he would thrill himself by pretending that he had not yet met Rebecca and that he would see her that afternoon for the first time.

The first time he touched her breasts he cried in his shame and delight. Can all this really have taken place in America? The trees rustled for him, as the rain did rain. One day, in New York, he bought her a silver friendship ring, tiny perfect hearts in bas-relief running around it so that the point of one heart nestled in the cleft of another. Innocent symbol that tortured his blood. She stood before him in the pale light in white bra and panties, her shorts and blouse hung on the hurricane fence of the abandoned and weed-grown tennis court and he held her, stroking her flanks and buttocks and kissing her shoulders. The smell of her flesh, vague sweat and perfume. Of course he was insane. She caressed him so far as she understood how through his faded denim shorts. Thus did they flay themselves, burning. What were they to do? Where were they to go? The very thought of the condom in his pocket made his heart careen in despair. Nothing was like anything said it was after all. He adored her.

She was entering her second year at Evander Childs that coming fall. He hated this school he had never seen, and hated all her fellow students. He longed to be Jewish, dark and mysterious and devoid of sin. He stroked her hair and fingered her nipples, masturbated fiercely on the dark roads after he had seen her home. Why didn't he at least *live* in the Bronx?

Any fool can see that with the slightest twist one way or another all of this is fit material for a sophisticated comic's routine. David Steinberg, say. One can hear his precise voice recording these picayune disasters as jokes. Yet all that moonlight was real. He kissed her luminous fingernails and died over and over again. The maimings of love are endlessly funny, as are the tiny figures of talking animals being blown to pieces in cartoons.

It was this same youth who, three years later, ravished the whores of Mexican border towns in a kind of drunken hilarity, falling down in the dusty streets of Nuevo Laredo, Villa Acuña, and Piedras Negras, the pungency of the overpowering perfume wedded to his rumpled khakis, his flowered shirt, his scuffed and beer-spattered low quarters scraping across the thresholds of the Blue Room, Ofelia's, The 1-2-3 Club, Felicia's, the Cadillac, Tres Hermanas. It would be a great pleasure for me to allow him to meet her there, in a yellow chiffon cocktail dress and spike heels, lost in prostitution.

One night, a huge smiling Indian whore bathed his member in gin as a testament to the strict hygiene she claimed to practice and he absurdly thought of Rebecca, that he had never seen her naked, nor she him, as he was now in the Hollywood pink light of the whore's room, Jesus hanging in his perpetual torture from the wall above the little bed. The woman was gentle, the light glinting off her gold incisor and the tiny cross at her throat. You good fuck, Jack, she smiled in her lying whore way. He felt her flesh again warm in that long-dead New Jersey sunlight. Turn that into a joke.

They were at the amusement park at Lake Hopatcong with two other couples. A hot and breathless night toward the end of August, the patriotic smell of hot dogs and french fries in the still air. Thin and cranky music from the carrousel easing through the sparsely planted trees down toward the shore. She was pale and sweating, sick, and he took her back to the car and they smoked. They walked to the edge of the black lake stretching out before them, the red and blue neon on the far shore clear in the hot dark.

He wiped her forehead and stroked her shoulders, worshiping her pain. He went to get a Coke and brought it back to her, but she only sipped at it, then said O God! and bent over to throw up. He held her waist while she vomited, loving the waste and odor of her. She lay down on the ground and he lay next to her, stroking her breasts until the nipples were erect under her cotton blouse. My period, she said. God, it just ruins me at the beginning. You bleeding, vomiting, incredible thing, he thought. You should have stayed in, he said. The moonlight of her teeth. I didn't want to miss a night with you, she said. It's August. Stars, my friend, great flashing stars fell on Alabama.

They stood in the dark in the driving rain underneath her umbrella. Where could it have been? Nokomis Road? Bliss Lane? Kissing with that trapped yet wholly innocent frenzy peculiar to American youth of that era. Her family was going back to the city early the next morning and his family would be leaving toward the end of the week. They kissed, they kissed. The angels sang. Where could they go, out of this driving rain?

Isn't there anyone, any magazine writer or avant-garde filmmaker, any lover of life or dedicated optimist out there who will move them toward a cottage, already closed for the season, in whose split log exterior they will find an unlocked door? Inside there will be a bed, whiskey, an electric heater. Or better, a fireplace. White lamps, soft lights. Sweet music. A radio on which they will get Cooky's Caravan or Symphony Sid. Billy Eckstine will sing "My Deep Blue Dream." Who can bring them to each other and allow him to enter her? Tears of gratitude and release, the sublime and elegantly shadowed configuration their tanned legs will make lying together. This was in America, in 1948. Not even fake art or the wearisome tricks of movies can assist them.

She tottered, holding the umbrella crookedly while he went to his knees and clasped her, the rain soaking him through, put his head under her skirt and kissed her belly, licked at her crazily through her underclothes.

All you modern lovers, freed by Mick Jagger and the orgasm, give them, for Christ's sake, for an hour, the use of your really terrific little apartment. They won't smoke your marijuana nor disturb your Indiana graphics. They won't borrow your Fanon or Cleaver or Barthelme or Vonnegut. They'll make the bed before they leave. They whisper good night and dance in the dark.

She was crying and stroking his hair. Ah God, the leaves of brown came tumbling down, remember? He watched her go into the house and saw the door close. Some of his life washed away in the rain dripping from his chin.

A girl named Sheila whose father owned a fleet of taxis gave a reunion party in her parents' apartment in Forest Hills. Where else would it be? I will insist on purchased elegance or nothing. None of your warm and cluttered apartments in this story, cats on the stacks of books, and so on. It was the first time he had ever seen a sunken living room and it fixed his idea of the good life forever after. Rebecca was talking to Marv and

Robin, who were to be married in a month. They were Jewish, incredibly and wondrously Jewish, their parents smiled upon them and loaned them money and cars. He skulked in his loud Brooklyn clothes.

I'll put her virgin flesh into a black linen suit, a single strand of pearls around her throat. Did I say that she had honey-colored hair? Believe me when I say he wanted to kiss her shoes.

Everybody was drinking Cutty Sark. This gives you an idea, not of who they were, but of what they thought they were. They worked desperately at it being August, but under the sharkskin and nylons those sunny limbs were hidden. Sheila put on "In the Still of the Night" and all six couples got up to dance. When he held her he thought he would weep.

He didn't want to hear about Evander Childs or Gun Hill Road or the 92nd Street Y. He didn't want to know what the pre-med student she was dating said. Whose hand had touched her secret thighs. It was almost unbearable since this phantom knew them in a specifically erotic way that he did not. He had touched them decorated with garters and stockings. Different thighs. She had been to the Copa, to the Royal Roost, to Lewisohn Stadium to hear the Gershwin concert. She talked about *The New Yorker* and *Vogue*, e.e. cummings. She flew before him, floating in her black patent I. Miller heels.

Sitting together on the bed in Sheila's parents' room, she told him that she still loved him, she would always love him, but it was so hard not to go out with a lot of other boys, she had to keep her parents happy. They were concerned about him. They didn't really know him. He wasn't Jewish. All right. All right. But did she have to let Shelley? Did she have to go to the Museum of Modern Art? The Met? Where were these places? What is the University of Miami? Who is Brooklyn Law? What sort of god borrows a Chrysler and goes to the Latin Quarter? What is a supper club? What does Benedictine cost? Her epic acts, his Flagg Brothers shoes.

There was one boy who had almost made her. She had allowed him to take off her blouse and skirt, nothing else! at a CCNY sophomore party. She was a little high and he—messed—all over her slip. It was wicked and she was ashamed. Battering his heart in her candor. Well, I almost slipped too, he lied, and was terrified that she seemed relieved. He got up and closed the door, then lay down on the bed with her and took off her jacket and brassiere. She zipped open his trousers. Long enough! Sheila said, knocking on the door, then opening it to see him with his head on her breasts. Oh, oh, she said, and closed the door. Of course, it was all ruined. We got rid of a lot of these repressed people in the next decade, and now we are all happy and free.

At three o'clock, he kissed her good night on Yellowstone Boulevard in a thin drizzle. Call me, he said, and I'll call you. I'll see you soon, she said, getting into Marv's car. I love you. She went into her glossy Jewish life, toward mambos and the Blue Angel.

Let me come and sleep with you. Let me lie in your bed and look at you in your beautiful pajamas. I'll do anything you say. I'll honor thy beautiful father and mother. I'll hide in the closet and be no trouble. I'll work as a stock boy in your father's beautiful sweater factory. It's not my fault I'm not Marvin or Shelley. I don't even know where CCNY is! Who is Conrad Aiken? What is Bronx Science? Who is Berlioz? What is a Stravinsky? How do you play Mah-Jongg? What is schmooz, schlepp, Purim, Moo Goo Gai Pan? Help me.

When he got off the train in Brooklyn an hour later, he saw his friends through the window of the all-night diner, pouring coffee into the great pit of their beer drunks. He despised them as he despised himself and the neighborhood. He fought against the thought of her so that he would not have to place her subtle finesse in these streets of vulgar hells, benedictions, and incense.

On Christmas Eve, he left the office party at two, even though one of the file girls, her Catholicism temporarily displaced by Four Roses and ginger, stuck her tongue into his mouth in the stock room.

Rebecca was outside, waiting on the corner of 46th and Broadway, and they clasped hands, oh briefly, briefly. They walked aimlessly around in the gray bitter cold, standing for a while at the Rockefeller Center rink, watching the people who owned Manhattan. When it got too cold, they walked some more, ending up at the Automat across the street from Bryant Park. When she slipped her coat off her breasts moved under the crocheted sweater she wore. They had coffee and doughnuts, surrounded by office party drunks sobering up for the trip home.

Then it went this way: We can go to Maryland and get married, she said. You know I was sixteen a month ago. I want to marry you, I can't stand it. He was excited and frightened, and got an erection. How could he bear this image? Her breasts, her familiar perfume, enormous figures of movie queens resplendent in silk and lace in the snug bedrooms of Vermont inns—shutters banging, the rain pouring down, all entangled, married! How do we get to *Maryland?* he said.

Against the table top her hand, its long and delicate fingers, the perfect moons, Carolina moons, of her nails. I'll give her every marvel: push gently the scent of magnolia and jasmine between her legs and permit her to piss champagne.

Against the table top her hand, glowing crescent moons over lakes of Prussian blue in evergreen twilights. Her eyes gray, flecked with bronze. In her fingers a golden chain and on the chain a car key. My father's car, she said. We can take it and be there tonight. We can be married Christmas then, he said, but you're Jewish. He saw a drunk going out onto Sixth Avenue carrying their lives along in a paper bag. I mean it, she said. I can't stand it, I love you. I love *you*, he said, but I can't drive. He smiled. I *mean* it, she said. She put the key in his hand. The car is in midtown here, over by Ninth Avenue. I really *can't* drive, he said. He could shoot pool and drink boilermakers, keep score at baseball games and handicap horses, but he couldn't drive.

The key in his hand, fascinating wrinkle of sweater at her waist. Of course, life is a conspiracy of defeat, a sophisticated joke, endless, endless. I'll get some money and we'll go the holiday week, he said, we'll take a train, O.K.? O.K., she said. She smiled and asked for another coffee, taking the key and dropping it into her bag. It was a joke after all. They walked to the subway and he said I'll give you a call right after Christmas. Gray bitter sky. What he remembered was her gray cashmere coat swirling around her calves as she turned at the foot of the stairs to smile at him, making the gesture of dialing a phone and pointing at him and then at herself.

Give these children a Silver Phantom and a chauffeur. A black chauffeur, to complete the America that owned them.

Now I come to the literary part of this story, and the reader may prefer to let it go and watch her profile against the slick tiles of the IRT stairwell, since she has gone out of the reality of narrative, however splintered. This postscript offers something different, something finely artificial and discrete, one of the designer sweaters her father makes now, white and stylish as a sailor's summer bells. I grant you it will be unbelievable.

I put the young man into 1958. He has served in the army, and once told the Automat story to a group of friends as proof of his sexual prowess. They believed him: what else was there for them to believe? This shabby use of a fragile occurrence was occasioned by the smell of honeysuckle and magnolia in the tobacco country outside Winston-Salem. It brought her to him so that he was possessed. He felt the magic key in his hand again. To master this overpowering wave of nostalgia he cheapened it. Certainly the reader will recall such shoddy incidents in his own life.

After his discharge he married some girl and had three children by her. He allowed her her divers interests and she tolerated his few stupid infidelities. He had a good job in advertising and they lived in Kew Gardens in a brick semi-detached house. Let me give them a sunken living room to give this the appearance of realism. His mother died in 1958 and left the lake house to him. Since he had not been there for ten years he decided to sell it, against his wife's wishes. The community was growing and the property was worth twice the original price.

This is a ruse to get him up there one soft spring day in May. He drives up in a year-old Pontiac. The realtor's office, the papers, etc. Certainly, a shimmer of nostalgia about it all, although he felt a total stranger. He left the car on the main road, deciding to walk down to the lake, partly visible through the new-leaved trees. All right, now here we go. A Cadillac station wagon passed and then stopped about fifteen yards ahead of him and she got out. She was wearing white shorts and sneakers and a blue sweat shirt. Her hair was the same, shorter perhaps, tied with a ribbon of navy velour.

It's too impossible to invent conversation for them. He got in her car. Her perfume was not the same. They drove to her parents' house for a cup of coffee—for old times' sake. How else would they get themselves together and alone? She had come up to open the house for the season. Her husband was a college traveler for a publishing house and was on the road, her son and daughter were staying at their grandparents' for the day. Popular songs, the lyrics half-remembered. You will do well if you think of the ambiance of the whole scene as akin to the one in detective nov-els where the private investigator goes to the murdered man's summer house. This is always in off-season because it is magical then, one sees oneself as a being somehow existing outside time, the year-round resi-dents are drawings in flat space.

When they walked into the chilly house she reached past him to latch the door and he touched her hand on the lock, then her forearm, her shoulder. Take your clothes off, he said, gently. Oh gently. Please. Take your clothes off? He opened the button of her shorts. You see that they now have the retreat I begged for them a decade ago. If one has faith all things will come. Her flesh was cool.

In the bedroom, she turned down the spread and fluffed the pillows, then sat and undressed. As she unlaced her sneakers, he put the last of his clothes on a chair. She got up, her breasts quivering slightly, and he saw faint stretch marks running into the shadowy symmetry of her pubic hair. She plugged in a small electric heater, bending before him, and he put his hands under her buttocks and held her there. She sighed and trembled and straightened up, turning toward him. Let me have a mist of tears in her eyes, of acrid joy and shame, of despair. She lay on the bed and opened her thighs and they made love without elaboration.

In the evening, he followed her car back into the city. They had promised to meet again the following week. Of course it wouldn't be sordid. What, then, would it be? He had perhaps wept bitterly that af-ternoon as she kissed his knees. She would call him, he would call her. They could find a place to go. Was she happy? Really happy? God knows, he wasn't *happy*! In the city they stopped for a drink in a Village bar and sat facing each other in the booth, their knees touching, holding hands. They carefully avoided speaking of the past, they made no jokes. He felt his heart rattling around in his chest in large jagged pieces. It was rotten for everybody, it was rotten but they would see each other, they were somehow owed it. They would find a place with clean sheets, a radio, whiskey, they would just—continue. Why not?

These destructive and bittersweet accidents do not happen every day. He put her number in his address book, but he wouldn't call her. Perhaps she would call him, and if she did, well, they'd see, they'd see. But he would *not* call her. He wasn't that crazy. On the way out to Queens he felt himself in her again and the car swerved erratically. When he got home he was exhausted.

You are perfectly justified in scoffing at the outrageous transparency of it if I tell you that his wife said that he was so pale that he looked as if he had seen a ghost, but that is, indeed, what she said. Art cannot rescue anybody from anything.

Steve Stern

"The Sin of Elijah"

Somewhere during the couple of millennia that I'd been commuting between heaven and earth, I, Elijah the Tishbite—former prophet of the Northern Kingdom of Israel, translated to Paradise in a chariot of flame while yet alive—became a voyeur. Call me weak, but after you've attended no end of circumcisions, when you've performed an untold number of virtuous deeds and righteous meddlings in a multitude of bewildering disguises, your piety can begin to wear a little thin. Besides, good works had ceased to generate the kind of respect they'd once commanded in the world, a situation that took its toll on one's self-esteem; so that even I, old as I was, had become susceptible from time to time to the *yetser horah*, the evil impulse.

That's how I came to spy on the Fefers, Feyvush and Gitl, in their love nest on the Lower East Side of New York. You might say that observing the passions of mortals, often with stern disapproval, had always been a hobby of mine; but of late it was their more intimate pursuits that took my fancy. Still, I had standards. As a whiff of sanctity always clung to my person from my sojourns in the Upper Eden, I lost interest where the dalliance of mortals was undiluted by some measure of earnest affection. And the young Fefer couple, they adored each other with a love that surpassed their own understanding. Indeed, so fervent was the heat of their voluptuous intercourse that they sometimes feared it might consume them and they would perish of sheer ecstasy.

I happened upon them one miserable midsummer evening when I was making my rounds of the East Side ghetto, which in those years was much in need of my benevolent visitations. I did a lot of good, believe me, spreading banquets on the tables of the desolate families in their coal cellars, exposing the villains posing as suitors to young girls fresh off the boat. I even engaged in spirited disputes with the *apikorsin*, the unbelievers, in an effort to vindicate God's justice to man—a thankless task, to say the least, in that swarming, heretical, typhus-infested neighborhood. So was it any wonder that with the volume of dirty work that fell to my hands, I should occasionally seek some momentary diversion?

You might call it a waste that one with my gift for camouflage, who could have gained clandestine admittance backstage at the Ziegfeld Follies when Anna Held climbed out of her milk bath, or slipped unnoticed into the green room at the People's Theater where Tomashevsky romped au naturel with his zaftig harem, that I should return time and again to the tenement flat of Feyvush and Gitl Fefer. But then you never saw the Fefers at their amorous business.

To be sure, they weren't what you'd call prepossessing. Feyvush, a cobbler by profession, was stoop-shouldered and hollow-breasted, nose like a parrot's beak, hair a wreath of swiftly evaporating black foam. His bride was a green-eyed, pear-shaped little hausfrau, freckles stippling her cheeks as if dripped from the brush that daubed her rust-red pompadour. Had you seen them in the streets—Feyvush with nostrils flaring from the stench, his arm hooked through Gitl's from whose free hand dangled the carcass of an unflicked chicken—you would have deemed them in no way remarkable. But at night when they turned down the gas lamp in their stuffy bedroom, its window giving on to the fire escape (where I stooped to watch), they were the Irene and Vernon Castle of the clammy sheets.

At first they might betray a charming awkwardness. Feyvush would fumble with the buttons of Gitl's shirtwaist, tugging a little frantically at corset laces, hooks and eyes. He might haul without ceremony the shapeless muslin shift over her head, shove the itchy cotton drawers below her knees. Just as impatiently Gitl would yank down the straps of her spouse's suspenders, pluck the studs from his shirt, the rivets from his fly; she would thrust chubby fingers between the seams of his union suit with the same impulsiveness that she plunged her hand in a barrel to snatch a herring. Then they would tumble onto the sagging iron bed, its rusty springs complaining like a startled henhouse. At the initial shock of flesh pressing flesh, they would clip, squeeze, and fondle whatever was most convenient, as if each sought a desperate assurance that the other was real. But once they'd determined as much, they slowed the pace; they lulled their frenzy to a rhythmic investigation of secret contours, like a getting acquainted of the blind.

They postponed the moment of their union for as long as they could stand to. While Feyvush sucked on her nipples till they stood up like gumdrops, Gitl gaily pulled out clumps of her husband's hair; while he traced with his nose the line of ginger fur below her navel the way a flame follows a fuse, she held his hips like a rampant divining rod over the wellspring of her womb. When their loins were finally locked together, it jarred them so that they froze for an instant, each seeming to ask the other in tender astonishment: "What did we do?" Then the bed would gallop from wardrobe to washstand, the neighbors pound on their ceilings with brooms, until Feyvush and Gitl spent themselves, I swear it, in a shower of sparks. It was an eruption that in others might have catapulted their spirits clear out of their bodies—but not the Fefers, who clung tenaciously to one another rather than suffer even a momentary separation from their better half.

Afterwards, as they lay in a tangle, hiding their faces in mutual embarrassment over such a bounty of delight, I would slope off. My prurient interests satisfied, I was released from impure thoughts; I was free, a stickiness in the pants notwithstanding, to carry on with cleansing lepers and catering the weddings of the honest poor. So as you see, my spying on the Fefers was a tonic, a clear case of the ends justifying the means.

How was it I contrived to stumble upon such a talented pair in the first place? Suffice it that, when you've been around for nearly three thousand years, you develop antennae. It's a sensitivity that, in my case, was partial compensation for the loss of my oracular faculty, an exchange of roles from clairvoyant to voyeur. While I might not be able to predict the future with certainty anymore, I could intuit where and when someone was getting a heartfelt shtupping.

But like I say, I didn't let my fascination with the Fefers interfere with the performance of good works; the tally of my *mitzvot* was as great as ever. Greater perhaps, since my broader interests kept me closer than usual to earth, sometimes neglecting the tasks that involved a return to Kingdom Come. (Sometimes I put off escorting souls back to the afterlife, a job I'd never relished, involving as it did what amounted to cleaning up after the Angel of Death.) Whenever the opportunity arose, my preoccupation with Feyvush and Gitl might move me to play the detective. While traveling in their native Galicia, for instance, I would stop by the study house, the only light on an otherwise deserted street in the abandoned village of Krok. This was the Fefers' home village, a place existing just this side of memory, reduced by pogrom and expulsions to broken chimneys, a haunted bathhouse, scattered pages of the synagogue register among the dead leaves. The only survivors being a dropsical rabbi and his skeleton crew of disciples, it was to them I appealed for specifics.

"Who could forget?" replied the old rabbi stroking a snuff yellow beard, the wen on his brow like a sightless third eye. "After their wedding he comes to me, this Feyvush: 'Rabbi,' he says guiltily, 'is not such unspeakable pleasure a sin?' I tell him: 'In the view of Yohanan ben Dabai, a man may do what he will with his wife; within the zone of the marriage bed all is permitted.' He thanks me and runs off before I can give him the opinion of Rabbi Eliezer, who suggests that, while having intercourse, one should think on arcane points of law . . ."

I liked to imagine their wedding night. Hadn't I witnessed enough of them in my time?—burlesque affairs wherein the child bride and groom, martyrs to arranged marriages, had never set eyes on one another before. They were usually frightened to near paralysis, their only preparation a lecture from some doting melamed or a long-suffering mother's manual of medieval advice. "What's God been doing since He created the world?" goes the old question. Answer: "He's been busy making matches." But the demoralized condition of the children to whose nuptials I was assigned smacked more of the intervention of pushy families than the hand of God.

No wonder I was so often called on to give a timid bridegroom a nudge. Employing my protean powers—now regrettably obsolete, though I still regard myself a master of stealth—I might take the form of a bat or the shimmying flame of a hurricane lamp to scare the couple into each other's arms. (Why I never lost patience and stood in for the faint-hearted husband myself, I can't say.) Certainly there's no reason to sup-pose that Dvora Malkeh's Feyvush, the cobbler's apprentice, was any braver when it came to bedding his own stranger bride—his Gitl, who at fifteen was two years his junior, the only daughter of Chaim Rupture the porter, her dowry a hobbled goat and a dented tin kiddush cup. It was not what you'd have called a brilliant match.

Still, I liked to picture the moment when they're alone for the first time in their bridal chamber, probably some shelf above a stove encircled by horse blankets. In the dark Feyvush has summoned the courage to strip to his talis koton, its ritual fringes dangling a flimsy curtain over his knocking knees. Gitl has peeled in one anxious motion to her starchless shift and slid gingerly beneath the thistledown, where she's joined after a small eternity by the tremulous groom. They lie there without speak-ing, without touching, having forgotten (respectively) the rabbi's sage in-struction and the diagrams in *The Saffron Sacrament*. They only know that the warm (albeit shuddering) flesh beside them has a magnetism as strong as gravity, so that each feels they've been falling their whole lives into the other's embrace. And afterwards there's nothing on earth—nei-ther goat's teat nor cobbler's last, pickle jar, poppy seed, Cossack's knout, or holy scroll—that doesn't echo their common devotion.

Or so I imagined. I also guessed that their tiny hamlet must have begun to seem too cramped to contain such an abundance of mutual af-fection. It needed a shtetl, say, the size of Tarnopol, or a teeming city as large as Lodz to accommodate them; or better: for a love that defied pos-sibility, a land where the impossible (as was popularly bruited) was the order of the day. America was hardly an original idea—I never said the Fefers were original, only unique—but emboldened by the way that wed-ded bliss had transformed their ramshackle birthplace, they must have been curious to see how love traveled.

You might have thought the long ocean passage, at the end of which waited only a dingy dumbbell tenement on Orchard Street, would have cooled their ardor. Were their New World circumstances any friendlier to romance than the Old? Feyvush worked twelve-hour days in a boot-making loft above the butcher's shambles in Gouverneur Slip, while Gitl haggled with fishmongers and supplemented her husband's mean wages stitching artificial flowers for ladies' hats. The streets swarmed with hucksters, ganefs, and handkerchief girls who solicited in the shadows of buildings draped in black bunting. Every day the funeral trains of cholera victims plied the market crush, displacing vendors crying spoiled meat above the locust-hum of the sewing machines. The summers brought a heat that made ovens of the tenements, sending the occupants to their roofs where they inhaled a cloud of blue flies; and in winter the ice hung in tusks from the common faucets, the truck horses froze upright in their tracks beside the curb. But if the ills of the ghetto were any impediment to their ongoing conjugal fervor, you couldn't have proved it by the Feyvush and Gitl I knew.

They were after all no strangers to squalor, and the corruptions of the East Side had a vitality not incompatible with the Fefers' own sweet delirium. Certainly there was a stench, but there was also an exhilaration: there were passions on display in the music halls and the Yiddish theaters, where Jacob Adler or Bertha Kalish could be counted on nightly to tear their emotions to shreds. You had the dancing academies where the greenhorns groped one another in a macabre approximation of the turkey trot, the Canal Street cafes where the poets and revolutionaries fought pitched battles with an arsenal of words; you had the shrill and insomniac streets. Content as they were to keep to themselves, the Fefers were not above rubbernecking. They liked to browse the Tenth Ward's gallery of passions, comparing them—with some measure of pride—unfavorably to their own.

Sometimes I thought the Fefers nurtured their desire for each other as if it were an altogether separate entity, a member of the family if you will. Of course the mystery remained that such heroic lovemaking as theirs had yet to produce any offspring, which was certainly not for want of trying. Indeed, they'd never lost sight of the sacramental aspect of their intimacy, or the taboos against sharing a bed for purposes other than procreation. They had regularly consulted with local midwives, purchasing an assortment of bendls, simples, and fertility charms to no avail. (Gitl had even gone so far as to flush her system with mandrake enemas against a possible evil eye.) But once, as I knelt outside their window during a smallpox-ridden summer (when caskets the size of bread pans were carried from the tenements night and day), I heard Feyvush suggest:

"Maybe no babies is for such a plenty of pleasure the price we got to pay?"

You didn't have to be a prophet to see it coming. What could you expect when a pair of mortals routinely achieved orgasms like Krakatoa, their loins shooting sparks like the uncorking of a bottle of pyrotechnical champagne? Something had to give, and with hindsight I can see that it had to happen on Shabbos, when married folk are enjoined to go at their copulation as if ridden by demons. Their fervent cleaving to one another (*dveykuss* the kabbalists call it) is supposed to hasten the advent of Messiah, or some such poppycock. Anyway, the Fefers had gathered momentum over the years, enduring climaxes of such convulsive magnitude that their frames could scarcely contain the exaltation. And since they clung to each other with a ferocity that refused to release spirit from flesh, it was only a matter of time until their transports carried them bodily aloft.

I was in Paradise when it happened, doing clerical work. Certain bookkeeping tasks were entrusted to me, such as totting up the debits and credits of incoming souls—tedious work that I alternated with the more restful occupation of weaving garlands of prayers; but even this had become somewhat monotonous, a mindless therapy befitting the sanatorium-like atmosphere of Kingdom Come. For such employment I chose a quiet stone bench (what bench wasn't quiet?) along a garden path near the bandstand. (Paradise back then resembled those sepia views of Baden-Baden or Saratoga Springs in their heyday; though of late the place, fallen into neglect, has more in common with the seedier precincts of Miami Beach.) At dusk I closed the ledger and tossed the garlands into the boughs of the Tree of Life, already so festooned with ribbons of prayer that the dead, in their wistfulness, compared it to a live oak hung with Spanish moss. Myself, I thought of a peddler of suspenders on the Lower East Side.

I was making my way along a petal-strewn walk toward the gates in my honorary angel getup—quilted smoking jacket, tasseled fez, a pair of rigid, lint-white wings. Constructed of chicken wire and papier-mâché, they were just for show, the wings, about as useful as an ostrich's. I confess this was a source of some resentment, since why shouldn't I merit the genuine article? As for the outfit, having selected it myself I couldn't complain; certainly it was smart, though the truth was I preferred my terrestrial shmattes. But in my empyrean role as Sandolphon the Psychopomp, whose responsibilities included the orientation of lost souls, I was expected to keep up appearances.

So I'm headed toward the park gates when I notice this hubbub around a turreted gazebo. Maybe I should qualify "hubbub," since the dead, taking the air in their lightweight golfing costumes and garden party gowns, were seldom moved to curiosity. Nevertheless, a number had paused in their twilight stroll to inspect some new development under the pavilion on the lawn. Approaching, I charged the spectators to make way. Then I ascended the short flight of steps to see an uninvited iron bed supplanting the tasteful wicker furniture; and on that rumpled, bow-footed bed lay the Fefers, man and wife, in flagrante delicto. Feyvush, with his pants still down around his hairy ankles, and Gitl, her shift rucked to the neck, were holding on to each other for dear life.

As you may know, it wasn't without precedent for unlicensed mortals to enter the Garden alive. Through the ages you'd had a smattering of overzealous mystics who'd arrived by dint of pious contemplation, only to expire outright from the exertion. But to my knowledge Feyvush and Gitl were the first to have made the trip via the agency of ecstatic intercourse. They had, in effect, shtupped their way to heaven.

I moved forward to cover their nakedness with the quilt, though there was really no need for modesty in the Upper Eden, where unlike in the fallen one innocence still obtained.

"I bet you're wondering where it is that you are," was all I could think to say.

They nodded in saucer-eyed unison. When I told them Paradise, their eyes flicked left and right like synchronized wipers on a pair of stalled locomobiles. Then just as I'd begun to introduce myself ("the mock-angel Sandolphon here, though you might know me better as . . ."), an imperious voice cut me off.

"I'll take care of this—that is of course if *you* don't mind . . ."

It was the archangel Metatron, né Enoch ben Seth, celestial magistrate, commissary, archivist, and scribe. Sometimes called Prince of the Face (his was a chiseled death mask with one severely arched brow), he stood with his hands clasped before him, a thin gray eminence rocking on his heels. He was dressed like an undertaker, the nudnik, in a sable homburg and frock coat, its seams neatly split at the shoulders to make room for an impressive set of ivory wings. Unlike my own pantomime pair, Enoch's worked. While much too dignified to actually use them, he was not above preening them in my presence, flaunting the wings as an emblem of a higher status that he seldom let me forget. He had it in for me because I served as a reminder that he too had once been a human being. Like me he'd been translated in the prime of life in an apotheosis of flames to Kingdom Come. Never mind that his assumption had included the further awards of functional feathers and an investiture as full seraph; he still couldn't forgive me for recalling his humble origins, the humanity he'd never entirely outgrown.

"Welcome to the Upper Eden," the archangel greeted the bedridden couple, "the bottommost borough of Olam ha-Ba, the World to Come." And on a cautionary note, "You realize of course that your arrival here is somewhat, how shall we say, premature?"

With the quilt hoisted to their chins, the Fefers nodded in concert—as what else should they do?

"However," continued Enoch, whose flashier handle I'd never gotten used to, which insubordination he duly noted, "accidents will happen, eh? and we must make the best of an irregular state of affairs. So," he gave a dispassionate sniff, brushing stardust or dandruff from an otherwise immaculate sleeve, "if you'll be so good as to follow me, I'll show you to your quarters." He turned abruptly and for a moment we were nose to nose (my potato to Enoch's flutey yam), until I was forced to step aside.

Feyvush and Gitl exchanged bewildered glances, then shrugged. Clutching the quilt about their shoulders, they climbed out of bed—Feyvush stumbling over his trousers as Gitl stifled a nervous laugh—and scrambled to catch up with the peremptory angel. They trailed him down the steps of the gazebo under the boughs of the Tree of Life, in which the firefly lanterns had just become visible in the gloaming. Behind them the little knot of immortals drifted off in their interminable promenade.

"What's the hurry?" I wanted to call out to the Fefers; I wanted a chance to give them the benefit of my experience to help them get their bearings. Wasn't that the least I could do for the pair who'd provided me with such a spicy pastime over the years? Outranked, however, I had no alternative but to tag along unobtrusively after.

Enoch led them down the hedge-bordered broadwalk between wrought iron gates, their arch bearing the designation GANEYDN in gilded Hebrew characters. They crossed a cobbled avenue and ascended some steps onto a veranda where a thousand cypress rockers ticked like a chorus of pendulums. (Understand that Paradise never went in for the showier effects: none of your sardonyx portals and myriads of ministering angels wrapped in clouds of glory, no rivers of balsam, honey, and wine. There, in deference to the sensibilities of the deceased, earthly standards abide; the splendor remains human-scale, though odd details from the loftier regions sometimes trickle down.)

Through mahogany doors thrown open to the balmy air, they entered the lobby of the grand hotel that serves as dormitory for the dead. Arrested by their admiration for the acres of carpets and carved furniture, the formal portraits of archons in their cedar of Lebanon frames, the chandeliers, Feyvush and Gitl lagged behind. They craned their necks to watch phoenixes smoldering like smudge pots gliding beneath the arcaded ceiling, while Enoch herded them into the elevator's brass cage. Banking on the honeymoon suite, I took the stairs and, preternaturally spry for my years, slipped in after them as Enoch showed the couple their rooms. Here again the Fefers were stunned by the sumptuous appointments: the marble-topped whatnot, the divan stuffed with angel's hair, the Brussels lace draperies framing balustraded windows open to a view of the park. From its bandstand you could hear the silvery yodel of a famous dead cantor chanting the evening prayers.

Inconspicuous behind the open door, my head wreathed in a Tiffany lampshade, I watched the liveried cherubs parade into the bedroom, dumping their burdens of fresh apparel on the canopied bed.

"I trust you'll find these accommodations satisfactory," Enoch was saying in all insincerity, "and that your stay here will be a pleasant one." Rubbing the hands he was doubtless eager to wash of this business, he began to mince backward toward the door.

Under the quilt that mantled the Fefers, Feyvush started as from a poke in the ribs. He looked askance at his wife who gave him a nod of encouragement, then ventured a timid, "Um, if it please your honor," another nudge, "for how long do we supposed to stay here?"

Replied Enoch: "Why, forever of course."

Another dig with her elbow failed to move her tongue-tied husband, and Gitl spoke up herself. "You mean we ain't got to die?"

"God forbid," exhaled Enoch a touch sarcastically, his patience with their naiveté at an end: it was a scandal how the living lacked even the minimal sophistication of the dead. "Now, if there are no further questions . . . ?" Already backed into the corridor, he reminded them that room service was only a bell pull away, and was gone.

Closing the door (behind which my camouflaged presence made no impression at all), Feyvush turned to Gitl and asked, "Should we have gave him a tip?"

Gitl practically choked in her attempt to suppress a titter whose contagion spread to Feyvush. A toothy grin making fish-shaped crescents of his goggle eyes, he proceeded to pinch her all over, and together they dissolved in a fit of hysterics that buckled their knees. They rolled about on the emerald carpet, then picked themselves up in breathless dishevelment, abandoning their quilt to make a beeline for the bedroom.

Oh boy, I thought, God forgive me; now they'll have it off in heaven and their aphrodisiac whoops will drive the neutered seraphim to acts of depravity. But instead of flinging themselves headlong onto the satin counterpane, they paused to inspect their laidout wardrobe—or "trousseau" as Gitl insisted on calling it.

Donning a wing collar shirt with boiled bosom, creased flannel trousers, and a yachting blazer with a yellow Shield of David crest, Feyvush struck rakish poses for his bride. Gitl wriggled into a silk corset cover, over which she pulled an Empire tea gown, over which an ungirded floral kimono. At the smoky-mirrored dressing table she daubed her round face with scented powders; she made raccoon's eyes of her own with an excess of shadow, scattered a shpritz of sparkles over the bonfire of her hair. Between her blown breasts she hung a sapphire the size of a gasolier.

While she carried on playing dress-up, Feyvush tugged experimentally on the bell-pull, which was answered by an almost instantaneous knock at the door. Feyvush opened it to admit a tea trolley wheeled by a silent creature (pillbox hat and rudimentary wings) who'd no sooner appeared than bowed himself out. Relaxing the hand that held the waived gratuity, Feyvush fell to contemplating the covered dish and pitcher on the trolley. Pleased with her primping, Gitl rose to take the initiative. The truth was, the young Mrs. Fefer was no great shakes in the kitchen, the couple having always done their "cooking" (as Talmud puts it) in bed. Nevertheless, with a marked efficiency, she lifted the silver lid from the dish, faltering at the sight of the medicinal blue bottle underneath. Undiscouraged, however, she tipped a bit of liver brown powder from the bottle onto the plate, then mixed in a few drops of water from the crystal pitcher. There was a foaming after which the powder assumed the consistency of clotted tapioca. Gitl dipped in a finger, gave it a tentative lick, smacked her lips, and sighed. Then she dipped the finger again, placing it this time on her husband's extended tongue. Feyvush too closed his eyes and sighed, which was the signal for them both to tuck in with silver spoons. Cheeks bulging, they exulted over the succulent feast of milchik and fleishik flavors that only manna can evoke.

Having placated their bellies, you might have expected them to turn to the satisfaction of other appetites. But instead of going back to the bedroom, they went to the open windows and again looked out over the Garden. Listening to the still warbling cantor (to be followed in that evening's program by a concert of Victor Herbert standards—though not before at least half a century'd passed on earth), they were so enraptured they forgot to embrace. Up here where perfection was the sine qua non, they required no language or gesture to improve on what was already ideal.

Heartsick, I replaced the lampshade and slunk out. I know it was unbecoming my rank and position to be disappointed on account of mere mortals; after all, if the Fefers had finally arrived at the logical destination of their transports, then good on them! What affair was it of mine? But now that it was time I mounted another expedition to the fallen world—babies, paupers, and skeptics were proliferating like mad—I found I lacked the necessary incentive. This is not to say I was content to stay on in Paradise, where I was quite frankly bored, but neither did a world without the Fefers have much appeal.

It didn't help that I ran into them everywhere, tipping my fez somewhat coolly whenever we crossed paths—which was often, since Feyvush and Gitl, holding hands out of habit, never tired of exploring the after-life. At first I tried to ignore them, but idle myself, I fell into an old habit of my own. I tailed them as they joined the ranks of the perpetual strollers meandering among the topiary hedges, loitering along the gravel walks and bridle paths. I suppose that for a tourist the Garden did have its attractions: you've got your quaint scale reproductions of the indus-tries of the upper heavens, such as a mill for grinding manna, a quarry of souls. There's a zoo that houses some of the beasts that run wild in the more ethereal realms: a three-legged "man of the mountain," a sullen be-hemoth with a barnacled hide, a petting zoo containing a salamander hatched from a myrtle flame. But having readjusted my metabolism to conform to the hours of earth, I wondered when the Fefers would wake up. When would they notice, say, that the fragrant purple dusk advanced at only a glacial pace toward dawn; that the dead, however well-dressed and courteous, were rather, well, stiff and cold?

In the end, though, my vigilance paid off. After what you would call about a week (though the Shabbos eve candles still burned in the celes-tial yeshivas), I was fortunate enough to be on hand when the couple sounded their first note of discontent. Hidden in plain sight in their suite (in the pendulum cabinet of a grandfather clock), I overheard Feyvush broach a troubling subject with his wife. Having sampled some of the outdoor prayer minyans that clustered about the velvet lawns, he complained, "It ain't true, Gitteleh, the stories that they're telling about the world." Because in their discourses on the supernatural aspects of his-tory, the dead, due to a faulty collective memory, tended to overlook the essential part of being alive: that it was natural.

Seated at her dressing table, languidly unscrolling the bobbin of her pompadour, letting it fall like carrot shavings over her forehead, Gitl ventured a complaint of her own. He should know that in the palatial bathhouse she attended—it was no longer unusual for the couple to spend time apart—the ladies snubbed her.

"For them, to be flesh and blood is a sin."

She was wearing a glove-silk chemise that might have formerly in-spired her husband to feats of erotic derring-do. Stepping closer, Feyvush tried to reassure her, "I think they're jealous."

Gitl gave a careless shrug.

At her shoulder Feyvush continued cautiously, "Gitl, remember how," pausing to gather courage, "remember how on the Day of Atonement we played 'blowing the shofar'?"

Gitl stopped fussing with her hair, nodded reflexively.

"Do you remember how on Purim I would part like the pages of Megillah . . . " here an intake of air in the lungs of both parties " . . . your legs?"

Again an almost mechanical nod.

"Gitl," submitted Feyvush just above a whisper, "do you miss it that I don't touch you that way no more?"

She put down the tortoiseshell hairbrush, cocked her head thoughtfully, then released an arpeggio of racking sobs. "Like the breath of life I miss it!" she wailed, as Feyvush, his own frustrations confirmed, fell to his knees and echoed her lament.

"Gitteleh," he bawled, burying his face in her lap, "ain't nobody fency yentzing in Kingdom Come!" Then lifting his head to blow his nose on a brocaded shirtsleeve, drying his eyes with same, he hesitantly offered, "Maybe we could try to go home . . . "

"Hallelujah!"

This was me bursting forth from the clock to congratulate them on a bold resolution. "Now you're talking!" I assured them. "Of course it won't be easy; into the Garden you got without a dispensation but without a dispensation they won't never let you leave . . . " Then I observed how the Fefers, not yet sufficiently jaded from their stay in heaven, were taken aback. Having leapt to their feet, they'd begun to slide away from me along the paneled walls, which was understandable: for despite my natty attire, my features had become somewhat crepe-hung over the ages, my rheumy eyes tending toward the hyacinth red.

Recalling the introduction I never completed upon their arrival, I started over. "Allow me to present myself: the prophet Elijah, at your service. You would recognize me better in the rags I wear in the world." And as they still appeared dubious, Gitl smearing her already runny mascara as if in an effort to wipe me from her eye, I entreated them to relax: "You can trust me." I explained that I wanted to help them get back to where they belonged.

This at least had the effect of halting their retreat, which in turn called my bluff.

"You should understand," I began to equivocate, "there ain't much I can do personally. Sure, I'm licensed to usher souls from downstairs to up, but regarding vicey-versey I got no jurisdiction, my hands are tied. And from here to there you don't measure the distance in miles but dozens of years, so don't even think about starting the journey on your own . . . "

At that point Gitl, making chins (their ambrosial diet had endowed her with several extra), planted an elbow in Feyvush's ribs. He coughed once before speaking. "If it please your honor," his listless tone not half so respectful as he'd been with Enoch, "what is it exactly you meaning to do?"

I felt a foolish grin spreading like eczema across my face. "What I have in mind . . . ," I announced on a note of confidence that instantly fell flat, because I didn't really have a clue. Rallying nonetheless, I voiced my determination to intercede with the archangel Metatron on the couple's behalf.

Who was I kidding? That stickler for the letter of the Law, he wouldn't have done me a favor if his immortality depended on it. Still, a promise was a promise, so I sought out his high-and-mightiness in his apartments in the dignitaries' wing of the hotel. (My own were among the cottages of the superannuated cherubim.)

Addressing him by his given name, I'm straightaway off on the wrong foot.

"Sorry . . . I mean Metatron, Prince of the Face (such a face!), Lesser Lord of the Seventy Names, and so forth," I said, attempting to smooth his ruffled pride. It seemed that Enoch had never gotten over the treatment attending his translation, when the hosts mockingly claimed they could smell one of woman born from a myriad of parasangs away. "Anyhow," putting my foot in it deeper, "they had a nice holiday, the Fefers, but they would like already to go back where they came."

Seated behind the captain's desk in his office sipping a demitasse with uplifted pinky, his back to a wall of framed citations and awards, the archangel assumed an expression of puzzled innocence. Did I have to spell it out?

"You know, like home."

"Home?" inquired Enoch, as if butter wouldn't melt on his unctuous tongue. "Why, this is their home for all eternity."

Apparently I wasn't going to be invited to sit down. "But they ain't happy here," I persisted.

"Not happy in Paradise?" Plunking down his cup and saucer as if the concept was unheard of.

"It's possible," I allowed a bit too emphatically. Enoch clucked his tongue, which provoked me to state the obvious. "Lookit, they ain't dead yet."

"A mere technicality," pooh-poohed the archangel. "Besides, for those who've dwelt in Abraham's Bosom, the earth should no longer hold any real attraction."

Though I was more or less living proof to the contrary, rather than risk antagonizing him again, I kept mum on that subject. Instead: "Have a heart," I appealed to him. "You were alive when you came here . . . " Which didn't sound the way I meant it. "Didn't you ever want to go back?"

"Back?" Enoch was incredulous. "Back to what, making shoes?"

That he'd lowered his guard enough to mention his mortal profession made me think I saw an angle. "Feyvush is a cobbler," I humbly submitted.

"Then he's well out of it." The seraph stressed the point by raising his arched brow even higher, creating ripples that spoiled the symmetry of his widow's peak. "Besides, when I stitched leather, it was as if I fastened the world above to the world below."

"But don't you see," I pleaded, the tassle of my fez dancing like a spider in front of my eyes till I slapped it away, "that's what it was like when Feyvush would yentz with his bride . . . " This was definitely not the tack to have taken.

"Like I said, he's better off," snapped Enoch, rising abruptly from his swivel chair to spread his magnificent wings. "And since when is any of this *your* business?"

Conversation closed, I turned to go, muttering something about how I guessed I was just a sentimental fool.

"Elijah . . . ," the angel called my name after a fashion guaranteed to inspire maximum guilt.

"Sandolphon," I corrected him under my breath.

". . . I think it's time you tended to your terrestrial errands."

"Funny," I replied in an insipid singsong, "I was thinking the same thing."

•   •   •

You'll say I should have left well enough alone, and maybe you're right. After all, without my meddling the Fefers would still be in heaven and I pursuing my charitable rounds on earth—instead of sentenced for my delinquency to stand here at this crossroads directing traffic, pointing the pious toward the gates, the wicked in the other direction, not unlike (to my everlasting shame) that nazi doctor on the railroad platform during the last apocalypse. But who'd have thought that, with my commendable record of good works, I wasn't entitled to a single trespass?

When I offered the Fefers my plan, Gitl elbowed Feyvush, then interrupted his diffident "If it please your honor—" to challenge me herself: "What for do you want to help us?"

"Because," since my audience with the archangel I'd developed a ready answer, "I can't stand to see nobody downhearted in Paradise. This is my curse, that such *rachmones*, such compassion I got, I can't stand it to see nobody downhearted anywhere." Which was true enough. It was an attitude that kept me constantly at odds with the angelic orders, with Enoch and Raziel and Death (between whom and myself there was a history of feuding) and the rest of that coldblooded crew. It was my age-old humanitarian impulse that compelled me to come to the aid of the Fefers, right? and not just a selfish desire to see them at their shtupping again.

Departing the hotel, we moved through whatever pockets of darkness the unending dusk provided—hard to find in a park whose every corner was illumined by menorahs and fairy lights. Dressed for traveling (Feyvush in an ulster and fore-and-aft cap, Gitl in automobile cape and sensible shoes), they were irked with me, my charges, for making them leave behind a pair of overstuffed Gladstone bags. Their aggravation signified an ambivalence which, in my haste to get started, I chose to ignore, and looking back I confess I might have been a little pushy. Anyway, in order not to call attention to ourselves (small danger among the indifferent immortals), I pretended I was conducting yet another couple of greenhorns on a sightseeing tour of the Garden.

"Here you got your rose trellis made out of what's left of Jacob's Ladder, and over there, that scrawny thing propped on a crutch, that's the *etz ha-daat*, the Tree of Knowledge . . . "

When I was sure no one was looking, I hauled the Fefers behind me into the shadows beneath the bloated roots of the Tree of Life. From a hanger in their midst I removed my universal luftmensch outfit—watch cap, galoshes, and patched overcoat—which I quick-changed into after discarding my Sandolphon duds. Then I led the fugitives into a narrow cavern that snaked its way under the Tree trunk, fetching up at the rust-cankered door of a dumbwaiter.

I'd discovered it some time ago while looking for an easier passage to earth. My ordination as honorary angel, while retarding the aging process, had not, as you know, halted it entirely, so I was in need of a less strenuous means of descent than was afforded by the branches of the Tree of Life. An antique device left over from the days when the Lord would frequent the Garden to send the odd miracle below, the dumbwaiter was just the thing. It was a sturdy enough contraption that, notwithstanding the sponginess of its wooden cabinet and the agonizing groans of its cables, had endured the test of time.

The problem was that the dumbwaiter's compactness was not intended to accommodate three people. A meager, collapsible old man, I'd always found it sufficiently roomy; but while the Fefers were not large, Gitl had never been exactly svelte, and both of them had put on weight during their "honeymoon." Nevertheless, making a virtue of necessity, they folded themselves into a tandem pair of S's and allowed me to stuff them into the tight compartment. This must have been awkward for them at first, since they hadn't held each other in a while, but as I wedged myself into the box behind them and started to lower us down the long shaft, Feyvush and Gitl began to generate a sultry heat.

They ceased their griping about cramped quarters and began to make purring noises of a type that brought tears to my eyes. I felt an excitement beyond that which accrued from our gathering speed, as the tug of gravity accelerated the dumbwaiter's downward progress. The cable sang as it slipped through my blistering fingers; then came the part where our stomachs were in our throats and we seemed to be in a bottomless free-fall, which was the dizzy, protracted prelude to the earth-shaking clatter of our landing. The crash must have alerted the cooks in the basement kitchen of Ratner's Dairy Restaurant to our arrival; because, when I slid open the door, there they were: a surly lot in soiled aprons and mushroom hats, looking scornfully at the pretzel the Fefers had made of themselves. I appeased them as always with a jar of fresh manna, an ingredient (scarce in latter-day New York) they'd come to regard as indispensable for their heavenly blintzes.

If the plummeting claustrophobia of the dumbwaiter, to say nothing of its bumpy landing, hadn't sufficiently disoriented my charges, then the shrill Sunday brunch crowd I steered them through would have finished the job. I hustled them without fanfare out the revolving door into a bitter blast of winter barreling up Delancey Street from the river.

"Welcome home!" I piped, though the neighborhood bore small resemblance to the one they'd left better than three-quarters of a century ago. The truck horses and trolleys had been replaced by a metallic current of low-slung vehicles squealing and farting in sluggish procession; the pushcarts and garment emporia had given way to discount houses full of coruscating gadgetry, percussive music shuddering their plate-glass windows. Old buildings, if they weren't boarded up or reduced altogether to rubble, had new facades, as tacky as hoop skirts on dowagers. In the distance there were towers, their tops obscured by clouds like tentpoles under snow-heavy canvas.

Myself, I'd grown accustomed to dramatic changes during my travels back and forth. Besides, I made a point of keeping abreast of things, pumping the recently departed for news of the earth, lest returning be too great a jolt to my system. But the Fefers, though they'd demonstrated a tolerance for shock in the past, seemed beyond perplexity now, having entered a condition of outright fear.

Gitl was in back of her husband, trying to straighten his crimped spine with her knee, so that he seemed to speak with her voice when she asked, "What happened to the Jews?" Because it was true that, while the complexions of the passers-by ran the spectrum from olive to saffron to lobster pink, there were few you could've identified as distinctly yid.

I shrugged. "Westchester, New Rochelle, Englewood, the Five Towns they went, but for delicatessen they come back to Delancey on Sundays." Then I grinned through my remaining teeth and made a show of protesting, "No need to thank me," though who had bothered? I shook their hands, which were as limp as fins. "Well, goodbye and good luck, I got things to do . . . "

I had urgent business to attend to, didn't I?—brisses, famines, false prophets in need of comeuppance. All right, so "urgent" was an exag-

geration. Also, I was aware that the ills of the century had multiplied beyond anything my penny ante philanthropies could hope to fix. But I
couldn't stand being a party to Feyvush and Gitl's five-alarm disappointment. This wasn't the world they knew; tahkeh, it wasn't even the
half of what they didn't know, and I preferred not to stick around for the
heartache of their getting acquainted. I didn't want to be there when
they learned, for instance, that Jews had vanished in prodigious numbers
from more places on the face of the planet than the Lower East Side. I
didn't want to be there when they discovered what else had gone out of
the world in their absence, and I didn't want to admit I made a mistake
in bringing them back.

Still, I wouldn't send them away empty-handed. I gave them a pocket
full of heaven gelt—that is, leaves from the *Etz ha-Chaim*, the Tree of
Life, which passed for currency in certain neighborhood pawnshops; I
told them the shops where you got the best rate of exchange. The most
they could muster by way of gratitude, however, was a perfunctory nod.
When they slouched off toward the Bowery, drawing stares in their period gear, I thought of Adam and Eve leaving the Garden at the behest
of the angel with the flaming sword.

I aimed my own steps in the direction of the good deeds whose abandonment could throw the whole cosmic scheme out of joint. Then con-
ceding there was no need to kid myself, it was already out of joint, I
turned around. Virtually invisible in my guise as one more homeless old
crock among a multitude of others, I followed the Fefers. I entered the
shop behind them, where a pawnbroker in a crumpled skullcap greeted
them satirically: "The Reb Ben Vinkl, I presume!" (This in reference to
Feyvush's outdated apparel and the beard that had grown rank on his re-
entering the earth's atmosphere.) But when he saw the color of the couple's scrip, he became more respectful, even kicking in some coats of
recent vintage to reduce the Fefers' anachronistic mien.

There was no law that said Feyvush and Gitl had to remain in the old
ghetto neighborhood. Owing to my foresight they now had a nest egg;
they could move to, say, the Upper West Side, someplace where Jews
were thicker on the ground. So why did they insist on beating a path
through shrieking winds back to Orchard Street via a scenic route that
took them past gutted synagogues, shtiblekh with their phantom con-
gregants sandwiched between the bodegas and Chinese take-outs, the

talis shops manned by ancients looking out as from an abyss of years? Answer: having found the familiar strange enough, thank you, they might go farther and fare even worse.

As luck (if that's the right word) would have it, there was a flat available in the very same building they'd vacated a decades-long week ago. For all they knew it was the same paltry top floor apartment with the same sticks of furniture: the sofa with its cushions like sinkholes, the crippled wing chair, the kitchen table, the iron bed; not that the decor would have meant much to Feyvush and Gitl, who didn't look to be in a nostalgic mood. Hugging myself against the cold on the fire escape, I watched them wander from room to room until the windows fogged. Then someone rubbed a circle in a cloudy pane and I ducked out of sight below the ledge. But I could see them nonetheless, it was a talent I had: I could see them as clearly in my mind as with my eyes, peering into a street beyond which there was no manicured pleasure garden, no Tree.

They went out only once. Despite having paid a deposit and the first month's rent, they still had ample funds; they might have celebrated. But instead they returned with only the barest essentials—some black bread and farfel, a shank of gristly soup meat, a greasy sack of knishes from the quarter's one surviving knisherie. Confounded by the gas range that had replaced her old coal-burning cookstove, Gitl threw up her hands; Feyvush hunched his shoulders: Who had any appetite? Then they stared out the window again, past icicles like a dropped portcullis of fangs, toward a billboard atop the adjacent building. The billboard, which featured a man and woman lounging nearly naked on a beach, advertised an airline that offered to fly you nonstop to paradise.

Hunkered below the window ledge, I heard what I couldn't hear just like I saw what I couldn't see—Feyvush saying as if to himself, "Was it a dream?" Gitl replying with rancor: "Dreams are for goyim."

At some point one of them—I don't remember which—went into the bedroom and sat on the bed. He or she was followed soon after by the other, though neither appeared conscious of occupying the same space; neither thought to remove their heavy coats. The sag of the mattress, however, caused them to slide into contact with one another, and at first touch the Fefers combusted like dry kindling. They flared into a desperate embrace, shucking garments, Gitl tugging at her husband's suspenders as if drawing a bowstring. Feyvush ripped Gitl's blouse the way a Cossack parts a curtain to catch a Jew; he spread her thighs as if wrenching open the jaws of a trap. Having torn away their clothes, it seemed they intended to peel back each other's flesh. They marked cheeks and throats with bared talons, twisting themselves into tortured positions as if each were attempting to put on the other's skin—as if the husband must climb through the body of his wife, and vice-versa, in order to get back to what they'd lost.

That's how they did it, fastened to each other in what looked like a mutual punishment—hips battering hips, mouths spewing words refined of all affection. When they were done, they fell apart, sweating and bruised. They took in the stark furnishings of their cold-water flat: the table barren of the fabric flowers that once filled the place with perpetual spring, the window overlooking a street of strangers and dirty snow. Then they went at it again hammer and tongs.

I couldn't watch anymore; then God help me, I couldn't keep from watching. When the windows were steamed, I took the stairs to the roof, rime clinging to my lashes and beard, and squinted through a murky skylight like a sheet of green ice. When they were unobservable from any vantage, I saw them with an inner eye far clearer than my watery tompeepers could focus. I let my good works slide, because who needed second sight to know that the world had gone already to hell in a phylactery bag? While my bones became brittle with winter and the bread and knishes went stale, and the soup meat grew mold and was nibbled at by mice, I kept on watching the Fefers.

Sometimes I saw them observing each other, with undisguised contempt. They had both shed the souvenir pounds they'd brought back from eternity. Gone was Gitl's generous figure, her unkempt hair veiling her tallowy face like a bloody rag. Her ribs showed beneath breasts as baggy as punctured meal sacks, and her freckles were indistinguishable from the pimples populating her brow. Feyvush, always slight, was nine-tenths a cadaver, his eyes in their hunger fairly drooling onto his hollow cheeks. His sunken chest, where it wasn't obscured by matted fur, revealed a frieze of scarlet hieroglyphics etched by his wife's fingernails. So wasted were they now that, when they coupled, their fevered bones chuckled like matches in a box. Between bouts they covered their nakedness with overcoats and went to the window, though not necessarily together. They rubbed circles, looked at the billboard with its vibrant two-some disporting under a tropical sun; then satisfied they were no nearer the place where they hoped to arrive, Feyvush or Gitl returned to bed.

Nu, so what would you have had me to do? Sure, I was the great kib-bitzer in the affairs of others, but having already violated divine law by helping them escape from *der emeser velt*, the so-called true world, was I now to add insult to injury by delivering them from the false? Can truth and deception be swapped as easily as shmattes for fancy dress? Give me a break, the damage was done: human beings were not anyway intended to rise above their stations. The Fefers would never get out of this life again, at least not alive.

So I remained a captive witness to their savage heat. I watched them doing with an unholy vengeance what I never found the time for in my own sanctimonious youth—when I was too busy serving as mighty mouthpiece for a still small voice that had since become all but inaudi-ble. I watched the mortals in their heedless ride toward an elusive glory, and aroused by the driven cruelty of their passion, achieved an erection: my first full engorgement since the days before the destruction of the Temple, when a maiden once lifted her tunic and I turned away. At the peak of my excitement I tore open the crotch of my trousers, releasing myself from a choked confinement, and spat my seed in a peashooter tra-jectory over Orchard Street. When I was finished, I allowed my wilted member to rest on the frigid railing of the fire escape, to which it stuck. Endeavoring to pull it free, I let loose a pitiable howl: I howled for the exquisite pain that mocked my terminal inability to die, and I howled for my loneliness. Then I stuffed my bloody putz back in my pants and looked toward the window, afraid I'd alerted the Fefers to my spying. But the Fefers, as it turned out, were well beyond earshot.

I raised the window and climbed over the sill, muffling my nose with a fingerless mitten against the smell, and shuffled forward to inspect their remains. So hopelessly entangled were the pair of them, however, that it was hard at first to distinguish husband from wife. Of course, there was no mistaking Feyvush's crown of tufted wool for Gitl's tattered red standard, his beak for her button nose, but so twined were their gory limbs that they defied a precise designation of what belonged to whom. Nor did their fused loins admit to which particular set of bones belonged the organ that united them both.

My task was as always to separate spirit from flesh, to extricate their immortal souls, which after a quick purge in the fires of Gehenna (no more than a millennia or two) would be as good as new. The problem was that, given the intricate knot they'd made of themselves, what was true of their bodies was true as well of their souls: I couldn't tell where Gitl's left off and her husband's began. It took me a while to figure it out, but ultimately I located the trouble; then the solution went some distance toward explaining their lifelong predicament. For the Fefers had been one of those rare cases where a couple shares two halves of a solitary soul. Theirs had indeed been a marriage made in heaven such as you don't see much anymore, the kind of match that might lead you to believe God Himself had a hand in it—that is, if you didn't already know He'd gotten out of the matchmaking racket long ago.

Cheryl Pearl Sucher

"The Quality of Being a Ruby"

Ruby Rothstein, twenty-three-year-old Mousketeer, hair dyed cellophane tangerine, rises from her unfit sleep to search for the lithium capsules she discarded weeks and weeks before. Nails fly, glasses break, pipes zetz, yet Guido LaSamba, her lover for the past eight days and seven nights, still runs that eyeball racecourse called REM-Zone Number One, unconscious to the serial dynamics of her hardware symphony.

"Matzoh balls," she roars, pulling on the seam of hair which Guido calls her matador's tail. She is failing, dropping altitude, sinking so fast her heartbeat is slowing, her pulse is disappearing, her toes tingling, her fingers freezing.

"I'm telling you I want to leave you," she continues as she tosses her antique slips aloft, "because if I don't you'll leave me first and I'm tired of being left." Lingerie floats in the air before collapsing onto the laundry piles barricading her étagere. No capsules fall out of her inverted pockets.

I'M TIRED OF BEING LEFT

Ruby knows that even if she finds her "matzoh balls" they will not do any good. They have to float in her bloodstream for seventy-two hours before attaining that magic median "7," smothering the typhoon leaving only an eye in its wake.

BECAUSE IF I DON'T YOU'LL LEAVE ME FIRST

Waves crash, roaring against the hollow hollow, beating LUBUMBA, that foreign rhythm which tells Ruby feeling is not enough, people cannot fly, Guido is certainly not enough. LUBUMBA is her father Isaac calling at six in the morning to ensure she is an early riser catching worms to show to his poker-playing klatch of American-born professionals.

"Why can't you write for *The New York Post?* Why can't you meet marriageable boys from good families instead of apaches from teepees?"

For Chanukah, Isaac bought Ruby a series of Judo classes at the West Side Jewish Y because he read in *Israeli Bond Monthly* that martial arts was the best way for an intelligent devout girl to meet a neurosurgeon.

"Why don't you listen to me, I'm your father. I'm not going to be here forever, who's going to support your bad habits when I'm gone?"

I WANT TO LEAVE YOU

Ruby moves towards the princess telephone lying on her bed. The receiver rests on a pile of unread magazines, unread books and an untyped term paper inscribed on blank rag. The LUBUMBA is moving closer. Soon it will be her only motion. The psychiatrist she visits once a week so she can stare at his transparent plastic skull filled with chocolate-covered expresso beans tells her she is suffering from anxiety neurosis. Isaac is paying him one hundred dollars an hour so she can listen to his grunts, tolerate his snores, interpret his closed eyelids and feel secure under his knowing nods. She spends her sessions deciding how she can crack open the skull so she can get to the chocolate-covered expresso beans.

YOU WILL LEAVE ME FIRST

Ruby Rothstein tiptoes through the fallout towards her telephone, wrapping her Memphis-inspired kimono about herself. Her fingers look like chicken bones, her elbows are sharp protrusions. The telephone, the telephone, her only destination.

BEING LEFT

Ruby's toenails are painted in the new French manicure. They look like Band-Aids to Guido who still sleeps, the jizm-soaked sheet scarving his genitals. Ruby resists the impulse to jump up and down on his pelvis, instead she tugs on the hand lying open like a lily on her carpeted floor.

"Guido."

She tickles his feet until he jerks awake. His snores gurgle, wheeze then die before becoming speech.

"Good morning, kid," he mutters all dreamy into the pillow. "I told you not to do that. It bothers the hell out of me."

"It's an emergency. I have to use the phone."

"What kind of good morning is that, babe?" he says, turning onto his elbows. Guido shakes his head so the black hair lying slick and flat against his neck brooms out like bat's wings. Ruby's heart skips a proverbial beat. She tries not to feel his thigh against her own. She knows he will flop his hand on her breast, a vague gesture which will become alert, fingertips scaling the topography of nipple.

TIRED

Ruby leans forward, eyes only for the lime lighted dial WE8-1707. Dr. Wiesotsky.

"You kill me," Guido says, pulling Ruby's hands from the phone cord. He holds her wrists tight so she can feel her blood dam. His eyes, speckled with sleep, burn olive through their bloodshot vitreous humour. Ruby knows his hands will travel to her flanks to knead the fleshy knobs he calls her "sponge cakes" before tugging her thighs so she will sit on top of his cock which is all muscle and syncopation. This morning she holds his hands in place.

"Guido, I'm telling you I want to leave you because if I don't you will leave me first and I'm tired of being left."

This doesn't even faze Guido because he is from California.

"Come on, babe, I don't understand what you're talking about. How can you leave your own apartment?" He moves his hands from her wrists to the soft concave bottom of her belly.

Normally Ruby would have laughed at the pun but her heart muscle is undergoing peristalsis. It burns, this pain, demanding relief. Finally Ruby understands why Isaac eats antacid tablets like peppermint pastilles and keeps a druggist's carton in the glove compartment of his Lincoln Continental. She believes she will be consumed by this fire unless she phones her shrink or moves up, out, beyond and away from the orthopedic mattress which was a gift from Isaac upon her initial dismissal from Hillside Hospital. He promised her a Mies van der Rohe chair if she would return to her analytic training and visit the St. Vincent out-patient clinic bi-weekly to undergo blood monitoring. Ruby promised, but she was seduced by the raw expansiveness of her loft space, how the cold chafed her skin. Morning light suffused her bedroom, reliquary to dawn's fugal chorus. Garbage cans rattled against grinding Dumpsters, trucks negotiated wounded potholes, horns honked as machine drills cracked overgrown cement blocks. This was Ruby's music, an urban exposition, harmony to dissuade her fevered blood and masquerade as requiem to diagnosis. So Ruby stopped taking her lithium and turned to a more uplifting remedy: the big C. The big C defied gravity, propelling her to tranquil heights where she reigned supreme, arbiter of destiny and queen of originality. Life became RUBESSENCE: the quality of being a ruby.

Ruby spent her mornings experimenting with loss of direction at a nearby modern dance studio. Afternoons were spent soaking her calloused feet in hot tubs. By evening, she was ready to don her shoulder pads, ring her ears, drop veils from her eyelashes, comb her seam of hair and paint her eyelids the color of hummingbirds' claws. Looking like an inverted triangle, she cabbed it to clubs where rock orders performed with menageries of exotic beasts. There she rendezvoused with men in moussed crewcuts who huffed and grunted and squinted after James Dean, exhaling cigarette smoke into their nostrils, leaning against walls waiting for the resurrection of their death lusts. Their leather felt lush against her rainbow-colored hose, their scotch-scented breath soft and aromatic as desert winds. When the clubs closed, she went home with one or the other, it didn't matter, for by dawn she would be alone, the men of soft leather dreaming of splendor in the grass. Dawn inspired her to work. In the cold sunlight she rolled to the rhythms of her unmonitored motion, exploring the hidden mysteries of mind's infinite space. Her assignments seemed to complete themselves.

But it didn't last. Down swooped the roller coaster, out of gas.

One morning she awakened feeling nauseous and slow. She had forgotten to remove her contact lenses before going to sleep and her corneas ached, pounding LUBUMBA LUBUMBA, that chronic beat, intensified by a migraine so severe she thought her cranium cracked along its suture joint. It was Guido in bed beside her. His nimble fingers danced a somnambulist's tango on her pubic cleft. The walls throbbed. In the ceiling's tin moldings she saw the commandment of her first comprehensive examination:

THOU SHALT FORSAKE ALL OTHERS THAN ME

Three weeks lay between the beginning and the end. Ruby stared at the books piled into a pyramid beneath her halogen floorlamp.

She hadn't planned on Guido.

She didn't believe that time would pass against her will.

When Dr. Wiesotsky emerged from his trance and tiptoed to his miniature refrigerator to get a Diet Dr. Pepper, he warned Ruby against falling in love.

"Falling in love isn't good for manic depressives experiencing anxiety neurosis. You want to be cured, don't you?"

She didn't know because knowing was the pragmatic sport of entertainment lawyers and investment bankers.

"Don't you want to get better?" her father Isaac asked each morning, his Yiddishisms laced with despair. "Don't you want to get better, *malgyreh*? Don't you know what you want? Are you taking your matzoh balls?"

Isaac started referring to lithium as "matzoh balls" when Ruby began blowing the steel whistle she kept for crank callers into the phone when he wouldn't stop his ceaseless meditation upon its wondrous properties.

"Don't you want to talk about it, babe?" Guido says, sitting upright on the mattress, his legs locked into a lotus position, his penis rising against his flat belly like a stamen from the flower.

"I want the telephone."

"Who do you want to call so badly you can't even give me a proper good morning?"

"The fire department. I want a fireman to come and rescue me from my own apartment."

"*Sangue de la Madonna!*"

LABUMBA BUM. These are the noises pulsing through Ruby's veins as Guido grabs her crotch and misses then grabs her calves just to grab. His fingers can hold one of her calves in each of his hands, so long are they and so lithe.

"You unplugged the phone last night, babe, don't you remember? You didn't want your father to wake you up in the morning."

Garbage cans clang against truck incinerators. Drivers shout to corner coffee-shop owners as they roll up steel canopies and fold back security gates.

"I have to make a call!"

Ruby lunges, lips chapped and chewed, blue eyes darkening to a deep violet. She stares at the disconnected wire and cannot remember unplugging the telephone. She cannot remember when she stopped putting her clothes away and stopped doing her laundry. She cannot recall when she ceased longing to look at Guido's pursed lips smiling contentedly in his sleep. She cannot remember when the pleasure started to pinch like a runner's ache in her side.

Guido rises and wrestles Ruby onto her back, straddling her as she lies face-up between his legs.

"How many buffalo does it take to screw in a light bulb?"

"What? Let me go!"

"How many buffalo does it take to screw in a light bulb?"

Guido's lips curve into a smile.

Ruby rolls out from under him.

"Guido, I don't want to screw in any light bulbs," she says, stuttering, placing his dancing hand on his penis.

With these words Ruby melts into the spiral swirling downwards. A long and dexterous hand elevates Ruby's entire being.

"He's got a third leg," Ruby's best friend Sheila whispered the night the pair went to the Lone Star Café and discovered Guido LaTango belly up to the bar, one hand hidden in his holster pocket. Ruby remembered his name because it sounded like Xavier Cugat playing the maracas. He was there with his brother Horatio. The pair were immigrant Italians from San Obispo, California with hair like prairie dogs and Eisenhower leather flight jackets. The quartet danced the Texas Two-Step until their clothes were damp and their legs flew independent of will or grace. When the clock struck three they descended upon the Empire Diner. As Ruby chewed Guido's earlobes, Sheila recited Yeats and Horatio pointed at the electronic time on his scuba diver's Pulsar. After cheeseburgers and eggcreams, the uncoupled pair waltzed into the night air while Guido flexed his noble length against Ruby's soft strength.

He stayed the night and the week.

"Babe, are you all right?"

"No, I'm not all right," Ruby says. "The room is doing a cartwheel. Be a pal and call WE8-1707. It's my doctor, he'll tell you what's going on."

"Why can't you tell me? Don't I know you?" Guido says, groping the mattress in search of his Camel 100's.

I WANT TO LEAVE YOU

Ruby's eyes flutter open then close. Her legs feel like Jell-O molds. She observes the way the pink skin of Guido's softening member catcurls onto itself. How lean he is and how dark—like the men in teen magazines whose portraits she clipped and posted onto her bulletin boards.

"Call!" she squeaks. Guido tickles her armpits, his predetermined source of instant access. When she doesn't giggle, he knows it is time to telephone.

"Not enough!" Isaac says when he calls. "The Italian is not enough for you!"

Guido LaSamba dials WE8-1707, then waits, raking his bangs back across his scalp.

"It's going to be all right, babe. It's going to be great," he says, lighting up with the New York University monogrammed lighter Ruby purchased when the only money she possessed was in the form of her university chargeplate. The smoke rises in tusks from his nostrils.

Guido LaSamba paces the length of the phone cord. He stares at Ruby, whose kimono has fallen open revealing skin the color of scalloped shells and ribs which rise higher than her breasts.

"Dr. Wiesotsky?"

The motion of merit, that downward double pike Ruby believed she could accomplish without fear or effort, suddenly seems untenable. Her legs have fallen out of the tuck position and she has bellyflopped over the edge. All those unread books and unaccomplished deeds will never transmogrify into the eruditions characteristic of the disease she inherited from her grandfather, Moishe Firestein, the Genius of Minsk. Ruby's mother, Sylvia, told her how Reb Moishe sat through the night before his talmudic texts sipping tea through a sugar cube, clutching his beard taut, his eyes open so wide they could see God's manifestations in the sacred parchment. No one told Ruby about the nights his eyes would not open. Nobody told her about the nightscape haunted by demons with pimpled noses and blood gefilte fish cleavers. For Ruby, the distillation of the illness was "Rubessence," the perfect calm of inspired originality, the longed-for union of the desired and the real.

"Is Guido a Jewish name?" Isaac asks each time he phones and hears someone singing "Celeste Aida" over the grumbling flush of a toilet.

"Is Guido what you want?" Dr. Wiesotsky asks at the beginning of each session. The last time she felt so good she believed she no longer had to crack open the skull to get at the chocolate-covered expresso beans. She said "yes" then walked over and reached through the nostrils to take a few.

"You're more involved than you think you are," Dr. Wiesotsky proclaimed, bringing to a halt Ruby's twenty-minute diatribe concerning her new sense of personal freedom. "People don't change overnight. Change takes a long time, sometimes prompted by medication, sometimes by dissatisfaction and frustration. But you, Ruby Rothstein, cannot tell me, your doctor, that a number of nights of uninterrupted sex has not created in you feelings of bonding."

Bonding. Tied by scratchy hemp, clutching at bodies with labial lips but unable to prolong joining. Bonding. Groping at night for the limb which will anchor, calm the tremolo rising when her blood boils afrenzy. Bonding. A yearning to run, leap, and jump out of her skin which resists a bonding she has never known. Is bonding a love that stays forever still or is it a forward motion which might, in the end, send her flying backwards?

"I don't know. I haven't been taking my lithium."

"You want to be a crazy person forever," Isaac asks, "so no one will ever want to live with you, a sick person? Do you want to be like Rhoda's daughter, Janet, who they found, her hair Cloroxed white, walking the pier at 42nd Street, dressed in her mother's underwear? You want to be so sick nobody will want to smell you? Why do you have to be such an action? Why can't you listen?"

The second night that Ruby slept with Guido he lay besides her blowing smoke rings in a series of collapsed hearts that rose towards her tin ceiling. Ruby watched their progression rather than the angular bones carving Guido's cheeks or the movement of his hand on her neck. He was talking and she wasn't listening. He was telling her he was engaged to be married to a computer programmer from Fort Lee named Dolores who had curly red hair. Dolores wasn't demanding, he said, but he wanted her so badly he could see her reflection in escalator guard rails. Guido said Dolores had gone to Palm Springs with her mother to contemplate their ensuing marriage. She had given him six months to get a white-collar job, but he was still working as a bicycle messenger on Wall Street, zigzagging his Peugeot 10-speed through the slalom course of limousines, taxicabs and moving vans. He said Horatio had taken him to the Lone Star Café that night to cheer him up because Dolores' mother said he was a never-amount-to-anything and Dolores needed to get away to know whether or not that was a temporary malaise or a permanent illness. Ruby couldn't listen: she liked not knowing. But yesterday Guido said his vacation from "Pedal-a-Gram" was over, Dolores was returning via Kennedy at seven P.M. and he had to take the train to the plane and this was goodbye.

LEFT

Guido feels his chest for pockets. Cradling the phone under his chin, he speaks into the receiver before crawling towards Ruby to search for her pulse. Her wrists are dry, coursed by faint veins. Her hand is limp and without color. The pulse he discovers is faint as his bicycle bell in midtown traffic.

"Ruby's ill," he shrieks into the receiver. "My name? Guido. Guido La-Triccio . . . I don't have a car . . . Listen, doc, I don't think I did anything. I told her to lay off the stuff . . . what stuff? You mean you are her doctor and you don't know how many lines she can do at one blow?"

The calm swells, Guido fondles the phone cord as he searches Ruby's face for some sign of recognition.

"What time is it? Is St. Vincent's still open? . . . But I have to pick up Dolores!"

Sounds swim, deepening the LUBUMBA, forest drums beating steady calls.

"Guido's all right, he treats me well, Dad," Ruby says to Isaac each time he asks. He threatens to stop paying her tuition if she doesn't stop seeing "that Mafioso."

LEAVE ME FIRST

It is graduation day. Ruby is starring in her own theme, Phi Beta Kappa and magna cum laude. These awards were bestowed upon the thesis she accomplished during her first and greatest flight into Rubessence. For three weeks she flew non-stop, percolating on pots of mocha java and Keith Jarrett's improvisational piano melodies. On graduation day, she boogied up to the president after he announced her name more times that that of the featured commencement speaker. In the audience was her coterie of lovers: the chairman of the philosophy department who had rendered Wittgenstein obsolete, the cellist who played Shostakovich when he couldn't sleep and ate horseradish on matzoh in bed, and the provost of Southern Connecticut State, twenty years her senior, who made love only after taking his blood pressure to make sure it had not risen above 110/70. On the podium, diploma in hand, Ruby felt like the instant winner of a McDonald's burger, the quality of being a Ruby in her red cap and gown.

"Hi, Ma!" she waved to Sylvia, flagging her diploma like a relay runner's baton. Sylvia wasn't there, however, she was in Fort Lauderdale receiving moccasin venom treatments for the residual paralysis resulting from the stroke which jammed her knees into knotted knobs and forced her into an electronic wheelchair to roll. Sylvia was never there but Ruby had learned to pretend. She could not hail her return nor protest for Isaac was forever telling her "your mother is a saint, not a person" and saints could be excused for not being there when there were more important issues like suffering to contend with. Sylvia's separation could be imagined into the difference.

"Goodbye!" they all waved from their seats. "Good luck!" The philosopher recently granted tenure, the cellist who had won that year's Naumberg competition, the provost who had become a father for the third time. A chorus of swells.

Guido dresses Ruby in her Eurythmics t-shirt and Matsuda pants. Ruby feels him pull her arms through the sleeves, kissing her brow before gently leading her head through the shirtneck. His long hands seem the hands of an artisan. Finding her crotch, he tickles the soft concave bottom of her belly before tugging on her lace underpants. Then he slides on her jeans which are so tight she can hear his exasperation. She remembers him naked. She imagines he will never leave her.

"Are we going to take the train to the plane, Guido?"

"Anything you say, kid," he mutters as he picks her up, elevating her entire being with one hand's grace.

Guido tiptoes over thumbtacks, hammers, nails and slips. He trips over an empty vial of pills whose orange container lies a sunburst on the floor. Ruby is flung in the air for a split second, all confetti, all light, before she falls back into Guido's arms. Guido prays in Latin as he kicks the door open and carries his bundle of eighty-eight pound Ruby down four flights of stairs.

Garbage trucks grunt, old ladies wheeling shopping carts hobble over potholes.

It was all a progressive somersault from the first steps taken down that marble staircase. Ruby never believed she would ever regain that altitude. The air felt like wands through her nostrils. Then the rhythms propelling flight began to slide a glissando towards silence. Her head started to swell. She felt like she was coming down with encephalitis, the engorgement of the fatty tissues of the brain. But actually it was the first coming of LUBUMBA, that foreign rhythm, that stone statue speech.

"Taxi!" Guido cries, raising his hand to hail a cab. He almost drops Ruby.

The sound of the cab screeching to a halt sounds like the ambulance which brought Sylvia home from the hospital the time they put her in the iron lung.

"I love you," she mumbles into Guido's shirt.

"Anything you say, kid," Guido responds, caressing Ruby's tangerine hair before tugging on her matador's ponytail. "Anything you say."

Benjamin Taylor

"Walnuts,
When the Husks Are Green"

from *Tales Out of School*

Free-wheeling up the drive on his bicycle, arms across his chest, with thrush-colored hair and olive aspect, rode the only grandchild of Liselotte Mehmel. Having stepped out onto the porch this afternoon to water her fuchsia, she watched the boy go past. Liselotte waved, but shook her head.

"Going home, going home," he called out to her, not stopping. Felix Mehmel was fourteen—with good and bad, everything, still to come—in the flat-calm summer of 1907. Arriving home, six blocks farther on, Felix took from behind the bicycle seat several books he had belted together and wedged there, while his mother regarded him from the front steps of the great house, consternation and delight mingling in a toss of her head.

"Felix Mehmel, are you going to spend your whole life just reading? I mean, just *reading* about everything?"

"Yes, ma'am."

He kissed away her frown, passed indoors and up the curving stair. An afternoon sun was spreading mullion shadows across the walls and onto the carpets. In the corner niche of the landing was a heavy milk-glass vase with harebells wound into a bouquet, Neevah's handiwork of the day before.

To the left and down the hall of the second floor was Felix's room. He flung open the door to find the brindle cat, Hildy by name, seated in a bar of light. Dispassionate, erect, she mewed once, more reproachful than friendly, and extended a simpering face to be stroked on her cheeks, scratched between her eyes.

"Stinker," Felix said, obliging.

Mrs. McClung, the cook, had been out to the fishmonger that morning, and there would likely be a scrap of pickerel or fluke to grace Hildy's dinner bowl. Was this the knowledge in which she privately smiled? Year by year, Felix thought, she'd been swapping youth for omniscience.

He threw off his steel-rimmed spectacles, lay down on the bed, opened a calf-bound volume, its pages foxed and brittle, that he'd taken from the book belt. Far gone already in nearsightedness, he preferred nonetheless to read without glasses, relishing the pleasant retinal stress as he went, his nose all but touching the page.

> Inur'd to suffer, and resolv'd to dare,
> The Fates, without my pow'r, shall be without my care.
> This let me crave—since near your grove the road
> To hell lies open, and the dark abode
> Which Acheron surrounds, th' innavigable flood;
> Conduct me thro' the regions void of light,
> And lead me longing to my father's sight.

Like walnuts when the husks are green, and darken at your touch, he took the impress of the words. But were they in like case, he and Aeneas? Aeneas at least could remember. Felix's struggling recollection pitched up this or that fragment of his own father, but these did not cohere. The clove scent of toilet water, the violent reek of the slop bowl: a dead father was both. Also, the noise of coins in his trousers pocket. The old-style watch with its burr-headed winding stem. The monogrammed fob on a length of black grosgrain. The pair of mutton chops, which were as nettle to your cheek. The sudden blaze of anger with never a warning. Even, once, the back of the hand . . .

Facts are facts. What has happened cannot be made not to have happened. A black rain fell, a rivening wind came on. An angry God rolled the waters of earth over Galveston seven Septembers before. Felix's father disappeared into that weather.

Leaving the boy to his abstraction, Hildy had taken a measured leap into the open drawer of the chifferobe, gazed blandly behind her, and begun to forage with her head buried and hindquarters bristling up. Bored suddenly—all Hildy's moods were at right angles to one another—she leapt to the bed and put her barbed tongue against the boy's cheek.

What had Gulf waters done with Aharon Mehmel? Did banqueting sharks pick him clean? Do the smooth-as-jade bones tumble in some distant surf? Or had the utter dark, below the deep, somehow—husbanded him?

It is reported that Jonah was not a perfect man either. But God furnished the great fish regardless. And Jonah supplicated God from its belly for three days and three nights. Then God spoke to the fish, and the fish vomited Jonah out on dry land. This is reported.

If three days alive in the belly of death, why not three years? If three years, why not six? Seven, why not? Why not Aharon Mehmel spat back whole into life? This question Felix did not dare to ask, but his dreams did. His dreams, unremembered by day, asked whether death might not be death after all but instead the great preserver. Like Jonah's fish . . .

"I'm out of sorts today," Felix told Hildy, sporting a new locution. "I'm restive, cross-grained, querulous." Such connoisseurship is what came of reading the dictionary straight through. His mother wondered if she oughtn't to take that book and throw it on the fire. Then perhaps he'd speak like other children. Fourteen years old and all of English had been through Felix Mehmel, a hankerer for the wizardry of words.

> Look round the wood, with lifted eyes, to see
> The lurking gold upon the fatal tree:
> Then rend it off, as holy rites command;
> The willing metal will obey thy hand,
> Following with ease, if favor'd by thy fate,
> Thou art foredoom'd to view the Stygian state:
> If not, no labor can the tree constrain;
> And strength of stubborn arms and steel are vain.

He closed his eyes and said aloud the first two couplets, then the second, and so on. By now it was not so much an undertaking as an instinct with him: he got things by heart. His learning was an appetite that grew by what it fed on. While still in taffety cuffs and collar he could recite the caesars from Gaius Julius to Romulus Augustulus. At ten he had sat down and mastered the names of all the lands of the earth along with their populations, natural resources, geographical features, mean annual precipitations, and etcetera. He was comprehensive, was Felix.

"Our boy got the mind of a sponge!" Neevah would inform marvelling grown-ups who came to call. With his contemporaries Felix was less successful. They didn't care about dynasties of China, explorers of the New World, prime ministers of England. No point in rattling off for them exportable produce of the Argentine pampas.

One morning near the end of the school term Wick Frawley, a freckle-faced setter-eyed boy who'd been held back a grade and was near sixteen, and had age and height if not intelligence to lord over his classmates, and was Felix's special tormentor, had blocked the door to the schoolroom and said, "Felix Mehmel, you walk like a girl!" He'd said it loud enough for everybody to hear, then demonstrated, prancing tiptoe in a circle with his arms expressively up. "Tippy Toes, that's your name." Everybody, even the one or two Felix thought were his friends, had heartily laughed.

Miss Claypoole, their teacher, had said, "Wick Frawley, you stop that this instant!" But not too sternly, it seemed to Felix. "And Felix Mehmel, *you* just quit provoking Wick. Ah, do please spare me your innocent looks, young man! I may have been born yesterday, but I stayed up all night, and I know that it requires two to make a situation!" Her bosom rose and fell with the great truth she'd uttered. "Boys and girls, take your seats!"

From his place in the second row, Wick kept turning around, first to wink and flutter his eyelids, then to brandish a fist. Felix passed a note up to him which read, in excellent Palmer method: *Let me alone, you Visigoth!*

Miss Claypoole broke off her instruction to declare that she would not tolerate the passing of notes in class. "Felix, Wick, to the cloakroom!" Everybody knew what that meant—a thrashing on the palms with her ruler. When the boys got to the unventilated cubicle, where a faint odor of sweat presided, Wick with narrowed eyes said, "After school, honey-bunch."

Then entered Claypoole with terrible swift sword and shut the cloak-room door behind her.

Felix could recollect a time before he understood that adults are former children, that children grow up to be adults. There had been children and there had been adults, and nobody ever got any taller or older, and everybody in this perdurable arrangement was as happy as could be. Now, swiftly, the changes came upon him: hair sprouting where the body forks, arms and legs splaying out, duskiness arriving in the voice.

That afternoon of early summer, a week or so after Decoration Day, there had come a knock at his bedroom door. He was busy. He was read-ing. What was this bother? The door swung open to reveal—Wick Fraw-ley.

"Hello, honeybunch."

The boldness of it dumbfounded Felix. Wick Frawley, here in the *sanc-tum sanctorum?* It was infamous. Summer meant not having to endure this tinhorn bully—his cretinous name-calling, his swaggering threats. On the last day of school Felix had tucked into Wick's satchel a little note which read: *Farewell, you thick and brutal ignoramus, you misbegot-ten clodpole, you dim-witted recreant!*

Not so dim, however, not such a clodpole, not so thick that he was un-able to figure out from whom the valediction came. "I told that old nig-ger woman downstairs me and you had some unfinished bidnis. I told her your marker's come due. She said mighty fine."

What he'd said to Neevah was something else entirely, something sugary polite. He'd inveigled Neevah into letting him up those stairs!

"Here in this pocket, I got me a stick knife. I use it very often. You know what for? Putting my mark on enemies. Sure, honeybunch. Right on their upper lip, so everybody can see, I write—WICK FRAWLEY WAS HERE. Shows up good."

"I haven't seen anyone with that on."

"Hee, hee," laughed Wick. "They all wear mustaches now. Have to."

"Well, I don't think I can grow a mustache." Felix wished to, but could not, disguise a quaver in his voice.

"That'll be your problem, honeybunch."

This Wick Frawley was a boy of no background, with a mother and father companionately married, as they say, meaning that neither church nor state had beheld their union. The Frawleys lived over to the north side, a sallow tow-haired common-law family of indeterminate size. Six or eight children could be seen of an afternoon to mope on the tumbledown front porch while in a yard choked with jimson weed a dozen or more aimlessly picked at one another. The truant officer had had to call more than once and carried appalling rumors back to town. He said the Frawley children fed from a trough, devil taking the hindmost. He said a state of nature obtained at that paintless ramshackle weatherboard house, the stronger offspring guarding their prerogatives while the weaker wasted away.

Felix had observed that the shoes Wick wore to school were out at the backs and had the tongues missing—erstwhile shoes. Also, that his clothes were sometimes too small and sometimes too big, and of an inevitable dirtiness. He didn't exactly stink; you could say he was piquant, odorous; you could say he smelled like geraniums. But it was the hands Felix most noticed—casehardened as those of a grown man. Felix did not wish to see, but saw, that these hands of his tormentor were very beautiful. Now Wick raised them, palms facing, in a gesture of mock conciliation. "Course, you can get yourself off the hook with me real quick like."

"By what means?"

"Hee, hee," laughed Wick. "You can fess up to being a girl inside them britches. Cause I don't put my mark on no girls, honeybunch."

To scream would be proof of what Wick alleged, so Felix did not let himself scream. Besides, that stick knife mightn't be an empty boast.

"Just take them britches down."

Whirling within himself, Felix said nothing, made no move.

"Lemme git a look, that's all," said Wick and whereas his voice had heretofore been all derision, now it harbored something different, a plea. "Lemme git a look." And the clenchfist of fear in which he held Felix was also, inexplicably, a caress. "Lemme." As in a dream Felix complied, not excluding the underdrawers.

"Aw, hell," said Wick, "I see a weener." And he pulled a mournful face.

"What are we gonna do about that? Better kiss your elbow, I think. Sure, honeybunch! Kiss your elbow, change your sex, don't you know that?"

Trousers down around his shoes, Felix said, "Impossible."

"Aw, try."

Admittedly there are truths unlearnable from the reference works. Was this one of them? Felix puckered up, straining towards one unattainable elbow and then the other as something humble, without a name, broke forth in him, something with joy in it: the dreamlike satisfaction of doing just as Wick bade him.

"Your weener's strange."

"In what respect?" asked Felix, who had but the indistinct memory of his father's naked person to go on.

"Well, it ain't all there. I'll show you what a good one looks like."

Wick now took out the uncircumcised real thing. "Mine's better, ain't it?"

"Yours is better, Wick." But Felix avowed silently that Wick's was *not* better. It looked like a sad case. It looked like a finished bloom of morning glory. It looked—well, just not how it ought to.

Now Wick pushed his foreskin forward, pulled it back. Forward, back; he was changing size. "Too bad you can't do this!" Forward, back, ever more quickly. Felix had studied his own privates in all phases, even rubbed himself, with pleasurable results, against the bedclothes, the window seat, the hook-stitched rug. But Wick's method, this stalwart back and forth, was—Felix surmised—something new, a discovery all of Wick's own.

"Join my club," the latter said. His dread blue gaze had lost the glint of meanness. Tending thus ardently to himself, pumping away, sighing, Wick acquired innocence.

"What kind of club is it?" Felix asked.

"Real private."

"How many members?"

"Just me, so far," said Wick, and moaned. "You'll be second. But honeybunch, the dues is *steep*."

"How much, may I ask?"

"Three dollars," said Wick, and gave out a groan, and cracked a lovesome grin. "Hey, feature *that*," he said, using his free hand to point. "I be-

lieve I see a boner on you! I *do* believe I see a boner! . . . Do what I do
. . . That's right."

The rusty pattern of freckles across Wick's nose, beheld hitherto as the
very ensign of evil, seemed now but a handsome detail in a scheme of
handsomeness. All malice, all mockery were gone from him. Beautiful
and good, he forged ahead to his conclusion.

So, too, did Felix, following as best he could Wick's lead while, in the
pulses, there rose a blood-boltered singing. He had a moment to wonder,
was something irreplaceable about to go from him? Or was this deep
source perpetual, bedded in the braving and original flesh? Yes, here in
tumult lay the truth of truths, surpassing knowledge, granting the vital
mean and measure.

Yes.

Outside, a cobalt light of day was sifting in through leaves of the sugarberry tree. Hildy at the windowsill had turned her back to the human
scene, averted her gaze. Upon the uppermost bough of the sugarberry an
eastern pewee was prinking himself. *Pee-ah-wee*, the bird sang, out of
reach. A breeze shifted the canopy of leaves. *Pee-ah-wee*, the bird sang.
Hildy's nostrils widened, Hildy lashed her tail. Grown old though she
was, she leapt for the upper bough as sidewise through leafage the pewee
darted away. Hildy gazed lornly after the bird, then cocked an ear forward. From treetop to treetop, through the surcharged afternoon, starting with the sugarberry and passing to the camphor and the osage orange,
had risen a thrumming of locusts.

A whole other life, sweet and perilous, bloomed in the mind. Were
Felix's accumulated school hurts, the torment of them laid up in mem-
ory, hereby to be annulled? Perennially outside, was he to pass in?
Strange and delicious, the feeling of inclusion in a secret.

Wick said nothing, only wiped his hand against the tail of his shirt,
and loured. Felix cast about nervously for a topic. "Are you a fancier of
cats, Wick? I know I am. Just look at Hildy, out on a limb. I never tire of
observing her, so dignified, so elegant. Others can keep their *canes fa-
miliares*, better known as dogs. That's my opinion. What's yours, Wick?"

"My opinion is, you owe me three dollars."

"Pardon? Oh yes, certainly, the dues. I'm afraid I haven't got them just
now, but most assuredly will by next week."

"You ain't in good standing till I get them three dollars."

"I certainly am eager to be in good standing."

Now Wick hitched up his pants in one motion. "Don't tell nobody about none of this, you hear? *Nobody*," he emphasized, gaining the door, and with a rakehell backward glance was gone.

S. L. Wisenberg

"Big Ruthie Imagines Sex without Pain"

She imagines it the way she tries to reconstruct dreams, really reconstruct. Or builds an image while she is praying. She imagines a blue castle somewhere on high, many steps, a private room, fur rug, long mattress, white stucco walls, tiny windows. She imagines leaving her body. It frightens her. If she leaves her body, leaves it cavorting on the bed/fur rug/kitchen table (all is possible when there is sex without pain)—she may not get it back. Her body may just get up and walk away, without her, wash itself, apply blusher mascara lipstick, draw up her clothes around it, take her purse and go out to dinner. Big Ruthie herself will be left on the ceiling, staring down at the indentations on the mattress and rug, wishing she could reach down and take a book from a shelf. She does not now nor has she ever owned a fur rug. But when Big Ruthie achieves sex without pain, she will have a fluffy fur rug. Maybe two. White, which she'll send to the cleaners, when needed.

She imagines sex without pain: an end to feeling Ruben tear at her on his way inside, scuffing his feet so harshly at her door, unwitting, can't help himself, poor husband of hers.

She thinks there must be a name for it. She has looked it up in various books and knows it is her fault. All she must do is relax. It was always this way, since the honeymoon. Of course the first months she told herself it was the newness. She is so big on the outside, so wide of hip, ample of waist, how could this be—a cosmic joke?—this one smallness where large, extra large would have smoothed out the wrinkles in her marriage bed? When all her clothes are size 18 plus elastic, why does this one part of her refuse to grow along with her? At first she thought, the membranes will stretch. Childbirth will widen. Heal and stretch, heal and stretch. But no. She has never healed, never quite healed. From anything. She carries all her scars from two childhood dog bites, from a particularly awful bee sting. I am marked, she thinks.

Ruben is the only lover she has ever had. "OK, God," Big Ruthie says, well into her thirty-fifth year, "I'm not asking for sex without ambivalence or sex without tiny splinters of anger/resentment. I am not even asking, as per usual, for a new body, a trade-in allowance from my ever-larger and larger layers of light cream mounds. I am not asking you to withdraw my namesake candy bar from the market, to wipe its red-and-white wrapper from the face of the earth. I have grown used to the teasing. It's become second nature, in fact. And I am not asking you to cause my avoirdupois, my spare tire and trunk to melt in one great heavenly glide from my home to Yours. I am only asking for a slight adjustment. One that I cannot change by diet alone. As if I have ever changed any part or shape of my body through diet. For once I am not asking You to give me something that just looks nice. Make me, O Lord, more internally accommodating." Big Ruthie, turning thirty-five, prays. Alone, in bed.

She is afraid.

She is afraid she will lose herself, her body will siphon out into Ruben's, the way the ancient Egyptians removed the brains of their dead through the nose. Ruthie wants to carve out an inner largeness, yet fears she will become ghostlike, as see-through as a negligee, an amoeba, one of those floaters you get in your eye that's the size of an inch worm. A transparent cell. Mitosis, meiosis. She will be divided and conquered. She imagines her skin as nothing more than a bag, a vacuum-cleaner bag, collapsing when you turn off the control. No sound, no motion, no commotion, all the wind sucked out of her. Still. A fat polar bear lying on the rug. Hibernating without end. No one will be able to wake Big Ruthie or move her in order to vacuum. No one.

She mentioned it once, timidly, to the Ob/Gyn man. He patted her on the knee. Mumbled about lubrication. Maybe the pain didn't really exist, Big Ruthie thought. Maybe it was her imagination and this was the intensity of feeling they talked about. But it is pain. It combines with that other feeling so that she wants it and doesn't want it, can't push this word away from her brain: Invaded. My husband is invading me. He makes her feel rough and red down there. As if he's made of sandpaper. Even with the lubricant they bought. It makes her want to cry and sometimes she does, afterward, turning her head away. How could her Ceci and Ellen fit through there and not her Ruben?

Still Big Ruthie imagines sex without pain, imagines freedom: f—ing out of doors. In picnic groves. She imagines longing for it during the day, as she vacuums, sweeps, wipes dishes, changes diapers, slices cheese for sandwiches, bathes her daughters, reads them stories. She imagines it like a tune from the radio trapped in her mind. It will overtake her, this sex without pain, this wanting, this sweet insistence. A rope will pull her to bed. Beds. Fur rugs. Rooftops. Forests, tree houses. She imagines doing it without thinking. Her family does nothing without thinking, worrying, wringing, twisting hands, with a spit and glance over the shoulder at the evil eye. At Lilith, strangler of children, Adam's first wife, who wanted to be on top. Who wanted sex without pain. Whenever she wanted.

Sometimes Ruthie begins. She might tickle Ruben. She might hope: This time, this time, because I started it, we will share one pure, smooth sweep, one glide a note a tune a long song, as sweet as pleasant as a kiss. She thinks, if she can conquer this, get over this obstacle, she of two children, a house and a husband—if she Big Ruthie can find her way to this sex without pain—then Ruben would be able to rope her, he would be able to lasso her from the next room, from across the house. She would rely on him, and on sex, on sex without pain. Then any man would be able, with a nod of his head, a wink of his eye, to pull her to him. Ruthie and Anyman with a fur rug, without a fur rug. Big Ruthie will advertise herself: a woman who has sex without pain. She will become a woman in a doorway, a large woman blocking a large doorway, foot behind her, against the wall, a thrust to her head, a toss, a wafting of her cigarette. Big Ruthie will start to smoke, before, after, and during.

Nothing will stop her. She will be expert. Till she can do it in her sleep. With her capable hands, with her ever-so-flexible back, front, sides, mouths. With the mailman, roofer, plumber; she could become the plumber's assistant, he, hers. She will go at it. She will not be lady-like. She will be a bad girl. She will swing on a swing in a good-time bar. She will become a good-time girl, wearing garters that show, no girdle at all, black lace stockings rounded by her thighs and calves, brassy perfume that trails her down the street. People will know: That is Big Ruthie's scent. She will have a trademark, a signature.

Big Ruthie, the good-time girl.

Fleshy Ruthie, the good-time girl.

Bigtime Ruthie. Twobit Ruthie.

Ruthie knows that other people have sex without pain. Men, for instance. Ruben. She has watched his eyes squint in concentrated delight. She herself sometimes cries out, the way he does, but she knows his is a pure kind of white kind of pleasure, while hers is dark, gray, troubled. It hurts on the outside just as he begins and moments later when he moves inside her. This was Eve's curse—not cramps, not childbirth, but this; hurts as much as what—as the times Ruben doesn't shave and he kisses her and leaves her cheeks and chin pink and rough for days. But this is worse.

But if she could have sex without pain—sex without secrets—she will have sex without fear, and without fear of sex without pain.

Then the thought of no sex at all will make her afraid, more than she is now of sex with pain, more than she is afraid of losing her body, more than she is afraid of never losing it, never being light.

Ruben said once she was insatiable. This is because she squirmed and writhed, wanting to savor everything, all the moments that led to the act, she wanted to forestall the act of sex with pain. When she has sex without pain, she will go on forever, single-minded of purpose. One-track mind. She is afraid she will forget everything—will forget the multiplication table, the rule for i before e, to take vitamins, when to add bleach, how to can fruit, drive, run a PTA meeting using *Robert's Rules of Order,* bind newspapers for the Scouts' paper drives, change diapers, speak Yiddish, follow along in the Hebrew, sing the Adom Olam, make round ground balls of things: gefilte fish, matzo balls. Ruthie will become a performing trickster, a one-note gal, one-trick pony, performing this sex without pain, her back arching like a circus artist on a trapeze, a girl in a bar in the French Quarter. "You cannot contain yourself," Ruben will say, turning aside. She will feel as if she is overflowing the cups of her bra. Her body will fill the streets. People will say, "That Ruthie sure wants it."

She tries to avoid it. So does Ruben. They are sleepy. Or the children keep them awake, worrying. There is less and less time for it. When they travel and stay in hotels, the girls stay in the room with them, to save money for sightseeing. Ruben still kisses her, in the morning and when he comes home from work, after he removes his hat.

But if she and Ruben could have sex without pain—there would be no dinner for him waiting hot and ready at the table. Big Ruthie would ignore all her duties. She would become captive to it. Body twitching. Wet. Rivulets. She would no longer be in control. No longer in the driver's seat, but in back—necking, petting, dress up, flounces up, panties down or on the dash, devil-may-care, a hand on her—"Sorry, officer, we had just stopped to look for—" "We were on our way home, must have fallen asleep—"

Sex would become like chocolate fudge. Like lemon-meringue pie. Like pearls shimmering under a chandelier. Or Van Gogh close enough to see the paint lines. Blue-gray clouds after a rainstorm. Loveliness. Would Big Ruthie ever sleep?

Big Ruthie's life will become a dream, a dream of those blue castles with long mattresses she will lie across, will f— in, far away, will never ever come back from, the place high on the improbable hill of sex without pain, the impossible land of sex without pain.

There in the castle she will find the Messiah himself. He too is insatiable. She will welcome him inside her. She will long for him, miss his rhythms when he departs her body. Up there in his castle, she will keep him from descending to do his duty for at least another forty years. In his land of sex without pain, she and he will tarry.

Biographies

Woody Allen has written three books: *Getting Even*, *Without Feathers*, and *Side Effects*; two plays for Broadway, *Don't Drink the Water* and *Play It Again, Sam*; and all or part of dozens of movies. He probably doesn't recall it, but he rented the apartment of one of the authors in this book to create the imaginary apartment of author Gabe Roth in *Husbands and Wives*.

Max Apple's stories have appeared in various magazines since 1972. His books of fiction and nonfiction are *The Oranging of America and Other Short Stories*, *Zip*, *Free Agents*, *The Propheteers*, *Roommates* and, most recently, *I Love Gootie*.

Saul Bellow is the author of twelve novels, and numerous novellas and stories. He is the only novelist to receive three National Book Awards, for *The Adventures of Augie March*, *Herzog*, and *Mr. Sammler's Planet*. In 1975 he won the Pulitzer Prize for his novel *Humboldt's Gift*. In 1990 Mr. Bellow was presented the National Book Foundation Medal for distinguished contribution to American letters. The Nobel Prize in Literature was awarded to him in 1976 "for the human understanding and subtle analysis of contemporary culture that are combined in his work." A long-time resident of Chicago, Mr. Bellow now lives in New England.

Harold Brodkey was born in Staunton, Illinois, and grew up in Missouri. Starting in the early 1950s, his stories appeared regularly in the *New Yorker* and other magazines. His many honors include two first-place O. Henry awards, a Prix de Rome, and fellowships from the National Endowment for the Arts and the John Simon Guggenheim Memorial Foundation. He is the author of several books, including *This Wild Darkness*, a memoir of his battle with AIDS, two novels, three volumes of short stories, *First Love and Other Sorrows*, *Stories in an Almost Classical Mode*, and *The World Is the Home of Love and Death*, and the extended meditation, *My Venice*. Mr. Brodkey, who died in 1996, lived in New York City with his wife, the novelist Ellen Schwamm.

Melvin Jules Bukiet is the author of three novels, *Sandman's Dust*, *After*, and *Signs and Wonders*, and two collections, *Stories of an Imaginary Childhood* and *While the Messiah Tarries*. His writing has appeared in the *New York Times*, the *Washington Post*, the *Los Angeles Times*, *Antaeus*, *Paris Review*, and many other newspapers and magazines. He is presently at work on a new novel titled *Strange Fire*.

Janice Eidus has twice won the prestigious O. Henry Prize for her short stories, as well as a Pushcart Prize, and is the author of four highly acclaimed books, the story collections *The Celibacy Club* (City Lights, 1997) and *Vito Loves Geraldine* (City Lights, 1990), and the novels *Urban Bliss* (City Lights, 1998) and *Faithful Rebecca* (Fiction Collective, 1987). She is co-editor of *It's Only Rock n' Roll: Rock n' Roll Short Stories* (David Godine, 1998). Her work has been widely published in magazines and anthologies throughout the world. She lives in New York City.

Nathan Englander is the author of *For the Relief of Unbearable Urges*, published by Knopf (April 1999).

Rebecca Goldstein graduated from Barnard College and received her Ph.D. in philosophy from Princeton University. She is the author of four novels, *The Mind-Body Problem*, *The Late-Summer Passion of a Woman of Mind*, *The Dark Sister*, and *Mazel*, as well as a collection of short stories, *Strange Attractors*. The recipient of various awards for fiction and scholarship, she became a MacArthur Fellow for her fiction in 1996.

Erica Jong is one of the few authors who writes fearlessly in just about any genre. She is equally at home in the worlds of fiction, poetry, memoir, and essays, and is developing a musical version of her third novel, *Fanny, Being the True History of the Adventures of Fanny Hackabout-Jones*. Her most recent books are *Inventing Memory: A Novel of Mother and Daughters* and *What Do Women Want?* A good question.

Binnie Kirshenbaum is the author of *Pure Poetry*, to be published by Simon & Schuster in 1999. She is also the author of two novels, *A Disturbance in One Place* and *On Mermaid Avenue*, and of two story collections.

Jerzy Kosinski was the author of, among other works, *The Painted Bird*, *Being There*, *Cockpit*, *Blind Date*, *Passion Play*, *Pinball*, and *The Hermit of 69th Street*. He received numerous awards, including the American Academy of Arts and Letters Award in Literature, the National Book Award, the Best Screenplay of the Year Award for *Being There* from both the Writers Guild of America and the British Academy of Film and Television Arts (BAFTA), and the American Civil Liberties Union First Amendment Award.

Michael Lowenthal is the author of a novel, *The Same Embrace*, and the editor of numerous anthologies, including *Obsessed* and *Flesh and the Word 4* (all available from Plume). His work has also appeared in the *New York Times Magazine*, the *Kenyon Review*, *Best American Gay Fiction*, and other publications. A 1990 graduate of Dartmouth College, he now lives in Boston. He has a (n)e(u)rotic attachment to the shaygetz.

Bernard Malamud was the author of four collections of stories—*The Magic Barrel*, *Idiots First*, *Pictures of Fidelman*, and *Rembrandt's Hat*; seven novels—*The Natural*, *The Assistant*, *A New Life*, *The Fixer*, *The Tenants*, *Dubin's Lives*, and *God's Grace*, and the unfinished *The People*. His many awards include two National Book Awards, the Pulitzer Prize, and the Gold Medal of the American Academy and National Institute of Arts and Letters. He served as president of the PEN American Center from 1979 to 1981, and taught for many years at Bennington College.

Leonard Michaels is the author of two collections of stories, *Going Places* and *I Would Have Saved Them If I Could*; a novel, *The Men's Club*; and a work of biographical fiction, *Shuffle*. His diaries from 1961–1995 will be published under the title *Time Out of Mind*. His stories have appeared in O. Henry Prize collections and *The Best American Stories*. He has been nominated for the National Book Award and the National Book Critics Circle Award.

Cynthia Ozick's essays, novels, and short stories have won numerous prizes and awards, including the American Academy and National Institute of Arts and Letters Straus Living Award, four O. Henry First Prizes, the Rea Award for the Short Story, and a Guggenheim Fellowship. She was also guest editor of *Best American Essays, 1998*. She lives near New York City.

Francine Prose is the author of nine novels, including *Hunters and Gatherers*, *Bigfoot Dreams*, and *Primitive People*, two story collections, and most recently a collection of novellas, *Guided Tours of Hell*. Her stories and essays have appeared in the *Atlantic Monthly*, *Harper's*, *Best American Short Stories*, the *New Yorker*, the *New York Times*, the *New York Observer*, and numerous other publications. She writes regularly on art for the *Wall Street Journal* and is a fellow of the New York Institute for the Humanities. The winner of Guggenheim and Fulbright fellowships, two NEA grants, and a PEN translation prize, she has taught at the Iowa Writers' Workshop, the University of Arizona, the University of Utah, and the Bread Loaf and Sewanee writers' conferences. A film based on her novel, *Household Saints*, was released in 1993.

Thane Rosenbaum is the author of the novel *Second Hand Smoke*, and the novel-in-stories, *Elijah Visible*, which received the Edward Lewis Wallant Book Award. He is the literary editor of *Tikkun* magazine, and writes essays, articles, and reviews for the *New York Times*, the *Wall Street*

Journal, the *Washington Post*, *Newsday*, the *Miami Herald*, and the *Forward*. He also teaches courses in human rights, and law and literature, at Fordham Law School, and creative writing at the New School.

While he applauds Melvin Bukiet's efforts in assembling this anthology, he is of the view that "as a people, Jews have only had mixed results with sex, so I'm not sure it's something we should keep working at." And as for the sex scene in "Romancing the Yohrzeit Light," he says, "I wouldn't try that sexual maneuver at home without proper supervision. I am a professional after all; I make no representations or warranties that you will end up fully satisfied."

Henry Roth's *Call It Sleep*, published in 1934 to mixed reviews, later became widely acknowledged as a classic of Jewish/American literature. After a half-century-long writer's block, Mr. Roth began an enormous project, *Mercy of a Rude Stream*; its component novels, *A Star Shines over Mt. Morris Park*, *A Diving Rock on the Hudson*, *From Bondage*, and *Requiem for Harlem*, were published starting in 1994 and received multiple honors. Mr. Roth died on October 13, 1995.

Philip Roth taught comparative literature—mostly at the University of Pennsylvania—and retired from teaching as Distinguished Professor of Literature at Hunter College in 1992. Until 1989, he was General Editor of the Penguin book series "Writers from the Other Europe," which he inaugurated in 1974 and which introduced the work of Bruno Schulz and Milan Kundera to an American audience. His lengthy interviews with foreign writers—among them Primo Levi, Ivan Klima, and Aharon Appelfeld—have appeared in the *New York Review of Books*, the *London Review of Books*, and the *New York Times Book Review*. He was born in Newark, New Jersey, in 1933 and has lived in Rome, London, Chicago, and New York. He resides now in Connecticut.

His books have received numerous prizes, including two National Book Awards, two National Book Critics Circle Awards, and the PEN/Faulkner Award. Since 1970 he has been a member of the American Academy of Arts and Letters.

Helen Schulman is the author of the novels *The Revisionist* and *Out of Time*, and a collection of stories, *Not a Free Show*. She is also a co-editor, along with Jill Bialosky, of an anthology of essays, *Wanting a Child*. Her stories, essays, and reviews have appeared in such places as *Time*, *Vanity Fair*, *Vogue*, *GQ*, the *Paris Review*, *Story*, *Ploughshares*, etc. She has written and co-written five commissioned screenplays. She presently teaches in the Graduate Writing Division of Columbia University.

Gerald Shapiro's first collection of stories, *From Hunger*, won the Edward Lewis Wallant Award for Jewish Fiction. He is the editor of the anthology *American Jewish Fiction: A Century of Stories*. His second collection, *Bad Jews*, will be published soon by Zoland Books.

Enid Shomer's work has appeared in the *New Yorker*, the *Atlantic Monthly*, *Poetry*, *Paris Review*, *New Criterion*, *Best American Poetry*, *New Directions in Prose and Poetry*, *New Stories from the South*, and many other magazines, as well as more than three dozen anthologies. A prize-winning poet and fiction writer, she is the author of three books of poetry, most recently, *Black Drum*, and of *Imaginary Men*, which won the Iowa Short Fiction Award as well as the Southern Review/LSU Fiction Prize. Shomer has received two fellowships from the National Endowment for the Arts, and three from the State of Florida, where she has lived for most of her life. She has served as Writer-in-Residence at the Thurber House, as Florida State University's first Visiting Writer, and is currently Visiting Distinguished Writer at the University of Arkansas. Shomer considers herself a Southern as well as a Jewish writer.

Isaac Bashevis Singer (1904–1991) was the author of many novels, stories, children's books, and memoirs. He won the Nobel Prize in Literature in 1978.

Gilbert Sorrentino is the author of some twenty-five books of poetry, fiction and, criticism. His latest novel, *Gold Fools*, will be published by Sun & Moon Press in 1999.

Steve Stern, DJM, author, most recently, of *The Wedding Jester*, a collection of stories from Graywolf Press, enjoys moonlight, fine dining, and Jewish self-loathing, seeks athletic woman to help him kick Franz Kafka as a role model. Responses via editor.

Biographies

Cheryl Pearl Sucher earned her MFA at the University of Iowa Writers' Workshop and also held a fellowship at Stanford University. She is the author of the novel *The Rescue of Memory* (Scribner hardcover/Berkley Signature paperback) and several award-winning short stories that appeared in the *Kenyon Review* and the *Southwest Review*.

Benjamin Taylor is the author of *Into the Open: Reflections on Genius and Modernity* and was awarded the Harold Ribalow Prize in 1996 for his novel, *Tales Out of School*. He has taught writing at Washington University in St. Louis and at the New School for Social Research.

S. L. (Sandi) Wisenberg's work has appeared in the *New Yorker*, *Ploughshares*, *Creative Nonfiction*, the *Miami Herald*, *Tikkun*, *Witness*, the *Chicago Tribune*, and many anthologies, including *Nice Jewish Girls: Growing up in America*, *Feminism3*, *The Pushcart Prize XXI*, and *Atomic Ghost*. She is the creative nonfiction editor of *Another Chicago Magazine*.

Credits